Creation Abomination

Alan W. Thompson

All Scripture quotations, unless otherwise indicated, are from The Project Gutenberg EBook of The King James Bible - www.gutenberg.org (Release Date: March 2, 2011 [EBook #10]).

Contents

Contents

Preface

I originally had the idea of Creation Abomination back in 1995. At that time, I wrote a detailed outline of the book, but then essentially let it sit on the shelf collecting dust for many years. I was inspired about 7 years ago to write my book and I started work both researching and writing. I spent a considerable amount of time doing research, as I wanted this to be as realistic and plausible as possible, with a supernatural twist. In the middle of 2016, I finished my novel and went through multiple rounds of edits.

I'd like to acknowledge friends and family who helped motivate me throughout this entire process. In particular, I'd like to thank my wife Juls, of almost twenty-five years, who gave me encouragement and time to work on my novel. She also devoted many, many hours editing and identifying areas that needed attention. Thank you for everything that you do!

CHAPTER 1

Annihilation
(Present Day)

In the early hours of the morning, the streets were completely empty in the downtown area of Los Angeles known as the Cleantech Corridor. Located on the eastern edge of downtown LA, a several-mile-long development zone adjacent to the Los Angeles River had been set apart by the Mayor to help realize his vision to establish Los Angeles as a leader of the clean tech revolution. Development had been underway for about two years, and while there were a good number of buildings completed, many remained under construction and roughly fifty percent had not yet begun. The remaining older buildings were comprised of light and heavy manufacturing facilities, warehousing, and food processing plants. Many of them had been standing for at least thirty-five years and were in serious need of attention. The majority of the windows had been broken and subsequently boarded up to prevent individuals from accessing the vacant buildings. The exteriors of the buildings looked old and tired with faded and peeling paint visible everywhere. Distinctively standing out against these faded, dull canvases, brightly colored gang symbols and words of hatred had been blazingly spray painted across most easily accessible surfaces. Parking lots adjacent to these structures were riddled with potholes and cracks. Careless citizens had used these abandoned properties as their own private dump, with numerous trash bags, old television sets, worn couches and other various carelessly discarded heaps of trash lying everywhere. Here and there, automobiles had been abandoned next to these buildings, some of them sitting directly on the ground, their wheels previously stripped off them, and many with windows that were missing or shattered by rocks or bricks. None of the older properties had much in the way of landscaping, except for a few scattered, unkempt bushes and trees. This was the part of Los Angeles that people wanted to forget about, had forgotten about, and showed the neglect of many years everywhere you looked.

In sharp contrast, and in many cases directly across the street, there were striking new structures that had been completed just months before, and multiple buildings actively under construction. The new, energy efficient, green buildings exuded innovation everywhere you looked. These buildings were constructed predominantly out of recycled materials such as stone and metal, and integrated other more natural products such as adobe and sandstone. State of the art techniques were incorporated into their construction such as passive solar design that oriented windows, walls and trees to shade windows and roofs during the hotter summer months, while letting in solar energy during the winter to provide heat. Efficient solar panels topped the majority of the roof surfaces, providing electrical energy for the buildings. Strategically placed sky lights were located to provide efficient day lighting to the buildings, increasing the amount of natural light used during the day, thus reducing the need for electricity. Beautifully landscaped campuses adorned the grounds, with large shade trees, flowering trees, bushes, and well-appointed gardens spread throughout. Aesthetic ponds, small streams and bridges were placed randomly, connected by bike and walking paths for employees to utilize. The architecture used in the design of these buildings was not the primary thrust of the Cleantech corridor, although there were businesses that were located here devoted to just that. Set apart to facilitate the incubation of green jobs and technology, it was envisioned as a way to revitalize this portion of the city, creating new jobs and tax revenues, and serving as an example to the rest of the world.

Located on the far eastern edge of the Cleantech corridor close to the river, laid the Cenetics facility and corporate campus. The campus itself was roughly seven acres in size, and was comprised of one main, four-story building sitting precisely in the center, with three smaller, two and three-story buildings located to one side. A large parking lot sat directly in front of the main structure and wrapped around the right side of the building. Surrounding the entire campus was a ten-foot-tall wire fence, topped off with razor-sharp barbed wire. A security booth sat close to the main road running adjacent to the property, located squarely in front of an electric security gate that would slide open for cars to come and go. Sitting within the security booth were two armed guards having an animated discussion about the previous night's sporting event. The driveway leading from the main road through the security gate ran approximately one hundred feet up to the two-story tall, glass front lobby of the main building, ending in a circular loop. At the center of the loop the driveway made in front of the lobby stood a fifteen-foot tall, bronze, impressionistic statue representing a DNA strand. Within the illuminated lobby it was easy to see two additional security guards. One of them was sitting lazily in front of computer screens, while the other stood hunched over, leaning against a wall and staring at his fingernails. It was the middle of the night in southern California, with a temperature of only fifty-two degrees. Being nearly 3:30 A.M., it was starkly dark and eerily quiet.

In the parking lot close to the main building, a man was lying awkwardly on the ground. He pushed himself onto to his knees and slowly stood up. Reaching back towards his left shoulder he stretched the neck of his sweatshirt down revealing his shoulder. He was not prepared for what he saw next. There were six gouge marks of the same size on the front of his shoulder, close to his chest, and blood was slowly oozing from each of the wounds. Shrugging his shoulder forward he saw six, virtually identical marks on the back as well.

"They almost resemble teeth marks!" he exclaimed. "But how is that possible?!"

Releasing his sweatshirt, he readied himself, and then sprinted roughly sixty feet to the wire fence that encircled the Cenetics campus. On the other side of the fence directly opposite where he stopped sat a large Chinese Elm tree. Directly above his head was a medium-sized branch that extended from the tree out over the security fence, onto which was tied a rope that hung lazily down and laid on the ground next to his feet.

"You've got to move now!"

Grasping the rope hanging from the tree, he started to climb up towards the branch overhead. The pain in his left shoulder was severe, but somehow, he was able to ignore it and kept climbing. Reaching the branch, he swung his leg over it, then the other, and slid his body along the length back towards the trunk of the tree. Looking beneath him, he saw that he had cleared the barbed wire fence. Instantly he unwrapped his legs and hung down towards the grass beneath him by his hands. Letting go he landed softly on the grass standing upright. Without wasting a second, he immediately turned and sprinted from the building down the main road leading directly away from the facility.

After running for about ten minutes as fast as his legs would carry him, his right hip began to cramp, undoubtedly from injuries he had experienced earlier that evening. As the seconds ticked away his sprint turned into a run, which ultimately turned into a jolting jog.

"You got to keep going," he angrily shouted at himself. He knew he needed to get as far away from the building as possible or he wouldn't survive the night.

A few moments later he thought to himself that it must be getting close - his time was almost up. Despite his injury, he was now approximately a mile and a half away from the facility. The pain was now almost unbearable as he tried to press forward. Suddenly, his hip gave out on him and he fell hard to the ground. With great effort, he pushed himself back up to his knees, readying himself to start moving again. He turned back to glance in the direction of Cenetics, and at that moment a tremendous flash of light burst into his field of vision. Blinded by the white beam, he turned his head away and braced for the shockwave that would inevitably follow the explosion.

Traveling at two thousand meters per second, a shockwave erupted outward from the center of the blast along with incinerating heat. Everything within a one-quarter mile radius of the blast was vaporized. At 10,000 degrees Kelvin not much was going to survive. Buildings, steel, concrete and trees...all gone. The blast dug a massive, bowl-shaped gouge into the earth about four hundred feet in diameter and almost twenty feet deep. Extending out to a half-mile radius was a scene of absolute destruction. The heat blast instantly ignited almost everything in sight. The heat was so intense that buildings were literally engulfed in flames. Walls of large, concrete structures were toppled to the ground, and large chunks of cement were strewn everywhere. Streets and roads were twisted and torn exposing deep gouges and cracks. What few trees remained standing were set ablaze or sat smoldering, the life literally burned out of them. It virtually looked like hell on earth.

Stretching out in a one-mile radius from the blast there were obvious signs of the intense level of energy and heat released by the detonation. The paint on cars and buildings was blistered, peeling and bubbling on all surfaces. Trees and other landscaping were burning or smoldering. Buildings sat burning, and secondary explosions occurred as gas mains and containers of chemicals detonated, sometimes in rapid succession. Glass was strewn out everywhere from windows of buildings. Several cars were sitting on their rims, as their tires combusted in flames, or just melted all together. Beyond one mile, burning debris comprised of wood and steel rained down from the sky igniting sporadic fires. Not one window facing the explosion within a three-mile radius remained intact.

Exactly one point two seconds after the detonation, a shock wave traveling at two thousand meters per second hit the man and he was thrown sideways into a dumpster behind a two-story brick building. He momentarily heard the explosion but then all sound vanished as the piercing noise hit his eardrums. With a struggle, he slowly crawled to his knees and looked back in the direction that the explosion came from. As he took in the devastation, blood oozed from both of his ears, and darkness slowly entered in from the outside of his vision until everything went completely black as he lost consciousness.

CHAPTER 2

Chance Encounter
(14 years earlier)

A soft, gentle, blue colored flame danced along the top of a short, silver metal tube roughly the size of a large cigar. The flame was approximately one inch in length and no more than a quarter inch in width at the base. The top of this shape came together in a sharp point that shifted back and forth ever so slightly. Encased within this blue outer shell was a somewhat brighter but also blue inner cone. The base of the inner cone was the same width as the outer tear drop shape, and extended upwards for about a half an inch converging into a rounded point.

Staring intently at the barely shifting flame coming from the end of a Bunsen burner was thirty-two-year-old William Mears, and the majority of his undergraduate class at the University of Southern California. Located in the front of the classroom, William sat on an adjustable stool behind a large black table. A metal pipe protruded up from the table's surface approximately two inches and ended in a rounded top. Extending on opposite sides of this pipe were two smaller metal tubes that narrowed down to a pointed tip in a stair step fashion, creating ridges along the metal tube. Close to the rounded top of the main tube were two metal handles to adjust the amount of natural gas that flowed through it. On one of the pointed tips, a rubber hose had been firmly slid into place transporting the gas from the pipe into the Bunsen burner. To the right of William was deep basin sink with a long, curved necked facet positioned directly above it. Directly behind him was a large screen extending down from the ceiling onto which was projected the images from the laptop sitting on the tabletop to his left.

Reaching towards the base of the Bunsen burner with his left hand, William slightly adjusted a knob, increasing the size of the flame slightly. In his right hand, he was tightly gripping a pair of metal tongs that held a small strip of magnesium between the tips.

"Alright everyone," William voiced to the class. "Watch very carefully as I place the end of the magnesium into the tip of the inner flame. You're going to see a very fast, violent reaction take place as the metal ignites."

With a grin on his face, William placed the tip of the magnesium strip into the blue flame coming from the end of the burner. Almost immediately, the magnesium caught fire and a blinding white light burst from the metal. The effect was relatively short-lived with the magnesium being consumed in roughly two seconds, after which the white light completely subsided.

"Pretty cool, huh?" he asked. His question was met with nodding heads and similar grins from his freshman class. "It's easy to see why magnesium is commonly used in fireworks, especially because it's so light weight."

Focusing back on his laptop he advanced the slide being projected onto the screen.

"Ok everyone, that should do it for today," he commented. "Please take note of your reading assignment for next class. And this Thursday, you will get the opportunity to play with fire a bit, now that you know what you're doing."

Immediately the sound of books shutting and backpacks being zipped filled the room, along with chairs sliding across the floor, as students packed up their things and headed for the door. In less than sixty seconds, William sat alone in the classroom looking down at his computer screen. He closed down the PowerPoint presentation with his mouse and started to shut down his laptop.

William was a student teacher at the University of Southern California in the Department of Biochemistry and Molecular Biology. He had received his master's in Molecular Biology three years earlier and was getting ready to start working on his thesis for his doctorate degree. Having also received his master's degree from the USC, William knew most of the professors, and more importantly, they knew William's work and ability, making him pretty much a shoe-in for a part-time job teaching undergraduate courses while professors focused on different research projects.

Standing up from his chair, William was six feet tall and had a fairly athletic build. He had participated in gymnastics for most of his younger life, and even spent a couple of years during his undergraduate work competing at the collegiate level. His hair was sandy blond, and he had dark blue eyes and fair skin. On the side of his face was an odd-shaped, dark, pink patch of skin extending from the outside corner of his eye down to the left-hand corner of his mouth, and from about half an inch in front of his left ear to the middle of his left cheek. The skin in this area was raised and rough in texture. As a teenager, William had a severe burn when messing around with a group of friends. They had gotten the bright idea to try and make homemade napalm, like what was used in the Vietnam War, out of simple, easily available materials in most homes. After creating almost half a soda can full of this volatile material, they thought it would be a "cool" effect to drop a lit firecracker into it to see what would happen. The outcome was something that ended up changing the course of William's life.

The other boys were already standing about twenty feet away in the middle of the street. Squatting next to the soda can sitting on the driveway of his parent's house, William lit the end of a firecracker and dropped it into the soda can. Immediately standing up he started to back pedal as quickly as he could towards the other boys. After covering about eight feet, he tripped on an edge of the sidewalk that was raised slightly higher than the driveway, falling backward onto the ground. Scrambling, he jumped up at the same instant that the firecracker went off. The force of the firecracker exploding inside of the can was sufficient to cause the outside of the aluminum can to split in two. Unfortunately, it ripped open in the same direction that William had tried to make his escape.

The sticky, white substance inside the can instantly caught fire, and sprayed outwards with violent force through the opening in the can. While there wasn't a tremendous amount of the substance that was propelled outwards, it was sufficient to do significant damage to William. About half an ounce, nearly a tablespoon, of this material flew through the air directly towards William who sat frozen, staring in astonishment. The flaming spray of napalm was heading right for his face. Realizing what was about to happen, at the last second William turned head sharply to the right and the flaming material narrowly missed hitting him in the left eye.

Being only fourteen years old, William didn't fully appreciate the chemical properties of the substance that they had concocted. Napalm is a very dangerous substance and burns anywhere from eight hundred to twelve hundred degrees Celsius. When this material is spread onto most surfaces, including skin, it is virtually impossible to remove. The most efficient way to remove napalm is to let it completely burn away; and this was unfortunately the only option for William. The flaming material essentially melted the skin and muscle away from his face, leaving pretty much only bone exposed through the gaping wound. It took multiple plastic surgeries and skin grafts to return William's face to a somewhat normal semblance of what it once looked like, but it left physical and emotional scars that would last a lifetime.

Absently, William reached up with his left hand and gently rubbed the scar on the side of his face. He was very self-conscious about the injury he had received and felt that it repulsed most people. It was this constant feeling of self-loathing that he had over his appearance that had motivated William from that point forward to focus on sciences in school. He always wished that there were some sort of a magical remedy that would have repaired the scars on his face to the point that no one would have ever known they existed. It was this fixation that had driven William into the field of molecular biology, and had given him the topic for his thesis: How to repair injuries that the body could not.

The human body is an amazing miracle of nature. Usually, the body has the ability to heal injuries when they occur such as scrapes, cuts, or even broken bones. However, when a catastrophic injury occurs to the body, there is not enough tissue to support the growth required to heal it. This is especially true of complicated organs in the human body. And a key part of this healing process is the ability of stem cells to provide a sufficient supply of new cells for the healing process to take place.

William picked up his papers and loaded them, along with his laptop into his computer case and started heading back towards the office he shared with some other doctoral candidates who were more or less indentured servants to various tenured professors. Deep in thought, he wound his way through the hallways to the stairwell and headed up one level. Upon reaching the third floor, he started shuffling through his bag trying to confirm that he had remembered to put his composition notebook in there. Focusing on his search, he rounded the corner close to his office and ran directly into a woman.

"Seriously!" she exclaimed, as all the contents she was carrying fell down to the floor with a loud clatter.

Completely surprised, William looked up and saw what he considered to be one of the most beautiful women he had ever seen. He stood there for a few seconds with his mouth agape and just stared at her.

"Well?" she prompted. "Aren't you going to at least say 'excuse me'?"

"Oh...ah...yes, I'm sorry. Please excuse me," he stammered. "I didn't even see you."

"Obviously," she said with a note of disdain in her voice. "Are you just going to stand there staring at me, or are you going to help me clean up this mess?"

Embarrassed by his juvenile demeanor, he turned bright red, but only for a moment. "Please, let me get those for you," he said as he squatted down and started to gather together the sprawl of books and papers that lay on the floor beneath them.

Having gathered everything into a neat stack, he stood up and presented them to the woman standing in front of him.

"Here you go," he said handing her the stack he had collected. "As good as new. Well, you may need to reorganize things a bit."

"Thank you," she said with a notably softened tone in her voice. "I'm sorry for snapping at you," she continued. "It's been a long day, and I've got a paper due tomorrow that I've barely started working on."

Having composed himself, William took a brief moment to assess the woman that stood in front of him. Likely in her early twenties, he surmised that she was an undergrad student - possibly in her Junior or Senior year. Based on the fact that she was in the science building, she was probably in an advanced science course. She was approximately six inches shorter than William, which would make her roughly five feet, six inches tall, and had a slender body frame. Her shoulder length, dark blonde hair was tucked neatly behind her right ear, and her eyes were a pale, light blue. She was fair skinned, but definitely had a darker complexion than William. She wore thin, black-framed glasses that made William wonder if they were actually for vision correction, or just for aesthetics, and as William had noted to himself earlier, her looks were absolutely stunning.

"My name is William," he went on. There was an awkward silence for about three seconds. "And your name would be?" he asked with a quizzical look.

This time it was her turn to be embarrassed as she turned a bright shade of red which took longer to clear than William's had.

"Tara," she finally responded.

"Well, very nice to meet you," he said while extending his hand to shake hers.

Tara shifted her stack of books and paper into her left hand and took William's hand. Her eyes met his and both of them stood staring at one another without saying anything. William thought to himself how soft and warm her hands were, and felt almost as if electricity was being exchanged through her touch. The corners of his mouth curved upwards forming a half smile to which Tara responded by turning yet another shade of red.

"I wonder what she's thinking," William thought to himself. "Who cares," he mused, "I think that I'm going to want to get to know her better."

Finally releasing their handshake, Tara held her stack of items closely to her chest and smiled back at William.

William needed to think of something to say to fill the silence. "I'm surprised that I haven't seen you around the science labs before. This is the third year of my doctorate and I also did my Masters here," he said. "You must be a senior, or possibly in a graduate program?" he asked.

"Actually, I'm technically a junior but will be a senior after the semester is up," she commented as they started making their way down the hallway.

"You must be in an upper division course, aren't you?"

"Well," she went on, "I'm actually taking my first biology class. Science and I don't get along very well and I have been putting off satisfying this GE requirement. So far, I haven't been doing very well at all," she admitted somewhat sheepishly.

This was the opportunity that William had been waiting for. "Really? Well, you're in luck! Science and I happen to get along very nicely," he joked. "Perhaps I could help tutor you a bit. It's the least I could do given the fact that I almost ran you over," he said with a smile.

"That would be really nice of you," she responded. "How much do you normally charge students when you tutor them?"

"Seriously?" he questioned her with apparent dismay. "I couldn't charge you."

Sensing his playful manner, she playfully responded. "Well, that just isn't going to do. I need to pay you something for your time and effort."

"I tell you what. Why don't you just agree to go out to dinner with me this weekend, and we'll call it even?"

Placing her right hand on her chin, she pretended to seriously consider his offer before answering. "It's a deal!" she exclaimed. "But you better be a good tutor!"

Pulling out a small notebook from her purse she neatly jotted down her name "Tara Cline" in meticulously elegant cursive, along with her email address and cell phone number.

Tearing the page cleanly from the notebook she handed it to William. "Here you go. I don't normally give out my phone number to strangers, but in your case, I'll make an exception," she teased.

Taking the paper from her he glanced at it for a moment. "Just making sure there are enough digits for the phone number," he said with a grin. "I'd hate to think that I wouldn't be able to get in touch with you. Especially after I've already come to the conclusion that you're someone that I would like to get know better."

That made Tara blush a third time. Dipping her head down slightly she looked up at William over the top of her glasses. "Oh, don't worry," she responded. "I'm pretty sure that I'd like to get to know you better as well."

Again, they stood looking into each other's eyes for a moment without saying a word. After what was probably no more than five seconds William decided that this was probably the best first impression he had made with a woman in his life and that he shouldn't press his luck.

"Alright then. I'll give you a call later this evening and we can figure out a time for our first tutoring session. And, of course, to schedule our dinner date."

With that last comment, William stood to the side and watched Tara walk past him finally disappearing as she rounded the corner. Closing his eyes, William nodded his head down slightly and made a fist with his right hand. "Yes!" he exclaimed in a hushed voice. "That was totally awesome!"

Tucking the piece of paper with Tara's information on it neatly into his front right pants pocket, William virtually danced down the hallway and opened up the door to the office that he shared with other students finding it completely empty. He slung his computer bag onto the desk and sat down in the chair in front of a desk facing the window.

"Time to get cranking," he muttered to himself.

He pulled his laptop out of his bag and opened it on the desk in front of him. Waking it up from sleep mode, the screen illuminated showing a desktop background image of a DNA double helix. On his screen was a Word document that he double-clicked, opening up a multi-page paper. The title on the top of the first page was "The Regenerative Properties of Adult Stem Cells."

William had been working on his thesis project for about two months and he knew that he had a very long way to go. Most doctoral students at the University had selected a relatively "easy" topic for their thesis project - one that wasn't terribly groundbreaking or difficult to accomplish. The most common one that fellow students had undertaken was to determine the purpose of a specific gene in a mouse by shutting it off during embryonic development. With the gene turned off, the result would be the lack of expression of a specific attribute when the embryo grew into a baby mouse. This would manifest itself in ways such as the size or shape of the mouse's ears, eye color, and possibly tail length. It was a technique that had been perfected many years before, so students couldn't simply reproduce the same results - they needed to come up with something unique that usually took the form of manipulating specific genes to create very particular results.

Rather than taking this relatively "safe" route that would have essentially guaranteed him to be awarded his doctorate degree, he decided to aim a little higher. He wanted his thesis project to be something that was actually valuable to society at large, and one that would benefit the lives of men and women the world over. William was determined that he was going to be the one who finally figured out how adult stem cells could be used to repair traumatic injuries that were seen as being unrepairable. The thesis of many scientists to date was that adult stem cells could be used to repair damaged tissues when introduced into the site of injury. However, no one had achieved any success in getting adult stem cells to produce the desired effect even in laboratory mice.

It was an extremely ambitious goal, and one that his professors cautioned him against making the primary thesis of his project.

Glancing at his watch, he noted that it was five forty-five PM.

"I'll work for about three hours and then give Tara a call to make our first date."

And with that, he pulled some papers out of his bag and started reviewing results from his last failed experiment.

CHAPTER 3

Recommendation

(Later that evening)

With a jolt, William snapped his head backward as he was awakened by the sound of a door slamming shut. Taking a deep breath, William stared at the man that stood in front of him with a silly grin on his face.

"Working late again, I see?" the man questioned.

Rubbing his right eye, William took another deep breath. "What time is it?" Without waiting for the man to answer he looked down at his watch and realized that it was already ten thirty PM.

"Crap!" he exclaimed. "I only meant to close my eyes for five minutes!"

He immediately reached into his front right pant pocket and pulled out the paper that Tara had given him earlier in the day with her contact information. "I'm such an idiot!"

"What's that?" the man inquired.

"None of your business Don," William barked.

"Well excuse me," he said in a sarcastic tone. "Just trying to be friendly."

"I know, sorry," William said in an apologetic tone. "It's just that I met this girl earlier and we really hit if off well. Actually, probably better than I ever have with a girl before. I promised that I would give her a call tonight to set a time for us to go out later this week."

"Is that all? I wouldn't worry about it. Besides, you don't want to come across as being desperate, do you? Well, in your case, you probably are really desperate, so maybe it doesn't matter."

"Ha, ha! You wouldn't have even known what to say if a woman asked you the time of day."

Both of the men laughed together and Don walked across the room and sat down in a chair sitting in front of an empty desk. William had known Don for the past three years. They had entered the doctoral program at the same time and had taken multiple classes with each other as they were both working towards their Ph.D. in Molecular Biology. Both of them were passionate about science and had become close friends.

"How's your thesis going?"

"Very slowly." With a frustrated look on his face he continued, "I've been able to extract and store the stem cells from the lab rat without any issues. Then I cultivate the cells to produce hundreds of thousands of them to inject them back into the rat once I have caused paralysis by severing the spinal cord. After I inject them into the subject the spinal cord starts to accept the cells and the healing process begins. Then after about six hours, the healing process stops for no apparent reason. All I've been successful at doing is mutilating over one hundred rats that I had to euthanize to put them out of their misery."

"Ouch! I'm glad that I'm not a rat!"

"Come on, be serious! It really isn't a laughing matter."

"I am. I mean, who'd want to be a rat at this university. By this time, you would have crippled my whole immediate and extended family. We'd all be wheeling around the building in these tiny little wheelchairs looking for cheese."

"Ok, ok...very funny!"

Don paused for a second, then proceeded in a more serious tone. "Maybe the problem is with the basis of your thesis."

"With my thesis? What do you mean?"

"Well, scientists have been trying to prove that adult stem cells can be used to heal injuries for several years. And in reality, they have achieved little to no success, right?"

"True. But I know that I'm on the right track. I just need to figure out why the healing process stops. If I can do that, I know that I'll be able to..." William hesitated for a moment and then continued. "It's just got to be right!"

At that point, Don turned back to the desk sitting in front of him and started thumbing through his notebook as if he was looking for something specific. After a few moments, he let out a large huff.

"What's wrong?" William inquired.

"Oh, I just remembered that I'm supposed to teach Professor Worley's biology lab tomorrow morning. The problem is I have an appointment with the department chair to talk about my own thesis. I've already rescheduled on him two times, so if I miss this one I'm certain that he'll string me up." Don paused for a second as if he was deep in thought, then continued. "Hey, you're free tomorrow morning, aren't you?"

"Come on Don," William implored as he spun his chair around to face him. "You can't keep asking me to take your student teaching responsibilities!"

With a sheepish look on his face, Don simply sat in his chair and smiled at William.

"Really! Are you going to try and stick me with your class again? What's does this make, the fifth time this semester already? Worley's going to catch onto the fact that I'm teaching your class more often than you are! Then you're going to be up a creek without a paddle."

"Have I told you what a good friend you are?"

"I'm not going to do it. You've got to be more responsible!"

"Now William...I don't know why you're pretending that you're not going to bail me out. Right buddy?"

"Yeah, yeah...whatever. You're just lucky that I could use the extra cash right now. It's Bio 1, right? Room three seventy-two?"

"Yup. You've really got a great memory," Don added. "A real genius in my esteem. You know, you're probably the...."

"Enough!" William interrupted. "I said I'd do it. Now stop bs'ing me and let me get out of here so I can get some sleep. I've got an early class that I have to teach tomorrow," he said sarcastically.

"By the way," Don continued, "it's an in-class lab tomorrow. Dissection!"

William audibly groaned and gave his friend a long, level glance. "You've got to be joking, right? Not only are you going to stick me with your biology class, but you're going to do it for a class that requires at least one hour of setup time, not to mentioned an hour to clean everything up."

"And here's the best part. Since it's their first dissection of the year, you get to find out first hand which students have the stomach for biology, and which ones..." he paused for effect, "are going to show you the contents of their own stomach!"

"You're a royal pain in the ass!" William asserted.

"Such harsh language my friend," he jested. "Do you kiss your mother with that mouth?"

"No, but I kiss YOUR mother with this mouth," he retorted.

Both of them broke into uncontrollable laughter at that

point. The art of juvenile put-downs was not lost on either of these men. At this point, William finished gathering together his things and started for the door. As he reached the door he turned back to look at his friend who was starting to pull out papers from his own bag to get down to some of his own work.

"Ok man, I'll catch you later," he called back.

Pausing for a brief second, Don finally responded. "Maybe you just need to think outside of the box a little."

"About what?" he questioned.

"Your thesis. My gut's telling me that you need to change your thesis."

"You've got to be insane," William said with an incredulous tone. "If I changed my thesis at this point it would set me back at least six months. I don't know about you, but I can't afford another six-month delay in my graduating if that is ever going to even occur. I have to stick with the plan that I've got."

"I'm not saying that you should change the entire thesis. Maybe you should look at the problem a little differently," he suggested. "Look at the constants and variables to see if there is anything that you can try differently. What do you have in common with all of the other scientists that have tried and failed so far?"

Thinking for a moment, William finally responded, "the stem cells."

"Right! Maybe that's the issue," he suggested. "Maybe using stem cells isn't the right path after all."

"Well, this has got to work because that's what my studies have focused on for the past five years. If it doesn't then I'm totally screwed." Pausing for only a brief moment, William continued. "Don't even go there," he warned in a humorous tone. "Don't even go there!"

"Who me?" Don replied in an innocent tone while he raised both of his hands upwards while shrugging his shoulders.

"Yeah right!"

Laughing, Don turned his chair back around to focus on the paperwork that was strewn out on the desk in front of him, and William opened the door and started walking down the hallway towards the stairwell. Reaching into his pocket he pulled out the piece of paper again that Tara had given him and glanced at his watch.

"Ten forty-five. Maybe it's not too late," he considered for a moment. "No, the worst thing I could do would be to call and wake her if she's already gone to sleep. I'll just call her tomorrow and apologize."

Irritated with himself, William opened the door leading into the stairwell, made his way to the first floor, and exited the building into the abnormally cool evening. Briskly, he walked across the parking lot to his car and hopped in. Immediately he turned the engine over, threw it into drive, and started back towards his apartment that was located just off campus.

CHAPTER 4

New Direction
(The Next Day)

William made his way to the science building just after seven o'clock in the morning. Biology one started at nine o'clock, and he wanted to ensure that he could swing by his office to pick up a few papers and still make it to the classroom in time to set up for the laboratory he had "volunteered" to conduct. After spending about ten minutes in his office answering a few emails, he made his way up to the third floor of the science building and entered room three seventy-two.

Despite the windows covering the entire length of wall on the opposite side of the room, it was relatively dark given the overcast sky. William reached to the right side of the door and flipped up the first of three light switches. Two rows of fluorescent lights positioned on the ceiling in the back of the classroom to his left flickered for a couple of seconds until all of them remained on illuminating the room. He flipped up the middle switch producing the same effect on the two rows of lights located in the middle of the room, and while they were still flickering he snapped up the last switch to turn on the remaining lights over the desk and table at the front of the room. There were five rows of tables fanning back from a large, elevated workspace surface that sat at the head of the room. Each row of tables had four pairs of chairs sitting in-between a storage cabinet and two drawers. An overhead projector was suspended from the ceiling approximately twenty-five feet from the front of the class. The table at the front of the classroom was raised to provide easier viewing for the students in the classroom. Behind the table and desk at the front of the class were three, enormous whiteboards that each had to be twelve feet in length. Sitting on a table located next to the windows at the front of the classroom was a large aquarium that contained no fewer than twenty live frogs. William grimaced slightly as he knew that these were going to be the subject of his student's laboratory in roughly one and a half hours.

Walking to the front of the room, William unslung his bag from around his right shoulder and rested it on the left side of the workspace. After unzipping his bag, he pulled out his laptop, opened it up and powered it on. While his computer was going through the boot process, he grabbed a VGA cable and plugged it into the backside of his laptop so he could project images through the overhead projector. Looking behind him, he realized the screen was still hidden in the ceiling. Located on the table next to his laptop was a small touch screen that responded with a soft beep when he reached forward and simply pressed with his forefinger. Immediately the screen lit up and displayed a message of "Welcome to Smart Screen for Learning." After a few moments, the screen displayed text reading "Power System On?" accompanied by two buttons: "Yes" and "No." William pressed the "Yes" button resulting in another soft beep, directly followed by the sound of an electric motor turning on which lowered a large white screen down from inside the ceiling. The projector mounted on the ceiling in front of him also turned on and started warming up.

Looking to his right, a neat stack of freshly copied laboratory packets sat on the table. William reached over and picked up three green colored sheets that were stapled together which rested on the larger stack of packets and read the title of the page.

"Frog Dissection Laboratory Instructions."

While reading through the printed instructions, William made his way around the room collecting various items that were identified as being required for the lab. After about ten minutes, he set down the instructions and surveyed the materials that were neatly organized on the table in front of him.

"Thirty dissection trays - check. Large box of dissecting pins - check. Large box full of scissors - check. Dissecting needles, rubber gloves, and forceps - check, check and check. Everything seems to be in order," he commented.

Then he ruefully looked over at the aquarium sitting next to the windows. "Aquarium full of live frogs to be sacrificed for science - check," he sadly remarked.

William understood the need for using animals to teach scientific concepts. And he especially knew the value of them for use in testing and research. But that didn't change the fact that he greatly disliked the idea of animals having to be killed, especially for something as mundane as a frog dissection. There were computer-based dissections that were equally as effective as the real thing. Unfortunately, the head of the Biology department thought that nothing was a good substitute for live frogs. Making matters worse, he knew that it was up to him to prepare the frogs for the students that would be making their way to the classroom in roughly thirty minutes. Turning back to the instruction sheet he reviewed the section on frog preparation.

"Well, I guess there's no reason to prolong this any further."

Taking a pair of scissors off the desk in front of him, he made his way over to the aquarium. There was a medium-sized cardboard box lined with plastic sitting directly to the left of the frogs, along with a bag of cotton balls and a jug with a label on it reading: 'Ether: Handle with Care'. To the right of the aquarium sat what looked like a large Tupperware lid that would neatly fit on top of the aquarium sealing in the toxic fumes. Reaching with his left hand, William picked up the jug and was about to unscrew the tightly fastened cap.

"Whoops. I almost forgot to open a window! Had the students came in and found me unconscious on the floor, they might have decided to dissect me instead of the frogs," he said to himself

Reaching across the table, William unlatched the window and swung it out widely to provide as much airflow as possible. Next, he placed one rubber glove on his right hand to avoid accidentally coming in contact with the nasty chemical. With his right hand, he reached into the bag of cotton balls grabbing roughly six of them and tightly wadded them in his fist. He then proceeded to unscrew the cap off the ether jug. Once the cover was removed, he quickly covered the opening with the clump of cotton balls and gently tipped the bottle onto its side allowing a portion of the ether to soak into the cotton. Immediately he screwed the lid back onto the jug and dropped the cotton balls into the aquarium with the frogs and covered it with the plastic lid to trap the fumes. Given the size of the aquarium, William reasoned that it would take a few minutes for the fumes to sufficiently accumulate and take effect on the amphibians. After roughly seven minutes he saw the frogs, in a relatively rapid manner, doze off and fall asleep, and after eight minutes none of the frogs were moving.

Knowing the students would be arriving in about twenty minutes, he quickly went to work euthanizing the animals. He reached over to the side of the tank and picked up a pair of sharp scissors with his right hand. This is where the plastic lined box was going to come in handy. He removed the lid from the top of the aquarium and grabbed his first victim with his left hand. Twisting to his left, he held the frog in position over the top of the box, opened the pair of scissors, and slid one of the blades into the frog's mouth until it rested in the corners. He positioned the second blade just beneath the base of the back of the frog's head to ensure that death was instantaneous and painless. With a flexing of his right hand, he swiftly brought the two blades together, grimacing as the top of the frog's head fell silently into the plastic lined box.

He considered for a moment how little blood there was from such a violent act, then placed the animal's body into one of the dissection trays sitting on the table. He then turned back to the aquarium and proceeded to repeat the same procedure until there were only three frogs left in the aquarium.

"This really is a bit gruesome...and all in the name of science," he joked to himself.

Reaching back into the glass box for the next frog, William noted that the animal twitched slightly when he picked it up.

"Perfect," he murmured. "They started to wake up already."

The very next moment the door to the classroom opened as the first student entered. Still holding on to the frog with his left hand he turned towards the door to see who had walked in and was shocked to realize that he recognized the student.

"Tara?" he offered in a somewhat dumbfounded manner.

"Well hello there, William! I figured that I wasn't going to see or hear from you ever again since you didn't call me last night," she asserted with more than a note of annoyance in her voice.

Realizing that he was still holding a half-conscious frog in his hand, he reached back and placed it gently into the aquarium and turned to face the obviously agitated woman standing in front of him.

"I'm really sorry," he implored. "I don't have a good excuse. I ended up working in my office last night and I must have been totally exhausted. I shut my eyes just for a moment and the next thing I knew it was ten thirty."

Tara walked slowly across the room, stopping about five feet in front of him and crooked her right eyebrow in a questioning manner.

"Really!" he continued. "I wanted to call you but I thought that you might have already gone to bed, and the last thing that I wanted to do was to wake you up from a dead sleep."

Reaching into his breast pocket of his dress shirt he produced the neatly folded paper that Tara had given him the night before.

"See?" he implored. "I brought this with me today and I was going to leave you a message right after I finished teaching."

Slowly, Tara's expression softened and a slight grin began to form on her face, which in turn shifted into a broad grin and her eyes twinkled.

"Got you!" she exclaimed.

Realizing that Tara really wasn't upset at him, he let out a soft sigh of relief and returned her smile.

"You actually had me worried there for a second," he said with his voice still a little bit shaky. Regaining a bit of his composure he continued. "What are the odds that you would be in the same class that I'm substituting?"

"I know, right?" she agreed.

"Well, now that we're together again, why don't we figure out when we're going on that date?"

"You know, William, teachers aren't really supposed to be fraternizing with students, are they? What would the Dean say?"

Grinning back at Tara, William shrugged his shoulders. "Well, since I'm only a student teacher, and not your normal one at that, I think that I'm going to be ok. Besides, I'm only subbing for this one class and won't be grading your lab practical."

Tara suddenly twisted the corners of her mouth downwards in an unflattering grimace.

"That is today, isn't it?" she groaned. "That's one of the main reasons that I have been putting off taking this course. I don't mind learning about Biology, but the thought of cutting up an animal disgusts me."

Tara then glanced over at the aquarium and box located to the right of William next to the windows.

"Don't tell me that you were just doing what I think you were doing," she stated flatly in an incredulous tone.

Without hesitating William responded. "Its just part of the job description. I don't like it either, but it has to be done."

At that point, William looked back at the aquarium to

find the three frogs had completely regained consciousness and were behaving normally, completely unaware that their lives had almost been prematurely ended.

"Well, looks like those three owe you a debt of gratitude. If you hadn't come in when you did, they would be just like the others," motioning to the three stacks of trays sitting neatly to the left of the glass box. "These guys are going to live to see another day!"

At that point, the door to the classroom opened again and a group of three students entered the classroom and took their seats.

"Why don't we pick this back up again after class?" Tara suggested.

Without waiting for William to respond, she turned around, walked back towards the other three students and took her seat. Looking up at the clock, he noted that there were about seven minutes until the class was supposed to officially start. He walked back to the front of the classroom and referenced the instructions again to determine the location of the PowerPoint he needed for the lab. Within less than thirty seconds he navigated to the appropriate URL, downloaded the presentation, and had the title page displayed in full-screen mode on the screen behind him. Looking down at his laptop he read the words 'Frog Dissection' accompanied by an image of a frog laying on his back.

By this point, most of the students had filed into the room and the noise level had grown to a gentle roar with everyone actively engaged in conversations with one another. Periodically, groans could be heard as students were undoubtedly discussing the events to come. Glancing up at the clock on the wall William saw it was time to start the class.

"Ok everyone, settle down. It's time to get started and we have a lot to do over the next two hours."

Immediately the noise subsided and William looked out across the classroom at the faces of the students, pausing momentarily when his eyes met with Tara's and he flashed a brief smile.

"Good morning everyone. My name is William Mears and I will be substituting your class today. As you can probably tell based on the screen behind me, we're going to be doing a frog dissection today. I'd like to ask everyone to come up to the front of the room and grab a lab practical packet from the stack on the desk, and then pick up a dissection tray with a frog. Please only take one tray for each pair of students."

Within a couple of minutes, all the students were sitting back in their seats with packets in hand, accompanied by a metal tray occupied by a recently deceased amphibian. Over the next five minutes, William reviewed the procedure the students were going to be following during their lab. Nearing the end of the instructions, a female student sitting in the front row of the classroom tentatively raised her hand.

"Yes, you have a question?"

"Ahh…yes. Sorry for interrupting you, but were these frogs just killed this morning. I mean were these frogs killed just so we could do our dissection today?"

William saw a deep look of consternation on the woman's face and knew that he needed to be somewhat sensitive in his response.

"In order for you to get the most out of the dissection

lab today, it is imperative that the internal organs be in as pristine condition as possible. That requires that the specimens are euthanized as close to the dissection as possible." William made special effort to refer to the animals as a 'specimen' and not a 'frog' in order to try and keep the discussion more pragmatic, and less emotional.

"Are there any other questions?" Pausing for a moment to confirm that the students were ready he continued. "Ok then, let's go ahead and get started. I'll be available to help you with any questions that you might have during the lab today."

With that, the students eagerly began reading the instruction packet and began the process of dissecting their frogs. William took a seat on a stool situated to his left, removed a notebook from his bag, and began to flip through its pages. Within just a couple of minutes, he was deeply engrossed in reviewing the results of his most recent series of lab trials for his thesis.

"November 18, 2004 - Experimental subject seventy-two: Typical results achieved during most recent series of tests. Spinal cord injury affected onto subject by severing spinal cord between second and third vertebrae using a surgical microscope and obsidian scalpel. Upon revival of the test subject, observed immediate and complete paralysis. Adult stem cells extracted from subject have been replicated in laboratory environment to produce in excess of one hundred thousand cells. Introduced stem cells into surgical site of spinal column in an effort to encourage natural regenerative behavior from cells adjacent to injury. Under low magnification of microscope, activity of neurons, axons and glial cells reflect increased regenerative properties, most likely produced by the introduction of adult stem cells. Increased cellular activity measured for a period of fifteen minutes after which time a notable decrease was observed. At twenty minutes post introduction of adult stem cells into subject, zero regenerative activity seen across all three cellular types. Conclusion: while introduction on adult stem cells encourages regeneration of nervous cells and tissues, this ability is...."

"PROFESSOR MEARS!" exclaimed a student sitting in the second row of the classroom. "I don't understand what I'm supposed to do at this point, can you help me?"

"Oh, I'm sorry," he apologized as he shut his notebook. "Of course, I can help you," he stated as he walked back to the second row.

"The lab packet says that we need to expose the lower abdominal organs to view the kidneys. I did that, but I can't tell where the kidneys are."

Looking down at the frog sprawled out in the dissection tray on the table, William picked up a metal pin and pointed at a small, light brown, peanut-shaped object located on the right side of the animal. "That's it right there. You know that this is the kidney because of how it is connected to the stomach and bladder."

"Got it, thanks."

William then turned his attention to the other students and started to walk up and down the rows surveying their efforts. As he walked down the aisle he saw that he was coming up to the lab station of Tara and her lab partner, a male who looked to be at least three hundred pounds situated precariously on top of his stool. As he approached the pair he noted that her lab partner was actively engaged in jamming a metal probe into the spinal column of the frog, much to the chagrin of Tara. The result of this action was predictable. The hind legs of the frog were twitching slightly, and sometimes, they would fully extend and then retract.

"And what do we have going on here?" William posed to the pair.

Immediately dropping the metal probe, the rotund student turned towards William with his face glowing brightly red.

"Ahh...I was...umm...."

"Having a little fun?"

"Ahh...yeah. Sorry," he apologized.

"What's your name?"

"It's Nathan, sir."

"Well Nathan, was that activity described in your packet as part of the dissection procedure?"

"No. We'll get back on task," Nathan muttered.

"That's good. I'd hate to see your laboratory partner get a poor grade on this practical because you were playing around rather than focusing on the directions."

Nathan immediately turned back to the packet to figure out what he needed to work on next. William shifted his gaze to Tara who looked very appreciative of his intervention.

"Professor?" she inquired. "If the frog is dead, how was Nathan able to get the entire leg to move?"

"Well, since the frogs are only very recently deceased, a slight electric charge remains in the spinal column cells of the animal. When a probe is pushed into the spinal cavity, it causes neurons to fire and transmit an electric charge. That electric charge, if strong enough, can travel the full length of the frog and cause the muscles to contract and the leg to twitch." Flashing a quick grin at Nathan he continued with his explanation. "In fact, you can get really dramatic results if you actually introduce electricity into the spinal tissues. You see, the entire nervous system of all living animals, and humans for that matter, uses electrical impulses to control all body movement."

Obviously impressed by William's answer, Tara showed him a broad grin. "I have another question for you professor."

He responded with a smile of his own. "Yes?"

"If electricity can cause the leg of a frog to move, couldn't you use electricity to help people who have been paralyzed to walk again? I mean, couldn't someone figure out how to control those 'electrical impulses' you described to make people walk and move like they could before they were injured?"

"That's a very insightful idea," he complimented.

William was thoroughly impressed with Tara's insight and inquisitive nature. Not only was she beautiful, she was also very smart.

"Unfortunately, being able to control electricity at such a microscopic level to facilitate specific motions isn't very feasible. In fact, the electricity would end up doing more harm than good."

"Bummer. I thought that I had come up with a medical breakthrough," she joked.

"That's very innovative thinking. Maybe I should have you help me with my thesis project."

"Oh, I doubt that. What is your thesis based on?"

"Well, funny enough, I'm actually working on developing a methodology to heal injuries or damaged tissues that the body can't repair fully on its own."

He realized that he was reaching up with his left hand to rub the scar on the side of his face and stopped short, then scratched his left ear as if that was what he intended to do in the first place. Sighing silently to himself, he continued.

"My thesis is based on exploiting the regenerative properties of adult stem cells to heal those injuries. It works for a short period of time, but then the healing process stops as if the stem cells have some sort of limited shelf life. It's very frustrating and I feel like I'm at a bit of an impasse," he admitted.

"Well, couldn't you use something other than the adult stem cells?" she inquired.

"That's what a friend of mine suggested to me just last night. The problem is what else could I use?"

Thinking for a moment on William's question, Tara finally responded. "What creates the adult stem cells?"

"Well, they just exist in every part of the body – organs, tissues, etc. And then they regenerate themselves to create new cells of the tissues or organs that they're found in."

"But they had to come from somewhere right? If these adult stem cells are so powerful, shouldn't whatever created them have at least the same abilities as they do?"

At that moment, it was as if a bolt of electricity shot through William's entire body. Immediately William knew the direction to take his research. He just had to figure out how to do it. Looking at Tara he beamed with excitement.

"What's wrong," she asked.

"Nothing's wrong, you're just brilliant!" he exclaimed. "I think that you just helped me figure out a new direction to take my thesis!"

"Really? I seriously doubt that."

"No really!" he explained. "I have been so focused on how adult stem cells had to be the answer to my problem, I never allowed myself to think about the answer that was staring me right in the face. For that matter, staring at all scientists who have been trying to do this for the past ten years. You see, adult stem cells have extraordinary abilities to regenerate cells and tissues. But it's the embryonic stem cells or ESCs that hold the real power. This might not even work, but at least this gives me a new path to take my research."

"Just trying to help out!"

Looking down at his watch, he realized that the students only had about twenty minutes to complete their labs. "Ok, you two, you've got to get busy if you're going to finish this lab. Back to work!"

As William walked back to the front of the class, his mind was racing with all types of ideas and possibilities. He couldn't wait to get back into the laboratory to start working with ESCs. He opened up his notebook and started feverishly jotting down his thoughts on the new direction to take his work.

Roughly twenty minutes later all the students were cleaning up their lab stations and gathering together their belongings.

"Alright, everyone. Hopefully this has been a good experience for you. Please remember that your packets are due in two days, this coming Thursday. If anyone has any questions, feel free to send email to your 'normal' student teacher," he stipulated, emphasizing the word normal with air quotes.

And with that, everyone started filing out of the classroom. Thirty seconds later William found himself sitting at the front of the classroom with only one student remaining behind. Picking up her book bag, Tara walked up to the front of the room, until she stood opposite of him in front of the table.

"So, what about that offer you made me?"

"Offer?" he questioned, then immediately realized what she was talking about. "Oh yeah, to help you with Biology. Well, what about that date?"

"First things first," she chided in a playful manner. "You help me with my frog dissection lab and then we'll see about that date."

"Deal! Where and when did you want to get together?"

"Well, the lab's due on Thursday morning. That gives us tonight and tomorrow. What works best for you?"

Thinking for a moment, William responded. "Tomorrow's totally shot for me. I've got two classes of my own to teach, and tests to grade. So, I guess that means tonight's the night."

"Ok then, let's meet at the library say around six o'clock?"

"Works for me. It's a date."

"No, it's a study session. Let's save the date for Friday."

"Deal!"

William then put the remaining items into his own bag, hefted it back onto his shoulder, and the two of them made their way towards the door.

"I've got to get back to the lab and start working on that great idea of yours. Thanks again!"

"Don't forget. Six o'clock sharp," Tara reminded him.

"Don't worry. There's no chance of me forgetting."

Both of them walked out of the classroom and parted ways heading in different directions.

CHAPTER 5

Pleasant Evening
(Later that week)

It was already fifteen minutes after six o'clock as William pulled up in front of an apartment complex about four miles away from the USC campus. The driver side door was already half way open as he threw the car into Park. In one deft move, he sprung out of the front seat swinging the car door shut with a loud thump. Placing his keys into his front left pocket he lightly jogged to the front of the building, spotted apartment number eight up a short flight of stairs to his right, and immediately ascended the stairs two at a time.

"Man, not a great way to start out our first date," William muttered to himself. "I'm always trying to maximize my time so that I can get every last possible thing done...but then I end up being late."

Reaching the top of the stairs he paused for a second, closed his eyes and took a deep, cleansing breath. After a few seconds, he opened his eyes and reached up with his right hand to knock on the door. Much to his surprise, before his knuckles were able to rap on the wood the door swung open and William nearly fell into the open doorway. Luckily, he was able to stop himself short.

Standing in the doorway was a woman that he had never met before.

"You're late," the woman complained. "Fifteen minutes to be exact. Isn't this your first date?" She paused for a moment, looking William over from head to toe and then continued. "Tara!" she shouted. "Mr. Wonderful finally decided to show up."

Dumbfounded by the verbal attack he just had suffered from a woman whom he had never met, he stood there with his mouth partially open as if he wanted to respond, but couldn't manage to utter a sound.

"Well? Are you going to say something or just stand there with that goofy look on your face?"

William still remained silent, but his irritation with this unfriendly woman was building. Rather than lashing out with a clever retort, he simply smiled back at her through gritted teeth.

"Whom do I have the pleasure of meeting this fine evening?" he finally offered in as pleasant a tone as he could muster.

Based on the facial expression that she returned, his tone of voice must not have been genuine enough. "Wait here," she commanded, and then spun around, retreating back into the apartment.

Watching the woman as she walked into the apartment, he thought to himself that he would have considered her fairly attractive if her personality hadn't gotten in the way. She was approximately five feet five inches tall and had a petite body frame. Her skin had a darkish, olive-colored hue to it. Her face was slender, with high cheekbones, her eyes were green and she had jet-black hair that hung about two inches past her shoulders. Yes, he definitely would have thought her attractive if he had seen her walking down the street, and possibly would have gone up to her if he spotted her at a bar. But based on his brief interaction with her, he knew that her beauty stopped at the surface of her skin.

As the woman disappeared around the corner, William found himself standing awkwardly on the doorstep. Not exactly knowing what to do next, he decided to just stand there and wait patiently. No more than thirty seconds after this rude greeting, Tara appeared around the same corner of the apartment with a broad, warm smile on her face. He returned her smile as his eyes met hers, and made a mental note to himself that he really felt a connection with Tara.

"Well hello there sir!"

As she approached William she held her arms open to give him an embrace. Without hesitation, he gladly returned the gesture and gave her a friendly hug. With their arms still loosely held around each other, William noticed that his greeter had come back from around the corner and stood in the middle of the hallway with her arms crossed staring at the two of them. Releasing Tara, he leaned back and looked into Tara's eyes.

"You look positively beautiful this evening," he complimented.

"Well, you're not half bad yourself. That is, of course, if I happen to overlook the two pens and highlighter hanging out of your front shirt pocket," she replied looking down towards his chest.

Reaching up with his right hand he confirmed that he hadn't removed the contents from his shirt pocket. Slightly embarrassed, he barely managed to suppress his face from turning a light shade of red.

"At least I'm not wearing a pocket protector," he joked.

Smiling, Tara reached forward and grabbed the bottom of the shirt pocket turning it up upwards so William could see it.

"Given the ink spots that have shown through your shirt, I think I know what to get you for Christmas this year."

This time William wasn't able to suppress the blush and his cheeks turned a bright crimson color.

"I'm sorry," he apologized. "I got caught up in the lab working on my project and completely lost track of time. I finally noticed that it was just after six o'clock, so I dropped everything and rushed right over. Obviously, I didn't even have time to change my clothes."

Tara let out a rich laugh while she leaned her head backward. Bringing her head back to her original position she looked at William directly in the eyes and took both of his hands. "Please, don't think twice about it. I'm simply giving you a bad time. I think it's wonderful how devoted you are to your work at the University. And besides...I'm kind of into dorks."

William's face broke into a smile. "Well then, you've hit the jackpot with me!"

Both of them laughed again, still holding hands as they stood in the doorway of the apartment.

"Ahem," interjected the woman standing at the other end of the hallway.

"Oh, forgive me Kim," apologized Tara. "William, let me introduce you to my roommate, Kim Dyson."

Still standing with her arms neatly folded in front of her, Kim shifted her weight onto her right foot. "Definitely attractive," William thought to himself, "but boy, I'd shoot myself if I had to be around this woman for any length of time."

"We've met," responded Kim in a cool, monotone voice.

William didn't say anything, but simply returned her ungracious tone with an irritated gaze. Tara finally broke the awkward silence.

"Well, we've probably got to get going if we're going to

eat any time before eight o'clock." Releasing William's hands, she turned around to face Kim. "I'll probably be out a little late this evening so don't wait up for me. And I will be as quiet as a mouse when I get home."

"Have a good time," she simply responded, then turned around and disappeared a final time back into the apartment.

"She's a real charmer, that one," William whispered under his breath.

"Shhh," Tara breathed quietly. "She might hear you."

Ignoring her caution, he continued. "I mean, I bet the boys are beating down her door to get some of the warmth and sunshine that she passes out. A real Miss Congeniality."

Smiling, and obviously suppressing laughter, she grabbed his hand again.

"Ok, you...time for us to go! Let me grab my jacket and we can head out."

Tara opened the closet door to her left, removed a light jacket, and shut the door again.

"Would you?"

Without a word, William took the jacket from Tara and held it open for her to slip her arms into.

"Alrighty then...we're off!"

Exiting the apartment, Tara shut the door and they made their way down the stairs. William guided them over to his car parked in front of the complex and held the passenger side door open for Tara.

"Quite the gentleman," she complimented.

William simply gave her a smile and a nod, and shut the door quietly once she was situated fully inside the car. He made his way around the car and hopped in the driver side, closing the door behind him. Immediately he put the key in the ignition, put the car into drive, and they were on their way.

"Ok," he said. "I've got to ask how you got hooked up with that one."

"Who Kim? Oh, she's harmless. She's definitely a little rough around the edges, but she's fine once you get to know her."

"Yeah, if you had any desire to get to know her."

"Oh stop!" she chided.

William simply responded back with laughter to which Tara joined in.

For about the next twenty minutes they drove through the city streets of Los Angeles towards a new Mexican restaurant that William had heard great reviews about from Don. Both of them were actively engaged in conversation the entire ride about fairly innocuous topics. Finally, William turned into the parking lot of an obviously new building located on the corner of two busy streets. He grabbed the first spot that he could find and hopped out of the car as soon as he turned off the engine.

"Now, you just wait there for me. We've already established that I'm a gentleman, so I better keep playing the part."

Running around the car he came to a stop next to Tara's window. Opening the door with his right hand he reaches into the car with his left to help her exit the vehicle.

"My lady," he intoned formally. "Might I escort you into this fine dining establishment?"

Taking his hand, she responded.

"Why thank you, kind sir. There aren't very many men left in this world with good manners. I'm going to have to keep my eye on this one. I wouldn't want to see him get away."

Having helped Tara out of the car, he shut the door and escorted her to the entrance of the restaurant. William immediately walked up to the greeter and let her know that he had a reservation for six thirty.

"Of course," the hostess responded. "You're about twenty minutes late, but we should be able to seat you right away. We're not that busy this evening."

Looking to Tara with a sheepish grin he shrugged his shoulders. "Story of my life. Always running behind."

After being escorted to their table, William and Tara both looked over the menu deciding on what they were going to order for their meal. After placing their order with the waiter, they sat taking in the Mexican décor of the establishment.

"I love the bright colors, and wood carvings," Tara said.

"Yes," William agreed. "Very authentic looking. At least it looks authentic."

"So why don't you tell me a bit about yourself, William? I'd love to hear about where you grew up, your family, your goals."

"Well, I grew up right here in Southern California. In Costa Mesa actually, so not that far away from where we are now. My father is a tax attorney and my mother is an elementary school teacher. She's done that for almost thirty years now. I have a brother who is four years younger than me, and everyone still lives in Costa Mesa except for me. We get together about once a month at our parents' house for a Sunday night dinner. It's kind of a tradition, especially during football season. We'll get together about five o'clock in the evening, my Mom will throw frozen a lasagna in the oven along with some French bread, and we'll watch Sunday night football together. It's really a good time and something that we've been doing ever since I can remember."

"That does sound like fun," Tara commented.

"You're welcome to join us if you'd like. A week from Sunday we're getting together to watch the Niners trounce the Dolphins."

Tara flashed William a big smile and let out a small giggle.

"What?" he asked.

"We're not even done with our first date, and you're already making plans for our second one."

"Well, I thought..." he replied, but Tara interrupted him immediately.

"Yes, I'd love to."

He returned her smile. "Excellent. Let's focus on this one to begin with, shall we?"

"Certainly. Tell me about your thesis. How have things been going this week?"

William smiled and his eyes widened.

"This has been an excellent week," he exclaimed. "I was dead serious about how your idea was a good one when you made me think of an alternative for adult stem cells. Over the last three days, I was able to conduct some preliminary tests with embryonic stem cells and saw a dramatic improvement in the regenerative process of the damaged cells. You see ESCs are what is called pluripotent, which means that they're immature, and not specific in function or designation. That means that they can develop into..."

"Excuse me," she interrupted. "In English? You lost me at regenerative."

"Oh sorry," he laughed. "To say it simply, ESCs haven't been programmed yet. They have the ability to turn into any type of cell in the entire human body. This ability makes them ideal, in my opinion, to heal injuries virtually anywhere."

"I see. That's what I thought," she jested. "Blurry potion you say?"

"Pluripotent," he laughed. "I know...it's a fifty-cent word."

"More like a fifty-dollar word if you ask me."

"I'm still a long way from proving anything yet, but I really think that this is going to be a good direction for my thesis. And who knows, maybe I'll actually be able to help people heal injuries."

Without thinking, Tara's gaze immediately dropped to William's left cheek at the scar he incurred in his youth. Almost jerking her head upwards, she looked back into William's eyes when she realized she was staring. His expression immediately changed, becoming self-conscious of the disfigurement his face bore.

"I'm sorry," she apologized. "I didn't mean to make you uncomfortable."

Taking a deep breath, William responded. "It's ok. Really! I've lived with this mark on my face since I was fourteen. You'd think that I'd be used to it by now."

Tara felt sincere compassion for William at that moment. While she had noticed the scar on his face before, she really hadn't thought much of it. To her, it really didn't stand out that much. But what she had failed to consider was the emotional scars that William likely suffered from the disfigurement.

"It happened to me when I was young and dumb. Some

friends and I were literally playing with fire, and unfortunately, it bit me in the ass. Well, in the face to be more accurate. This is about as good as it's going to get. I had multiple skin grafts and surgeries, but there's only so much that science can do."

Knowing the answer to her question already, she asked anyway. "That's why you chose the thesis that you did right?"

"More specifically, this is the main reason why I chose the field of molecular biology. I figured that there really should be a better form of treatment for injuries like this. This has been one of the driving forces in my life. It pushed me in the direction of math and science, and guided me into the field that I'm trying to get my doctorate in."

"That you *are* going to get your doctorate in," she positively corrected.

"Exactly," he agreed.

After pausing for a moment, he continued.

"You really gave me an insightful idea. There's only one problem though."

"Oh, what's that?"

"Supply. You see...there is a very limited supply of human ESCs that scientists are able to use in their research. On August 9, 2001, George W. Bush signed the Human Embryonic Stem Cell policy that placed significant restrictions on the use of ESCs for research purposes. Any ESCs that were derived prior to nine o'clock p.m. on August 9, 2001, can be used in research and receive Federal funds. Any research utilizing ESCs that were derived after that date and time are not considered for Federal funding. As you can probably imagine, it created a virtual gold rush for the limited supply by most major research facilities in the United States. Everyone wanted access to cells that would qualify for Federal funding."

"So, does that mean that you can't move forward in your research?"

"Not exactly. Everything that I'm doing right now focuses on using ESCs of laboratory mice. The problem comes once I have perfected my methodology with rodent ESCs, and I'm ready to start working with human ESCs. While USC has a good number of human ESCs stored in the Cryo freeze, their use is pretty much restricted to only tenured professors."

Thinking for a moment, Tara asked what she thought was an obvious question. "Couldn't you just base your research on the ESCs of mice?"

"I could, but that would mean that someone else would come along and figure out how to perfect this with humans. I don't want to sound too prideful, but this is my baby. I want to take this beyond trials with mice and actually perfect it in human subjects."

"So, what does that mean for your research then?"

Without hesitating, William responded. "It means that I might have to go about securing human ESCs in a more nefarious manner."

Tara gasped at William's suggestion. "Do you mean to steal them?" she probed.

"The thought had occurred to me."

"Oh, you better not say anything about this to my dad. He'd blow a circuit."

Feeling that the conversation was getting a little too intense, William thought it might be a good idea to switch the topic a bit.

"Enough about me. Let's talk about you now. Tell me about your background and family."

"Hmmm," Tara mused. "Let me think. Well, I'm an only child. My mother died of cancer when I was only four years old. That meant that my dad had to raise me on his own."

"He never remarried?"

"Nope. He always jokes with me that my mother ruined him. He was so in love with her that he knew no one else would ever be able to take her place."

"Wow. He sounds like a great guy."

"He is. In fact, he's one of the most generous and thoughtful people that I know."

"What does he do?"

"He's a minister for a local Christian church. He was a minister before he and my mom met. In fact, that's how they met. She attended a service that he was leading. As they explain it, it was love at first sight."

"I didn't think that ministers could get married," William pointed out.

"You're thinking about Catholic Priests. A minister can marry, and most actually do."

"Ah, so that's why you were saying that your father would pop a gasket if I told him that I was thinking about obtaining ESCs in a less than legal manner."

"Stop it! You're not going to steal anything. I'm sure if you talk with one of your professors, they'd be more than happy to help you."

"Maybe," he considered. "But it never hurts to have a backup plan."

"Anyways...my father raised me by himself, and really gave me everything that I could have ever wanted. Most importantly, he loved me."

"Do you see him very often?"

"Every Sunday at church. We moved here from Iowa about eight years ago. He lives just over in Santa Monica. You'll have to come with me to church sometime and I'll introduce you to him."

William visibly flinched at her suggestion.

"You do go to church don't you," she inquired.

"Well...I...ummm..." he stammered.

"Do you believe in God?"

"It's not that I don't believe in God, it's just that I don't feel that there is any proof of his existence."

"No proof?" she pressed. "Proof of God is all around us. He's everywhere that you look. He's in life itself."

She paused for a thoughtful moment and then continued.

"Maybe you don't actually see God in person, but evidence of his existence is irrefutable."

"Ok...Ok! Don't get all worked up. I didn't say that I don't believe in God. I just don't think that there is sufficient empirical evidence of his existence. So, I guess that I'm more of an agnostic," he quickly added to try and placate the situation.

Laughing out loud, Tara responded.

"You really are a scientist, aren't you?"

She paused for a moment looking thoughtfully at William across the table. She reached for her water glass and started to rub her index finger around the rim of the glass in a pensive manner.

"Uh-oh. What are you cooking up in your head?"

"Me?" she responded as innocently as possible.

"Yes, you."

"Oh nothing," she stated in an offhand manner. "Nothing at all."

"Yeah. That's what's got me worried."

At that point, both of them started to laugh again and the waiter brought their food to the table. They spent the next hour and a half sharing different experiences from each of their lives, laughing, and learning more about each other over dinner and drinks. At the conclusion of the meal, William escorted Tara back to the car, once again opening her car door for her.

"Such chivalry. I probably shouldn't expect this continue for very long, should I?" she asked, as he was about to shut her door.

"Of course you should. My parents taught me to always treat a lady with respect. Some people say that it's too old fashion. I think that some things never go out of fashion."

He closed her door, walked back around the car and jumped in from the driver's side.

"You really are a good guy," Tara remarked.

William smiled back at her, started up the car, and proceeded to drive Tara back home. About twenty-five minutes later he pulled up in front of her apartment complex. Once again, he hopped out of the driver seat to open her door for her and escorted her up the flight of stairs back to her apartment.

"I really had a wonderful time with you tonight," Tara commented. "A really, really, wonderful time."

Without giving William a chance to respond, she reached up with her right hand, cradled his face, and leaned forward to give him a kiss. William met her lips with his in a soft kiss that lasted for only about five seconds. As they pulled apart from each other they both had a smile on their face. William reached down with his right hand and took her hand in his, squeezing her fingers gently.

"You've got my number, right?" she inquired.

"Sure do!" he replied.

"Ok then, be sure to use it."

Releasing her hand, he started down the stairs and stopped halfway, turning back to face her.

"Don't worry, I'll be certain to use it," he replied.

Tara then opened her door and watched William walk back to his car and drive off slowly down the street. Smiling, she slowly closed the door and turned off the porch light. As she turned to walk back into the apartment she gave a quick gasp as she made out the dark outline of a person standing at the end of the darkened hallway leading back towards the bedrooms.

"Kim! You scared me to death."

Without a word, Kim walked forward slowly out of the dark shadows of the hallway into the light coming from the ceiling fixture next to the front door. Coming to a stop roughly eight feet from Tara, she leaned up against the wall with her arms crisscrossed in front of her, held tightly to her chest. Tara could not make out the features of her face clearly, but she could make out enough to tell that her roommate wasn't in the best of moods. With her head tilted downwards, her brow cast a dark shadow across her face making it impossible for her to see Kim's eyes. Unexplainably, Tara felt a chill start from the middle of her back, crawling upwards until the top of her head tingled. She felt as if the woman standing in front of her was someone she hadn't even met before which intensified the tightening sensation she felt in her stomach. Kim didn't move or say a word...she just stood there glaring at Tara.

"Kim?"

Without a word, Kim reached over to the light switch on

the wall and flipped on a larger, bright light in the middle of the hallway.

"Oh, I'm sorry Tara," she apologized. "I was sound asleep in bed, and then the next thing I knew I was standing in the hallway looking at you. What time is it? Did you just get home?"

The previous impression that Tara had of being confronted by a stranger immediately left as she saw her friend standing in the hallway in her pajamas and she let out an audible sigh.

"You scared me to death Kim!"

"I'm sorry. I really don't know how I even got here. I must have been sleepwalking or something. How was your date?"

"I had a really great time," she responded. "But I'm very tired. I'll tell you all about it in the morning."

Tara walked past Kim down the hallway towards her bedroom door. As she passed by her roommate she felt like someone, or something, was staring at her. Opening her door, she turned back to Kim.

"You better get back into bed yourself. Goodnight Kim."

"Goodnight Tara," she responded in a monotone voice.

As Tara entered her room she closed the door behind her.

Kim remained in the hallway and reached back over, flipped off the light switch, and stood silently in the dark hallway staring at the closed door to Tara's bedroom.

CHAPTER 6

Breakthrough
(A Few Months Later)

William sat alone in the laboratory located in the Biology building at the USC campus. It was approximately eleven thirty p.m. and he was struggling to keep his eyes open. Sitting at a desk in the front of the room, William was typing notes into his personal journal.

February 18, 2005 – The last few months have been comprised of professional successes and failures. I have spent the majority of my time holed up in the lab working on my thesis project, trying to make progress. I was able to achieve considerable progress in leveraging ESCs to encourage the reparation of damaged tissues and cells in laboratory mice.

In order to create a structure onto which to introduce the ESCs into the subject, I was able to leverage a biodegradable gelatin-based scaffold made from synthetic polyethylene glycol. This precisely built structure provided the ideal foundation onto which to introduce the ESCs in close proximity to existing healthy cells, and successfully promoted growth along the microscopic scaffolding structure.

However, I now find myself at a bit of an impasse with regard to advancing my research. While the introduction of ESCs promoted an increase in the level of cell restoration and the duration under which it occurred, eventually, and usually within one hour of the introduction of ESCs, the cellular activity decreased until stopping completely. Further, the immune system of the mouse has been very problematic. While ESCs should be readily accepted into the subject, the immune system eventually seems to recognize them as a foreign entity and ultimately fights against and kills the ESCs.

William leaned back from his laptop rubbing his eyes, and then ran his fingers through his hair scratching the back of his head. He paused momentarily thinking about the last passage that he typed.

"There's got to be something that can be done to prevent the mouse's immune system from rejecting the ESCs," he thought to himself. "But what? Simply matching the blood type of the ESC donor mouse to that of the host mouse isn't working. There's something else going on at a genetic level."

Similar to humans, mice are complex organisms. Matching the blood type should increase the likelihood of acceptance by the host mouse by ensuring the at least the blood's antigen proteins are similar. However, this has proven insufficient as the immune system continues to reject the cells.

Additional research is required, but unless there is a way to ensure that the host mouse will not reject the ESCs, further progression down this path will...

Suddenly, William took in a sharp, abbreviated breath with his fingers still hovering over his keyboard, virtually frozen in place. His eyes widened and his mind raced. An increasing feeling of excitement began to rise in his chest as the muscles in his forearms tightened. He began to take shallow breaths as he thought through his revelation.

"If the mouse won't accept ESCs from any other mouse...I need to use ESCs from the same mouse!" he enthusiastically exclaimed.

Leaping up from his stool, he would have fallen to the floor if he hadn't been able to grab a hold of the table in front of him. Steadying himself he paused for a moment in deep thought.

"THAT'S IT!" he finally shouted. "I'm SOOO stupid!!"

Slapping the lid of his laptop shut, he tossed it into his bag along with a few papers scattered across the top of the table, slung it over his shoulder, and bolted for the parking lot. After making it to his car, he turned the engine over and accelerated so fast that the tires screeched leaving nearly four feet of rubber on the ground. Keeping an eye out for any cops, he drove as quickly as possible over to Tara's apartment.

Upon arrival, he hit the brakes coming to an abrupt stop, with the front right tire edging up slightly onto the curb. He jumped out of the car slamming the driver side door, ran up to Tara's building and ascended the stairs two at a time. Immediately he starting to loudly knock on the front door of the apartment and then froze. Grimacing, he slowly glanced down at his watch and realized that it was twelve fifteen AM.

He stood there silently, straining his ears to see if he could sense any activity within the apartment.

"Maybe they're still asleep," he hopefully thought to himself.

Sadly, he heard the familiar sound of footsteps gradually getting louder as someone approached the front door from within the apartment. The footsteps paused as the person was likely looking through the peephole to see who had come calling so late in the evening. The sound of a chain being unhooked startled William, followed almost immediately by the sound of the deadbolt being flicked aside. The next instant, the door flung open and William found himself confronted by a very angry looking woman, who regrettably was not Tara.

"What in the hell do you think you're doing!" she barked.

"I'm so sorry Kim!" he apologized. "I just figured out something that I've been working on for quite some time and I couldn't wait to tell Tara. I can come back if she's still sleeping."

"Oh no, you don't! You woke me up, so let's go and wake up Tara too!"

William readied himself to protest, but Kim immediately turned around and stomped back down the hallway towards Tara's door. Stopping in front of her door, she began to roughly pound on it with her closed right fist.

"Tara! William's here and he said that he's got to tell you something...NOW!"

Sighing to himself, William stepped into the apartment and shut the front door. He scowled at Kim who returned his annoyance with an icy stare.

"TARA," she yelled while knocking on the door, "WILLIAM WANTS TO TALK WITH YOU!"

After a brief moment, the door opened and Tara walked out into the hallway, none too happy to have been woken up. By the look of her hair, and the moistened section of the collar of her pajamas, she had been sound asleep for quite a while already.

Before giving Tara a chance to talk, William took the opportunity to try and diffuse the situation.

"I'm sorry Tara! I was working late in the lab..."

"Obviously!" Kim interrupted.

Ignoring her he continued. "And I think I was able to make a breakthrough." Flashing a closed smile while sheepishly shrugging his shoulders, he tried to look as apologetic as possible.

"Oh, it's ok," Tara replied. "Let's go into the kitchen and you can tell me all about it.

"ARE YOU KIDDING ME?!" Kim protested, obviously upset by Tara's calm response. "He woke me up from a dead sleep!"

"I'm sure he didn't mean to," she abjectly said in an attempt to placate Kim's anger. "I'm sure that he would have waited until the morning if he had realized how late it was."

"You...I...he...Oh, forget it!" Kim stammered.

She threw her hands in the air, stomped down the hallway and slammed the door behind her.

William glanced at Tara and visibly grimaced in response to her roommate's reaction. Tara silently motioned for William to follow her as she walked into the kitchen located at the other end of the apartment. Sitting down at the table, Tara lightly rubbed at the corners of her eyes, neatly folded her arms in front of her and crossed her legs. William stood next to the table not saying a word until Tara gestured to the chair sitting opposite from her.

After taking a seat, he leaned towards Tara and clasped his hands atop of the table.

"I figured it out!" he whispered. "At least I think I figured it out."

"You figured what out?"

"Remember me telling you about how the immune system of lab rats was essentially identifying the ESCs as a foreign body and was eradicating them from the host?"

"In English," Tara responded with a blank stare.

"Oh, sorry. A mouse's immune system will attack anything in the body that it thinks is an enemy. Similar to when your white blood cells attack a virus like a cold. That's what has been preventing me from being able to repair an injury. It thinks that the ESCs that I'm introducing are invaders, like bacteria."

"Ok...I follow you."

"Well," William continued, "I was making some notes in my journal when I came to the realization about how to get around the mouse rejecting the ESCs. All I need to do is to use the actual Embryonic Stem Cells of the same mouse. That way, there's no reason that it would be rejected."

Tara thought for a moment on what William just explained.

"Oh, I think I get it," she said while raising an eyebrow. "That would mean that the white blood cells wouldn't attack the ESCs since they 'belonged' there right?"

"Exactly! Up until the point that the white blood cells attack, the ESCs haven't been showing any sign of deterioration or decline. My thinking is that if we can prevent the mouse's immune system from fighting them that they will continue to regenerate complimentary tissue leading to a complete restructure or healing of the injury."

"So where do you get ESCs from?"

"Well, that's what makes mice so perfect a test subject. All I need to do is to extract ESCs from a mouse embryo. It only takes about nineteen days for the embryo to develop into a baby mouse, and then another six to ten weeks for it to grow into adulthood. That means that within as little 9 weeks I would be ready to validate my hypothesis."

Tara sat for a moment considering what William had just explained.

"What are you thinking about?"

"Well. I understand what you're saying about how this would work with mice – I totally get it. But the whole point of your research is to be able to help humans, right? How are you going to get the cells from human embryos? Wouldn't you have to, what was the word, 'extract' them before the human was even born? If that's the case, you wouldn't be able to help anyone who is currently alive right?"

William paused for a second contemplating what he had just heard. While her question was so simple, Tara had unknowingly identified a critical issue, likely *the* critical obstacle to be overcome with his hypothesis.

"I hadn't really thought about that," he admitted.

After thinking for a moment, he could only come up with one answer, but he knew that Tara wasn't going to like what he had to say.

"What?" she asked. "You're not telling me something."

After waiting for another thirty seconds, William finally responded.

"Well, there is one way that I could get the embryonic stems cells."

"What's that?"

"I would need to create an embryonic clone of the human for whom we needed the ESCs. About four or five days after fertilization, human embryos reach what is called the blastocyst stage. During this stage, we can harvest the ESCs from the embryo. At this point, the ESCs are what is called pluripotent, meaning, that they're unspecified and can develop into any of the more than two hundred and twenty cell types that comprise the human body. This characteristic, as well as the fact that under specific circumstances ESCs can regenerate themselves indefinitely, is what makes them an ideal candidate for my research."

"Wait a second. In all that scientific mumbo jumbo, didn't you say 'harvest' the ESCs from the embryo? What happens to the embryo when they are harvested?"

A strong feeling of consternation swept across William. Not knowing how else to respond, he just simply answered.

"The embryo is destroyed in the process."

Tara's expression changed from one of keen interest to one of complete apprehension and disgust.

"YOU KILL THE BABY?"

"The cells are destroyed. It really isn't a baby yet. It has the ability to develop into a baby, but it isn't really alive at that point of development."

Tara stood up abruptly from her chair, staring at William with her hands planted firmly on her hips.

"You're joking, right? An embryo *is* a life form. So essentially, you would be killing a baby...that's completely unacceptable."

"Think of the good this will bring. All of the people that will benefit from if it actually works. I know that you have strong reservations about this..."

"STRONG?! Try vehemently against!"

"Ok. I get it. You disagree with this as an approach. But what if the research that I'm working on might be applied to a good friend of yours who was paralyzed in an accident? Or what if you had a child with a heart deformity that my work could not only treat, but also cure the defect that they are contending against? I agree there are ethical questions about scientific research, but you have to take into consideration the greater good. Think of the thousands, potentially millions of lives that will be saved."

Tara stood there motionless, considering what William had said. After a few moments, her body language visibly changed as she removed her hands from her hips and took her seat again. Before William could say anything, a thump followed by the sound of glass breaking came from the hallway just outside of the kitchen startling both of them. William jumped up from his chair and rounded the corner leading to the hallway ready to do battle. As he stepped into the hallway he was surprised to find Kim kneeling on the ground picking up pieces of glass.

"Are you ok?" William pressed. "What happened?"

"Oh, I'm just a klutz," she responded without even looking up at William. "Ouch...dammit!" she suddenly exclaimed.

Standing up from her crouched position, Kim cradled her right hand in her left. Based on the amount of blood pooling into her palm, she had obviously cut herself seriously. A deep scowl cut across her face and as she gruffly pushed past William making her way to the kitchen sink.

"Oh Kim!" Tara empathized. "Is it bad?"

"Yup. I did myself a good one."

Turning on the faucet with her uninjured hand, Tara let the cool water rinse the blood from her hand, and gently flushed out the wound in her palm.

"What happened?" William asked again.

"Well, I was in my room trying to fall back asleep, but you two were talking so loud that I wasn't able to drift off to sleep. I got out of bed and was going to come and ask the two of you if you could talk a little quieter, and then accidentally knocked one of the picture frames off of the wall."

Pulling her hand back from the running water, it appeared as if the majority of the bleeding had stopped. Holding her hand in a slight cupping shape over the sink, she gently stretched her fingers outwards. When she got to the point of almost having her hand fully open, some of the fatty tissue from the inside of her hand protruded up through the gash in her palm. Tara visibly turned gray at the sight of her injury.

"You've got to keep this elevated above your heart, and you're going to need some stitches," he advised while holding her hand above her shoulders.

Kim tried to pull away from William, but he refused to let her go.

"Tara, can you check and see if you have any gauze? We should wrap this so nothing gets into the cut and causes infection."

Without saying a word, Tara jumped up and headed back down the hallway.

"Watch out for the glass!" William cautioned. "You don't have any slippers on."

William watched as Tara carefully circumvented the glass on the floor and disappeared into the bathroom. After about five seconds she returned with a first aid kit.

Rummaging through the box she found a tightly wound roll of medical gauze and handed it to William. Taking the bandage from Tara, he undid the end of the gauze and started to gently wrap it around the palm of Kim's hand.

"We don't want to wrap this too tight. If the wound starts to bleed again the gauze will end up sticking to it when it dries, and that won't be very pleasant to pull off." William paused for a second to survey his handy work. "That should do for now."

"Does it hurt?" Tara gingerly pried.

"It really stings, but it's not that bad." Kim looked at William, giving him an odd smile. "Thanks for helping me take care of this," she said in an almost grateful tone of voice.

"No problem, but we've got to get you fixed up."

"Do you really think that I need to get stitches?" she protested.

Amused, William responded. "Well, based on the fact that the tissue on the inside squished up through your cut when you opened your hand...yes, you need to get stitches."

"Well, I've got to get dressed. I'm not going to the hospital wearing my fuzzy blue pajamas."

"I'm coming as well," Tara chimed in. "Give us a quick second."

"Sure thing," William responded. "I'll just clean up the glass from the hallway."

Both Tara and Kim disappeared down the hallway and William retrieved a dustpan and broom from underneath the kitchen sink. Kneeling down, he quickly swept up the pieces of glass into the dustpan and stood up. At that moment, he looked at the spot on the wall where the picture had been hanging. He had expected it to be positioned at about waist level, maybe a little bit lower, where Kim could have hit it with her hand as she walked down the hall. To his consternation, there was a hook on the wall where the picture had been hanging at about shoulder height. Perplexed, he flipped over the broken frame lying in the dustpan and saw a thin metal wire stretched across the back of the frame.

"There's no way she accidentally knocked this off the wall as she was walking towards the kitchen," he thought silently to himself. "She must have been eavesdropping on our conversation, clinging to the wall to stay hidden from our view."

William abruptly snapped his head to his left and found Kim standing in the hallway no more than two feet away, silently staring at him. Startled by her sudden appearance, he audibly sucked in a quick breath and took a step backward.

"Something wrong?" she inquired in a manner that hinted at the fact that she knew exactly what he had been thinking.

"Wrong?" he responded in a flustered manner. "Oh no, nothing's wrong. You just startled me."

"Good. By the way, I wanted to tell you that your idea of using embryonic stem cells is a really good one. I think that you should focus on making that work."

Before William could respond, Tara emerged out of her room. "Ok, let's get you to urgent care before it gets even later!"

Kim turned to follow Tara as she headed out the front door and paused for a moment. Tilting her head sideways she gave William a sidelong glance over her left shoulder.

"You coming?" she almost purred.

The expression on her face made William's skin crawl, and the sound of her voice made his stomach churn. Without saying anything else, she walked out the front door following Tara.

William stood there for a moment, and then followed them both down the stairs. Sitting in her car with the driver's door open, Tara started the engine and immediately hopped out and turned towards William.

"Why don't you just let me take her down to the hospital. No need for all of us to stay up late."

Before William could voice his disapproval, Kim chimed in.

"Good idea Tara. Let's go!" she agreed as she opened up the passenger door and hopped in.

Before shutting the door, she looked at William standing next to the car with a confounded look on his face.

"I guess we'll see you later?" she whispered before getting into the front seat.

Still perplexed, William looked over at Tara and motioned towards the back of the car.

"Why don't you let me go with you to the hospital," he began. "That way I can at least keep you company while you wait for Kim."

"Oh, it's ok. Really. And besides, it will give her a bit of time to cool off."

"That's probably a good idea," William conceded. "Is she always this angry?"

Kim thought for a brief moment then responded. "Actually, she's usually in a fairly good mood. Come to think of it though, she has seemed to become more and more distant over the past few months, and very quick to lose her temper."

"Distant in what way?"

"Being in the same room as me, but not really being present. She seems to easily lose interest in things we are talking about, and I often find her lost in thought or just looking in front of her like she is staring at something, but nothing is there. Something is definitely a little off with her and I can't put my finger on it."

Looking through the rear window at Kim to confirm she was still in the car, he leaned closer to Tara and spoke in a hushed tone.

"I don't think that Kim was telling the truth about how the picture fell off the wall."

"What do you mean?"

"Well, when the two of you went to change into some clothes, I noticed where the picture was hanging that had fallen the floor. There's no way that Kim could have accidentally hit that as she walked by. It was too high."

"So, what are you saying happened then?"

"I think she was eavesdropping on our conversation," he proposed.

"Eavesdropping? Don't be ridiculous. Why would she be listening in on us talking about your thesis? Don't you think you're being a bit paranoid?"

"Maybe. Even still, I want you to be more careful around her. Especially what you say."

"Whatever you say. I really should get her to the hospital. I'll give you a call in the morning."

"Alright." He paused for a second and continued. "Tara, please don't be too upset about my idea to create an embryonic clone. In all likelihood, I won't be able to even create one. I mean it should work with a lab rat since it's been done many times before. And proving that my theory works, even if just on mice, should be sufficient to get me my doctorate. But taking it to the next level of cloning a human will be nearly impossible."

"It's ok William. I was really taken aback by the idea of destroying a human embryo. You've got to remember my upbringing. But I do agree with you that this idea could potentially save many, many lives."

William was visibly relieved by Tara's comments. "It's really good to hear you say that."

With that, Tara leaned over, gave him a quick kiss, and started back towards the driver side door. As she went to get back in the car, William glanced back at Kim through the rear window to find her looking back at him over her left shoulder. Despite the fact that the interior light in the car was on, her face was concealed by shadows making it difficult to see her eyes. However, he was able to make out that she was wearing a thin smile on her face. After a brief moment, she turned around facing forward.

Walking back up to the sidewalk, he watched as the car pulled away from the curb and headed out into the chill, dark night. As the car rounded the corner, William made his way back to his own car and drove back to his apartment.

CHAPTER 7

Partner

(Later that Evening)

While it was only eight a.m., William had already been working for over four hours in the laboratory. After leaving Tara's apartment he intended to go back to his home and get as much sleep as possible before starting the next day. However, after lying in bed for two hours staring at the ceiling, he figured that he might as well go in and continue working on his thesis.

The science building was just starting to bustle with students as they came scrambling in for their first class of the day. The lab that William was working in was usually unoccupied until about eleven o'clock on Thursdays. To William's surprise, the door in the back of the room unexpectedly swung open and his friend Don came striding into the lab.

"What's shaking?" Don asked.

"Not too much. What are you doing here this early? Normally you don't get out of bed until ten in the morning. Are you feeling ok?"

"Ha ha! Yes, I'm fine. I would have still been sleeping but I got a call this morning around five a.m. from this girl that I've been seeing."

"You? Dating a girl? Since when have you ever been serious about just one girl?" he questioned feigning amazement.

This time it was Don's turn to laugh. "Yeah, yeah. I know. I guess I've not been too monogamous before. But there's something different about this one."

A broad grin crept across William's face. "Welcome to

the club, my friend. It's about time you grew up a little bit. Who is she?"

"No one that you'd know I'm sure. She's an undergraduate student that I literally bumped into over at the student union about four weeks ago." He thoughtfully paused and then continued. "It really was a total accident that we met. I was grabbing a couple napkins from the counter, and when I turned around we collided."

"Very graceful of you!"

Ignoring his comment, he continued. "Well, of course I dumped the contents of my cup, half of which ended up on her. Amazingly, she wasn't even mad. She just started to laugh."

"I would have smacked you upside the head."

"At any rate, that's how we first met. I gave her my phone number so I could at least pay for her shirt that I ruined. She called me that same night and asked me to go out for a cup of coffee – of course this time, she wanted to drink it rather than wear it. And the rest is pretty much history. We've been seeing each other pretty much every day since. She's very sweet, and gorgeous of course. Did I mention that she was gorgeous?"

"Ah...yeah. I think you did," he replied smiling. "So why did she call you so early this morning. Doesn't she know what a slacker you are?"

Overlooking his comment, he responded. "She actually called me from the emergency room of the hospital."

"Yikes!" William exclaimed. "I hope that she's ok."

"Yeah, she ended up being fine. She had to go in for some stitches because she cut her hand pretty bad"

William froze for a second not believing what he was hearing, standing there with a dumbfounded look on his face.

"What's wrong," Don pressed.

"You said she cut her hand correct?"

"Yeah."

"Was it her right hand?"

"Yes. But how do you know that?"

A ton of emotions flooded William's mind and he sat down roughly on the stool behind him. After a few seconds, he spoke.

"Her name isn't 'Kim' by any chance, is it?" he asked while he hoped to himself that he was completely wrong.

"Dude! How do you know what her name is?"

Tilting his head backward he let out a sigh and then responded. "I was there when she cut her hand. Kim is Tara's roommate!"

Visibly surprised, Don also took a seat on a stool next to him. After about five seconds he finally responded.

"Wait a second! The girl that you've been telling me about, Tara's roommate, who you said was a total psycho, is actually the same girl that I'm dating?!"

William broke out into loud laughter. "I'm afraid so my friend!"

Don paused for a second and then started laughing himself. "It figures!"

Still laughing, William continued. "Well, I guess we have different tastes in women."

"I'm certain of that," Don replied. "I'm amazed though. She's nothing like the girl that you've described. Kim is extremely nice, considerate, and very into me."

"I guess 'love' does weird things to people. Well in your case, I guess 'lust' has clouded your judgment."

"What were you doing over at their apartment so late last night? Kim said that she cut her hand around one thirty in the morning."

"Well, last night I was working late in the lab on my thesis. As I was jotting down some notes I had a revelation about what would make my thesis successful."

"Don't keep it to yourself!" Don exclaimed throwing up his hands in the air. "What was your breakthrough?"

"Remember how I was describing to you that the host lab rat kept rejecting the ESCs when I introduce them."

"How could I forget? You've been whining about that for the past two months!"

Ignoring Don's jab, William continued. "The lab rats would initially accept the ESCs and the injured area would start to show an increase in regenerative processes. After about thirty minutes those processes would begin to slow, then stop entirely. The rat's immune system was rejecting the cells. That's when it hit me. Rather than simply introducing the ESCs of some random rat, why not use the ESCs of that same rat?!"

Don thought for a brief moment, then a broad grin creased his face. "Brilliant my friend!"

"That's exactly what I thought!"

"So, let's think through this. You're going to extract the ESCs a specific point in the fertilization process, but in the process of extracting those ESCs you will destroy the rat embryo, won't you?"

"True. That's why I need to create an embryonic clone of the rat! I'll extract the ESCs from one of the embryos, and let the other embryo develop into a baby rat. Then once it's approximately twenty days old, I can inflict a dramatic injury and then introduce that same rat's ESCs to the injury site."

Don paused again thinking through the logic. An even broader grin appeared on his face.

"I want in!"

A bit surprised, William looked at Don in a quizzical manner.

"Don't you have your own thesis project to worry about?" Don inquired.

"Absolutely. But the scale of what you're going to do, let alone the significance of your research if you were successful, would easily justify two graduate students working together on this, don't you think? Besides, if you continue to work on this alone it will be years before you're ready to present to the board.

"And think about this. Professor Mabel who's sponsoring my thesis project has been successfully working on cloning mice for the past two years. I'm certain that he'd be willing to share his research, putting us significantly down the path of proving out your theory."

William seriously considered the proposition, while Don sat there with an excited look of anticipation on his face. Finally, William flashed a sidelong grin.

"You're in!" he exclaimed while extending his right hand. Don quickly grasped the extended hand and firmly squeezed it. "But you owe me big time!"

"Sure thing," Don replied with an excited tone in his voice. But let's not stop there. Why don't we prove that not only does this work with lab mice but has applications for humans as well?"

"Don't get ahead of yourself. While I'd like to prove that this has applications for humans, actually creating a human embryonic clone has never been accomplished. Let's just start with the rodents and then see where things take us."

Reaching up with his up with his right hand, he rested the tips of his fingers on the scar that marred his visage.

"Trust me...I'd love to show how this could benefit mankind."

"So, where do we start?"

"Why don't you head over to Professor Mabel's office and feel out if he'd be willing to share his research? I'll contact the board and get their approval to add you to the project, and then we'll get cooking."

"Perfect!" Don proclaimed. Jumping off the stool he firmly grasped William's hand again. "Thanks for including me in this! We're going to be famous you know. And rich!"

"There you go again, getting ahead of yourself. We've got a ton of work to do. Let's focus on that and fame and fortune will take care of itself."

Don smiled, turned, and briskly walked out the back door of the classroom. Finding himself in the hallway, Don quickly made his way to the stairwell, descended two flights of stairs and exited the back of the building heading towards the parking lot. As he jumped into the front seat of his car he pulled out his cell phone and made a quick call.

"Hello," the response came through on the cell phone in a female voice.

"I'm in," he announced. "He agreed to let me work with him on his thesis."

"Excellent!" the voice replied. There was silence for about ten seconds and then the voice continued. "He wasn't suspicious of your intentions, was he?"

"Not at all. In fact, he welcomed my assistance." Don paused for a second then continued. "I'm really glad that you suggested that I offer to assist him. I think that William is really onto something big here."

"Bigger than you can imagine," came the response.

"Now, start getting busy on work. You're not going to make your millions sitting and gabbing with me."

"Absolutely." Don paused for a brief moment before continuing. "You know what? I think that I might be falling for you Kim."

"Yes. Me too. Now, focus on what the job at hand. We've got lots to do and little time to do it."

CHAPTER 8

Extraction
(Two Months Later)

William and Don found themselves working late on a Saturday evening in a lab located in the biology building of the USC campus. Don was hunched over an electron microscope while William stood next him staring at the image being displayed on the computer screen. Leveraging a robotic arm with a microscopic needle attached to the end, William very carefully, painstakingly, maneuvered the needle to the outer edge of a circle shown on the screen. Pausing for a second, William leaned back from the keyboard, turning to face Don.

"It's hard to believe that it's only been two months since we started working on this. And now, here we are about to extract ESCs from the first mouse clone embryo."

"Exciting, I know! Are you ready to do this?"

"Absolutely. You've got vials ready with the Trypan Solution to inject the ESCs into once we've extracted them, right?"

"Roger! The Cryo Freezer is ready as well. The vial containing a cell pellet is already in place for us to suspend the genetic material."

"Ok. Here I go!"

Very carefully, William typed instructions into the keyboard for the robotic arm to insert the microscopic needle two microns past the outer cell wall to the specific location in the rat blastocyst where the ESCs were located. Once the instructions were typed in, he hit the enter key. Looking at the robotic arm it was impossible to see that it had moved at all, but the images reflected on the computer screen very clearly showed the needle penetrate through the cell wall, extending into the mass. Both men audibly exhaled.

"Looks like the integrity of the cell wall is intact," Don commented. "Ready for extraction?"

William simply nodded, purposefully typed in three keystrokes and hit enter. The next moment a very quiet, humming noise came from the robotic arm. Liquid visibly moved from the center of the blastocyst adjacent to the end of the microscopic needle into the needle itself. William made five more keystrokes and the needle retracted from the cell wall back to its original position. The moment that the needle was fully removed from the cell wall, the blastocyst appeared to almost collapse upon itself and the cell wall disappeared entirely.

"And that's what we call a textbook extraction," William commented.

Don quickly walked to the right side of the robotic arm and opened the top of the Cryo freezer.

"Ready to receive the specimen," Don commented.

"Ready to deliver. The vials in the right location correct?" William inquired.

"Yup. Receptacle twenty-three dash 'B'."

William nodded and typed in eleven keystrokes on the keyboard and struck enter. This time the robotic arm that previously appeared to have been sitting motionless moved dramatically away from the encasement where the blastocyst had been located. It turned sideways and in on itself and the multi-articulated-arm twisted in the direction of the Cryo freezer. As the arm extended over the open top of the freezer, the tip of the arm rotated ninety degrees downwards, and then extended down into the box.

Within a small glass tube located in the freezer, a tiny clear globe rested delicately on the bottom, barely visible to the human eye. The tip of the arm extended outwards from the arm, into the vial, and ever so gently touched the clear ball. Another computer screen located adjacent to the first showed contents of the vial magnified two million times normal size, and you could easily see the tip of the microscopic needle.

"Ready to deliver genetic material."

And with that, William hit enter once again, which was immediately followed by another gentle humming from the robotic arm. Looking at the image on the screen you could clearly see the liquid contents transfer from the needle tip into the clear globe.

Again, both men audibly expressed their breath.

"Get ready to close the lid," William instructed.

Don simply nodded in response. After making six additional keystrokes, the needle withdrew from the tiny clear ball into which it expelled its contents. As the needle exited the outside of the ball, unlike the blastocyst that essentially disintegrated, the exterior clear wall remained intact. William hit return one more time and the robotic arm fully removed itself from the top of the Cryo freezer and returned to its original position. Immediately, Don closed the lid of the freezer and clamped the lid shut.

"Perfect! Absolutely perfect!" William exclaimed.

"You're telling me! You made me practice that no less than twenty times this afternoon. We could have already been home and sleeping."

"But the practice paid off!"

"So, how long do you think we need to wait until we can introduce the ESCs into the cloned mouse?"

William thought to himself for a brief moment.

"Well, Junior over there," he stated as he motioned over to the small metal cage containing a tiny white mouse located atop a table, "is already five days old. He shares the exact same genetic code as the embryo that we just extracted the ESCs from. He's got another fifteen to go until he's 'officially' an adult mouse. If we start culturing the ESCs that we extracted in ten days, we should have sufficient numbers to begin the therapeutic healing process when Junior is exactly twenty days old."

"Nothing like a tight time schedule." Don paused briefly then continued speaking. "It's going to be a lot tougher, and I mean A LOT tougher, once we move onto our second stage of testing. Human embryos are infinitely more complex than that of a rodent. Just figuring out how to effectively freeze human ESCs and then thaw them for our research is going to a herculean effort. No researcher in the world has been able to accomplish this without causing irreparable damage. And what about us procuring a large enough supply of embryos? Ever since the Human Embryonic Stem Cell policy was signed into law, researcher's ability to access these has become extraordinarily difficult."

"All things that I'm aware of," he replied in a calm manner. "We're just going to have to deal with things the best we can. And right now, we need to deal with the job at hand and at least prove out that this works with a lab rat."

"Yeah, I know," Don whined. "I just can't help but think about the bigger picture."

"Why are you so fixated on us moving into human trials?"

"Because this is where the real benefit can come from

this research," Don replied. He purposively lowered his gaze until it rested on William's scarred cheek. "You of all people should want to move as quickly as possible to human applications."

"If it proves out to work," William added.

"When it proves out to work," Don corrected. "Your hypothesis is right. Your logic is sound. This will work on humans, I just know it!"

"How can you be so sure?"

"I don't know how I know, but I do. My gut is telling me that this will work."

"Well, I hope you're right. And yes, trust me, I'm keenly aware of the benefit this will have for mankind. And I will likely be a key beneficiary of it!"

"Totally agree with you. We're going to be rich!"

A slight frown appeared on William's face. Tilting his head sideways he responded.

"I wasn't talking about the money, I was talking about applying this myself so I can get rid of this," he declared motioning to his right cheek. "We will likely make lots of money from this as well, but that's not my primary motivator."

Don feigned chagrin at William's comment. "Of course, we're going to help millions of people. But shouldn't we also benefit financially in a huge way by being the two scientists who figured it out? I'm all for helping out humanity, but there's no reason that we shouldn't benefit, in a very big way, while we do."

William laughed briefly at Don. "You're a mercenary, aren't you? Well, I'm certain that we'll get fame and fortune if we're successful. It will just be a natural byproduct."

The two men sat silently for a moment staring at each other until finally, William broke the silence.

"So, why don't we start preparing the lab to culture the ESCs that we extracted? It's going to take us at least five full days to get everything ready."

Don twisted to his left and reached into his book bag. When his hand emerged, it was grasping a black and white, composition notebook. "Here's Professor Mabel's lab notebook. He's detailed all of the steps required to maximize the number of ESCs that we can culture in preparation for our next step."

"I can't believe that he actually let you take that from his office!" Don gasped in disbelief.

"Well," he stated in a somewhat furtive manner, "he didn't really give me permission to remove it."

"WHAT!" Don barked. "You stole this from his office?!"

"One might say that I 'borrowed' this from him," Don replied with a sheepish grin on his face. "Besides, he's given me full access to all of his work. What's the big deal if I take his notebook versus taking a quick picture of the pages we need?"

Holding his head William responded. "For one, if you lose a couple of photocopied pages, you don't lose the last two years' worth of research that Professor Mabel has invested. I can't believe that you would be so brazen as to take his journal without even asking if that was ok."

"Means to an end," he dryly replied.

"I guess. You'd better be extraordinarily careful with that. Go make a quick copy of the pages that we need and then put it back in your bag. I'm going to be very nervous until you return that back to his office."

"Yes mother," Don muttered as he stood up from his chair and walked to the front of the classroom where a copier was located. Two minutes later he took his seat again and roughly slid the photocopied pages across the tabletop to William.

"That'll do pig...that'll do," William quoted.

Both men laughed for a moment and silently began reading the pages covering the topic of culturing ESCs.

"This doesn't look too difficult," William asserted.

"Nope," Don agreed. "Not difficult at all."

Pausing thoughtfully for a moment, Don set the pages he had been reading down on the tabletop.

"Question for you."

"Sure. What is it?"

"How are we going to get access to all of the human embryos that we need for stage two?"

"We're going to have to petition the University Hospital and Biology Departments for access. We can probably ask Professor Mabel make a request for us, especially since he sits on the board."

"That's going to seriously take forever!" Without hesitating, Don continued speaking. "You know...I have access to the primary storage freezer in the Biology wing where all of the embryos are stored."

Before he could continue, William jumped in.

"Don! We're not going to steal them!"

"Yeah, you're right. That wouldn't be a good idea." Purposively pausing for effect for about ten seconds, Don continued. "It's really too bad. If we can show that this works with lab rats, we might not ever get a chance to prove this out with humans. And what's going to happen is some 'well connected' postgraduate student or another professor picks up our work where we left off, and then they'll get all the glory, just because they had access to a supply of embryos."

William sat for a moment thinking to himself, while Don watched him intently. After about one minute William finally responded.

"First things first. Let's see if this works on our friend 'Junior', then we'll cross the bridge of how we get access to enough human embryos."

"Agreed," Don quickly replied. Feeling that he had positioned things as well as he could for the moment, he changed gears back to the task at hand. "So, what's next? Should we start prepping the culture dishes?"

Rubbing both of his eyes with the tips of his fingers, William sighed. "I'd love to keep working, but I can barely keep my eyes open as it is. Why don't we call it a day and start again first thing tomorrow?"

"Sounds good to me."

"Oh, and be sure that you drop off Professor Mabel's notebook before you head home. I'd don't want to have any part of you 'accidentally' spilling something on it or losing it altogether."

"Sure thing. Let's get stuff picked up and then we can head out."

About twenty minutes later the lab was roughly in the same condition that they had found it ten hours earlier when they started working. As they both started towards the door, William's stomach audibly groaned for lack of food.

"Oh yeah, we should probably get something to eat as well. We haven't had anything since about one-thirty this afternoon."

Don laughed. "Sounds like a burger run to me."

Both men walked out the door in the rear of the classroom, flipping the lights off as they exited.

CHAPTER 9

Experiment
(Two Weeks Later)

William and Don found themselves working late again. This time it was just past midnight. They were sitting opposite each other on either side of a table that was covered with a menagerie of papers and various pieces of laboratory equipment. Directly between them sat a large dissection tray containing a white mouse. Despite the fact that the tray was not covered with some sort of a top, there was no chance that the mouse lying motionless before them was going to escape.

The mouse's bare skin was exposed starting directly behind the ears, extending about one inch down the back where it had recently been shaven in a thin line. While there was no blood, the back of the rodent's neck laid wide open, directly exposing the spinal column of the subject. One of the discs close to the base of the head had been carefully removed, and small retractors had been used to keep the two vertebrae separate from one another. Normally this would have directly exposed the spinal cord of the mouse. In this case, however, the spinal cord had previously been severed by a laser scalpel, so nothing was visible in the one-millimeter wide opening.

Sitting directly to the right of the dissection tray, a small, robotic arm sat on the tabletop. At the end of the arm was a small container housing the ESCs that William had extracted just fifteen days prior. The ESCs had already been cultured and were suspended in a liquid solution to keep them intact.

"You're certain that the gelatin scaffold has been

positioned directly on either end of the spinal column?" William queried.

"Check."

"And you provided enough material across the gap for the ESCs to bind and cellular growth to occur?"

"Yes," Don answered, this time a little bit perturbed. "We've got everything set up perfectly Will. Let's begin with the administration of the ESCs to the target site."

"I just want to be one hundred percent certain that everything is perfect," he countered. "I know that this is unlikely to work the very first time, but I'd like to rule out 'user error' from the mix of variables." He paused for a moment after taking a deep breath. "Here we go!"

William methodically typed in several keystrokes on the keyboard causing the robotic arm to move slowly towards the dissection tray, stopping about two millimeters short of the surgical site on the mouse. Looking at the monitor located to his right, William realized that they had forgotten to turn on the camera for the electron microscope located at the tip of the robotic arm.

"See!" he exclaimed. "Knew we had missed something."

Laughing, Don reached over to the side of the device and flipped a switch upwards. A brief moment later the computer screen flickered and the image of the surgical site appeared at normal size.

"Let's go ahead and magnify this just a bit," William commented as he typed in a few instructions on his keyboard. Within three seconds the image on the screen went completely black. "That's five hundred thousand times magnification."

"Not a whole lot to look at, is it?" Don commented.

Without replying, William typed in a few more

commands and almost instantly images came into focus on the screen. One-third of the left-hand side of the screen was filled with the yellowish, white mass of the spinal cord. At this magnification, they could see individual cells that comprised the spine. To the right of the mass, they could see the sinewy, almost string-like helix structure that formed the scaffolding stretching out into the blackness that represented the gap between the two ends of the severed spine.

"That's one million times magnification. Gives you a little bit more to look at, yes?"

Don smiled and nodded his head. "Ok, let's get ready to introduce the ESCs onto the scaffolding structure. But be careful!" he cautioned. "You need to place them directly on the spinal cord where the gelatin is touching it. That's the only way that the ESCs will have a chance to adopt the characteristics of the mouse's spinal cord."

"Really?" William responded in mock surprise. "I didn't know that."

Not waiting for a response, he typed in a few commands into the computer and a distinct click was heard as the motion of the robotic arm switched over to manual operation. Grasping the joystick William readied himself to begin the delicate task of maneuvering the tip of the microscopic needle to the very exact spot where the spinal cord and scaffolding came in in contact with one another.

Holding his breath, he gently moved the control stick forward. Movement was not perceptible in the robotic arm to the visible eye, but the imagery on the screen showed the needle come in from the top of the screen. It was steadily, albeit slowly, moving closer to the edge of the severed spine.

"Careful not to touch the scaffold!" Don blurted.

"Geez, Don!" William exclaimed. "All I need is for you to startle me and I'll end up stabbing the mouse in the heart!"

Obviously embarrassed by his actions, Don turned a bright shade of red.

"Sorry," he apologized.

Taking a deep breath, William took ahold of the joystick once again and began to slowly manipulate it, deftly negotiating around the scaffolding until the tip of the needle hovered precisely over the spinal cord. Bumping the controls slightly to the left, the needle crept even closer until it was positioned directly adjacent to the scaffolding material and the spine. Not wanting to tempt fate any further, he switched control back over to the computer, typed in a few commands and the needle microscopically moved forward until the tip barely, almost imperceptibly, touched the actual spine of the mouse.

"Nice work," Don complimented.

William nodded in agreement. "Ok, now to start introducing the ESCs onto the spinal column."

After typing in a few commands, a quiet humming noise came from the robotic arm, similar to when they were initially performing the extraction. A moment later you could see a small portion of the liquid flow out of the end of the needle and onto the surface of the spinal cord. While ESCs themselves were barely visible at this magnification, you could see them spread out across the surface of the spinal cord as well as onto the gelatinous scaffolding.

"Alright, one location complete. Only fifteen more to go."

"This is going to be a long night, isn't it?" Don complained.

"Quit your whining," William joked. "You knew this was going to be a lot of work when you signed up for it."

"Yeah, but I thought I was going to at least be able to get two hours of sleep each night."

For the next three hours, William and Don repeated the same procedure at various locations all around the circumference of the spinal cord. Finally, the last of the genetic building block material was discharged onto the subject.

"That's it!" William declared. Looking at his watch he let out a heavy sigh. "Almost four a.m."

Don reached with both arms over his head, arching his back as he stretched out his aching muscles. "That took longer than I thought it would. But at least we're finally done."

"Agreed."

Having removed all of the various instruments and objects that lay around the dissection tray, Don walked over to the back of the lab where an incubator for cell culturing was located. He opened the door and called over to William.

"Why don't you grab the tray and we can tuck it safely into the incubator?"

Without responding, William picked up the tray and carefully made his way over to where Don stood waiting.

"Ok Junior," he whispered to the mouse. "It's up to you now."

He then slid the tray into the incubator and Don closed the door.

"So, what do you think? Head home and grab a couple hours of sleep and then meet back here at eight a.m.?"

Obviously tired, Don rubbed his eyes and in a somewhat dejected tone replied, "sure...why not!"

William laughed and smacked his partner on the back. "Come on man," he encouraged. "If this works, we should be able to see some cellular regeneration in the mouse's nerves within four hours. Then again, if we don't see anything, at least we'll know that our first attempt didn't work."

"You're such a ray of sunshine, aren't you?" Don commented as both men started for the door.

"Yup, I'm the eternal optimist!"

CHAPTER 10

Unsettling Encounter
(Very Early the Next Morning)

It was nearly four-fifty the morning when Don found himself virtually staggering into his apartment, physically and mentally drained from all of the night's activities. As he shut the door behind him, he tossed his keys into a ceramic bowl that sat on top of a small, rectangular table located approximately three feet into the entryway. Reaching to his left, he flipped the switch to turn on the light directly overhead to illuminate the hallway. The light turned on, and then immediately started to emit a buzzing noise as it grew brighter and brighter, until the hallway was ablaze with a dazzling, blinding white light which caused Don to close his eyes and turn his head away. Suddenly, the light bulb exploded with a loud pop, sounding almost like a gunshot, sending tiny pieces of glass in every direction and the hallway went immediately dark.

"HOLY CRAP!" Don exclaimed as he opened his eyes and gazed up towards where the light in the ceiling used to be.

He immediately reached up to his hair with both hands and started brushing his fingers through it vigorously to dislodge any glass that might have landed on him. Next, he brushed his shoulders and his arms until he was satisfied that he had removed any shards.

"What on earth would have caused that to happen," he reasoned in his head. "As soon as I flipped the switch a power surge must have hit. I should go check and see if the entire apartment is out or just this one circuit."

Walking slowly down the hallway he could hear the tiny

shards of glass crunching beneath his shoes. Making his way into the kitchen he reached with his right hand towards the wall and firmly held the light switch between his thumb and index finger.

"Hopefully we don't get the same result," he muttered to himself as he prepared to turn on the light.

With a twist of his wrist, he flicked the light switch upwards, turning his head back towards his left shoulder just in case. Absolutely nothing happened; the kitchen remained in darkness.

"This is all that I need," he complained. "Well, screw this, I don't need light to sleep. I'll take care of this tomorrow."

Out of force of habit, he flipped the light switch back to the off position and immediately sighed when he realized what he had just done.

The apartment was very dark, but enough light was coming in from the kitchen window that he could make out enough details to prevent him from walking into walls. Even still, he reached out with his left hand to gauge where the doorway was to the hall leading back to his bedroom. Slowly he walked down the hallway towards his room that sat immediately at the end. As he got within about four feet of the door he noted to himself that the door was sitting slightly ajar. And to his surprise, he realized there was a very faint flickering of orange light coming through a crack in the door. Perplexed by what he saw, he approached the door warily, readying himself to do battle in case there was an unwanted intruder in his room.

A very soft, almost humming like noise could faintly be heard coming from the room. As he got closer the humming noise turned into a soft, almost chant-like whispering coming from behind the door. He slowly reached out for the doorknob with his left hand and eased the door back into the room. His right hand was already doubled up into a rock-hard fist and drawn back to his side in case he needed to unleash it to protect himself.

With the door less than halfway open, he saw the source of the flickering light. On his dresser were five lit candles of varying heights, clustered closely together in a small circular pattern. Decidedly alarmed, he quickly opened the door the remainder of the way so he could try and catch whoever had lit the candles off guard.

To his utter amazement, he found the outlined silhouette of a woman sitting with her legs crossed squarely in the middle of his bed. His eyes quickly adjusted to the shimmering light coming from the candles on his dresser, and he was able to ascertain that it was Kim sitting on his bed.

She was wearing a very sheer, almost see-through gown. Looking at the reflection in the mirror behind her, it became obvious to Don that she wasn't wearing anything beneath her gown, as the candlelight accentuated the form of her body and curves. She slowly, almost rhythmically undulated her body back and forth while she whispered in a melodic manner to seemingly no one. He strained his ears to try and make out what she was saying, but the sounds coming from her mouth were unrecognizable, almost as if she was speaking some different, almost guttural accented language.

Stepping into the room, he unclenched his fist and let his right arm lower slowly to his side. He could sense the adrenaline that was coursing through his veins and realized that his heart was thumping in his chest. Despite being relieved that the intruder wasn't really an intruder, he was completely mystified at the scene that he saw before him. As he moved closer to the dresser the candles suddenly flickered and Kim emitted a low, almost animal-like groan. He immediately turned back to Kim and saw that she now sat motionless on the bed, excepting her neck and head that were circling in a counterclockwise direction.

Don reasoned to himself that Kim must be sleepwalking, and is completely unaware of where she was or what she was doing. He quietly sat down on the bed to her left and reached with his left hand to try and gently wake her up. The instant that his hand touched her shoulder she immediately jerked backward and sucked in a deep breath through clenched teeth as if being in pain. Don's hand immediately recoiled in surprise, almost causing him to fall off the bed onto the floor. Regaining his balance, he leaned forward towards Kim, positioning his mouth close to her left ear.

"Kim," he faintly whispered and paused for a couple of seconds.

There was no response.

"Kim," he stated again, but this time a little bit louder.

Still...no response.

"KIM!" he sharply spoke.

Instantly, Kim's eyes opened and her head snapped in the direction of where Don was sitting. Her lips curled backward exposing her teeth, and a deep, almost creature like growl erupted from the back of her throat. Her pupils were completely dilated and appeared totally black, and when they locked with Don's there was nothing familiar in the lifeless gaze. He sat motionless staring at his girlfriend not knowing what to do next.

The growling noise subsided and Kim appeared almost statuesque sitting in the center of the bed. The room was eerily quiet except for the ever so faint noise coming from the flickering flames of the candles. Both of them sat there motionless for what was likely sixty seconds.

Still at a loss for what to do, Don decided to try and wake her up. He realized that both of his hands were drawn to his chest in a protective manner. Purposively, he lowered them into his lap and then cautiously reached out with his right hand towards Kim's left cheek. As his hand neared her face, the light in the room seemed to increase. Glancing briefly back at the candles on the dresser he realized that the height of the flames had almost doubled in size. Refocusing back on Kim he extended his arm, gently touching her cheek and neck.

Without any warning Kim lunged forward at Don shrieking, forcefully knocking him backward off of the bed and noisily onto the floor.

"DO NOT TOUCH ME!!" she sharply cried. "NEVER TOUCH ME!"

Don was utterly terrified by what was happening. Without taking his eyes off Kim, he quickly scrambled to his feet, pulling himself up off the floor by grabbing the corner of the dresser with his right hand. As he hoisted himself to a standing position his shoulder slammed into the corner of the dresser, jarring it backward. The force of the impact was substantial enough that the candles on the dresser momentarily wobbled back and forth, and finally tipped over onto the surface of the furniture. As the candles fell the flames extinguished, leaving the bedroom in complete darkness.

Sharp aches of pain emanated from Don's shoulder. He

hastily jumped towards the window to pull up the shades in an attempt to provide some illumination. Instead of grabbing the cord to open the shades, he accidentally grabbed the window treatments themselves, pulled them completely off the window, and they fell in a loud clatter of noise.

Turning back towards the bed he was caught completely off guard by what he saw in front of him. Enough light was coming through the window from outside that he could clearly see Kim. To his surprise, he found her sobbing uncontrollably with her head buried in her hands.

Almost instinctively, he leaped back to the bed and placed his left arm around her shoulders in a consoling manner. As he did so, she heavily leaned into his body and the intensity of her cries increased to such a level that she was almost virtually gasping for air.

"Kim," he whispered to her softly. "Are you ok?"

She didn't respond but seemed to bury her head and shoulders even deeper into his embrace. Don wrapped his other arm around her and held her close to him trying to calm her down. After about thirty seconds Kim's sobbing lessened a bit and he attempted to try and talk with her to figure out what was wrong.

"Kim, what just happened? What are you doing here?"

Kim slowly leaned back from Don looking up at his face. Her cheeks were with streaked with tears and her eyes were puffy and red from crying. Don noticed that her pupils were no longer dilated and he saw the familiar gaze of the woman that he was falling in love with.

"I...I..." she stammered in an attempt to respond but then broke back down again crying.

"It's ok," Don softly spoke. "Take your time."

About thirty seconds later Kim tried again.

"I...I don't know," she whimpered. Looking up into Don's eyes again she continued. "I have no idea how I got here. I don't know what I'm doing, and I have no idea what I'm even wearing," she said motioning to her attire.

"You scared me to death," Don responded.

"What happened?" she inquired.

"I got home about ten minutes ago and the power was out. I was just heading back to my room to crash for the night, and as I got closer to my door I could hear you talking, almost chanting."

"What was I saying?" she pressed in an alarmed manner.

"I have no idea," he admitted. "Whatever you were saying it wasn't in English. I couldn't understand anything you said."

"I don't understand."

"Neither do I. You had lit some candles," he commented motioning towards his dresser. "And...well..." he paused for a moment.

"What?" she demanded. "What is it?"

"I don't know how to say this, but you attacked me."

Kim stared at him in disbelief. "I attacked you?"

"I was going to try and wake you up and when I touched you, you lunged at me and threw me to the floor."

"How...what...I don't understand."

"Neither do I," he admitted. "It must have been some type of sleep walking, or maybe you were having some sort of a freaky dream. Whatever it was, I'm glad that it's over. Do you remember anything?"

"I really don't. The last thing I remember was falling asleep in my bed back at my place. Next thing I know I was sitting here on your bed feeling more scared than I ever have in my life...and completely cold. But not cold like a temperature, but cold to my core, feeling like there was almost no life in me."

"It's ok," Don replied in a comforting manner. "Let's get you into some pajamas and you can just sleep here tonight. We can talk about this more tomorrow."

"If it's ok with you, I really don't want to talk about this again. Just the idea of trying to remember what happened horrifies me for some reason."

"Alright then, let's just get you to bed."

Kim slid over and sat on the side of the bed. Don stood up and made his way back towards his dresser. As he pulled open the top drawer to pull out some sweats and a t-shirt for her to wear, he noticed that there was a thin layer of sand covering a portion of his dresser where the candles were situated. Looking closer it appeared that faint patterns had been drawn in the sand itself. While it was difficult to make out the shapes completely, Don could have sworn that the outline of a star sat circumscribed within the center of a circle. Not wanting to alarm Kim any further, he simply ran his hand across the top of the dresser, removing the shapes that had been scrawled.

Returning to the bed he found Kim sitting quietly, slumped forward slightly. She was obviously weary from the events of the evening and could barely keep her eyes open.

Gently, he lifted up her arms and removed the see-through gown that she had been wearing. Normally, he would have taken a moment or two to gaze at Kim's body, but the concern he had for her welfare prompted him to immediately pull the t-shirt over her head, carefully pulling her arms through the sleeves. Laying her back gently onto a pillow he slid the pair of sweatpants over her feet and pulled them up to her waist. Satisfied that she was ready for bed, he pulled the covers up to her shoulders.

Walking around to the other side of the bed he quickly removed his clothes until he was only wearing his underwear and slid into the left side of the bed. He was amazed at how exhausted he was. He briefly glanced over at the digital clock by his bedside and noted that it was already five-o-five in the morning.

"I guess a couple hours of sleep is better than none" he ruefully thought to himself.

Closing his eyes, he quickly felt himself drifting off to sleep. Within a matter of three minutes, his breathing slowed as he slid into a deep slumber.

Kim, who had already drifted off to sleep, rolled slowly onto her left side. Taking a deep breath, her eyes momentarily opened revealing fully dilated pupils, and then slowly closed as she exhaled.

CHAPTER 11

Viable Alternative
(Later in the Morning)

The sound of a car horn blaring outside abruptly awoke Don from a sound sleep. After reaching up to rub both of his eyes, he drew his hands back towards either side of his head, arching his back and tightening up his legs muscles as he stretched out his body out for a full five seconds. Letting out a large exhale, he rolled over to his left side and found that the other half of his bed was empty.

"Where did she go?" he silently thought to himself.

"Kim!" he loudly called out as he sat up in bed. "KIM!"

He sat quietly, straining to hear a response, but there was only a deafening silence.

He glanced to his left to see the digital clock sitting on the nightstand, and leaned forward to clearly see the time.

"Ten-o-five!!" he exclaimed. "Crap. I totally overslept!"

Leaping out of bed he hurried into the bathroom where he hastily brushed his teeth, gargled some mouthwash to take the bite out of his breath, splashed water on his face and tried to comb his hair into place. After realizing that no amount of simple brushing his hair was going to make him more presentable, he leaned over and splashed four handfuls of water onto his head. This time his hair yielded to his will, somewhat, and lay mostly in place. Shrugging his shoulders, he made his way back into the bedroom where he pulled on a pair of jeans and threw a polo shirt over his head. Sitting down on the edge of the bed he pulled on a pair of socks, stuffed his feet into his shoes, and made his way to the kitchen.

"Ten-o-eight," he muttered under his breath. "So late."

Upon opening the refrigerator, he spotted a bottle of orange juice that he quickly grabbed, opened, and gulped down no less than one-third of the container. He tossed the orange juice back into the fridge and slammed the door shut. Reaching to his right he opened a kitchen cabinet, grabbed the last breakfast bar sitting in the box, and stuffed it into his front pocket. After grabbing his wallet and keys, he exited the apartment walking as fast as possible to his car parked directly in front of the building.

About eight minutes later Don found himself pulling up to the science building at the college campus. Before turning off the engine he glanced at his radio to see the time.

"Ten eighteen," he remarked. "That's got to be some kind of new record!"

Within a few moments, he found himself in the stairwell bounding upwards two steps at a time. Reaching the second floor he tried to compose himself a bit and walked in a little more sedate manner to one of the doors. Taking a breath, he opened the door and walked into the laboratory that he and William had been spending what seemed to be virtually every waking moment of their lives for the past few months.

Upon entering the room, he saw the familiar site of William hunched over the eyepiece of an electron microscope. William's head immediately jerked in the direction of the door and greeted Don with a broad grin that seemed to cover his face from ear to ear.

"You've got to take a look at this! Get over here!" he implored motioning dramatically with his right hand.

Don hurriedly walked to the side of the room where William was located and quickly surveyed the scene. The laboratory mouse, that had been the focus of their prior night's activities, lay motionless in the tray it had been placed in, and the lens of the electron microscope was situated roughly over the back of the mouse where they had severed the spinal cord. William took two steps backward allowing Don to position himself in front of the scope. Leaning forward he peered into the eyepiece with his right eye.

"So, what exactly am I supposed to be looking at?" he queried. "I'm pretty much seeing exactly what we saw last night. Black space where the spinal cord used to be."

Pushing Don aside, William looked into the eyepiece and grunted under his breath.

"Oops. I accidentally turned the magnification down."

Reaching to the side of the electronic microscope he flipped a switch and intently looked through the sight.

"There you go. It's unbelievable!" he trumpeted.

Don leaned forward again, scrutinizing the image being displayed. After a few moments, he leaned back with an unimpressed look on his face.

"I still don't see anything."

Obviously frustrated, William let out a garbled choking sound from the back of his throat. Reaching over to the monitor located on the table he turned it on and then flipped another switch located on the right side of the microscope. The small image that was visible through the eyepiece was now displayed on the large, twenty-four-inch monitor.

William pointed at the screen where the total blackness met up with the off-white color of the severed spinal cord. "You see," William exclaimed in an excited tone pointing at the screen. "Right there, can you see it?"

"I'm still not seeing anything worth getting excited about."

"Look harder."

Don stepped closer to the screen, placed his hands on the table and nearly pressed his nose up to the screen. After staring intently at the screen for about ten seconds, he turned his head and looked at William.

"What's on the lens of the scope?" he asked as he turned back to the screen, pointing at a faint white haze that appeared on the edge of the spinal cord next to the black void. "It looks like there is something obscuring the picture."

William crossed his arms in front of his chest with a same silly grin from ear to ear. Frustrated with his silence, Don turned back to the screen.

"Tell me!" he insisted. "Don't just sit there with that stupid look...."

Don abruptly stopped talked mid-sentence, leaving his mouth hanging open as he stared at the screen, with an expression of complete disbelief on his face. After about fifteen seconds he pointed with a shaky index finger at the hazy portion of the image.

"I don't believe it," he uttered. "It's working, isn't it?"

"You bet your ass it's working! And even better, you can see it working at this level of magnification! The 'haze' that you referred to is actually cells of the spinal cord being regenerated at an accelerated rate and literally climbing up the scaffolding that we placed between the two severed ends."

"What is the scale of the image?" Don anxiously pressed.

"That area of haze which is about the width of your thumb on the screen is roughly ten to the minus two millimeters."

"And what's the growth rate?"

"Right now? It's growing at a rate of about one-thousandth of a millimeter, every fifteen minutes."

Don cocked his head sideways as he tried to do the calculation in his head.

"Don't strain yourself," William joked. "I already did the math. That translates to roughly one millimeter every twenty-four hours."

Wide-eyed and with his mouth still hanging open, Don turned his head to stare again at William. "And how wide is the gap between the two ends of the spinal cord?"

"Two millimeters."

"That means...."

"Exactly! In roughly forty-eight hours, both ends of the spinal cord should be reconnected." He paused for effect before continuing. "That means that in just two days' time we should have results that tell us if the new spinal tissue is transmitting neural impulses."

"You did it! I can't believe it, but you freaking did it!"

"Not yet," William replied, "but things are looking really good!"

"That's the understatement of the year. This is unbelievable! This is going to be one of the biggest breakthrough medical advances in modern history."

"I think you're getting a little bit ahead of yourself. And besides, just because we have connected two pieces of tissue, doesn't mean that we have returned normal function to the spinal cord. This mouse may yet still be paralyzed for the rest of his life."

"So, what do we do now?"

"About all we can do now is wait," Don admitted. "And make sure that this mouse getting sufficient hydration and nutrition so it doesn't die. All we need is to starve this poor creature to death before we get our results."

"And once we get the results? And if it proves successful, then what?"

"Then you and I have got to write up a very comprehensive thesis."

Don paused for a moment deep in thought. After about sixty seconds of silence, his expression changed to one that resembled the cat that just ate the canary.

"What are you scheming up in your brain?" William wearily questioned.

"Let's go for it," was all he said.

"Go for what?"

"Let's go for the whole thing."

"What whole thing?"

"Who cares about healing a mouse, let's prove out that this works on humans!"

William paused for a moment while he reasoned through the complete ramifications of Don's statement. Slowly, he began to shake his head back and forth in disapproval.

"It would take too long. And besides that, it might not even work." William paused for a moment puzzling through the logistics of this line of thinking. "In order to show that this works on humans, we're going to need a large supply of human embryos. Imprinting the genetic code onto a mouse embryonic clone is one thing, but doing so on a human embryonic clone, is another story entirely."

"The human gene catalog contains just under twenty-three thousand genes. The mouse gene catalog contains just over twenty-two thousand genes. There really isn't that much of a difference. We were able to figure this out for mice, with a little help from Professor Mabel's work. Who says that doing this on a human will really be that much more difficult?"

"It will be trial and error and we'll burn through hundreds of embryos while we figure it out. And in case you forgot, ever since the Embryonic Stem Cell policy was signed into law, the supply of embryos has virtually dried up. I don't know about you, but the last time I was in Wal-Mart, they were fresh out of human embryos.

The right corner of Don's mouth twisted sideways as he let out a brief blast of air from his nostrils with an audible harrumph.

"I don't think I like the sound of that," William commented. "What scheme are you concocting in your head?"

"Me?" Don replied with feigned innocence as he raised his eyebrows.

"Yup, you!"

"Well, I guess we'll have to go somewhere else other than Wal-Mart to pick up our supplies. And lucky for us, I know just the place."

"What are you talking about?" Don skeptically asked.

"Let's just say that I know where there is a very large supply of frozen embryos just waiting for us."

"Where?"

"Do you remember Shauna?"

"The girl that you dated before Kim, right?"

"Yup. Do you remember where she works?"

William's head leaned forward as his eyes widened in shock. After a brief moment, he responded.

"At a fertility clinic."

"Exactly. Remember when I told you about our late-night adventures at the clinic?"

"How can I forget? Do the letters 'TMI' mean anything to you?"

Don ignored his comment and went on.

"Well, after we had our fun, she gave me a little tour of the facility. You wouldn't believe the high-end laboratory equipment that they have in that place. One of the things that she showed me before we left was the large Cryo freezer where they keep all the embryos of the patients that are trying to get pregnant. There were easily over fifteen hundred samples in there."

"Absolutely not!" William immediately blurted out. "We are not going to steal the embryos. And besides, these embryos aren't even designated for research purposes. If we were caught trying to steal them, we'd be thrown in jail for a long time."

"That's why we'll have to be careful," Don replied. "If your research stops with the healing of a mouse, sure you'll get your doctorate. You'll be lauded for a short period of time as making a big breakthrough. You might even be referred to as the grandfather of a new medical era. But someone else is going to pick up your research, apply it to humans, and they will be the one that reaps all of the rewards. And why? Because they used your research and your brain as a stepping stool to achieve greatness. Why should we let someone else get all of the fame and glory?"

William thoughtfully paused for a moment letting Don's words sink into his brain. Realizing that his words were having the desired impact, Don pressed even harder.

"Imagine this. You're standing before the USC board to present and defend your thesis on the application of human ESCs to heal irreparable injuries. And your case study?"

Turning his left hand over with the palm facing up, he extended his fingers in the direction of William's face. Unconsciously, William reached with his left hand and gently touched the scar on his cheek.

"Exactly," Don answered. "You have applied your research to yourself, showing first-hand the potential of your breakthrough."

Pursing his lips, William's left hand slid down to his chin that he held between his thumb and index finger, remaining motionless for roughly thirty seconds. Removing his left hand from his chin, he placed it in his pants front pocket.

"We'd have to be very careful to not get caught."

"Absolutely!"

"And we'd have to have our own Cryo freeze in which to store the embryos that nobody else knew about."

"Of course!"

"And heaven help me if Tara finds out. She'd probably turn me in herself."

"We'll keep this just between you and me," Don replied in a hushed tone. "No one else would need to know. And once we figure out how to suppress the genetic expression of an embryo, imprint your genetic code onto it, and create an embryonic clone of yourself, *then* we'll petition the laboratory to release to us a small handful of embryos that have been designated for use in research. And we'll use those embryos in your 'official' research."

"That's actually a really smart idea."

"Of course it is," Don joked. "You don't have me helping you based on my good looks alone do you?"

"Good looks huh? Let's just say that it's a good thing we're going to create an embryonic clone of me rather than you. I don't think the world could handle two of your ugly mugs running around."

"So, what do we do next?" Don posed.

"First things first. We've got to prove out that this procedure worked on Junior here. Once we've done that, we've got to figure out how to actually procure those embryos from the fertility clinic."

"Tell you what. You focus on getting Junior jumping around again, and let me worry about getting my hands on our supply of embryos."

CHAPTER 12

Validation

(Two Days Later)

Both men found themselves in the laboratory again. On the table in front of them lay a sedated mouse in the center of the table, surrounded by various pieces of scientific equipment. The mouse was still shaved bare from the base of its skull, down the length of its back, to the point that the tail connected to its body. Along the exposed, pink flesh of the rodent was no fewer than twenty-five miniature electrodes housed within a special strip of tape adhered to the animal. Tiny wires trailed from the base of the tape and were connected to a biopotential electrode sensor. A small screen on the device itself showed an image representing the tape to which it was connected.

"Explain to me how this is going to work," Don inquired.

"The tape that is adhered to the animal's body has tiny electrode sensors that are spaced every two millimeters. When an electrical impulse is transmitted along the spinal cord, a very small charge, less than a single millivolt, is discharged and detectable by the electrodes. The screen will actually reflect the strength, location, and speed of the charges as they traverse the spinal cord."

"Excellent. So, we'll be able to determine whether the impulse is transmitted the length of the spinal cord, if it slows down or dissipates in strength as it approaches the injury site, and ideally is relayed to the brain."

"Exactly. And the converse is true too. We can measure the response of the brain and the consequential impulse transmitted to the mouse's extremity as we try to solicit a response. The thing to keep in mind is that the electrical impulse passes through a neuron in roughly seven milliseconds, far too quickly for us to see visually at real-time speed. To account for this, I've set the electrode sensor to represent the impulses at roughly one hundred times slower the speed than they actually occur. That way, we'll be able to visualize the impulse's location based on which part of the screen lights up, and the intensity based on the brightness and color of the light."

"Let's get started!" Don exclaimed, smiling in anticipation.

William reached out with his right hand and placed it on a small, obscure black box with a red button located on the top. A small wire protruded from the back of the box, across the table, and connected to an electrode placed directly on the skin of the mouse's back right thigh where a bare spot had been shaved. Taking a deep breath, William lifted his right index finger and hovered about one-half inch over the button.

"This is it," he hopefully stated.

Both men stared intently at the animal in front of them. Lowering his finger, William depressed the red button on the box sending an electrical charge down the length of the wire and into the mouse's body through the electrode. Almost immediately, the back-right leg of the mouse twitched sharply and the toes curled downwards.

"DUDE!" Don declared. "IT WORKED!"

William stood there silent for a moment, letting the reality of the situation sink into his brain. With his mouth slightly agape, Don stretched his neck forwards while he raised his eyebrows in an attempt to prod him for some sort of response. Don didn't have to wait very long.

"YES!!!!" William exclaimed at the top of his lungs, clenching his right fist and raising it high above his head. "It freaking worked!"

"You've got to control your language," he gibed.

Clearly ignoring Don's comment, he turned his attention to the biopotential device.

"Let's take another look at that. Frankly, I wasn't even looking at the screen – all of my attention was directed at the mouse."

William pressed a button immediately beneath the screen to replay the measurement of electrical impulses. Immediately on the far-right side of the screen a bright orange LED light illuminated, followed by another bright orange LED light about half a second later immediately adjacent. This same sequence repeated itself across the entire length of the screen from right to left. In each case, the LED light was the same, bright orange hue. When the light made it to the far left of the screen an audible chirp came from a speaker on the side of the sensor, indicating that the impulse navigated the full length of the tape. Instantaneously after the chirp, the light immediately illuminated adjacent to the light located furthest to the left, and then the next, and the next, until the lights completed the return journey back to the right side of the screen. Arriving where it initially began the sensor emitted another chirp.

"Brilliant!" Don approved. "Absolutely brilliant!"

"It actually worked," William repeated almost in complete disbelief. "And the strength of the signal didn't dissipate at all. That means that the spinal cord is completely healed."

"You know what this means? Time to move onto phase two."

"Phase two?" William questioned.

"Human trials!"

"Why don't we just take the victory that we have? We've cemented our names in medical history at a minimum with this discovery."

"True," Don responded.

Lifting his right hand up towards his chin, he began to pensively scratch at the front of his neck while looking up towards the ceiling. After a few moments, he continued.

"Very true. But by not taking this to the next, obvious level with the successful application to humans, we're going to simply be opening up the door for someone else to take all of the glory. And for that matter, all of the money that comes along with it."

William pursed his lips for a moment as he thought about their previous conversation. With a brief sigh, he finally spoke.

"What exactly do we need to do?" he finally yielded.

A large smile appeared on Don's face, as he was barely able to contain his excitement.

"Actually, I've got everything already pretty much figured out. I went to the fertility clinic that Shauna works at a few nights ago to determine the easiest way for us to break in. As luck would have it, there's a door located behind the building without a lock on it that leads into a small receiving area. Once we're inside, we can freely access the rest of the clinic, including the Cryo freeze where they store all of the embryos."

"Doesn't sound like they have much going on in terms of security, does it?"

"Well, I guess they think that people wouldn't want to break into a fertility clinic. They don't keep money there, and who in their right mind would want to steal frozen embryos?" he asked with a smirk on his face.

"That would be us!" William chortled back.

"There is one minor catch though."

William crossed his arms in front of his chest preparing for the worst.

"What's the catch?" he tentatively inquired.

"This has to be a three-person job. We need one person to hang around the back of the building and keep an eye out for any passerby's, one person to actually go into the clinic to retrieve the embryos, and a third person to drive the getaway car."

"That's really cliché."

"I know...right? Like an old-school bank robbery."

"More like the 'Apple Dumpling Gang'," William joked.

"Are you Don Knott's, or am I?"

"Anyways," William replied ignoring his question. "I don't see why we can't just park the car in the back of the building."

"That's the other catch."

"Another catch? This just keeps getting worse. What else do we have to deal with?"

"There aren't any cameras behind the clinic, but there are security cameras on both of the streets that run on either side of it. If we drive our car in there..."

"They'll capture our license plate," William finished his sentence.

"Exactly. Or if we covered it up, they would at least get the make and model of the car that could be traced back to us. Which means that we'll have to go in on foot. And, we'll have to wear ski masks as well, just to ensure that they don't get a picture of our faces."

"Don't you think it would just be easier if we parachuted in, and then escaped through the sewer system?"

Don laughed. "Ok, I get it. It's not going to just be an easy 'lay-up' to the basket. But it really isn't going to be that tough."

William paused for a moment to think through all the information that he just received. After roughly thirty seconds he continued his conversation with Don.

"So, who's the third man?"

"Well," Don hesitated.

"Who is it?" William demanded.

"I was thinking we could use Kim."

Both of William's eyebrows crawled up his forehead while he pulled his chin inwards to his chest, obviously not trying to mask his surprise at Don's suggestion.

"Kim? Really?"

"Yes, really! Besides, she already knows about our plans."

Clearly surprised, William firmly crossed both of his arms in front of his chest, glaring directly at Don.

"How does she already know about our plans? I thought that this was supposed to be 'top secret'...only between you and me."

"You know how it is...I pretty much tell Kim everything. She's actually shown a keen interest in what we're working on for some reason as of late. Initially, our work seemed to bore her, but over the last few weeks she has been more and more attentive to my blabbering. At first, I thought she was making fun of me, but her questions and comments are getting more insightful. Don't tell me that you haven't mentioned our plans to Tara?"

"No, I haven't," William simply replied. "I told you that she is somewhat conflicted over the idea of working with human embryos to prove out my theories. If I were to tell her, 'by the way, we're going to steal some embryos to further our work', that definitely would not go over well."

"I hate to say it, but we'll just need to keep her in the dark about our plan."

"Don't you think that Kim has mentioned anything to her? Or at least would mention this if we actually asked her to help us?"

"I think we're ok. Kim was actually the one that suggested that she help us out. I know that you don't like her very much..."

"Understatement," William instantly replied.

"...but, she really sees this as a great opportunity for me. And I asked her not to share this with Tara. I'm pretty certain she'll keep her mouth shut."

"She better...or my goose is cooked."

"You worry too much."

"And you don't worry enough!"

"That's why we make such a good pair. We are a good balance."

"Alright, so let's assume that Kim is the third man...ahh...better make that woman. When do we actually go and 'procure' the embryos?"

"Well, it's Wednesday, and the sooner we do this the better. Why don't we plan on doing this on Saturday night?"

"Do what on Saturday night?" a female voice chimed in from the back of the laboratory.

Instantly William's chest sunk into his stomach as he turned to look towards the back of the room. Unknown to

William and Don, the door to the laboratory was now open, and Tara and Kim were just entering the room together.

"Do what on Saturday night?" Tara innocently asked again.

William instantly froze not knowing what to say or how to respond. Fortunately for him, Don picked up the question without missing a beat.

"A double date," he simply responded. "Will and I were thinking that it would be fun for the four of us to go out on Saturday and have some fun."

William glanced at his friend with an expression of disbelief on his face, which he immediately covered by smiling and then shifting his glance back to the two women who were now standing directly in front of them.

"That does sound like fun!" Tara agreed. "What do you think Kim, maybe grab a quick bite and a movie? Anything to get these two out of the science room and back into our lives."

"Sounds good to me." She shifted her inquisitive gaze momentarily to William and then looked directly at Don.

"Are you ready?" she asked.

"Ready for what?"

"Our lunch. Don't tell me that you forgot."

"Oh geez," he replied looking at his watch. "It's already noon. Let me grab my coat. Will, are you ok with things if I head out with Kim?"

"Sure. I just want to run a few more tests and then put everything away."

"If you don't mind, I'll keep you company," Tara proposed.

"Of course not, I'd love the company. This will only take a few minutes and then we can get some lunch as well."

"Ok you guys," Don called out as he and Kim were already starting to walk towards the door. "We're going to head out. Will and I will finalize our plans for Saturday night and let you know what we're going to be doing."

With that final comment, Don and Kim walked out of the door and into the hallway outside of the lab. Waiting about twenty seconds until he was positive that they were out of earshot, Don turned to Kim.

"Hey, where did you go this morning? I was worried about you after last night."

"Oh, I'm sorry. I woke up and you looked so tired I figured I would just let you sleep. Don't worry...everything is ok. I think I must have been sleepwalking or something, or had a really bad nightmare. I'm totally fine. So, how did everything go today?"

"Perfect. Better than perfect. The procedure worked."

"That's great news!" She briefly paused thinking to herself and then continued. "Is William on board with the next step?"

"I think so. He was a little concerned when I suggested to him that you would be in on it, but I think I convinced him that it would work out."

"So, what's the plan?"

"Well, we're going to break into the clinic late Saturday night, or early Sunday morning depending on how you want to look at it, just like you suggested."

"Excellent. I think that would work best. There will be few if any people out and about in the early hours of the morning. By the way...nice cover up with the double date idea. It might make things a little more interesting in terms of preparation, but we'll be able to manage. Once we finish our 'date', William will need to drop Tara off at the apartment so we can attend to our late-night activity."

"Are you sure that you want to help us out with this? What if we get caught?"

"You worry too much," Kim replied.

Before he could respond, she grabbed the collar his shirt with her right hand, roughly pulled him towards her and planted her lips solidly on top of his. After a brief kiss, she parted her mouth slightly and bit his bottom lip.

"Ouch!" he exclaimed. He immediately put his hand up to his mouth to touch his lip, and when he pulled it away there was a small drop of blood on his index finger. "You actually drew blood!"

Kim tightened her grip on his collar and pulled him close to her again. This time she sucked on the small abrasion on his lip.

"Mmmm," she purred. "Maybe we should just bypass lunch altogether?"

Without giving Don a chance to respond, she grabbed his hand and walked down the stairs, almost dragging him behind her.

CHAPTER 13

Progress
(The Next Day)

Tara had a sympathetic expression on her face as she stared at the laboratory mouse that lay motionless on the table in front of her. Unconsciously, she started to reach her right hand towards the mouse with her fingers extended.

"I wouldn't do that if I were you," William cautioned.

"He just looks so pathetic," she replied, stopping short with her hand approximately three inches from the animal. "Are you sure he's ok? He looks so uncomfortable with all of the wires connected to him."

"Oh, he's fine. Actually, he's much better than he was twenty-four hours ago when he was completely paralyzed. The sedation should be starting to wear off right about now, and I'd hate for you to get a nibble taken out of one of your fingers."

William had just unplugged a USB drive from the measurement device. Gripping it firmly between his index and thumb he held it directly in front of his face pointing it at Tara.

"What's that?"

"This, my dear, is proof that my thesis works. That I've been able to successfully heal an injury that has been up to this point unfixable."

"That's incredible!" she exclaimed. "That means that you just need to finish your write up and then you can present..." she paused for a second, "...I mean, 'defend' your thesis to the Biology Board for your doctorate!"

William paused a moment before responding. 'She's

right', he thought to himself. 'I really could present this to the Board and be done with my doctorate degree. But someone else would just use my groundbreaking work as a springboard. I really need to take this to the next, most logical application and prove that my thesis works on humans. I need to come up with some sort of excuse or delay so Tara doesn't become suspicious'.

"What's going on in that head of yours?" Tara finally said.

"Sorry," he apologized. "I'm just thinking through all of the additional tests, trials, and validation studies that need to be completed before I can present this to the Board," he quickly commented. "I don't want to claim victory prematurely in case I overlooked something. And it would be extraordinarily embarrassing if I went to present my findings, just to have them find a flaw in my research, or to have someone disprove that my procedure worked. I've got to be one hundred percent certain that my thesis is accurate and can easily be defended."

"How long do you expect that to take?"

'This is my opportunity to buy myself some time', he reasoned in his head.

"It's hard to say," William replied. "A doctorate takes a minimum of two years to complete, and that's a best-case scenario. Typically, it takes three or more years, and I've only been at this for about one and a half so far."

Tara let out an audible sigh. "You mean that you could be at this for another two years?"

"Hopefully not, especially with how much progress I've already made. But it may take an additional six months…twelve at the outmost."

Tara's shoulders slumped slightly, however, realizing

what she had done she quickly pulled them back and flashed a big smile at William.

"Well then, I guess that you've got to keep yourself motivated. It's not a sprint, right?"

"Exactly," William replied. "However, I don't intend on doing this forever. So, I'll be working as smartly as possible!"

"Well, you're not going to be able to work at all if you don't get something to eat."

"Agree. Let me just get our little friend here back in his cage and we can head out."

Reaching over to the side of the tray that contained the mouse, William picked up a pair of leather gloves. Holding the glove in his left hand, he slid his right hand in and made a tight fist after it was fully inserted. He repeated the same procedure with the left glove, and then held both of his hands in front of his face, with his palms facing himself, as a surgeon would who had just scrubbed up in preparation for a surgery.

"Now I'm ready to handle the mouse. And these," he described while extending the fingers of both of his hands to emphasize the fact that he was wearing gloves, "will keep my fingers safe from this little bugger's teeth."

Reaching into the tray he gently scooped up the mouse in his right hand, cradling it on its back. With his left hand, he firmly gripped the wires and edge of the tape that was adhered to the bare skin on the mouse's back.

"Can you hold the tail for me?" he asked. "I want to make sure that the tape comes off cleanly."

"I thought you said I shouldn't touch the mouse without some sort of protection!"

"Two things," William advised with a smile. "First, I have

the mouse firmly in my control, so I won't let him bite you. And secondly, you're going to be holding the mouse on the opposite end of where his teeth are."

Tara reached forward with the intent to hold the mouse's tail so William could peel the tape off of the animal. A fraction of a second before she was about to touch the tail...

"AAAAHHHHH!!!" William screamed.

Startled, Tara jumped backward from the mouse emitting a high-pitched cry, and William immediately began laughing.

"You're terrible," Tara admonished. "Absolutely terrible."

"I'm sorry," he apologized. "I couldn't resist. Ok, go ahead and hold the tail and we'll get this mouse back into his cage."

A bit more hesitantly, Tara reached forward expecting William to try and scare her for again. This time, however, he remained quiet, allowing her to grip the animal's tail between her right thumb and index finger.

"Now, go ahead and lightly pull the tail away from the body."

Once William saw that she had complied with his request, he gently, but firmly, pulled the tape and wires towards the mouse's head. The adhesive on the tape slowly released its grip on the animal's skin and after about five seconds had completely come off. With a satisfied smile on his face, William placed the tape on the table next to the device. Turning to his left, he reached out with his left hand, opened the door on the top of a small mouse cage and gently slid the mouse into the cage.

"All safe and sound," he commented.

Picking up the cage he returned the mouse back to a shelf in the front of the classroom.

"William, I have a question for you."

"What's that?"

"Well..." she hesitated momentarily and averted her eyes towards the windows.

"Is everything ok?" he prodded.

"Oh yes, everything is fine."

"Then why are you acting so nervous?" he pressed.

Tara took a deep breath before continuing. "I was wondering if you wanted to have dinner with me on Friday night."

"Sure," he simply responded. "But why were you nervous about asking me to have dinner with you?"

"I was hoping that we could have dinner at my father's house," she quickly blurted out.

William smiled at Tara and quietly laughed. "Is that what you're getting yourself worked up about? Having me meet your father?"

"I didn't want you to think I was pressuring you," she sheepishly replied. "But we've been dating for the past ten months, and things seem to be going really well. And...well...that we're getting pretty serious, so I figured that it was probably time that you actually got to meet my dad."

Tara paused for a second and visibly held her breath waiting for William to respond. While she knew that their relationship had been going very well, she was worried that William might get upset at her for assuming that he wanted to meet her father.

A broad smile creased William's face. He reached out and took Tara's left hand in his right. He stopped for a second realizing that he still had the leather gloves on and quickly pulled them both off and tossed them onto the table. Again, he reached forward and took Tara's hand in his and looked directly into her eyes.

"You know what?" he offered. "I think you're right. Things have been going pretty good for us."

He took her other hand in his and stood directly in front of her with about six inches separating them.

"And I think it is about time that I get introduced to your father. You've told me so much about him, and I'd like to meet the man that raised such a wonderful woman."

Tara instantly blushed as she flashed William a playful smile.

"Perfect," she simply stated. "He's invited us both over to his house this Friday night. I'd really like you to get to know him better. I've told him all about you and he's anxious to finally meet you!"

William inched forward slightly until his nose was about one inch from hers. Still holding her hands, he lowered them downwards, released them, and slid his hands slowly around her waist. She responded in kind by wrapping her arms around his midsection.

"What exactly have you been telling him about me?"

"Oh, not much. Just that you're a kind, handsome, brilliant scientist, that I love very much."

"Well, at least you're being truthful," he joked as he pulled her closer so he could gently kiss her lips.

"You bet. Let's head out and get something to eat for lunch or I'm going to pass out. My blood sugar level is seriously low."

Ignoring her, William kissed her again solidly on the lips.

"Ok, ok...cool your jets! There will be time for that later," she suggested. "Let's go grab some food and we can talk more about you meeting my dad."

"Alright," he relinquished. "But we'll definitely continue this 'conversation' later tonight," he countered.

Releasing Tara from his embrace, William reached over to the table, slid his notebook into his computer bag, and they headed for the door in the rear of the classroom.

"You sure you don't want to continue this 'conversation' now?" he virtually pleaded. "I know of an excellent storage closet just down the hallway."

"You're terrible," she admonished. "Don't you know that good things come to those who wait?"

Flashing a big smile, William took Tara by the hand and escorted out into the hallway.

CHAPTER 14

An Introduction
(Later That Week)

It was roughly seven thirty in the evening and the Southern Californian August sky was a blaze of vibrant colors as the sun was beginning to set. Bright oranges, pinks, and purple colored wispy clouds that stretched out towards the horizon were framed artfully between palm trees lining either side of the street. People lazily walked here and there on the sidewalk, idly chatting and enjoying the near-perfect weather and dazzling sky. William and Tara made their way slowly through residential streets on their way to Tara's father's house. His home was located fairly close to the beach in El Segundo, not far from the Los Angeles International Airport.

"Isn't the sky just gorgeous?" Tara asked. "We should drive along the beach for a few minutes before going to my father's house."

"Don't tell me that you're getting cold feet about me meeting your dad?"

"Oh no, not at all," she quickly countered. "I used to take the 'round about' way to get home all the time so I could enjoy the scenery. Sometimes it would take me an extra thirty minutes to get home. I figure, if you live in paradise, you might as well take advantage of the views."

"Ok, but let's not take too long. Your dad is expecting us at seven forty-five and I want to be certain to make as good of a first impression as possible. Where do you want me to go?"

"Go ahead and turn right at this next stop sign, and head out to Rosencrans Avenue where we'll turn left. Then just follow that down until we hit the ocean – you can't miss it!"

Within a couple of minutes, they had made their way towards the beach and sat patiently at a stoplight facing the ocean. If the view was spectacular before it was now absolutely breathtaking. Colorful hues in the sky reflected brilliantly off the shimmering ocean as if fresh paint had been brushed across the skyline, running off into the horizon and leaking onto the water. Seagulls glided gracefully across the constant breeze flowing from the shore out to the ocean and often appeared as if they were frozen in midair, not moving forward or backward, or even flapping their wings. William stared off into the horizon in an almost hypnotic-like trance.

"You can go now," Tara gently prodded. "The light's green."

"Oops!" he exclaimed while shrugging his shoulders upwards.

After navigating the left turn he continued to drive at a relatively slow pace, frequently looking out the passenger side window to peek at the beach and ocean.

"Doesn't get much better than this."

"It sure doesn't," William agreed.

After driving for approximately one mile, Tara instructed William to take his next left heading back into the residential area where her father lived. Roughly five minutes later, William pulled the car into the driveway, put the car in park, and turned the engine off.

"I still can't believe you used to live this close to the ocean."

Tara simply smiled at William, opened her door, and exited the car. William quickly followed suit and walked around the car to meet her in front of the walkway leading up to the front of the house.

"This is it!" he stated while grabbing her left hand with his right. "Let's go meet Dad!"

The two of them walked the short distance to the front door and stepped up onto the porch. Tara reached with her right hand to grab the doorknob, but the door opened before she could grab hold. Luckily, William had a firm grip on her other hand; otherwise, her momentum would have caused her to fall into the entryway of the house.

A large man, easily two inches taller than William stood in the doorway with a broad grin on his face. He was a relatively stocky, heavyset man, with a broad chest and thick forearms. He wore a plaid, button up shirt and a pair of blue jeans with a brown belt. His head was balding and had the crimson color of someone that had stayed out in the sun too long. His stark, white hair emphasized the reddish hue on top of his head and on his cheeks. He wore a pair of eyeglasses with a thin, gold frame holding the lenses in place. William couldn't help but picture the man in front of him with a large, bushy white beard, wearing a red outfit and riding in a sleigh.

"Tarz!" the man exclaimed as he rushed out of the door and embraced his daughter in a massive bear hug.

William thought he could literally hear the wind whoosh out of her lungs as the man enveloped her in his massive arms.

"Oh daddy," Tara virtually squeaked, not being able to voice loud opposition. "You're going to crush my ribs!"

Encouraged by her protestation, he picked her up off the ground and squeezed her for a full five seconds with her feet dangling before setting her gently back on the ground. Releasing her from his rough embrace, he turned his attention to William.

"And you must be William," he bellowed.

"Yes Sir!" he quickly replied.

"Rich Cline," he advised. "No need to call me 'sir', just plain old Rich."

"Sounds good to me, Rich. It's a pleasure to meet you finally."

Rich firmly took William's hand in a rough, but warm handshake.

"Likewise," he agreed. "Why don't you both come inside? I've got meat on the grill in the backyard that I need to go tend to."

The three of them walked into the house with Tara closing the front door behind them. Rich made his way quickly across the entryway, through the kitchen and out a sliding glass door that led out onto a small wood deck situated beneath a garden window above the kitchen sink.

"Go on," Tara prodded him. "This is a great opportunity for you to bond with him. Men always bond around the barbeque, don't they?"

William laughed as he purposively walked towards the sliding door leading outside. The glass door was open and the screen was shut closed to keep annoying insects out of the house. William grasped the screen door with his right hand and began to struggle with it to get it to slide to the left.

"You've got to jiggle it a bit and lift at the same time," Rich called out from the deck. "That screen's been giving me problems for years…"

"And Dad's too cheap to fix it!" Tara chimed in from the kitchen.

"Frugal my dear. The word is frugal...not cheap."

William followed Rich's directions and with a bit of effort, was able to slide the screen door enough to the left to slide sideways onto the deck. After making his way through the opening he struggled again, but was finally able to close the screen door.

"Have a seat and we can get to know each other a bit better."

William made his way to a patio chair situated to the right of the barbeque, close to the deck railing. Taking a seat, he glanced at a small flowerbed adjacent to the house about eighteen inches in depth and six feet in length. After a brief moment, he looked back at Tara's father who was actively engaged in flipping and basting steaks on the open grill.

"Tara tells me that you're a priest, err, I mean minister for a local church. Sorry about that, I always get them confused."

"No problem. To tell you the truth, most people do."

"How long have you been a minister for?"

"For the past thirty-two years."

"Wow! That's quite a long time. You must really enjoy it."

"It's definitely my calling in this life," he agreed. "I first became a minister at age twenty-two. I always felt that this was the right place for me. Tarz tells me that you're a brilliant scientist that's getting close to finishing your Ph.D."

"I wouldn't go that far, but yes, I'm a scientist. And while it's still going to take me a bit more time, I do think that I see the light at the end of the tunnel for me completing my doctoral degree."

"Tarz has tried to tell me about your thesis, but frankly, I haven't been able to follow her very well. Something to do with healing rats using ESP?"

William laughed out loud at his comment.

"ESCs," he corrected. "Not ESP. Although, it would be something to cure an injury with my only thoughts from my head."

Rich laughed in response to the comment.

"So, you're working with embryonic stem cells huh?"

"Yes," William agreed cautiously. "In fact, just this week we were able to successfully treat a laboratory rat with a severe spinal cord injury with ESCs. The spinal column was completely healed and we were able to measure brain activity and neural impulses."

"How did you get the ESCs for the treatment?"

"Well, we actually created an embryonic clone of the mouse in the laboratory. We collected ESCs from that specimen and then created an exact duplicate at the genetic level. Once the mouse grew into adulthood—which by the way only takes a few weeks0—we inflicted an injury to the spinal column and were able to heal it through treatment with the ESCs."

"That's really amazing!" Rich commented. "It sounds like you're well on your way." He paused for a moment and then continued. "What do you think are the applications of this type of treatment to humans?"

William's chest immediately tightened from concern that Tara's father would have some moral objections. He took a deep breath before attempting to answer his question and hopefully assuage his concerns.

"There could very well be human applications for this treatment. However, it's is probably going to be several years, if not decades, before we can even hope to replicate what we did with the mouse. Being able to gain access to ESCs for a specific person may possibly turn out to be an impossibility."

"Hold that thought for a second."

Rich quickly turned the steaks over on the grill and basted them again. Leaning back towards the screen door, called out to Tara.

"Hey Tarz!" he bellowed. Why don't you grab some plates and silverware? It's gorgeous out here tonight so let's just eat on the deck."

He turned to glance back to William and paused for a moment. After what was a seeming eternity, he finally began to talk.

"You know William, scientists are always hell-bent on figuring out what is and isn't possible. What they can and can't achieve. Pushing the envelope of knowledge, breaking through barriers and discovering new things. One thing that I don't believe is ever seriously considered is whether or not those barriers should even be tested. There are some areas that man really shouldn't be dabbling. It's not their domain, it's His domain," he asserted while looking up towards the sky and pointing upwards with his right index finger. "I'm not trying to be contentious with you, but how do you or any other scientist plan on getting *embryonic* stem cells?"

After taking only a moment, William directly answered his question.

"Well, the most likely method would be to create an embryonic clone of the individual that needed the ESCs."

"Hmmm..." he thoughtfully replied. After another moment, he continued. "So essentially, you would be creating a human life form that could develop, if allowed, into a baby."

"Well, we would only allow the embryonic clone to develop to a specific stage, at which point we would harvest the ESCs to be used for medicinal purposes."

"But if you didn't stop the development process, the embryo would develop into a human life correct?"

William glanced downwards at his lap while he took a deep breath before replying.

"I guess it would. But we wouldn't allow...."

"So essentially," Rich interrupted, "you would be performing a type of abortion...from a certain point of view. Let alone, you would be stepping into the role that up until this point God has previously been the only player. You would be creating life."

Tara emerged from the house carrying a stack of plates with silverware and napkins sitting on top of them, and immediately sensed the heightened tension between the two men.

"So, what are you two talking about?" she asked cautiously.

"Oh, William was just telling me about his research he is working on. Very interesting. Although, I think there might be some ethical and moral concerns with the approach that he is taking."

William's eyes locked with Tara's and she could sense the anxiety he was feeling.

"Daddy, William is focusing on lab rats right now. That's it! Don't make a mountain out of a mole hill ok?"

Rich glanced back at William and could see that his comments had the desired effect on him. Turning back to Tara he continued.

"Ok, ok...I'll ease up. I only wanted William to consider the potential ramifications of his research. I mean, up until this point God has been the *only* architect when it comes to creating human life. While William might not take his research down this path himself, it definitely will open the door for others to carry the work forward."

"I understand your position, sir...I mean Rich," he corrected. "When you think about it, however, didn't God give us our minds, our intellect, and desire for knowledge? Aren't we just using the tools that He has given us and progressing down a path that He would have thought that we would naturally have taken?"

"Touché," he responded with a smile. "And a good point at that. Tarz, why don't you bring those plates over here and we can get them loaded up with some tasty food? William, would you mind grabbing the salad sitting on the top shelf of the refrigerator?"

"Sure thing," William quickly replied as he stepped around Tara and walked back into the kitchen.

"Oh, and can you grab some juice or water from the fridge and bring that out with you as well?" Rich called into the house.

William emerged back from the kitchen with a salad bowl and drinks in hand. The steaks had already been removed from the grill and were sitting neatly on the plates that were resting on the patio table.

"Here we are," William announced as he took his seat next to Tara.

Tara reached over and rubbed his knee to reassure him that everything was going to be fine.

"Alright. How about I offer a blessing on the food," Rich asked.

Without waiting for a response, he bowed his head and closed his eyes.

"Dear Lord," he started. "We are grateful for this bounty before us. We acknowledge Thy hand in all things and gives thanks unto Thee for all we have. Please bless this food to our good health, in Thy name, Amen."

"Amen," both Tara and William spoke at the conclusion of the prayer.

"Ok...let's dig in," Rich announced. "William, why don't you have the first taste? It's been marinating for the past four hours in my 'secret' sauce. Tell me what you think."

William responded by picking up his fork and steak knife and cut off a good size piece of meat. Rich anxiously watched him for a reaction as he put the food in his mouth and started to chew.

"Oh!" he exclaimed. "This is excellent...and juicy. Wow!"

"You're not just saying that, are you?" he prodded.

"Absolutely not. This is superb!"

"I'm glad you're enjoying it."

Rich took a bite of his own steak and while chewing continued his conversation with William, having to talk around the meat in his mouth.

"So, tell me about you and my Tarz," he mumbled in-between chews. "It sounds like you two are in a pretty serious relationship. Do you think that you might be asking me for her hand in marriage sometime in the near future?"

William virtually choked on the piece of steak he was trying to swallow as he was surprised at how direct and forward Tara's father was.

"Daddy!" Tara complained.

"Now, now Tarz...I'm your father. And it's my place to

understand his intentions. You're my little girl and I will always be looking out for your best interests."

William had already recovered from the initial shock of his question and readied himself to respond. He reached over and took Tara's hand in his and looked into her eyes.

"Yes, things are definitely pretty serious between the two of us." He turned his gaze back to her father and then continued. "I love your daughter, and I think the world of her. She brings out the best in me. In fact, helps me to be a better person in general. I don't have a crystal ball as to what the future has in store for us, but I'm confident that our future is very bright."

A large grin creased Rich's face.

"Very well said," he simply stated. "Hold on a second, I've got something that I wanted to give both of you."

Obviously excited, Rich jumped up from his seat and darted back into the house. About thirty seconds later he emerged with a small white box in his right hand. After taking his seat, he carefully handed the box over to Tara.

"What is it, Dad?"

"Go ahead and open it. It's something that I picked up for you on my trip to Jerusalem a couple months ago."

Tara opened the box to reveal the contents. Sitting neatly inside the box, resting gently on a swatch of cotton, were two almost identical golden pendants of curious workmanship. The pendants had two triangles interconnected with each other, both circumscribed within a circle. One of the pendants was connected to a thin gold necklace, obviously meant for a woman to wear, while the other hung on a slightly thicker, more masculine looking chain.

"They're beautiful," she exclaimed.

"I'm glad you like them," Rich replied. "These are referred to as 'Talisman', and are believed to provide good luck and protection for those that wear them. By themselves, they're just a piece of jewelry. But when a Jewish High Priest consecrates them, it charges them with magical powers. This one is specifically the 'Seal of Solomon'. The triangle pointing upwards represents good and the triangle pointing downwards represents evil. As a talisman, this one, in particular, is believed to be all-powerful, and was worn by people seeking protection from fatalities, threats, and to be protected from all evil."

"This is a great gift, thank you," Tara replied.

"Originally, I thought you would wear one and I would wear the other," he continued. "However, seeing how well you and William are getting along, and getting a good feel for William's character, I think that it would be more appropriate for you and him to wear them."

"Oh," William started to protest. "Please don't change your plans on account of me. You should keep..."

"I'll have nothing of it," he replied. "I want the two of you to have these. It will give you even more of a connection with one another. Remember, love is more than just an emotional and physical connection...it is a spiritual connection."

"That is so thoughtful, thank you, dad!"

"There's a catch though," Rich commented with a very serious look on his face. "I had both of these talismans consecrated at the same time. As such, they're bound to one another, much like how you and William are bound in love. Once you both put these on, you need to wear these at all times and in all places. If one of you fails to wear them, it will weaken the protection that it provides you, and could potentially weaken your relationship." He dramatically paused for a moment and then proceeded. "At least, that's what they tell me," he said with a chuckle.

Tara smiled very broadly while she reached into the box to remove both of the pendants.

"I love it! Take this," she said handing one of them to William. "You put this one around my neck, and I'll hook the other around yours."

"I guess I don't get a vote in this, do I?" William muttered in a dejected tone of voice.

"Of course not," Rich replied. "One thing that you've got to figure out if you haven't figured it out by now, is that a woman always gets her way."

William held open the clasp and unhooked one of the ends of the necklace. Separating the two ends of the chain, he reached both hands around either side of Tara's neck and tried to reconnect the clasp. After a couple moments of not being able to latch it, he stood up to peer around the back of her head so he could visually see how to hook it on. After a brief moment, he connected the end of the necklace and let the clasp securely close.

"It's beautiful!" Tara remarked glancing down. "Ok, your turn now."

Having more experience latching necklaces, she was able to hook his on her first attempt. Once the clasp securely held the necklace around William's neck she leaned backward to admire the jewelry.

"It looks perfect on you."

William looked downwards towards the pendant hanging on the chain around his neck, reaching with his right hand to grasp it to get a better look. The instant that his fingers touched the pendant, William felt an overwhelming sense of nausea. His vision darkened dramatically and he felt like he was starting to spin in a counterclockwise direction. He shut his eyes briefly, and when he opened them he caught a glimpse of a dark, shadowy figure in the periphery, lurking just beyond his field of vision. While he couldn't distinctly see the figure, he sensed an overwhelming feeling of anxiety and coldness, and his heart began to race.

He turned towards the shadowy figure to try and get a clear look, but when his field of vision focused on where he thought it was located, it was no longer there. He stared for a moment, almost as if in shock, and tightly squeezed his eyes again. When he opened them, the feeling of nausea was gone.

"William, are you ok?" Tara asked with an obvious tone of concern in her voice.

"Yes, I'm fine. I think I just had a head rush, like when you're sitting down for a long period of time and when you get up everything starts to go black and you feel dizzy. It's the weirdest feeling."

"How strange. Are you sure you're ok?" she pressed still concerned.

"Yes, I'm fine," he reassured her.

"Even still, maybe you should go and lie down just to be safe."

Rich stared intently at William, almost as if trying to read his mind. He looked around his backyard for a moment, and then returned his gaze back to William.

"Tarz is probably right, why don't you go and lie down on the couch for a few minutes to make sure everything is good. We're pretty much done with dinner. We'll clean up the plates and get dessert out. Ice cream can cure anything that ails you, so if you're not back to normal, I'll give you a double helping."

William simply nodded and walked back in the house and sat down on the couch in the living room.

Once William was clearly out of earshot, Rich turned to his daughter.

"Tarz," he hissed in a quiet whisper. "When you put the pendant around your neck, did you have any of the same sensations that William felt?"

"Nothing at all. Is there something wrong?"

"I don't know yet." He paused for a moment and then continued. "I wasn't just being dramatic about the story behind the talisman. They are in fact real artifacts from Jerusalem, and I had a real High Priest consecrate. The physical reaction that William had almost immediately after the talisman was hung around his neck indicates to me that someone, or something, could be watching William."

"Watching him? Is he in danger?"

"I'm not certain yet, but you should keep a close eye on him paying particular attention to anything strange that you might see, especially in his behavior. It's one thing to be watched by something evil, but it's another thing entirely to be under its influence."

"Dad, William is as normal as he has always been. I can't believe something 'evil' is watching him."

"Even still, please keep an eye out. And let me know if you experience anything similar yourself. Promise me!"

"Ok, I promise. Now let's get inside so I can check on William."

Tara stood up from her chair and left her father, along with all of the dirty plates outside. She quickly made her way into the living room and found William sitting on the couch with his right leg crossed neatly in front of him and his ankle resting on his left knee.

"Is everything ok?"

"Totally," he responded. "I feel completely fine. How about that dessert?"

Tara let out a sigh of relief, leaned over and threw her arms around William's neck, holding him in a tight embrace.

"I can't breathe," William squawked.

"Sorry," she laughed while releasing him from her clutches. "You just scared me when you zoned out. You let me know if you feel light-headed or dizzy again, alright?"

"Really, I'm..."

"Promise me!"

"Ok, I promise."

"Thank you," she replied. Standing erect again she took William's hand and pulled him up from his seat. "Let's go get some of that dessert now."

William simply smiled and let Tara lead him back into the kitchen. As he was exiting the living room he felt for a brief moment that same, oppressive presence he felt when sitting on the deck. The next moment later it was completely gone again and William dismissed it from his mind.

CHAPTER 15

Break In
(The Next Evening)

"Are you sure you won't stay the night with me," Tara almost begged while making a big pouty bottom lip to try and convince William to change his mind.

"You know that I would love to," William replied, feigning disappointment, "but I have to head into the lab by six tomorrow morning to take care of some things that I've been procrastinating on."

William leaned forward and pressed his lips against Tara's for a few moments while he wrapped his arms around her waist.

"I really had a fun time tonight. We should go on a double date with Don and Kim again."

"Yeah," she agreed. "Dinner was good, and the conversation was very engaging." She paused for a moment before continuing. "And I'm so happy that you're wearing the Talisman that my Dad gave us."

"I don't want to bring bad luck upon us do I?" he chided.

Tara laughed in response. "Well, you had better get going if you're going to get any rest before having to go into the office."

Tara stepped back into the doorway of her apartment while William turned and skipped swiftly down the stairs and headed for his car parked directly in front of the complex. Stopping, he turned and blew Tara a kiss before hopping into his car.

He inserted the key into the ignition and turned the engine over. Within a few moments, he was driving down the street and around the corner.

Glancing down at his watch he grimaced.

"Already twelve fifteen," he muttered. "Don is going to think that I got cold feet and backed out."

With a sense of urgency, he pressed the accelerator downwards until he was moving along at about forty-five miles an hour in a thirty-five zone.

"Don't get a ticket, but you've got to hurry," he thought silently in his head.

Within about fifteen minutes he found himself driving on predominantly abandoned city streets in the downtown area of South Los Angeles to the predetermined location that he was going to meet up with Don and Kim. They had decided that it would be safer to park their cars about half a mile from the clinic, and for William and Don to head in on foot. No need to draw extra attention to themselves at that early hour in the morning. The plan was for Kim to stay with the cars until they returned with the stolen embryos.

Two minutes later William turned right onto a side street off one of the main roadways. His heart nearly jumped out of his chest when he immediately saw a Los Angeles police car driving toward him on the opposite side of the road. He held his breath while he drove past the vehicle and anxiously watched in his review mirror as the police car turned left down the same road that William had just come from. As soon as the cop had disappeared from his view he let out a dramatic 'whoosh' from his lungs. He could still feel his heart pounding a mile and minute, and the slickness of sweat on the palms of his hands as he gripped the steering wheel tightly.

"You better keep yourself under control," he whispered through gritted teeth. "There's no second chances tonight."

After driving for another couple of blocks, William made the final turn onto a darkened side street and drove for about one hundred yards before pulling over to the side of the road, put his car in park, and turned off the lights and engine.

He furtively glanced around the buildings on either side of the street. He was in a light industrial area of downtown Los Angeles. Both sides of the street contained various places of business from a gas station to a local pizza joint. All the lights were off and there was no indication that anyone in the immediate area was awake. Looking over to the opposite side of the road he recognized the shape of Don's black car.

Almost immediately after spotting the car, he opened his side of the car, cautiously slid out and quietly closed the door behind him. The dome light of the car remained dark, as he had smartly remembered to switch off the light so it didn't illuminate when he opened the door. He quickly traversed the street and came up to the driver side window of Don's car.

The window was unrolled and he found Kim sitting in the driver's seat staring back at him. She momentarily glanced down at the necklace that hung around William's neck before returning her gaze back to meet that of Williams.

"We almost thought you weren't coming," she said with a distinct tone of disapproval in her voice.

"Yeah, yeah...I know," he defended. "Tara tried to get me to stay, but I told her that I had to be into the office early tomorrow. Are we ready?"

Don leaned over from the passenger seat so William could see his face that was creased with a broad grin and had a strong sense of excitement in his expression. "Absolutely!" he almost chortled.

"This isn't supposed to be fun!"

Don simply laughed as he turned back to his side of the car and reached for the door handle.

"Did you turn off the light?" William blurted out in a sharp hiss.

"Relax my friend. You need to take a chill pill or else we're going to do something stupid and get caught."

Pulling on the door handle he swung the passenger door open and William let out an audible sigh realizing that they had, in fact, turned off the map light in their car. Kim simply shook her head in disgust at his behavior.

"You're going to stay right here and wait for us, right?" he pressed Kim.

Kim pretended to be surprised by his statement as a perplexed expression appeared on her face.

"Wait a second! I'm not coming with you?" she asked.

"Ha ha, very funny," he responded, realizing that she was making fun of him.

He turned and walked around the back of the car until he stood on the sidewalk. After quietly shutting the car door, Don walked towards William carrying a black duffle bag.

"You've got the Styrofoam cooler and dry ice?" he asked motioning to the bag that Don was carrying.

"You bet," he enthusiastically responded.

"Alright then...let's start making our way towards the clinic." William glanced down at his watch for a moment. "It's just after twelve thirty. It will take us about ten minutes to get to the clinic, hopefully only ten minutes at the clinic, and ten to get back again. That means we should be ready to go just after one o'clock."

"Sounds good to me. Let's start moving."

Without another word, both men started walking down

the darkened side street at a brisk pace. Then had specifically chosen this road to be their primary path because it ran directly parallel with the street on which the clinic was located, and a short, virtually invisible alleyway gave them an easy way to get into the rear parking lot. The long stretch of road also gave them the ability to see cars early enough for them to hide behind something to ensure that they weren't seen.

William felt extremely nervous and he anxiously looked around him, trying to see in all directions at the same time. Don reached over and softly put his right hand on William's left shoulder in a reassuring gesture.

"Relax," he whispered. "Everything is going to be fine."

After walking for about seven minutes, Don pointed to the left at the entrance to the alleyway that lay between two small buildings. Thirty seconds later, both men were walking down the dark passage leading to the back of the fertility clinic. The path was only about five feet wide, and windowless buildings loomed over them on either side.

As they got towards the back of the two buildings, the pathway widened a bit, then opened up entirely revealing a small parking lot located adjacent to the one-story building.

Suddenly, a loud clash erupted from behind them to the right, causing both men to visibly jump in response. Don reached and grasped William's right forearm and held him tight, which turned out to be a good thing as William was readying himself to start running. Both men stood completely motionless as they warily searched the shadows for the source of the sound.

"Don't move a muscle," Don quietly warned.

Roughly five seconds later another clatter of metal and

glass came from the backside of the building that was on their right. Both stood motionless, staring intently at the shadows. The next moment later a small, dark silhouette started moving towards them close to the ground. As it moved closer, the light from the quarter moon in the sky revealed their potential assailant as a small cat.

Both men let out an audible sigh of relief.

"Damn cat!" Don quietly spouted. "I damn near soiled myself!"

"I thought I smelled something odd," William offered. "But then I realized it was the familiar scent of your breath. What was the name of that toothpaste you don't use?"

Don flashed a quick smile at William as both men let out a muffled laugh. Without hesitation, they both resumed walking towards the back of the clinic where a black, non-descript door was located at the top of 3 concrete steps.

Don motioned to William to pause where he was. He stealthily looked around the area in the rear of the building and glanced over to the parking lot to ensure that there wasn't anyone or anything watching. Satisfied that they were alone, he cautiously ascended the three steps and reached forward firmly grasping the cold, steel doorknob. Holding his breath, he meticulously began turning the knob in a clockwise direction. Much to his relief, the handle smoothly turned as he twisted his right wrist. A moment later the knob stopped and Don glanced backward at William who was intently staring him.

"Here we go," he simply stated.

Turning back to the door he slowly pulled on the handle and the door freely began to swing back towards the steps. Don stepped carefully to his right allowing the door to open wide enough for him to slide into the interior of the building. Without a word, he disappeared into the blackness of the building.

William stood motionless at the bottom of the steps, simply staring into the dark doorway. The next instant, Don popped his head out from the building and feverishly motioned for him to follow.

"Stop lollygagging and get your butt in here," he barked.

William snapped his backward as if he had just been slapped.

"Sorry," he whispered, as he quickly climbed the three steps and entered into the darkness.

"Stay here for just a moment and allow your eyes to adjust."

William dutifully paused for what seemed an eternity, waiting for his vision to adapt to the dark environment. Roughly forty-five seconds later, he was able to start making out shapes of cabinets, bookcases, and filing cabinets.

"You good?"

William simply nodded his head in reply.

"Alright then. We know what we need to do. You go up to the front of the clinic and retrieve the key from the doctor's office, just to the left of the reception area. I'll stay here at keep watch on the back of the building."

Again, William nodded in acknowledgment, but still stood motionless.

"You sure you're ok?"

Taking a deep breath, William simply nodded again and then started walking down the hallway past several open doors leading into examination rooms. Pausing for a moment he glanced into a room on his left. He could make out the shape of a stainless-steel examination table that was undoubtedly covered by sanitary paper. Located directly behind the table was a cabinet with several doors and drawers, and a stainless-steel sink located on the top. To the right was an office chair sitting on casters and a wastebasket for safe disposal of biohazardous materials.

Suddenly, William felt a strange sensation that he was not alone. He slowly, deliberately started to turn his head to his right to look back down the hallway. As his head rotated on his neck, the awareness of another person grew stronger and stronger. He became aware of a stinging, almost burning sensation located on the top of his chest against his skin. Once able to look squarely back down the hallway, he thought he saw a dark, almost imperceptible shadowy figure located at the end. There was a brief moment of recognition as he perceived that this figure was the same one he had encountered previously, except this time, it wasn't just in the periphery of his vision, but was now in his direct field of sight. As he strained his eyes to try and focus on this motionless shape, the burning on his skin began to intensify, and the room started to spin in a counterclockwise direction.

William's stomach lurched as a strong feeling of nausea swept over him and his vision started to darken. Reaching upwards with his right hand towards his neck, he slowly drew out the Talisman that hung at the end of the necklace beneath his collared shirt. As the ornament adorning the chain slipped out from beneath his shirt, a brilliant, almost blinding light filled his vision. Staggering backward he was barely able to catch himself with his left hand on the doorway, narrowly escaping falling to the ground. He closed his eyes at the intensity of the light and shook his head violently for a brief moment. When he opened his eyes the dark figure that had previously occupied the hallway in front of him was gone, as was the sensation of nausea.

William felt his heart beating violently in his chest from the adrenaline that was flooding into his bloodstream. His eyes darted apprehensively in every direction, searching for the would-be assailant to no avail. All he found was a darkened hallway and silence.

Glancing downwards towards his chest he saw the Talisman. Grasping it, he thought his fingers could still feel the warmth coming from it and the burning sensation still lingered in his chest. He looked around him erratically, trying to catch an image of the figure that he had just witnessed, but found nothing. Standing there motionless for a few moments, William's nerves calmed down, his breathing slowed, and his heart rate returned to normal. Taking a deep breath, he forced himself onwards toward the front of the clinic.

Immediately to the left of the doorway leading into the waiting room, William saw a short hallway that led to the doctor's office. Without hesitating, he walked into the office, circumventing the two chairs that sat immediately in front of a wooden desk, and crouched down in front of several drawers. He pulled open the long, horizontal drawer that lay immediately beneath the desk and peered inside. Nestled amongst paperclips, pens, and some spare change, he found what he was looking for: a small set of keys hooked onto a metal ring.

Reaching into the drawer he scooped up the keys with his right hand, stood up, and made his way back to the doorway leading into the office. Pausing at the door, he peered out expecting to find someone, or something, waiting for him. Instead, he found the same darkened hallway that he had previously occupied. Walking as fast as he could, he made his way back towards the rear of the office and found Don standing silently, peering back through a partially cracked door into the dark night.

Realizing that he had returned, Don turned and looked at William with an odd expression on his face.

"You look like you saw a ghost," he grunted. "What happened?"

"Nothing," he simply stipulated. "The quicker we get this done the better. Let's find that Cryo freezer."

William reached for the Styrofoam cooler that Don held in his hands containing the dry ice. Don recoiled for a moment not allowing William to take it from him.

"Are you ok?" he pressed.

"Yes, just give me the cooler," he demanded.

Obediently, Don relinquished the cooler and both men walked towards a door on the right side of the room that led to a storage area where the embryos were kept.

Upon entering the room, they observed the large, stainless steel door that was affixed to a massive freezer unit. Without a word, William approached the freezer door with the previously acquired keys in his right hand. Gripping the lock with his left hand, he slipped the first key into the lock and effortlessly turned it clockwise. With a quiet 'click', the top of the lock popped open and William unhooked it from the steel fastener on which it was hanging.

"Good guess," Don commented.

Without hesitation, William twisted the steel ring on which the lock was hung until it was horizontal with the ground and lined up perfectly with the opening in the steel metal plate that was attached with small hinges to the freezer door. He quickly flipped the metal plate forwards, grasped the large door handle that was oriented vertically on the surface, and pulled it sharply towards him. With a sharp click, the door swung open and a puff of freezing cold air erupted from the freezer in a white cloud of vapor.

As the white vapor cleared, the lights on the inside of the freezer revealed the spacious interior which housed hundreds, if not thousands of tiny vials neatly arranged on dozens upon dozens of shelves. Towards the interior right side of the unit stood three towers standing atop four caster wheels allowing for easy maneuvering, each housing no fewer than twenty-five drawers. William walked approximately four feet to the first of these three towers, pulling out one of the drawers to reveal neatly labeled vials, suspended through small openings in the bottom. Each drawer contained no fewer than fifty individually labeled vials. William removed one of the vials and turned it sideways to read the label:

'Patient: Jonathan Sparks
Specimen collected: September 29, 1985'

He turned back towards the entrance to the freezer to find Don, who had followed him into the interior, standing there with a large smile on his face.

"Jackpot!" Don exclaimed. "Look at all of these!"

William reached down and removed the top of the Styrofoam box.

"There must be five thousand samples in here," Don continued. "How many do you think we should take?"

"As many as possible," William answered in a cool, level tone. "I don't want to have to break back into this place if we run out. And once they discover the theft, you can be certain that they will take better precautions to protect them."

"Let's start loading up then."

With William holding the container, Don worked as fast as possible to load as many of the vials as possible. After about two minutes the Styrofoam container was filled nearly to the top.

"I think that's got it."

"How much does it weigh?" Don inquired.

Hefting the box in his arms William replied, "at least twenty pounds...maybe even twenty-five."

"Alright then, put the lid on and let's get going. No reason to dillydally around."

William nodded in agreement and slid the top of the container into place. Both men exited the freezer and Don shut the door behind them.

"Grab me some of that medical tape off of the counter. I want to be certain that this lid doesn't come off and we start dropping our valuable cargo."

Don reached over and pulled a length of about twenty inches of tape, connected the one end to the side of the container, and pulled the other up and over the top affixing it to the opposite side. He repeated this procedure about four additional times.

"That should do it then. Let's head out," William ordered.

Without another word, both William and Don walked back to where they had entered the rear of the clinic. After approaching the door, Don cracked it slightly to peer back into the rear of the property, and after a brief pause swung the door fully open.

"All clear," he offered.

Don led the way down the stairs with William following closely on his heels. Walking as quickly as their feet would carry them, they found themselves in the dark alleyway between the buildings leading back to the street where they had initially parked.

As Don rounded the corner to the right, William experienced an oppressive feeling that stopped him immediately in his tracks. Turning back in the direction towards the clinic, he again experienced an almost vertigo-like sensation accompanied by what was becoming a familiar sense of nausea. As he peered back down the darkened alley he again felt as if there was another presence concealed by the shadows glaring back at him. Instinctively, he reached towards the necklace that hung around his neck. To his surprise, before he even grasped the necklace the feeling of dizziness and nausea parted and the entity that he felt was watching him was no longer there.

He paused for a moment and then proceeded to pull the Talisman from beneath his shirt again. This time there was no blinding light, but a sense of calm and well being swept over him. He paused for another moment and let the pendant softly rest on the outside of his shirt rather than tucking it back in.

The next moment Don came running back around the corner, almost running directly into William.

"Why did you stop?" he demanded. "Did you see something?"

"It's fine," he reported. "Let's just get back to the car and get out of here."

Don nodded in agreement and both men started back down the street towards where they had originally left the cars. After about four minutes they spotted the two cars parked where they had left them.

Upon reaching the back of Don's car, Kim exited the driver side door and stalked back towards where they were both standing. Arriving at the back of the car, she first looked and Don, and then glared over at William. Her eyes glanced down at the Talisman that he wore on the outside of his shirt and immediately shot back up meeting William's gaze.

"About time you got back," she stated, without breaking eye contact with William. "Did you get them?"

William silently nodded down towards the cooler in his arms.

Sensing the tension that was obviously present between his girlfriend and William, Don reached for Kim's left hand and grasped it.

"Ok then," he stated as he pulled Kim towards him. "No reason to stand around here. Let's go home."

Kim stopped staring at William and met Don's gaze with an icy stare to which he unconsciously recoiled. The next moment a grin appeared on her face and she looked back over at William.

"You remember the plan, right? Just take the samples back to your apartment tonight, and then bring them with you when you go to the lab. That way you won't raise any suspicions by paying the university a visit at two in the morning."

"Yes, I remember."

"Good," she replied. "Don, get in the car and let's head home."

Don obediently followed her instructions and started walking towards the passenger side of the car. Upon reaching the door he looked back at William.

"Don't speed either. It would be a hard thing to explain to the cops why you got five hundred frozen embryos," he laughed.

"No worries. The speed limit is my friend."

William walked across the street to his car, opened up on the back door on the driver side, and slid the cooler into the back seat. Being extra careful, he pulled the seatbelt around the container and snapped it into the buckle. He quickly shut the door, hopped into the front seat and started the engine. Glancing back over towards Don's car he again met Kim's gaze. She was staring intently at him through her open window. A sly grin creased her face and she slowly pressed the accelerator and drove down the street.

William waited for them to be almost out of view before putting his car in drive and starting his journey home.

CHAPTER 16

Epiphany
(Four Months Later)

William found himself behind a large desk in the office that he shared with a few other graduate students. Don was slumped over in an easy chair on the far side of the room quietly snoring. The Christmas break had already started and they were among very few people still on the USC campus. Adding to their solitude was the fact that it was twelve-thirty on Tuesday morning. Fighting off the drowsiness that was starting to hit him as well, he was working on updating his laboratory journal with the events of the day.

September 26, 2006 – Over the past four months we have figured out how to successfully thaw the experimental human embryos, as well as accurately mapping and identifying the genetic blueprint of a host. However, we have been thwarted at determining a process by which to imprint that blueprint onto the 'host' embryo to create ESCs that would be genetically compatible with the subject. Leveraging previous research studies, we have been able to suppress the existing genetic code within embryos. However, once the target genetic blueprint is imprinted onto the embryo the cell walls begin to deteriorate (usually within fifteen minutes), allowing for cytoplasmic contact across distinct cells, resulting in the destruction of the embryo within thirty additional minutes.

Don let out an abrupt noise, almost a loud snort, which startled William momentarily. After mumbling softly to himself he shifted onto his right side and began to quietly snore again. William returned his attention back to his computer screen.

> In order for ESCs to be successfully extracted, the embryo itself needs to stay intact for a period of roughly eight hours. This period of time would allow for the imprinting process to take hold and for cell division to begin taking place. The critical time to extract the Embryonic Stem Cells is after cell division has begun and before they differentiate themselves into one of the three primary germ layers (ectoderm, endoderm, and mesoderm), from which all two hundred and twenty cell types in the human body are derived. Since ESCs can propagate themselves indefinitely once removed from the embryo, a sufficient number of cells should be capable of being cultured for use in the treatment of injuries. If there was only a way to ensure that the integrity of the embryo cell walls could be maintained long enough to harvest...

William paused for a second to think about what he had just written down. "All I need to do is extend the amount of time the cell walls remain intact," he mused in his mind. "Just long enough for..." and he paused for a moment. "OH MY GOD!" he exclaimed, slamming his hand down on the desk creating an earsplitting bang.

Don violently jerked awake at the sudden commotion resulting in him tumbling off of his chair and landing on the floor with a distinct thud.

"What the hell is wrong with you?" Don shouted as he picked himself up on off the floor and sat back down on the chair he was previously occupying.

"I love keeping lab journals!"

"What are you talking about?"

"Just the whole process of documenting your work, logically discussing successes and failures, creating a means whereby you can..."

"Seriously," he implored, "what the hell are you talking about?"

Taking a deep breath, William paused to collect his thoughts before responding.

"I was just writing about how we've been unable to successfully imprint the genetic code onto the embryo in order get the specific blueprint expressed. And then it hit me."

"I'm going to hit you if you don't tell me what you're talking about!"

"All we need to do is strengthen the cell walls! Just enough for them to retain their integrity for say twelve hours. This would be enough time for the embryo to fully integrate the genetic code, and for us to extract ESCs before they begin the transformation process into germ layers."

Sitting up in his chair Don raised an eyebrow at William. "Ok, you've got my attention. How do we do that?"

"Sugar," he replied. "Glucose to be more specific."

Don just stared at him blankly.

"Come on," William chided him. "It's simple cellular biology. The magnitude of a given cell walls integrity is directly related to the level of glucose present in the cell, or in our case, surrounding the cell. By adding the right amount of glucose into the solution that the embryo is suspended, we should be able to effectively create a barrier around each of the cells giving them enough time to accept the genetic imprint, and then for us to extract those elusive ESCs."

"Well, my friend," he replied in a jovial tone, "I'm certainly glad that one of us is a genius! It sounds like it could work."

"It's got to work. Otherwise, I think we're stuck!"

"So, when do we start?"

"No time like the present!"

Don glanced over at the clock hanging on the wall. "Seriously? It's twelve thirty-five in the morning."

Rather than responding, William jumped up from his chair and virtually ran out the door and headed down the hall towards the lab. After waiting about sixty seconds, Don rose from his chair and laboriously walked down the hallway and entered the lab, where he found the Cryo-freeze door open and William carefully removing a frozen embryo.

Shutting the door William spun around and started walking towards the side of the laboratory where their equipment was neatly laid out across two sets of tables. He glanced momentarily at Don and flashed him a quick grin.

"Took you long enough to get here," he chortled.

Don managed a weak smile in return while he rubbed at sleepy dust in the corners of his eyes. "So, what's the plan?" he grunted without any enthusiasm.

"Well, we've got to thaw one of the embryos. That will take about thirty minutes. Can you grab me the vitrification solution from the drawer over there?"

Don complied with his request and set the vial in front of William.

"Now, this solution already had a glucose Molar mass of one point zero. We need to increase that to approximately three times the amount to ensure sufficient coverage across all cell membranes. Since the vial contains fifty milliliters of liquid, we need to add," he paused for a second while he did some quick math on his calculator, "twenty-two grams of sugar to the solution."

William walked over to a shelf containing jars and vials of various substance and returned with a small jar of sucrose. Very carefully he placed some filter paper on the gram scale, zeroed it out, and added granules of sugar to the scale until the display read "22.00 grams."

"Grab one of the sterilized test tubes and place it on the rack," he commanded as he motioned to the countertop in front of him.

Silently, Don walked over and put a pair of rubber gloves on to ensure he didn't contaminate the experiment, removed a test tube from the plastic container, and placed it in the receptacle that was connected to the electron microscope.

"Thank you, sir," William offered.

William then very carefully took the vitrification solution and poured it into the newly placed tube. Without being asked, Don walked around the table and took his place on William's right side. Satisfied that all of the solution had been poured into the tube, William then meticulously folded the filter paper on which the sugar had been measured in half, and gently poured the crystalline granules into the test tube, where they immediately dissolved into the solution.

"Ok, let's introduce the embryo into the solution now."

Don carefully placed the end of a pipette into the vitrification solution to capture a tiny drop. Next, he looked into the microscope that was focusing on the vial containing the frozen embryo. He painstakingly inched the end of the pipette into the vial, using the microscope to guide his path to the edge of the frozen embryo that was suspended within it. Meticulously, he moved the end of the pipette next to the embryo, and with a very slight movement, the embryo was enveloped into the drop of solution at the end of the pipette. He warily removed the pipette from the vial and placed the end of it back into the vitrification solution. William was already looking through the electron microscope to oversee the transfer of the embryo into the solution.

"Good to go?" Don inquired.

William simply nodded in reply, to which Don responded by gently squeezing the bulb at the end of the pipette to transfer the embryo into the solution.

Both men held their breath for a brief moment.

"Ok," William whispered. "It's in the solution. Now we just need to wait for the embryo to thaw and we can turn off the epigenetic tags on the embryo and then imprint mine."

Don turned towards William with a look of great anticipation on his face.

"If this works, we're going to be filthy rich! There are so many applications for this. Every biochemical company out there is going to be clamoring to hire us. Or better yet, to license the rights to leverage our discovery. We need to make certain that we patent this entire process!"

"Don't get ahead of yourself," William cautioned. "And besides, if this does work, the University owns the rights to the research. Furthermore, I'm doing this so we can help out mankind. The money will take care of itself, but the good that this discovery can do is what this is all about."

Don raised an eyebrow speculatively at William and finally broke out laughing.

"I guess you're right."

"About what?"

"That the money will take care of itself. Even if the University owns the rights to the research, you and I are going to make billions off of this!"

"Always the altruistic one, aren't you? There's more to life than just money," William commented.

"Yup. And that's more money!" Don barked.

Both men laughed for a brief moment, and then sat quietly for a couple of minutes. William glanced down at his watch and grimaced.

"We've still got twenty minutes until the embryo's ready."

"What time is it," Don pressed.

"One thirty in the morning."

Don let out an audible sigh and slumped in his seat. After another moment, he continued with William.

"If this does work, what is the next step?"

William silently motioned towards his right cheek.

"If we're able to successfully imprint my genetic code onto the embryo, we are going to test whether they have the same regenerative effect on my cheek as they did on the lab rat."

"You're not going to try and repair the entire scar all at the same time, are you?" Don incredulously inquired.

"Of course not. I'm not stupid!" he replied. "I'm going to test it on a very, very small portion of my cheek. Then if that proves successful, we'll go for the whole enchilada."

"Crazy," Don commented with a slight cringe on his face. "Are you going to do that yourself?"

"Of course not. You're going to be the one operating the scalpel."

Don visibly turned green at the thought of cutting into his friend's cheek with a surgical knife. William suddenly burst out laughing after he gotten the desired effect from his friend.

"Don't worry. I've got a good friend over at the medical center on campus that works with burn victims and he's already agreed to handle the procedure. I've told him that it's essentially a skin graft, but that I'll be providing him the material to graft into the affected area."

"But it's different than a normal skin graft, right?"

"Correct. Essentially, he'll remove the scar tissue down to the point where he finds healthy skin, and would then apply the ESCs in what amounts to a paste. Once applied to the wound they will pick up genetic instructions from the healthy cells, and the body will automatically give the ESCs direction on transforming into the ectoderm germ layer. Then the body should be able to successfully grow new skin, which when completed, should be virtually perfect."

"What if it doesn't work? Won't you potentially be left with an unsightly injury that is worse than you currently have?"

"That's why we have to be absolutely certain that everything heals perfectly when we first test it on a small area."

William briefly glanced down at his watch and smiled.

"Ok, let's verify that the embryo is completely thawed and we can begin the imprinting process."

William looked intently through the electron microscope for what seemed an eternity, but what was really only a couple of minutes. Finally satisfied he stood upright with a smile on his face.

"Ready to suppress the current genetic expression!" he exclaimed.

Quietly, William walked over to the cold storage unit and removed a small vial with a green label on the outside.

"What's that?" Don asked.

"It's a synthetic solution containing RNA that turns off all of the genes in the embryo. Once they have been turned off, we can then introduce the synthetic RNA that I've engineered based on my own genetic code to imprint the 'unspecified' embryo with my gene sequencing. If the cell wall integrity is maintained, it should result in the creation of a perfect embryonic clone of myself."

William took off the stopper of the vial and carefully removed exactly ten milliliters from the solution with a surgical syringe. He placed the syringe into a robotic delivery device that he would use to maneuver the end of the needle to the exact location in the embryo to deliver that payload.

"Here we go!"

Pressing a couple of buttons, the needle was inserted into the vial containing the now viable embryo. Looking at the digital image displayed on the screen in front of him, he skillfully guided the tiny needle to the edge of the cell wall of the embryo. Without any extra fanfare, he inserted the needle just into the outer lining of the cells and injected the solution.

"And now we wait," William stipulated. "It takes about three hours for the embryo to begin accepting the genetic code, and an additional two hours for the complete integration of genetic code."

"And we need to be *here* in order monitor the entire process so we can extract the ESCs, *if* this is successful, at *just* the right moment, *correct?*" Don speculated.

"That's correct."

"Figures," he complained. "You had to wait to have this breakthrough until the wee hours of the morning with both of us completely exhausted, didn't you? Would it have been too much to ask for you to have your 'ah ha' moment at nine in the morning, right after we finished a large breakfast?"

"You crack me up! Alright, what do you want to do for the next few hours?"

Don reached into his bag, pulled out a deck of cards and began shuffling them. After three shuffles of the deck, he started to deal out cards for the first of what was likely to become many games of cards.

############################

Approximately three hours later, Don was getting ready to deal out another hand of cards. William leaned back on his stool, stretching up towards the ceiling with both of his hands, letting out a slightly muffled groan. Having finished stretching, he brought his left wrist in front of him to glance at his watch.

"What time do you have?" Don inquired.

"It's almost four thirty," William announced at the same time he was yawning. "Let's take a look and see how things are progressing."

William shifted his chair back towards the electron microscope and began to intently stare at the digital image shown on his screen. The next moment later he started shaking his head, letting out a disgruntled huff as he exhaled through his nose.

"What's wrong?" Don asked.

"I don't see any activity."

"So, what does that mean?"

"Well, most likely it means that the genetic imprinting didn't take. That, or it has already been successfully integrated into the embryo, but we haven't allowed enough time for that."

"How do we know for sure?"

"We need to take some fluorescent imaging of the RNA to determine if the sequencing matches the sequencing of my own genetic code." William reached over to the side of the electron microscope to turn on the scanner that would read the genetic expression of the embryo. "This will take about five minutes to complete. Then we can compare the gene clusters of the embryo side by side with those of my own genes. We should know pretty quickly whether this worked or not."

Both men sat in silence for the next four minutes simply staring at the digital image on the screen. Suddenly, a soft beep was emitted from the machine and an icon appeared in the bottom right corner. William used the mouse connected to the device to position the cursor over the icon and dragged it onto a magnifying glass. Instantly, an image was displayed on the screen that represented the various spatial patterns of the gene expression of the embryo. William then clicked on a link on the top of the screen labeled 'Compare', and navigated to a directory where he had located spatial patterns of his own DNA previously. He selected the file labeled 'William_DNA_SEQUENCING_10152003' and clicked open.

Within thirty seconds the machine displayed a second set of spatial patterns side-by-side with each of the corresponding patterns from the embryo for easy comparison. Both men stared at the screen in complete silence for about thirty seconds. Finally, Don said something.

"So, what are we supposed to be looking at?" he questioned.

"We're supposed to be comparing the patterns of the one image to the other one. If they're the same, then we have created an exact match." William scratched his head for a second and then continued. "Let me take a closer look," he commented as he leaned forward to look through the two eyepieces of the electron microscope.

As he adjusted the fine focus on the microscope something on the periphery of his vision caught his attention and he backed away from the lenses momentarily to see if he could identify the source. After a few moments, he leaned back in to view the image once again. As his eyes focused on the interior of the embryo, William felt a slight tingling sensation on his chest beneath his shirt.

Consciously, he reached towards his chest and felt the Talisman beneath his shirt, noting a sensation that could only be described as heat.

"What's wrong?" Don questioned.

William leaned back to look at Don and paused again for a brief moment before responding.

"It's nothing," is finally said in an unconvincing tone.

Again, he leaned back down to look through the lenses of the microscope. The next instant William saw a dark shadow enter into his view from the left-hand side of his field of vision until it almost completely consumed the image shown through the eyepiece. It looked as if it was oozing into the microscopic image of the embryo, slowly disappearing until the shadow was completely gone and all that was left was the image of the embryo again. As soon as the shadow had dissipated, the sensation of heat coming from the amulet ceased.

"Did you see that?" he exclaimed.

"See what?"

"The dark shadow on the screen. It appeared out of nowhere and then disappeared into the embryo."

Don look at William with an incredulous expression on his face.

"I don't know what you're talking about," he stated. "I was looking at the screen the entire time and didn't see anything."

"Seriously? It was right there," he argued pointing at the eyepiece.

"Maybe it was an eyelash or something that crossed your line of vision."

"Across both eyes at the exact same time? And in the exact same place?"

"I have no idea," Don finally answered.

"Never mind. It's probably nothing," William stated dismissively as he rubbed again at his shirt where the Talisman lay. "Let's compare the two images now. I think enough time has passed."

Both men stared at the screen and the series of images that appeared side by side for about three minutes.

"It looks like the same image. Are you sure you selected the right file?" Don finally inquired.

William sat silently, staring at the screen with a growing expression of disbelief on his face.

"Hey!" Don pressed. "Did you choose the right file?"

William still looked fixedly at the screen. However, the

corners of his mouth began to turn slightly upwards as his eyes began to widen.

"Well, what's the deal?"

William turned his head slowly until his eyes met Don's gaze. The slight upturning of his mouth was now a big, toothy grin.

"You're kidding me?"

With his eyes still locked with Don's, he leaned backward on his stool and folded his arms in front of him.

"It's an exact match!" he proclaimed.

CHAPTER 17

Persuasion
(The Next Morning)

Closing his apartment door behind him, Don tossed his bag onto the couch and started making his way down the hallway towards his bedroom. Despite it being nine o'clock in the morning, he had every intention of flopping himself on his bed to grab a few hours of sleep before meeting back up with William to start writing up all of the test results and determining next steps.

He reached for the doorknob to push the door back in the room, but before he could grasp it the door swung open by itself. Don nearly fell forward into the room but was able to catch himself by placing his right hand on the trim around the door. Standing squarely in the doorway before him with her hands folded neatly underneath her chest was Kim. She was wearing one of his dress shirts with only the third button down from the top fastened. The singly fastened button wasn't doing a very good job to cover up Kim's body, and as far as he could tell, she wasn't wearing anything else.

"Holy crap," he exclaimed. "You scared me to death!"

"Don't be so dramatic," she dismissively stated as she rolled her eyes. "I assume you have a good reason for getting home so late?"

"Actually, I have a phenomenal reason. In fact, I have such a great reason that you're never going to guess."

Staring flatly into his eyes she simply responded with, "well?"

Don raised his eyebrows a bit in response to her flippant response and then decided to let it go.

"We were able to successfully imprint Will's genetic code onto the embryo," he stated triumphantly. "We did it! We created a clone!"

Kim pursed her lips together slightly as if deep in thought, and her eyes almost seemed to go completely blank for an instant as if she wasn't even in the room. The next moment later her gaze fixed solidly on Don's before responding.

"Did you notice anything," she paused for a second before continuing, "odd?"

"Odd? What do you mean?"

"Did you see anything out of the ordinary?"

Don thought to himself silently for a few moments before responding.

"Nothing strange...no, nothing really..." and he paused.

"What?" Kim demanded.

Taken aback by Kim's demanding voice Don physically backed away from her a few of steps.

"What did you see?" she pressed.

"I didn't see anything. Everything seemed normal. William on the other hand, claimed that he saw some type of dark shadow when he was looking through the microscope that disappeared from view."

"Was he wearing that Talisman than Tara gave him?"

"What's that got to do with..." he replied, but stopped short as Kim's icy glaze seemed to almost bore into the back of his skull.

"Was he wearing the Talisman?" she demanded in an even icier tone that the first time. She had also taken a step forward and was now standing almost toe-to-toe with him.

Swallowing hard Don finally responded, "yes...err...I think he was. Why?"

Kim's expression instantly changed, and the iciness of her stare had shifted to one that was more alluring, almost seductive. She raised her right hand and brushed the backside of her index and middle finger against his left cheek.

"It's not important," she purred as she slid her left hand around Don's waist and pulled him closer to her until their noses almost touched one another. "What is important is that you were successful."

She paused for a moment and then gently pushed him back with her right hand on his chest. Don just stared at her with a look of confusion on his face.

"You remember what we talked about right?" she whispered. "It important that William doesn't hold you back. He's in this for altruistic reasons. The real reason," she stated as she grasped the front of his shirt in her right hand, "is that you're doing this is for the money. You're going to be rich beyond your wildest dreams."

"But this really is Will's research. This is all based off on ideas."

"Nonsense! He would be lost without you. The only reason that he's gotten this far is that you're helping him. Have you talked to him again about how you're going to make money off of this research?"

"Just three or so hours ago."

"And?"

"He's still pretty much committed to focusing on helping others," he conceded.

Kim tilted her head downwards and looked up at Don through strands of hair that lazily lay across her face.

"He's going to lock you out," she whispered. "He's going to push you out and claim all of the research for himself."

"But that wouldn't..."

"Listen to me!" she interrupted. "He's going to push you out and take your name off of the research. You can't let that happen! He's just using you and then he's going to kick you out!"

Kim paused for a second to let the gravity of her statement take its full effect.

"We talked about this remember?" she continued. "The only way that you can ensure that you get what's due to you is to take the research. Half of it belongs to you anyways."

"But all of the research is meaningless without having the embryos. I can access the same equipment in other labs on campus, but without the embryos, I can't replicate the same results."

Kim drummed the fingers of her right hand thoughtfully on the point of her chin, stopped suddenly, and stared deep into Don's eyes.

"Then you will have to steal some of the embryos then."

Don looked down briefly before returning back to Kim's gaze and he apprehensively bit his bottom lip.

"I guess you're right?" he almost suggested.

"Of course I'm right!" she angrily blurted out.

"But what if I get caught?"

"So what?" she replied, as she visibly worked to control her temper. "What's he going to do? Go to the police and let them know that someone stole embryos from him that he himself had previously stolen? He's not going to go to the police. He won't do anything!" she stated very matter-of-factly.

Don thought to himself silently about the situation while Kim calmly stood waiting for him to come to what she knew was a foregone conclusion. Finally, he took a deep breath and responded.

"I guess you're right," he conceded.

"Yes. It's the only way. And once you've gone your separate ways, nothing is going to stop us from changing the world."

Kim paused again, looking into Don's eyes that now had an appearance of surrender in them. She again advanced forward, taking his left hand and sliding it up the front of her body until it came to a stop on top of the single button holding the dress shirt she wore loosely around her unclothed body.

"Well, now that that's decided," she purred as Don slowly unfastened her shirt. "Let me give you your Christmas present early this year," she whispered as she slowly pulled Don back into the bedroom, shutting the door behind them.

CHAPTER 18

Dissolution
(Later That Day)

William sat at the front of the laboratory busily typing notes on his laptop. He was completely alone in the room, and most likely the only person in the building. He paused for a moment to glance at his watch.

"Three-thirty," he muttered under his breath in an obviously irritated tone. "Just once it would be nice if Don could show up on time.

As if his comments had magically summoned him, Don bounded into the room at almost the same instant that William completed his sentence. Turning around, he looked sharply him and exhaled loudly through his nostrils in disapproval.

"I know, I know," Don offered. "I'm late...again."

"Just over one and a half hours late," he announced in objection. "Really Don! There's still a ton to do, and I need you here working with me."

Don walked up to the table directly across from where William sat. He crooked a sideways smile at him before speaking.

"I...ah...well, I got a little distracted," he said sheepishly.

William returned a raised eyebrow back at him and then cracked a smile. Both men chuckled for a moment and Don finally took a seat next to William.

"I would have been here sooner, honestly. I had every intention of jumping into bed the instant I got home and catching a quick nap." He paused momentarily and then continued. "Well, I guess I did jump directly into the bed. The sleeping part is what a failed to follow through on."

"T M I," William cautioned. "I don't want to hear any of the specifics."

Ignoring his friend's request, he continued. "The instant I walked into my apartment, Kim was on me like white on rice."

"I get it!"

"Like a fat kid on chocolate cake."

"I GET IT!"

"Like flies on…"

"ENOUGH ALREADY!" William screamed. "Let's get back to the task at hand."

"Ok, ok. I just wanted to make sure that you understood why I was late. You're being such an inquisitive scientist, I know you like to have all of the information surrounding the situation."

"Again, too much information!"

Don laughed hard for a few moments, gained his composure, and took on a more serious look.

"Ok then," he offered. "Where are we at?"

"Well, I've pretty much documented all of the events of last night, err, I'm mean early this morning from our test. Now we need to start formulating our plan of attack to consistently validate our procedure and results. I'm thinking that we will probably have a couple more months of testing and validation before I can take my work to the Biochemistry Board to present for my thesis."

"Our thesis," Don corrected him.

"Sorry, our thesis," William agreed. "We've still got a ton to do! And unfortunately, it's going to be repetitive, and not terribly exciting. It's very anticlimactic. We achieved a scientific breakthrough which is going to change the world as we know it, but we can't celebrate until we have proven beyond a shadow of a doubt that it's reproducible."

"Anticlimactic is an understatement," he bemoaned. "Well, I guess we better get started."

Don paused for a moment as if deep in thought and then continued.

"By the way, I agree with you that we're going to change the world. This is truly a quantum leap forward in biochemistry. We are going to change the medical industry for decades to come."

"Absolutely! Let me just finish up this paragraph and we can start mapping out a timeline for next steps."

William began typing on his laptop again, engrossed in his thoughts, while Don sat shifting back and forth on his stool. Noticing his uneasiness, William stopped typing and turned to face Don.

"What's bothering you?"

"You know," Don replied. "This is an opportunity for us to make a colossal amount of money."

"Really? Are we back to this? Don't worry about the money! Let's focus on the getting everything perfect with the research, and the money will take care of itself."

Noticeably perturbed by his response, Don postured himself in his chair until he was sitting up straight, and then leaned in towards William.

"What's the big deal? It's our idea...well...it was *your* idea, but *our* painstaking hard work and perseverance that brought us to where we are today. Why shouldn't we be rewarded for our efforts?"

"We will!"

"Don't be so sure! The University is going to get their hands all over this. We should start taking steps to ensure that we're protected. That they can't just take our work, put their name on it, and then collected billions in residuals from all of the future monies that this will generate."

"The university is not going to steal our work. But we do owe them for everything that they've provided. If it weren't for their labs and equipment, we wouldn't be anywhere near where we are today."

Don abruptly stood up from his chair, turned his back on William and walked three steps in the opposite direction before stopping. Roughly five seconds later he turned back around and folded his arms across his chest.

"I think we should come up with a list of items that the university needs to agree to in order to ensure that we get our fair share. I'm not saying that they won't get anything, I just want to make sure that we get a good chunk as well!"

"Don," William protested as he stood up from his chair. "We're not going to try and dictate terms. And we're not doing this just so we can get rich. We're doing this for the pure science! To advance the knowledge of human science, for the better of mankind."

"You're naïve!" he accused.

"And you're paranoid!" he shouted back.

"I'm not willing to go along with your philanthropic plans and just giving away our research!" he proclaimed as he took two purposeful steps towards William.

"Sorry Don," he objected while standing up from his seat, "but you don't really have much say in the matter. This is my baby. It was my idea! It was my thesis! This is my project and I've just let you come along for the ride!"

Both men were now standing directly in front of one another, only separated by no more than eighteen inches. Don's cheeks were visibly flushed in anger, and if it weren't for the fact that he had his arms crossed in front of his chest, his hands would have been shaking. Neither of them said a word for a seeming eternity, but in reality was probably no longer than thirty seconds.

"Fine!" Don hissed through clenched teeth. "We're done!"

"Don't be so childish!"

"You're the one who's not willing to listen to reason," he retorted severely.

Neither man spoke a word, but stood motionless, staring menacingly at one another. Finally, Don diverted his eyes away from William's icy stare and took a step backward.

"I guess this is it then," he stated with an air of finality.

"I guess so," William replied.

Don the abruptly took two steps back towards William and shook his clenched fist in his face.

"You'll be sorry that you pushed me out! You'll see!"

Don then turned back around and stormed towards the back of the room. William just stood there motionless and watched his best friend violently pull open the classroom door and slam it behind him.

Walking at the quickened pace, Don made his way towards the stairwell, bounding down the stairs two steps at a time. Reaching the bottom of the stairs he threw his weight into the push plate of the door, forcing it open with a great amount of force.

Much to his surprise, he spotted Kim patiently standing beside his car in the parking lot. After a brief pause, he made his way across the parking lot, stopping short of his girlfriend who was looking at him with a satisfied expression on her face.

"How's everything going?" she inquired feigning an innocent look on her face.

"Wonderfully," he sarcastically replied. "What are you doing here?"

"I just had a feeling that you needed me," she calmly replied. "Did you talk with Will about making money off of your research?"

"Yes," he grunted. "He's being stupid. He doesn't realize how much money we can make off of this work."

He paused for a moment to gather his thoughts and then continued.

"I let my temper get the better of me and I said some things which I shouldn't have. I need to go back and apologize so that..."

"No. You don't!" Kim succinctly stated.

"But I told him that I didn't want anything to do with the research. I can't just walk away though."

"Why not?" she pressed. "You're as smart as he is, and this is as much your work as it is his. We talked about this already, didn't we? You knew he was going to force you out, and now all you need to do is complete the work on your own."

Don opened his mouth to protest, but Kim quickly took a step forward placing the fingers of her right hand on his lips.

"Don," she purred. "We've got this under control. All we need to do is to get our hands on a few of those embryos and we're in business."

"Kim," he complained. "I don't think..."

Instantly Kim's hand jumped from his lips and roughly gripped his chin, forcefully squeezing it between her fingers and thumb, almost to the point of inflicting pain. The next moment later her grasp loosened and she playfully, but forcefully, slapped him on his left cheek.

"Sweetheart. This is the path that we are now on. Let's head home so we can start making some plans of our own."

Without giving him a chance to object, Kim walked back around the car, opened the door, and sat in the passenger seat.

"You coming?" she stipulated more as an order than a question.

"I guess so," he finally relented.

And with that, Don climbed into his car and they drove away from the biology building and completely out of sight.

CHAPTER 19

Unsanctioned Activities
(Four Months Later)

Approximately four months later, William found himself sitting alone in a small, windowless room in the medical research building of the USC campus. His right legs began to bounce restlessly as he glanced downwards at his watch on his left wrist. He had been sitting here for nearly forty-five minutes already waiting for his friend to show up.

Taking a deep breath, he lifted the lid off the small white cooler that sat squarely in his lap to look at the contents for probably the tenth time since he sat down. As verified multiple times previously, a clear glass jar with a silver lid secured tightly on top sat neatly in the center of the cooler with multiple packages of dry ice holding it in place. Satisfied that everything was as it should be, he returned the lid back to the top of the cooler and looked at his watch again.

"If Carl doesn't show up soon, I'm going to have to return this to the cool storage facility back at the lab," he muttered quietly to himself.

"Sorry I'm late," the man commented apologetically as he swung open a door leading into the room. "But better late than never, right?"

"No worries Carl," William convincingly lied.

Carl was a relatively short, unassuming man somewhere in his mid-thirties. He was likely no taller than five feet, six inches tall, and his lack of height was emphasized by the fact that he was nearly as round about the waist as he was tall. He wore thick, black-rimmed glasses, and sported what could be best described as a friar haircut given that he had started going bald in his senior year of high school. His forehead was glossy with sweat that seemed to constantly roll off his brow regardless of it being hot or cold. All in all, he wasn't a very pleasant man to look at, but what he lacked in appearance he made up for in brilliance. Carl was one of the leading experts in the treatment of severe burn victims in the United States. And this was what brought William here today.

While most people would purposively avoid looking at the disfiguration, Carl intently, almost eagerly, regarded the scar that marred the left side of William's face. After a brief moment, he glanced down at the white cooler that sat on his lap and a broad grin creased his round face.

"Is that what I think it is?" he ardently asked.

"Yup. The past four years of my life are contained within this beer cooler that cost no more than three bucks!"

"Well alrighty then," he announced while rubbing his hands together in anticipation. "Let's get down to work. Follow me!" he ordered.

Obediently, William stood up, carefully cradling the cooler in his arms to ensure that he didn't upset the contents, and followed the other man down the hallway. After about twenty feet, Carl grasped the handle of a door on the right side of the hallway, opening it back into the room and walked in. As William entered the room he quickly became aware that they were standing the middle of an operating theater. The room resembled the shape of an amphitheater with a surgical table located at the head of the room, and tiered seating emanating outwards in a half circle. Normally this is where procedures were performed where students and other spectators could watch. Now, however, the room lay eerily quiet without any other occupants except for the two men who just entered.

Carl walked over to a large stainless-steel sink and began vigorously washing his hands and arms all the way up to his elbows with a thick, green, surgical disinfectant. After about sixty seconds of scrubbing, he carefully rinsed off his arms and hands and gently dried them off with a sterile white towel.

"Go ahead and hop up on the table," he asked pointing over to the stainless-steel platform in the middle of the room. "As you can see, I've already got everything prepped which is why I was late coming to get you."

As he walked towards the table, William looked around at the various smaller tables that were clustered closely about containing various objects. Carl stood next to a table that had a green cloth resting on it, with the ends wrapped back up over the top covering the contents. He reached forward and meticulously unfolded the two ends that met at the middle backward revealing a menagerie of surgical devices, blades, and probes.

The reality of what was about to transpire suddenly hit William, and he thought that his heart was literally going to explode out of his chest.

Realizing his anxiety, Carl approached William, looking at him intently.

"Are you sure you want to go through with this? If it will make you feel better we can postpone or get more people to assist in the procedure."

Taking a deep breath William steadied himself.

"No...I'm ready," he confidently stated. "And I want to keep this as quiet as possible. If the Biology Board found out about this they would kick me out of the University."

"And me right with you," Carl added with a lighthearted chuckle.

"Don't worry. I'm not going to let anyone know who helped me do this."

"Thanks," he replied with an obvious note of relief in his voice. "I'd really hate to be out of work right now. And don't worry," he continued, "I know exactly what I'm doing. We don't need anyone else to assist with the procedure."

"Then let's get started!" William stated.

"Great. Go ahead and take off your shirt and hop up on the table."

William complied with his request, removed his shirt and took his place lying horizontally on the table. Carl carefully shaved William's face and washed it with a sterilizing disinfectant. Satisfied that his patient was prepped, he slid a couple of towels beneath William's head and neck. Finally, he reached over to one of the tables and returned with both a large syringe containing a pink liquid in a clear vial, as well as a small tube that looked like it might contain toothpaste.

"This is a topical anesthetic," he commented holding up the tube, "which will completely deaden the feeling of any pain on your face. Once this takes effect I will use this," he continued holding up the syringe, "which is an injectable anesthetic to ensure that you don't feel anything as we work multiple layers of skin to entirely remove the scar tissue on your cheek."

"It's critical that we remove all of the damaged skin and cells to get the maximum results," William cautioned. "That will likely mean that you will need to remove some of the healthy skin just to be certain."

"You're certain that this will work, right? I mean, once we've done this there is no turning back."

"Yes, I'm positive," he confidently replied. "I've already tested it three times," he announced pointing to the edge of his scar back towards his left ear. "Each time the skin completely grew back and was totally healthy. You even verified that the skin and cells were almost as if they had never been injured," he reminded Carl.

"True," he agreed. "But we're going from the outermost layers your skin, down through the inner layers of the dermis. This is a very invasive procedure and could leave you more disfigured that you already are."

"I realize the risks," he advised. "With that said, let's move forward."

"Alright then...let's begin then," Carl replied.

Methodically, Carl pulled on a pair of white surgical gloves. He next unscrewed the cap off the end of the tube containing the topical anesthetic and carefully squeezed it onto the fingertips of his right hand. Satisfied that he had a sufficient amount, he began to liberally apply it to scar and surrounding areas on William's left cheek.

"Let's give it about ten minutes to fully take effect," Carl cautioned. "So, how's your girlfriend doing? It's Kara, right?"

"Tara," he gently corrected. "She's doing great. We're doing great!"

"Why isn't she here?" Carl quizzically asked.

"Tara doesn't know that I'm doing this. I want this to be a complete surprise. Besides," he admitted, "if she knew what we're about to do she would probably report me herself to the school board!"

"I love it! This will absolutely surprise her. How are you going to explain all the bandages on your face though?"

"Based on previous tests, it will likely take two weeks for the skin to complete repair itself."

"That's it?!" Carl incredulously demanded.

"Yup," William asserted. "Embryonic stem cells are the future of medicine. They have unparalleled regenerative properties. And they work with lightning speed."

"That still doesn't tell me how you're going to explain the bandages."

"I've already told Tara that I have to go back East for three weeks to attend a couple of seminars and a conference. That will give me time for my cheek to completely heal."

"Gotcha. Where are you really going to be?"

"Actually, I was hoping that I might be able to crash at your condo down by the beach," he hopefully conceded.

"Sure thing," Carl happily replied. "And that will allow me to closely watch your recovery, and take care of any 'issues' that might arise. What ever happened to that other guy you were working with? Ron, I think his name was."

"Don," William corrected again. "You really have a tough time with names."

"Yeah, sorry. What ever happened to Don?"

William's brow furrowed momentarily before replying.

"We had a bit of a falling out I'm afraid. Suffice it to say that we had irreconcilable differences on our approach which forced us to go our separate ways."

"That's too bad," he responded. "I thought he was a pretty funny guy."

Carl glanced at the clock hanging on the wall close to the door. Realizing sufficient time had elapsed, he turned back to William with that same broad grin on his round face.

"Alright, let's start the procedure. It's critical that you remain as still as possible. I don't want to make any mistakes."

William lied motionless on the surgical table as Carl reached back over to another table and returned with the syringe. Using extreme care, he carefully placed the needle on the top-most edge of the scar and gently slid it beneath the surface of the skin, into his tissue.

"You might feel a slight pinch, but there shouldn't be any pain. Do you feel anything?"

"No. Not a thing."

A look of satisfaction appeared on Carl's face as he gently pushed the end of the syringe forwards until a total of one cubic centimeter had been injected. He slowly removed the needle and methodically repeated the injections approximately every one-half-inch around the edge of the scar. Upon completion of the last injection around the periphery of the scar, he then proceeded to push the needle directly into the main body of the scar tissue and delivered exactly one cubic centimeter of the anesthetic. He repeated this procedure eight additional times forming an 'X' pattern across the tissue, and then returned the now empty syringe to the table.

"Still doing ok?" he questioned.

"Everything's good," William replied.

"Now things get interesting," Carl commented in a fervent manner.

After reaching over to the table, he returned with a surgical scalpel and another instrument that had the appearance of a medieval torture tool. It was a steel rod with a small blank handle on one end of it, and a textured, almost honeycomb looking blade on the other end.

"What is that?" William blurted out in an alarming tone.

"I assume you're inquiring about this," Carl replied hefting the scary looking tool in his right hand. "This is a curette. They come in many shapes and sizes and have very different purposes. This one is meant for use in the excision of skin and tumors. This is what I will use to remove the scar and any other tissue."

William swallowed hard and his eyes nearly bulged out of his skull.

"That's a pretty frightening device."

"It does the job. Oh, I almost forget," he casually commented reaching back to the table and grabbing a pair of binocular looking glasses, "better make sure that I can see what I'm doing," he joked.

"Uh yeah, please," William agreed. "Let's be certain that you can see exactly what you're doing!"

After affixing the surgical loupes onto his head and adjusting the dials located on the sides to focus, Carl began the procedure.

Initially, he stretched the skin on William's face to easily view where the scar tissue ended and the healthy skin began. After about three minutes surveying the scar, he once again stretched the skin on the top edge of the scar, but this time he meticulously maneuvered the sharp edge of the scalpel to what he believed to be the point where the damaged skin ended and healthy skin began.

As he sliced through the flesh, he cautiously increased the tension on the skin to widen the incision. In a cleaving motion, he carefully dug deeper into the flesh, carving away millimeter by millimeter until he got down to the point where he felt the damaged tissue ceased.

"That's a little deeper than I had originally thought we'd

have to go," he commented. "I cut through the epidermis of course, but also entirely through the dermis and into the subcutis. Hopefully, we won't have to go any deeper than this anywhere else, or else we're going to start running into veins."

Without another word, Carl painstakingly repeated the same procedure around the entire circumference of the scar until he met back up at the top where he initially began. In total, it took him approximately ninety minutes to complete.

"I'll be right back," he commented. "I need to take a quick bio break."

"WHAT!" William exclaimed.

"Just kidding," he laughed. "Just keeping the mood light."

"Very funny."

"Stop talking. You're not supposed to be moving at all remember?"

William grunted back in response. Carl placed the scalpel back on the table and returned with a small probe that had a flat edge at the end.

"I'll use this to tease back the tissue enough for me to slide the curette underneath. Then I'll very carefully separate the damaged tissue from the healthy underlying tissue across the full breadth of the scar."

At this point, William's fists were tightly clenched at his sides and his jaw ached from holding his teeth together. He wanted to close his eyes, but at the same time, he was intrigued by the whole scientific nature of what was happening. As such, he intently watched each movement and expression that Carl made.

This time, Carl started at the bottom of the scar tissue closer to William's chin. He started to separate apart the tissue at the initial incision point, digging beneath the scar itself. Thanks to the magnification glasses that he was wearing, Carl was able to very clearly see his handiwork without having to get uncomfortably close to his patient. After about fifteen minutes of teasing back about a half-inch flap of skin, he gently placed the medieval-looking implement underneath the tissue and meticulously started moving it back and forth in a saw-like motion.

I small trickle of blood ran down his cheek but was easily caught on the towels lying beneath William's head. The injectable anesthetic had a strong coagulation property that minimized the amount of bleeding during the procedure. It wasn't until he started running the excision blade horizontally beneath his skin that any noticeable bleeding was seen.

Carefully, Carl removed the curette from beneath the flap of tissue, and while holding the skin upwards towards his patient's eyes he peered through the magnification lenses to survey his handy work. Satisfied with the results achieved, he repeated the process of removing damaged tissue for the next two hours.

Finally, the width of the flap of skin diminished as it came to a point at the top of the scar beneath William's eye. Carl placed the curette blade back onto the table and returned with a pair of forceps. Spreading the handles apart he then slid one side of the forceps beneath the tissue and closed the handles to firmly grip the flesh. Then, as he gently pulled the tissue away from the patient, he separated the remainder of skin that connected the scar tissue with a probe and fully removed the scar.

As he pulled the forceps back from his patient, William stared in disbelief at the size of the tissue that was just removed.

"Kind of looks like pepperoni doesn't it," Carl joked.

William suppressed a laugh as he tried to remain motionless on the table, resulting in him lightly coughing.

Carl placed the tissue into a small, stainless steel container located on another table close by, and turned back to William.

"Time for phase two!" he advised in great anticipation.

Carefully, Carl removed the surgical gloves he was wearing and repeated the procedure he had initially conducted by washing his hands up to his elbows, rinsing, and the donned a new pair of gloves.

Reaching over to another table, he then removed the lid from a white cooler, reached into it, and returned with a small clear jar containing what could be best described as a 'goo-like' substance. Carefully he unscrewed the lid and looked at the gelatinous material contained on the inside.

"This is it, huh? This is the secret sauce that will change the world as we know it? I can't wait to see how this works."

Reaching back to the table he gripped the scar tissue that he had removed from William's face with the forceps and placed it onto a gram scale to accurately measure how much the tissue weighted.

"Remember," William spoke in a hushed tone. "You only need to have 'approximately' the same amount of ESCs in terms of weight and volume compared to the scar tissue. The human body is a miraculous thing and will only use what it needs. Any extra material should be expelled. But if we don't use enough, then we won't get the desired outcome."

"So, in other words, apply liberally?"

"Right. Not too liberally though. I don't want to be oozing for months!"

"Stop talking," Carl cautioned. "Let's get back to business now."

Having measured the weight of the tissue, Carl now placed a petri dish on the scale and zeroed it out. Next, he began to scoop the jelly-like material into the petri dish until it read exactly the same weight as the damaged flesh. Satisfied that he had the minimum amount, he then added roughly twenty percent more and gave a satisfied grunt.

He carefully removed the dish from the scale and turned back to William. With extreme care, he began to spread the material uniformly across the open wound on his face, paying particular attention to get contact with all of the underlying skin. After about twenty minutes of painstakingly painting his patients face with the gel, he took a step back and removed his glasses.

"It's done," he announced. "Now we just need to dress it and get you back to my condo so you can rest. How do you feel?"

"I'm a little bit tired, but that shouldn't be a surprise. And my teeth hurt from clenching them so tightly. But other than that, I feel great."

"Well, you shouldn't feel any discomfort for about two more hours when the anesthetic will start to wear off. Then we'll see how you feel."

Carl placed a special coverlet bandage over the wound on William's face.

"This will keep any outside material from contaminating your injury while it heals, and at the same time not touching the injury at all."

Satisfied that the bandage was secured properly, he helped William sit up and slide into a standing position on the floor.

"Take a moment to steady yourself before trying to move. All we need is for you to fall and pull the bandage off, along with that precious compound your wearing, and all of this will be for naught."

"You got it."

After a brief moment, William carefully pulled his shirt back on and buttoned it up the front.

"All set?" Carl questioned.

"Yup. That's one small step for man, one giant medical advance for mankind! Let's get out of here."

###############################

"Are you sure that William won't be in the lab?" Don cautiously asked.

"Positive," Kim replied. "He tried to keep everything so secretive, but I have my ways of getting information. He's probably still under the knife over at the medical center. There no one around so let's get moving."

Don and Kim exited their car in the parking lot outside of the microbiology lab building and made their way to the exterior door. Don was carrying a small white cooler. Without saying a word, they started making their way up the stairs. Don was about to open up the door leading into the hallway on the second floor when Kim abruptly grabbed his hand.

"Wait a moment," she hissed. "There's someone inside."

Don stood motionless in the stairwell and could feel his heart wildly beating in his chest. He looked into Kim's face and noticed that her eyes looked vacant. After roughly thirty seconds, Kim cracked open the door and both of them peered down the hallway. At the far end, a janitor was pushing a mop bucket with the handle of his mop. He stopped at a classroom door, opened it up, and entered.

"Ok, let's move," Kim commanded.

"How did you know that there was someone in the hallway," Don incredulously demanded.

"Don't ask stupid questions," Kim replied in a growingly impatient tone of voice. "Move!"

They slipped through the doorway, walked down the hall and entered the second door on the right. Quietly closing the door behind them they found themselves inside a completely empty laboratory room.

"Where are they?" Kim demanded.

Don motioned over to the back corner of the room where a stainless-steel door rested in front of a large cryogenic freezer. Grasping his hand, Kim practically pulled him across the room until they were both standing in front of the freezer. Don purposively lifted the handle and swung the door outwards revealing the contents inside.

Various packages and boxes were neatly arranged on shelves in the freezer, each having specific labels detailing the contents. The freezer was large enough for both of them to walk partway inside. Don led them into the freezer and reached to grab a large cardboard box in the back-left corner.

"Hopefully, Will has not moved the embryos," he cautioned.

Don lifted the box outwards revealing dozens of rows of test tube holders, each containing fifteen vials. And each of the vials contained one of the stolen embryos that Don and William had previously taken from the fertility center. Without a word, Kim opened up the white cooler containing dry ice, and they began to load it up with roughly seventy-five vials.

"That should be enough. Let's put that box back in place and get out of here," Don noted. "With any luck, he won't even notice that we took anything."

Kim regarded Don with almost a look of disgust.

"Who cares if he finds out? Let's get out of here so we can start executing our plan!"

Don simply nodded in agreement. After returning the box to its original location, they carefully shut the door and made their way back across the lab to the door. Without pausing Kim opened the door and entered the hallway.

"What the hell are you doing?" Don angrily thought to himself. "What if the janitor is out there?"

Suddenly, Kim sharply turned around to face Don and placed her right hand lightly on his cheek.

"Don't question what I do," she threatened. "And never, ever, doubt me again!"

Don had a dumbfounded expression on his face. "How did you...I mean...I didn't say..."

"Just call it a woman's intuition," she simply replied. "Now let's get these to a safe place and start the next phase."

CHAPTER 20

Triumph
(Three Weeks Later)

A tiny sliver of light cracked through the curtains and cascaded down across a large, open family room, coming to rest on a light tan leather couch. While it was only five o'clock in the late afternoon, the sun had already made significant progress in its descent towards the horizon. The sound of seagulls could be heard amidst the periodic lapping of waves against the sandy shore of the Southern California coastline.

Listening to the hypnotic, soothing sounds of the ocean, William was stretched out on the couch. Reaching up over his head with both hands, he began to arch his back and let out almost a growl like noise as he tensed his muscles and then relaxed them. Slowly, he slid his legs off the side of the couch and sat upwards into a sitting position.

The room was relatively dark, excepting the light coming from a fluorescent fixture in the kitchen, as well as the beam of sunshine breaking through the curtains that now rested directly on a bandage adorning his left cheek. Sensing the heat on his skin, he unconsciously reached towards his cheek and stopped short of touching the bandage. He had spent the last three weeks judiciously caring for his self-inflicted wound, and he wasn't going to accidentally cause a setback now.

William thought about the planned events of this evening with great anticipation. Everything had been progressing as they had hoped. The gel containing his own ESCs that had been administered on his injury had performed extraordinarily well. The hypodermis and dermis layers had completely healed within the first seven days of application. The epidermis layer, however, mended at a much slower pace. He was a bit concerned that things were coming down to the wire in terms of timing. Tara expected William to be returning home on a flight back from his conference around seven o'clock. And making things more complicated, she insisted on picking him up at the airport.

Standing up from the couch he made his way into the kitchen, opened the refrigerator, and removed a can of Dr. Pepper. After cracking open the seal on top of the soda, he took a long drink of the ice cold soda inside, reveling in the sensation of it sliding down the back of his throat. After removing the can from his lips, he gently wiped the moisture off them with the back of his right hand. The sound of a door opening behind him caused William to turn around to see the source.

"As promised," the man commented while shutting the door behind him. "Five o'clock on the dot!"

"You da man Carl!" William replied. "You da man!"

Carl smiled as he set his leather backpack on the kitchen table.

"Tonight's the night! And we've got no time to waste. I've got to drop you off over at LAX so you can meet Clara at the baggage claim."

"Tara," William corrected. "How can someone so smart not be able to remember something as simple as a person's name?"

"I've chosen to allocate my brain cells to other, more important facts and figures," he joked. "Why don't you come over and take a seat?"

Without delay, William made his way over to the table

and flopped himself down in one of the chairs. Turning to his right he faced Carl, who was busy removing small notebook and a magnifying glass from his bag.

"Alright then, let's get started," Carl announced.

Leaning towards the patient, he reached out with both of his hands and started to gently peel the edge of the coverlet bandage that covered his left cheek. Carefully and methodically, he made his way around either side of the bandage, unsticking the adhesive until finally he reached the top and lifted it entirely off of his face. Carl intently stared at the skin beneath the bandage without saying a word. He picked up the magnifying glass to scrutinize things more closely, and then opened his notebook and jotted down a couple of notes.

"Well?!" William blurted out. "How does it look?"

"Patience my friend. We need to be thorough."

Setting down his pen, he returned his attention back to William's cheek. With his left hand, he slowly ran his fingers across the surface of his face.

"Amazing!"

"What?"

"The texture of your cheek is completely smooth. It's almost as if I'm touching a baby's bottom it's so smooth. The coloration of the skin is even and consistent across the entire region. And wow...it's white. Not really a surprise since this skin has never been exposed to the sun."

"That's good, right?"

"Absolutely," Carl chortled. "Hydration appears to be normal. Let's check sensation."

Reaching back into his back he pulled out a small metal probe and gently poke the side of William's cheek.

"Ouch!"

"How about this?"

"Ow...careful!"

Carl meticulously tested and retested virtually every square millimeter of the surgical site with the same results. Next, he walked over to the refrigerator and removed an ice cube from the freezer. After sitting back down he placed it on his cheek.

"It's cold," William exclaimed.

Again, Carl repeated this test across the entire surface of his cheek with the same results. He then walked over to the sink and half-filled a glass with water and placed it in the microwave.

"Thirty seconds should about do it."

The microwave made a beeping noise signifying that it had completed its task, and after removing the glass, Carl sat down next to William. Lifting the glass, he placed the bottom corner of it lightly on William's cheek.

"It's warm."

Carl set the glass back down on the table and ceremoniously shut his notebook. He turned back to William with an intense expression of excitement.

"It worked," he almost cried. "Not only did it work, but it worked almost perfectly."

"What do you mean 'almost' perfectly?"

"Take a look for yourself..." he commented while handing William a mirror.

William tilted it sideways so he could take a look at his cheek for the first time since the procedure. What he saw in the reflection caused him to catch his breath.

All indications of the previous injury were completely gone. There was no roughness or dark pink discoloration that is usually associated severe burns. As he ran his fingers across the surface he marveled at how smooth it was. While he did not have a dark complexion by any means, the starkness of contrast between the newly repaired skin and the rest of his face was striking.

"The disparity in color will lessen as your new skin gets exposed to the sun," Carl commented as if he had just read William's thoughts.

Holding the mirror closer to his face he focused on the delineation between the old and new skin. There was a very thin border of skin between the two different areas that were slightly darker than both the new and old skin, denoting where the scar had been removed from his face.

"Will this go away?" William inquired pointing at the location.

Carl took the magnifying glass and carefully inspected the area in question. After about sixty seconds of careful observation, he sat back in his chair and set the magnifying glass back on the table.

"I don't think so," he admitted. "When we removed the scar tissue we went right up to the border of where the healthy cells began and there was no way of not damaging the good cells in this process. Those cells had to heal themselves on their own, resulting in a very, very slight scarring of those tissues."

William thought for a moment and then smiled.

"I guess I can live with that!" he finally surmised.

"I agree. And besides, if we wanted to try and eliminate the appearance of any scarring, we would have to completely remove all of your skin! That way, there wouldn't be any seam!"

"Ouch! That doesn't sound very appetizing to me!"

"I wouldn't think so!"

"So, what is your professional opinion?" William pressed. "Is it a success?"

Without hesitation, Carl responded.

"Absolutely! This is truly an amazing discovery!"

"Thank you, my friend. Thank you for everything that you helped me with...and for the risk that you took doing so," he graciously added.

"This was the chance of a lifetime for me. I can't wait for this to become broadly available. This is going to completely change the lives of many, many people."

Standing up from chair William reached forward and enthusiastically shook Carl's hand. Carl stood up and gave William a rough hug and slapped him on the back.

"You've got to get going, my friend. It's almost six o'clock and we've got to get you to the airport. Do you have your bag packed?"

William smiled and walked down the hallway and into one of the bedrooms. Shortly thereafter he returned to the kitchen carrying a large piece of luggage.

"I even stopped doing my laundry for the past two weeks so it would be more believable."

"Good thinking! Let's get going!"

##############################

Rocking back and forth, Tara impatiently stood by the escalator leading down to the baggage claim area from the terminals. It had been three weeks since she had seen William and she couldn't wait to throw her arms around him. According to the arrivals screen, his flight landed twenty minutes ago so he should be coming down any moment.

Pulling a large piece of luggage and carrying a small bouquet of flowers, William silently snuck up behind Tara and parked his bag. He stealthily positioned himself directly behind her and wrapped his arms around her body, placing the flowers in her immediate field of vision.

Startled, Tara voiced a high-pitched gasp, but quickly recovered when she realized who had surprised her. With a big smile on her face, she turned around with the intent of wrapping her arms around William and planting a giant kiss on his lips.

As Tara turned around to face William, her breath caught and her mouth gaped open as she tried to feverishly process what her eyes were beholding.

William patiently watched Tara and simply smiled, waiting for her to say something. After about thirty seconds of silence, she finally did.

"WILL!" she exclaimed. "Your face...it looks...it isn't...I don't know..."

William started to laugh and smiled very broadly. Suddenly, Tara's eyes welled up with tears and she began to cry in an almost uncontrollable manner.

"It's ok," he consoled her while wrapping his arms around her body. "It's ok...really!"

Tara embraced William with such a tight hug that he almost had difficulty breathing. After a couple of moments, she loosened her grip and leaned backward so she could look into his face.

"Your face. I mean your cheek. How is this possible? What happened to your scar?"

"Remember my research project? Well, let's just say that it was a success."

"Oh my goodness!" she exclaimed. "You look beautiful!"

Tara paused for a moment and then continued talking in a rushed manner.

"I don't mean that you weren't beautiful before. There wasn't anything wrong with you. But now," she paused for a second not able to express her feelings. "Oh, I better just stop talking," she finally admitted, "or I'm going to have to pull both feet out of my mouth."

"It's ok," he reassured her. "I won't take it personally."

"When did this happen? I thought you were at a conference!"

A slight expression of guilt ran across William's face.

"There really wasn't a conference," he admitted. I just told you that so I had a good reason to not see you for a few weeks."

"Where did you have this done?" she almost demanded. "Who did this? Is it permanent?"

"Slow down, slow down," William assured her while pulling her tightly against his body. "I'll explain everything on the way home."

Looking up at William, Tara placed her right hand on his cheek and gently rubbed it. Then sliding her hand behind his neck, she turned his head slightly and lovingly kissed his cheek.

"Ok," she chided. "You've got a lot of explaining to do."

CHAPTER 21

Dissertation

(Middle of May 2007)

Standing in the shade beneath an oak tree outside the Department of Biochemistry, Tara busily primped William's clothes as he prepared himself to defend his doctoral dissertation that was scheduled to begin in just ten minutes. Just four weeks earlier, he had contacted the Biochemistry Board to schedule a time for him to present his doctoral dissertation. It turned out to be an extremely busy four weeks. Normally, the Board was scheduling dissertation defenses two to three months out. However, one of William's advisors was extremely keen on him presenting, given he had been working for so long, and scheduled the defense to occur in just one month's time.

William had put the final touches on his presentation only sixty minutes prior, and it was a mad dash for him to shower, throw on his clothes, and make his way back to the USC campus in time.

"Stop fussing," Tara ordered as she dragged a brush roughly through William's tangled hair. "You've got to at least appear as if you're a professional."

"Ouch!" he complained, grabbing the brush out of Tara's hands. "Let me do this!"

He ran the brush back through his hair three more times and then handed it back to Tara. "How does that look?" he hopefully inquired.

Tara took a step backward and looked him over thoroughly from head to toe. William was wearing brown leather shoes, khaki pants, a blue dress shirt and a dark brown corduroy jacket. Finally, she gave him a weak smile that looked more like a grimace.

"I guess it's got to be good enough," she sighed.

William then reached into the bag containing his computer and pulled out a white, plastic object which had an elastic band stretched from one side to the other. Tara looked at the item in his hand and frowned.

"Do you really think that you should be so theatrical? I mean you are presenting to a distinguished group of professors about a very serious topic. Isn't this going to come across as cheap and silly?"

"Not at all," he confidently responded. "Besides, they all know me pretty well, so this shouldn't surprise them very much."

Still frowning, Tara threw her hands up in the air in resignation.

"You know best," she added.

Then she wrapped her arms around him and planted a kiss solidly on his lips.

"Knock them dead!"

Smiling in response, William turned on his heels, started towards the building, and then turned around and approached Tara.

"Did you forget something?" she inquired.

Standing again in front of Tara, William took both of her hands in his, as a broad smile appeared on his face.

Tara stared into his eyes with a somewhat quizzical expression on his face.

After about sixty seconds of silence, William took a deep breath and slowly lowered himself down onto one knee.

Tara's breath caught as she realized what was about to happen, and tears started to well up in both of her eyes.

"Tara, my angel," he stated in a level tone. "It's no secret that I'm in love with you. In fact, I don't know if it is possible for a person to care for another person more than I do you. But then, the next moment later I realized that my love for you continues to grow upon itself."

Despite the tears rolling down Tara's cheeks, a considerable smile covered her beaming face.

"While my life had meaning before I met you," he continued, "it is now filled with purpose. A direction which has guided me along a certain path, and one that I hope will continue to influence all of the days for the rest of my life."

William paused for a brief moment then reached into his front right pocket. When his hand emerged, it was holding a black velvet jewelry box. While his voice conveyed poise, his hands visibly shook as he attempted to open the box to reveal the contents.

Finally, the lid was pulled back and a beautiful engagement ring came into view. It was a brilliantly white diamond of considerable size, surrounded by two rows of sparkling round diamonds.

Tara bit both of her lips as she stared intently into William's eyes.

"Tara, would you do me the honor of becoming my wife?"

"Yes, YES! Absolutely yes!" she exclaimed while squeezing his hands tightly.

William then carefully took the ring from its case and slid it gently on Tara's wedding finger.

"You have made me one of the happiest individuals on the earth today", he declared. "Absolutely the happiest man in the world".

Tara wiped some of the tears that were rolling down her

cheeks, pulled William close to her, and then laid a passionate kiss on his lips.

"This is such a wonderful surprise", she exclaimed. "I love you so much!"

William then wrapped his arms around Tara and embraced her for about five seconds. Then he suddenly snapped his head back with an anxious expression on his face.

"I almost forgot that about my presentation! I've got to go!"

Releasing Tara, he turned towards the building, paused, and then turned back to face Tara again.

"I'm sorry, but I have to run!"

"Go...GO!" she implored. "We'll talk about this later. You go in there and knock their socks off!"

At that, William turned and nearly sprinted into the building.

##############################

Making his way to the third floor, William walked down a short hallway that led to the School of Biochemistry offices and entered through the main door. Sitting behind a large mahogany desk was a very petite looking woman who had to be in her late fifties or early sixties. Noticing that he had entered the office, the tiny woman peered up at him through what had to be trifocal glasses and greeted him with a welcoming smile. A name placard in front of her read 'Denise Pack'.

"You must be mister Mears," she announced.

"Yes, thank you. I'm here to present my dissertation to the board."

"We've been expecting you. Go ahead a have a seat," she stated while motioning over to a couple hardwood chairs on the right side of the room. "I'm sure they will be with you shortly."

Obediently he walked over and sat in one of the chairs, setting his bag down with a heavy thud. William positioned his right leg across his left knee and folded his arms neatly in front of him while he waited to be summoned. The room was deathly silent, excepting a large clock that hung on the opposite wall across from where he sat. Each movement of the second hand resulted in a loud click noise that seemed to echo in his ears.

After waiting for about three minutes, the phone rang on Denise's desk.

"Yes," she responded. "Right away," and she hung up the phone.

Turning slightly to face William, she stood up from her chair and walked around the desk.

"They're ready to see you now. Please follow me."

William jumped up from his chairs and followed her through a doorway to the right of her desk. They walked down a short hallway leading to a closed door with a sign hanging on it that read: 'Dissertations in progress. Please do not disturb." Denise stopped about five steps short of the door and turned back to William.

"Just go right on through there young man. And good luck!" she wished him.

"Thank you," he graciously responded and walked towards the door.

Before opening the door, he glanced backward to confirm that Denise had started making her way back to her desk. He then reached into the inside breast pocket of his jacket and removed the white plastic object he had previously taken from his bag. Pulling the elastic band away from the plastic, he placed what closely resembled the white 'phantom of the opera' mask on top of his face, fully covering up his left cheek. Satisfied that it was securely fastened, he took a deep breath, turned the knob of the solid wood door in front of him and entered the room.

As he entered, William glanced around the surprisingly large room to take in his surroundings, and more importantly, to ascertain to whom he would be presenting. He knew that his audience was going to be somewhat varied, comprised of former advisors, committee members, and colleagues. In total, there were eight people present that were there to evaluate his work, presentation, and ultimately vote on whether or not he should receive his doctorate degree.

A large screen hung down from the ceiling in front of a series of whiteboards at the front of the room. To the left of the screen sat a podium where he was to hook up his laptop to navigate the presentation. There were two rows of narrow, short tables facing the front of the room where the audience was located, and large windows lined the left wall through which bright sunlight beamed.

The group of individuals had been busy talking when William entered the room but now sat silently as they all looked at him with amused expressions on their faces. Obviously, the mask that he was wearing had grabbed their attention as he had hoped. He couldn't wait to see their faces when he made the 'big reveal' at the climax of his presentation.

"Good afternoon ladies and gentlemen," William

gracefully announced as he walked over to the podium and began to set up his laptop. "I'd like to thank all of you for gathering here this afternoon for me to present and defend my doctoral dissertation 'Healing Through Somatic Cell Nuclear Transfer, or: Therapeutic Cloning'. I'm certain by the end of our time together that you will have come to the conclusion that not only should I be awarded my doctoral degree, but that my research will change the course to medicine for many decades to come."

Sitting in the middle of the first row sat a man who looked to be fifty years of age. He had messy, dark black hair, and a scraggly dark beard and mustache. The color of his skin was fair white, and he had deep, dark green eyes that stared intently at William behind black-rimmed glasses. William recognized him as Dr. Koenraad Schmidt, head of the Biochemistry Department at the University.

"And thank you," Dr. Schmidt replied in a thick German accent, "for coming here today my good sir. We are anxious to hear your findings and for you to make your defense."

He paused for a moment scrutinizing William.

"I do have to say," he continued, "I'm somewhat confused by the strange mask that you're wearing. Is there a purpose for this?"

Feeling a bit self-conscious about his choice, he took a deep breath and responded.

"Dr. Schmidt," he began. "I do realize that this may seem a bit out of the ordinary, and well, shall I say over the top. However, I guarantee that by the end of my presentation that my purpose for wearing this mask will make sense to each and every one of you. So please, indulge me a bit, and with your permission, I will begin my presentation.

"Please begin," Dr. Schmidt replied, gesturing somewhat impatiently for William to take his place behind the podium.

"Thank you," he began as he walked up to the podium and picked up the remote to advance slides in his presentation. "Assuming all of you have had a chance to review my thesis which I provided two weeks ago, I would like to begin by telling you a story. This is a story about a man who experienced an accident early in his life that left him disfigured. As a young boy, a mishap resulted in my experiencing fourth-degree burns on my left cheek," he explained motioning to the mask that he wore. "This injury was very substantial, extending completely through my skin and into the underlying fatty and muscle tissue, leaving my face severely scarred."

William then advanced the presentation and displayed some of the original photographs that doctors had taken of his injury immediately following his accident as a child. A couple of the audience members visibly cringed at the image shown on the screen.

"I saw multiple specialists, underwent several skin grafts, reconstructive surgery...pretty much exhausted all of the options that medical science had to offer in an attempt to repair this injury. Unfortunately, there is only so much that could be done, and after a certain point it was about as good as it was ever going to get."

He advanced the presentation again to display an image of his scarred face taken just a few days before he and Carl underwent the procedure. He paused for a moment for effect and then continued.

"This is a face that all of you are familiar with. This is how you have always known me. In fact, I'm certain that many of you have grown so accustomed to this scar that you practically don't even see it any longer when we meet," he commented motioning to some of his colleagues that he worked with on a weekly, if not daily basis.

"For me, however, this disfigurement is something that I have not grown accustomed too. This deformity is something that I've had to look at in the mirror every day of my life. And I'm not the only one. There are thousands, tens of thousands, of individuals that have experienced similar injuries, who deal with dissatisfaction every day of their lives because of their appearance. Today, I am here to tell you that people need not suffer any longer because of this."

William paused for a moment, caught up in the emotion of his message. Both of his eyes started to tear up and he gently rubbed away the moisture with a white Kleenex. Looking across his audience, all of them were listening intently, each leaning forward in their chair.

"Now you might say we've had medical advances over the last twenty plus years since I had my accident and we can do a lot more now than we ever had. However, even with our most modern medical advances, treatments, and cures, we still are not able to give a little child the respite from the ridicule that they experience on playgrounds or in the classrooms from other children. Or the confidence that they should have by seeing a reflection they are not embarrassed by. There is only so much we can do."

He paused again for a moment, walked back towards the podium, and set his left hand on the top of it. Taking another deep breath, he continued.

"That, my esteemed board members and colleagues, is about to change. Today you are going to hear about an advance that is so radically revolutionary, you are barely going to accept that it is true."

Dr. Schmidt leaned backward in his chair and folded his arms stiffly in front of him.

"Mr. Mears, you do realize that this isn't a dramatic reading for a part in a school play correct?"

William smiled at him and held up his hand.

"Don't worry. I'll be getting into my thesis very shortly."

"I do hope so," he growled back in response.

Ignoring the interruption, William picked right back up where he left off.

"The primary focus of our discussion this afternoon is Therapeutic Cloning. More specifically, leveraging Embryonic Stem Cells in the healing process. There has been quite a bit of research performed with stem cells previously, showcasing their regenerative properties and potential role in medical treatments. Unfortunately, the extent to which these cells can be utilized has been somewhat limited, especially in the treatment of human beings. I too initially went down the path of leveraging stem cells as a means to repair injuries, and I too experienced that same limited results as other scientists."

"This failure, and I do look at this as a failure, caused me to search for another answer...another path if you will. After many, many hours of thought and deliberation, I finally had my 'ah ha' moment. We all know that normal stem cells have limited regenerative abilities. We have tried to push the boundaries of these abilities unsuccessfully. However, what types of cells seem to have limitless regenerative boundaries?"

William paused for a moment and slowly shifted his focus across each member of his audience. Finally, he stopped which his vision locked with that of a woman who had just successfully defended her doctoral thesis.

"Embryonic stems cells," she stated in an unconfident manner.

"Exactly!" he nearly shouted. "Embryonic stem cells, really the building blocks of all the cells of our body, possess incredible regenerative properties. Unfortunately, use of ESCs in the healing process hasn't yielded the promising results that would have expected, have they? Why is that?" William asked searching again across his audience.

This time, he didn't give anyone the opportunity to respond.

"That's because the ESCs were from someone else!" he announced enthusiastically. "The ESCs that we have attempted to utilize came from some external source. Why is that?"

Dr. Schmidt's expression had visibly changed over the past few minutes from one of near contempt to one that was keenly engaged in the words he was hearing. He silently raised his right hand with his index finger pointing upwards towards the ceiling. William simply nodded his head in response.

"Because it is impossible to access Embryonic Stems Cells of a human that is alive today. And there are a mere handful of people that had ESCs drawn from the umbilical cord after the birth of a child. But research with those ESCs has also proven unsuccessful."

"Correct!" William agreed. "Why do you think that is?"

"I guess it is because ESCs present in the blood contained within an umbilical cord are not the same Embryonic Stem Cells that formed a human body."

"Exactly!" he nearly cheered. "While these are ESCs, they do not have the same properties of the ESCs that are present when life is first formed. There is a specific moment once an egg is fertilized and an embryo is formed that *true* Embryonic Stem Cells are present. And these ESCs exist for only a very short period of time in a pluripotent state before they differentiate into the three primary germ layers from which our skin, bone, and muscle are formed. These are the ESCs that we want...these are the ESCs that we need!! But how can they be obtained? We all know that the process of extracting ESCs from an embryo completely destroys the embryo. That doesn't bode well for the future population of the human race, does it?"

His audience responded in a light round of laughter and then quieted down so William could continue.

"Even if ESCs could be extracted without destroying an embryo during the gestation process, it isn't remotely feasible to accomplish across the entire world's population as children are being conceived, is it?"

All heads in the room nodded in agreement.

"So, then that left me with only one possible path to pursue. There is only one possible source where Embryonic Stem Cells *could* be extracted that would be the right *type* of ESCs, that were, in fact, the *exact* ESCs that were present for any human being on the planet today."

Dr. Schmidt silently stood up from his chair with an expression of awe and disbelief on his face. He stood their silently for a full thirty seconds before speaking.

"You have figured out how to create an exact duplicate...an embryonic clone of a human being!" he said in disbelief.

"Not only have I figured out how," he grandly

announced as he reached up to the mask lying on his face. "I have done it!" he exclaimed.

The next instant he removed the mask from his face by pulling it upwards and over the top of his head.

A collective gasp filled the room they viewed for the first time the perfect skin on William's face where the disfiguration used to be. Each member of the room shifted their view back and forth between the image on the screen displaying the previous scar, and William's face now appearing virtually perfect. One of the women in the room walked forward and placed her hand on his cheek and gently felt the smooth, perfect skin.

"Oh my God!" she exclaimed. "This isn't possible!"

William stood beaming with self-satisfaction at everyone in the room. The woman who had walked forward stepped backward towards her seat, tightly clasping both of her hands in front of her. William then shifted his gaze back to Dr. Schmidt who stood with an extraordinarily satisfied expression on his face. After a few moments, he finally spoke.

"Well done William. Well done!"

CHAPTER 22

Implantation
(Three Days Later)

A black Nissan slowly made its way through the downtown area of Los Angeles late on a Saturday evening. It was roughly two o'clock in the morning and there were very few cars in the industrial area of Los Angeles. Rounding a corner, the automobile made its way down a dark side street for approximately two hundred feet until quietly pulling over to the side of the road. The headlights turned off along with the sound of the engine, leaving the car sitting silently in the nearly complete darkness.

After about sixty seconds the passenger side door of the car slowly opened, then swung directly outwards away from the car without the interior lights illuminating. The next moment later a slender leg extended out from the car covered in a dark nylon stocking, and a woman's shoe rested silently on the pavement. A hand then reached upwards to grip the roof of the car and a woman slid out, stood up, and then noiselessly shut the door behind her. The driver's door then opened and a man crept out of the car without making a sound, carefully shutting the door behind him.

Staring impatiently at the man, the woman hastily motioned for him to join her. Silently he complied, walking around the car to meet her.

"Forgetting something?" Kim hissed quietly.

"Oh," Don replied apologetically turning back to the car.

He opened up the rear door, briefly leaned inside, and reemerged holding a white cooler in his hands.

"I guess we wouldn't get very far without these," he commented in a lighthearted manner.

Not amused by his attempt at humor, Kim rolled her eyes while sucking in a quick breath before responding.

"No, we wouldn't. Let's get moving...they're waiting for us!"

Both of them made their way to the sidewalk and walked silently down the darkened street. After about thirty seconds, they came upon a narrow alleyway leading away from the street bordered by a wooden fence on either side.

"This is it," Don breathed as quietly as he could.

He recognized this alleyway as the path he and William had taken several months ago when they first broke into the fertility clinic to steal embryos for their research.

Without responding, Kim turned sharply and walked down the alley giving Don no other option than to scurry behind her as quickly as he could. After a few moments, they both stood in an open space located behind several buildings. Directly in front of them lay the fertility clinic that they had previously visited. Don clutched the cooler tightly against his body, resulting in a light squeaking sound from the side rubbing up against his jeans. Kim glared at him coldly in response and then motioned for him to continue following her.

Arriving at the concrete steps at the rear of the building, she cautiously ascended them and stood quietly next to the rear door of the clinic. Without a word, she lightly knocked on the door three times. The next moment later the sound of someone walking inside the building could faintly be heard. The source traveled back towards the rear door then abruptly stopped. Don anxiously held his breath, staring at the door handle that slowly began to turn counter-clockwise until a soft click was heard signifying that the latch had cleared the strike plate. The door opened slowly outwards revealing a pitch-black interior.

"You're late," a hushed, almost frantic whisper came from inside. "Hurry up and get in here."

Without a word, both Kim and Don entered through the doorway and into the building. Once they had cleared the doorway the unseen voice quickly shut the door and latched the deadbolt.

"Give your eyes a moment to adjust," the faceless voice requested.

Roughly sixty seconds later Don's eyes had adapted to the seemingly pitch-black interior of the building and he was able to make out features of the room more easily. Turning to his left he clearly saw the source of the voice that had bid them to enter the clinic. A man, roughly six feet tall, wearing a white lab coat, was standing in front of them with his hands clasped tightly in front of him at about waist level. His eyes were darting nervously back and forth, obviously exhibiting his discomfort with the situation.

"I think we're good now," Kim barked. "Let's get this taken care of."

The man standing in front of them visibly flinched in response to her voice. After quickly recovering his composure he started walking back into the clinic and motioned for them to follow.

"This way then," he encouraged.

They walked a short way down the hallway and entered a room on the left-hand side that was already open. Once both Kim and Don had entered the room, their host shut the door behind them and flicked the light switch. The fluorescent lights above them flickered momentarily until completely illuminating the room with what was at first a blinding white light.

"A little warning next time," Kim snarled.

"Sorry," the man apologized again. "This whole thing has got me a little nervous."

"You're Jonathan, right?" Don asked not really questioning who the man was, but wanting to try and ease the tension a bit. "We spoke on the phone."

"Yes," the man in the white coat replied.

"Excellent. Well, I've got everything that you'll need right in here," he declared patting the white cooler he was holding.

"Perfect. This is a little out of the ordinary. I mean, normally we perform the entire in vitro fertilization process in-house. People don't normally bring us embryos that have already been fertilized for us just to implant. Where did you get these?"

Kim glared at Jonathan with such intensity and he visibly recoiled away from her stare.

"We're not paying you to ask questions. Just to perform the procedure. And we don't need to know your name!"

Jonathan swallowed hard in response and Don shifted uncomfortably where he stood. After an awkward moment of silence, she continued.

"And if I remember correctly, our contact is paying you quite handsomely, yes?"

He quickly nodded in agreement.

"He already paid me half up front, and said he would pay the other half once the embryos were implanted."

"Perfect," she now purred. "Where do you want me?"

"Over there on the examination table. I'll need you to

take off your skirt and nylons, and there's a medical gown for you to put on as well," he explained motioning over to a counter where the paper covering lay neatly folded. "I'll just step out of the room for..."

Without wasting any time, Kim immediately began disrobing in front of the two men without any sense of self-consciousness or proprietary, loosely wrapped the paper gown around her waist, and took her position on the examination table.

"You'll probably want me to place my feet in these," she theorized, pointing to the stirrups that were attached to two movable steel poles at the end of the table.

"Ah.... yeah..." Jonathan stuttered.

Lifting both of her legs upwards, she placed her feet into the stirrups and lay back on the table with her legs spread apart. Jonathan glanced over at Don with a helpless expression on his face, to which Don simply shrugged his shoulders in response.

"Alright then, I've got everything we need already set up," he commented motioning over to the metal tray that sat atop a poseable arm. "All I really need are the embryos and we can get started."

Don took the lid off the cooler and handed it to Jonathan. After peering inside of the container, he looked up at Don and smiled.

"Everything looks to be in order. I'll assume that the embryos you're providing are in fact healthy and viable. Otherwise, this isn't going to work."

"Oh, they're viable," Don replied. "Trust me, I oversaw the process directly myself."

Jonathan reached into the cooler and withdrew a test tube holder containing six small vials that he set down gently on the counter. He then opened up a small refrigerator and removed a syringe containing a clear liquid inside. After putting on a pair of glasses that had magnification lenses on the end, he carefully inserted the syringe into the first test tube and squeezed out a couple of cubic centimeters into the bottom. He repeated the process five more times and returned the syringe back to the counter.

"I'm simply depositing some ionized water into each of the vials. The embryos are at a temperature of negative one hundred and ninety-six degrees Celsius. The liquid, which is exactly at fifty degrees Celsius will gently raise the temperature so as not to damage…"

"I'm not interested in a play by play scientific analysis," Kim snapped. "How long until you can put them inside of me?"

"About fifteen minutes," he simply responded.

"Fine. Wake me when you're ready," she ordered as she closed her eyes.

The next fifteen minutes passed by in virtually complete silence. Jonathan spent the time busily preparing a microscope to visually inspect the embryos to confirm they were viable and ready for implantation, and Don simply stood there rocking back and forth. After roughly five minutes Kim reached out her hand without opening her eyes and grabbed Don roughly on his forearm.

"Just stand still!" she barked. "You're driving me crazy."

"Sorry," he apologized.

About five minutes later, Jonathan finally spoke up.

"I think we should be about ready. Let me just verify that the embryos have successfully thawed and we should be able to begin."

Jonathan took the first vial from the holder and placed it onto a special apparatus connected to a microscope on the counter. He flicked a switch on the side of the microscope and a small screen turned on showing a blurry image. Reaching up towards the adjustment knobs on the side of the microscope, he twisted the dials slightly until the image of a tiny, pink blob clearly appeared on the screen. Jonathan briefly analyzed the screen and then turned to Don.

"This one looks to be in excellent condition," he stated.

Don looked visibly relieved by the revelation.

He repeated the process five more times with the same result. Each of the tiny vials contained a viable, healthy embryo.

Kim opened her eyes, sitting upwards until she was in a half-seated position resting her body weight on both elbows.

"I'm not getting any younger! Can we start?"

"Of course," Jonathan replied. "I now need to draw each of the embryos into this catheter, which I will then insert inside of you in order to implant the embryos into your uterus."

Carefully, Jonathan gently depressed a tiny bulb located on the end of the catheter and inserted it into the first vial. Using the image displayed on the screen, he placed the end directly adjacent to the embryo itself and released the tiny bulb, gently drawing the embryo itself into the end of the catheter suspended in a drop of fluid. He then turned towards Kim, and taking a position at the end of the table, inserted the catheter into her body, guided it past her cervix and into her uterus. Once again, he gently squeezed the tiny bulb on the end of the catheter and then removed it. Jonathan then meticulously repeated the procedure until all five of the remaining embryos were successfully implanted into her uterus.

"And that should do it," he finally stated. "Now it's important that you remain still for the next sixty minutes to ensure that the embryos have as good a chance as possible to embed themselves into your uterine wall."

"An hour!" Kim incredulously stated.

"Sorry, that's what it's going to take. You can't be too careful!"

Groaning, Kim lowered herself back into a laying position on the table and closed her eyes again.

"Thank you," Don commented. "We really appreciate your help on this."

"No problem," Jonathan stated as he began to clear away the various tubes and items that he had used for the procedure. "I still don't understand why you're being so secretive about this. I mean people undergo in vitro fertilization every day. Why all the cloak and dagger stuff to do this in the dead of night, and paying cash?"

"Let's just say that we don't want to draw too much attention to ourselves," Don coolly replied. "This is actually part of..." he cut himself off roughly realizing that he was sharing too much information and gave a furtive glance at Kim who still laid motionless on the table with her eyes closed.

"It doesn't matter why...suffice it to say that we have our reasons," he finally continued. "We just need..." and he cut himself off again as something caught his eye out of the corner of his vision. "Did you see that?" he demanded.

"See what?" Jonathan nervously inquired sensing that something wasn't right.

"I'm not sure. It thought I saw something out of the corner of my eye."

He paused for a moment, searching around the room for whatever it was that he had seen. Unable to see anything he resumed.

"I was just going to..." and he froze again, searching the room wildly.

"What?!" Jonathan demanded in a concerned tone.

"I saw something again. But this time it was larger."

The fluorescent lights in the room began to flicker slightly, and the sound of the low, deep rumble was barely audible in the background. Both men looked around the room with a panicked expression, and Kim still lay motionless on the table. Suddenly, the lights in the room flickered on and off and a loud noise pierced the room as if a car moving at a high velocity had just struck a tree.

"THERE!" Don shrieked, pointing to the side of the room behind Jonathan. "DID YOU SEE THAT?!"

Jonathan jumped forward, looking behind him and was just able to catch a dark, shadowy figure in his field of vision before it disappeared. He positioned himself directly behind Don.

"YES! I SAW THAT! WHAT'S HAPPENING?"

The lights in the room went completely out and both of them stood motionless in the complete darkness, desperately straining to try and see anything. The next instant the light in the room fluttered on momentarily, revealing the dark, murky outline of a figure which seemed to come out of the corner of the room and move slowly towards the examination table. The low tone that was barely audible previously was now easily and continuously heard, sounding like the heavy bellow of thunder after a lightning strike. The light flickered on again and the outline of the first figure seemed to be dissolving into the body of Kim who still lay completely motionless. As the shadow appeared to completely absorb into her body, Kim's eyes opened wide and an unearthly scream burst out of her mouth. Her arms and legs violently shook as her entire body convulsed.

The lights flashed again, and another figure crept out of the walls, sliding across the room, oozing into Kim's convulsing body, causing her to shake even more violently than before. One of the steel rods onto which the stirrup was attached broke off of the table as she extended her leg and it flew across the room piercing the wall. Another dark figure came out of the wall and started to enter the uncontrollably shaking frame of Kim. This time, it seemed as if the shadow met with some resistance, and appeared as if it was forcibly pushing its way into her body. Blood streamed out of the corner of her mouth. Both men stood there helplessly not knowing what was occurring or what they could even do.

Finally, the sixth shadowy entity appeared in the corner of the room. The size of this figure was easily twice as large as the five previous ones and seemed to purposively stalk towards Kim's body that was uncontrollably thrashing in convulsions on the table. For a brief moment, it seemed as if the figure paused at the side of the table and peered at the two men who were now frantically hugging each other and screaming themselves. A low, guttural sound came from the creature in front of them sounding like some demonic beast. It turned its attention to Kim, and seemingly reached forward with its right hand and pierced directly into her abdomen area. Kim responded even more violently than before, thrashing viciously, and howling in utter agony as the dark shadow dissolved into her body.

Once the massive shadow had completely disappeared, the booming sound of thunder immediately ceased, the lights went out, and Kim lay motionless on the table as if her life had been ended. Both men stood there clutching one another in complete silence, straining their eyes to try and see Kim. Suddenly, the light in the room turned on and Kim sat straight up and opened her eyes. Don took a step towards her and noticed that her pupils appeared completely dilated. He took another step towards her and cautiously reached out with his right hand to touch her arm. As his fingers barely pressed up against her skin she sharply turned to face him and screamed so loudly he clenched his eyes and covered his ears. The lights suddenly flickered off leaving the room in darkness...and then came back on roughly five seconds later.

Slowly, Don opened up his eyes to find Kim lying back down on the table with her hands neatly folded in front of her. He rushed to her side and grasped her hand.

"ARE YOU OK?" he frantically cried.

Kim slowly opened up her eyes, sat up, and turned her head quizzically at him before responding.

"Of course, I'm ok," she commented in almost a casual manner. "Why are you screaming?"

Don turned to look at Jonathan who stood back in the corner with tears streaming down his face as he shook his head. Turning back to Kim he grasped her hand between both of his.

"Why?" he demanded. "Don't you know what just happened?"

"I just took a nap for the last sixty minutes. Big deal! What are you so worked up about?"

"You don't remember anything? You were screaming, and convulsing like you were having a seizure. Seriously, it just happened!"

"I don't know what you're talking about," she replied, shaking her head in disbelief. "Can we go now? I don't want to spend the entire evening here."

Don turned back again to Jonathan who had gathered himself somewhat and was drying his eyes.

"Jonathan, you saw..."

"I don't know what I saw!" he blurted out. "All I know is that I want the two of you to get the hell out of here right now!"

"But..."

"Seriously! I want you to leave NOW!"

Don turned back to Kim who had already gotten up off the table and was beginning to dress. After having put her clothes back on, she started to walk towards the door and paused for a moment to look at Jonathan.

"Nothing happened here tonight...right?" she demanded.

Visibly afraid of Kim, Jonathan quickly nodded his head in agreement and he moved away from her, pressing his back against the wall.

"Good," she replied. "Don, let's go!"

###############################

One hour later, Jonathan was still finishing cleaning up the examination room and was getting ready to leave. Hearing a sudden noise behind him, he spun around to see what it was.

"GEEZE!" he exclaimed. "You nearly scared me to death, Dr. Schmidt. What are you doing here?"

"Did everything go as planned this evening?"

"Yes. I implanted the embryos! But let me tell you, I'm not signing up to do this ever again!! Something strange, something unexplainable occurred! Something..."

"Something what?"

"Something evil happened here! I have no idea what it was, but I've never been so scared in my life." He paused for a moment and then continued. "You don't have any idea what I've just been through. It was...was..."

"It was what?"

"Oh, forget it," he virtually whimpered. "You've got the rest of my money, right?" he inquired as he made his way around Dr. Schmidt to grab a couple of remaining items off of the counter.

Dr. Schmidt turned as Jonathan walked past him, reached forward with both of hands, and rested them on his shoulders.

"Don't worry son," he uttered in a hushed tone. "You'll get what's coming to you."

The next moment later Dr. Schmidt grabbed the other man's head between his hands and with a violent, twisting motion, snapped his neck, and his lifeless body silently slid down to the floor.

"You'll get exactly what you deserve!"

CHAPTER 23

Night of Nights
(Evening of December 22, 2007)

It was approximately six thirty in the evening and William found himself standing in front of a mirror in the men's restroom, busily fidgeting with a dark purple tie that was hung around his neck. As he cinched up the knot to his neckline he regarded the reflection in the mirror, and let out a huff of breath loudly in exasperation. The small end of the tie hung lower than the wide portion by about two full inches. Pulling the knot downwards he feverously began working to tie his neckwear for the fourth time.

A light knocking on the restroom interrupted the silence.

"Do you need any help," Tara offered in as helpful a manner as possible from behind the closed door.

"Fine!" William blurted out as he walked towards the exit.

Opening the door he found Tara standing in front of him with an inviting smile on her face.

"Wow," he exclaimed stopping in his tracks, "you look positively ravishing!"

Tara was standing in the hallway wearing a black, full-length evening gown. In response to his compliment, she turned slowly to her left in a circle causing the base of the dress to artfully flare outwards. The gown itself was strapless, leaving her shoulders and arms bare. Her dark blonde hair was delicately arranged, with large ringlets cascading down onto the top of her shoulders. A jewel-encrusted belt was wrapped around her waist, accentuating the slimness of her figure. And as always, she wore the curious looking amulet that her father had given to both her and William. It hung gracefully on the end of a delicate gold necklace, with the two interconnected triangles circumscribed by a circle lying flat against her skin.

"Why thank you, kind sir!" she announced in a Southern drawl. "I must say that you look mighty handsome yourself."

"I will, once I get this tie figured out."

"Let me take a look at that."

Tara reached forward, undoing the tie, and then carefully arranged the two ends around William's neck at varying lengths. After a few quick flicks of her hand, she slid her left hand up to the base of the knot and cinched it up snugly to his neck. Taking a step back, she admired her work with a broad smile of satisfaction.

"That should do nicely!"

Looking downwards at the tie hanging around his neck, William saw the that the tie laid properly against his white dress shirt.

"How'd you learn to do that?"

"Years of practice. My father could never get his tie on straight either!" she playfully chided.

"How do I look?" he inquired taking a couple of steps backward.

Tara purposively looked him over from top to bottom before responding.

"Like I said before, you look very handsome. I might even take you home with me after the party tonight!"

"Can you believe that it's only been six months since I was awarded my doctorate? And now, here I'm about to go out and talk with the employees of Mears Laboratory!"

"Why yes, I can, Dr. Mears."

"I know that there are only ten employees so far, but it's really amazing that we got funding so fast and were able to secure office space at this biotech incubator. Now if we can just get our hands on a large quantity of embryos we'll be able to start making some incredible breakthroughs with my research."

"Haven't you been able to find a reliable source yet?"

"No," he conceded. "And when I'm able to find one, they have such stringent restrictions in place on how many you can request, that I'm only able to get a small handful. Some laboratories don't even return my phone calls."

"Don't the other research facilities realize the importance of your work?"

"To them, I'm just another research scientist with a big idea. Even still, it does seem odd that so many sources that other scientists at the university have successfully used for years all seem to have simultaneously dried. It's almost as if someone is working against me," he mused. "I'm probably just being paranoid."

"Just a bit," Tara playfully laughed.

"Alright then. We've got to get out there and address the team before they get too restless. My dear!" he intoned formally as he crooked his left elbow outwards toward Tara, who responded by interlocking her right arm around his. "Let's be on our way."

The two of them walked down a short hallway that curved slightly to the right then came to a stop in front of two large wooden doors at the end. Taking a deep breath, William reached out with his right hand and pulled the door back into the hallway, allowing Tara to enter first before following himself.

As he walked into the room, William found himself standing in the large lobby of the biotech incubator, with the ceiling extending upwards the height of two stories. Music filled the air from a small CD player boom box that was appropriately playing 'She Blinded Me with Science." On the far right side of the lobby was a large, curved staircase that arched elegantly upwards in front of enormous glass windows covering the entire exterior wall. The view through the windows was spectacular given that they were up ten stories from street level. The sky was already darkening as it was about quarter after six in the evening. Lights from other buildings could be seen off into the distance for several city blocks.

Oil rubbed bronze spiral spindles adorned the stairs, topped with a glossy, dark oak handrail. To the right of the stairs sat a small, circular table with two contemporary black leather chairs on either side. There was also a large black leather sofa sitting in between the chairs and a small oak reception desk with a name placard reading 'Tara Cline' sitting on top of it. To the left of the stairs sat a long, rectangular table covered with enough drinks and appetizers to feed a group of thirty,

Two women and seven men, all in their mid-twenties and early thirties, who were busily talking with one another, occupied the lobby. A fair skinned, red-headed woman who was easily as tall as William, and probably twice as heavy, leaped up from one of the black chairs with a broad grin on her face. She wore a black skirt that William thought humorously to himself was far too short for a woman of such girth.

"It's William!" she exclaimed. "Our fearless leader has arrived!"

The talking in the room immediately silenced as everyone turned in response to the announcement.

"Thanks for announcing me Carol," William graciously replied.

"My pleasure!" Looking around with a big grin on her face, she continued. "I hope you don't mind," she joked, "but we got started already."

Both William and Tara walked over to join the group in conversation and laughter. The team was comprised of graduate and post-graduate students from the University that William had worked with in one capacity or another over the past few years. Everyone in the room was actively engaged with the group as a whole. William prided himself on the fact that he was able to have formed such a close-knit team in a relatively short period of time. They all genuinely liked and respected one another, and for the most part, there were not any prima donnas.

Tara walked over to the table where all the goodies sat and returned with two full wine glasses. Handing one to William she leaned forward to whisper in his ear.

"Don't you think you should make some sort of speech," she gently encouraged him.

"Absolutely, but I wanted to wait for..."

The door to the lobby suddenly opened inwards and in walked an older gentleman in his fifties.

"Speak of the devil!" he jokingly commented.

"And he doth appear," Dr. Schmidt calmly replied.

Tara turned back towards the door and her eyes locked with those of the recently arrived guest. Dr. Schmidt met her gaze and then slowly shifted his sight down towards her bare neckline where the amulet she wore gently rested next to her alabaster skin. His eyes instantly narrowed, almost squinting like one would do when trying to see something clearly when the bright sun was glaring directly behind it. Smoothly, he shifted his sight back up to her face and then refocused his attention back to William.

"Glad you could make it!"

"I wouldn't miss this for the world. It's not every day that one of your students achieves such a level of success. You should be very proud of what you have accomplished."

"Oh, thanks. I couldn't have come this far without your assistance. Your connections with the incubator really helped us out!"

"Happy to oblige," he replied as he clasped his hands behind his back.

Leaning forward slightly he continued.

"You'd be amazed at what I'm willing to do in the name of science."

Tara, who was already holding William's left hand, apprehensively squeezed his fingers in response to the comment. Sensing her anxiousness, Dr. Schmidt flashed her a quick smile in a feigned attempt to make her feel more at ease.

William just laughed in response and reached up with his left hand to lightly touch his left cheek with the back of his fingertips.

"Yes. I'd have to say that I was willing to go to great lengths in the name of science as well! Please," he continued while motioning to Dr. Schmidt, "take a seat. I was about to make a brief speech to everyone."

"Thank you," he simply replied.

Without another word, Dr. Schmidt walked over towards the reception desk and turned to face the staircase and windows with his hands still clasped behind him.

"You ok?" William asked Tara in a hushed voice. "I got the feeling that something was bothering you."

"Don't worry about it," she replied. "It's nothing...really. Now, go ahead and give your speech."

William gently squeezed her hand before releasing it, walked towards the windows and ascended up seven steps on the staircase before stopping and turning to face the audience

"May I have your attention please," he loudly stated, while tapping the end of a silver fork against a crystal flute filled with sparkling champagne. "I promise, I won't take very long, but I wanted to take a moment to say something to all of you."

The room immediately quieted and everyone turned their attention to William, who was standing at the edge of the staircase with both of his hands resting gently on the handrail. The night skyline of the city was nicely framed in the large, two-story-tall windows immediately behind him.

"First of all, I wanted to thank everyone for joining the team. It's hard to believe that only four months ago I was just a team of one, but now we have a team of ten."

"Eleven!" Carol declared loudly. "Don't forget Tara!"

"Oh yes, sorry. I didn't mean to leave you out," he apologetically replied flashing a grin in Tara's direction. "In reality, it's a team of eleven. Tara has played an instrumental part of our operation keeping everything running smoothly."

The room filled with a light round of applause to which William raised both of his hands in response.

"Please, hold your applause until the end or I'm never going to get through this."

He paused for a brief moment to collect his thoughts and then continued.

"Four months ago, I, along with the guidance of Dr. Schmidt," he stated motioning over to where the gentleman motionlessly stood, "had the idea that I needed to start a company based on my research at USC. This idea quickly grew into a full-fledged business plan with which we were able to secure a total of three million dollars of funding!"

Another round of applause erupted in the room, accompanied by a couple hoots and hollers. William simply laughed, waiting for the room the quiet again, and then continued.

"We have made substantial progress in the last three months. Securing this fabulous office space, bringing each of you onboard, and let's not forget all of the scientific breakthroughs that each of you have contributed to in immeasurable ways."

As William continued with his speech, Tara walked over to the black leather chair situated furthest to the right and adjacent to the window, and rested her right arm lightly on the top of the chair.

Standing there listening to William, a sensation of dizziness abruptly swept over her, causing her to rest her arm more heavily on the back of the black chair. The next moment, something caught her attention out of the corner of her eye off in the distance outside of the building. Turning her head to try and locate whatever it was that she saw, she looked out the large windows across the top of several shorter industrial buildings roughly eight to ten blocks away, and focused on an area containing several large warehouses situated close to the river.

As she intently stared at the building, she had a slight sensation of heat on the top of her chest. Reaching up with her left hand, she gently laid it on the amulet that hung from the gold necklace around her neck, sensing immediately that the heat was emanating from the adornment itself.

She glanced down momentarily to try and focus on the jewelry when something outside caught her attention. Almost as if in an explosion, a giant black cloud seemed to erupt out of the rooftop of one of the warehouses. Large dark wisps that could only be described as black smoke began swirling directly above the rooftop, gradually spreading outwards in a counterclockwise motion, reaching upwards to the sky. Straining to identify something, anything, in the blackness, she momentarily caught a glimpse of what appeared to be wings. Then she saw them again, but this time with what appeared to be an elongated, almost snakelike looking figure.

With her eyes affixed on the scene outside of the window, she was unaware of William as he continued with his speech – and completely oblivious of the fact that Dr. Schmidt had made his way over to her, standing at most two inches directly behind her in a somewhat menacing manner. Ominously, he placed both of his large, rough hands on either of her shoulders while leaning in closely to whisper in her ear.

"Beautiful, isn't it?" he intoned in a rough, almost growl like hum.

Tara let out an audible gasp but didn't avert her eyes from the swirling funnel of blackness now reaching outwards across five city blocks.

Removing his right hand from her right shoulder, he gently placed it beneath her chin, applying a light pressure to force her to turn her gaze to meet his own.

"What do you see?" he probed, staring intently into her eyes.

Frozen with fear, Tara couldn't pull away from him or shift her gaze from his eyes. Within the dark pupils staring at her, she saw the same swirling blackness she had just observed in the night sky. The total darkness that was staring past her eyes into the back of her skull seemed lifeless...almost evil.

"I...I..." she stammered helplessly.

"You what?!" he growled. "Something catch your eye?"

Still unable to shift her gazed, she felt acutely aware of her heart racing in her chest, and she could feel the heat of the amulet against her skin more intensely than before. She stood there completely motionless as if paralyzed.

Narrowing his eyes, Dr. Schmidt continued.

"You know what tonight is don't you?" he pressed. It's December twenty-second, the longest night of the year. Do you know what makes it so special?"

He paused for a moment to give Tara an opportunity to respond. Unable to move, all she could do was increase the frequency and depth of her breathing.

"This is the night of nights. Tonight is a very special day for Father – it's His highest holy night of the year. It's a time for a celebration of His new beginning. This is the night that He begins to take back this wretched world, and stake His claim on the hearts, no...on the souls of men."

He slowly, almost gently, allowed her head to turn back towards the windows to gaze again at six large tendrils of black haze emanating from the roof of a warehouse, reaching upwards to a height of about five hundred feet and then curving back downwards towards the earth, abruptly ending into the dark, murky waters of the river. Five of the vine-like gaseous columns of darkness were relatively thin, maybe fifty feet in diameter. However, the sixth column was massive, with a diameter of nearly two hundred and fifty feet.

The smaller threads almost seemed to shimmer, pulsate if you will, as they danced across the surface of the water. The next instant, the base of one of the thinner columns widened momentarily as if something was entering into it, and then pulsed through the full length of the column as if a boa constrictor had just swallowed a rat, and entered into the top of the warehouse. A few seconds later, another tendril widened and pulsated, and another, until each of the five passageways appeared to have transported something from the murkiness of the water, through the air, and into the warehouse.

The next moment later the largest of the black conduits began to stretch outwards at the base, allowing for a seemingly massive, unseen object to exit from the water and enter into what could be best described as a large artery. However, as this object slid through the length of the tube, there appeared to be dark, almost sludge-like liquid ooze from the walls. As it neared the end of the passageway atop the roof of the warehouse, all six of the vine-like tendrils began to lift up from the water surface, and retract back through the air towards their source. As the massive, unseen object entered into the top of the warehouse, the six fibril-like strands suddenly raced outwards, away from the building, and dissipated slowly into the darkness of the night.

Unable to speak, and completely overcome by what she had seen, Tara swayed back and forth while her eyes rolled back into her head, and she unconsciously slid into the arms of the good doctor.

###############################

A few moments earlier, in a dark and dusty warehouse, Kim laid back across the top of a stainless-steel table. Sweat beaded furiously down her forehead and soaked the hospital gown that lay loosely across her naked body. Her legs laid spread apart, and her ankles rested in two steel stirrups on either side of the table. Another large, square table was situated roughly four feet to the side of the table that she occupied. There were a total of five bassinets that lay in a circular pattern centered on the square table, with a sixth one situated in the center.

Don was standing close to Kim on her left side. He wore a dark, almost cape-like gown that hung loosely from his shoulders. He furtively reached out for her left hand but had it knocked roughly aside by Kim who glared at him in a menacing manner.

Without any warning, Kim threw her head backward as she quickly pushed herself up onto her elbows, straining what looked to be every muscle in her body. The hospital gown which had previously covered her body, slid roughly onto the floor exposing an overly sized and oscillating pregnant stomach.

Instinctively, Don reached forward to take her hand.

Slowly and purposively, she rolled her head sideways until her eyes met his.

"DO NOT TOUCH ME!" she howled through tightly gritted teeth.

Don recoiled slightly but knew that he couldn't abandon her. He was going to have to deliver the six children that Kim bore within her womb.

The next moment later, a loud, deep humming growl filled the air, and quickly became louder, and louder, until reaching an almost deafening level. Looking upwards, towards the ceiling of the warehouse, Don viewed a dark, circular looking object that began to stretch outwards in every direction, shimmering as it grew. The only way that Don could describe what he saw in the air above him was that he was looking at some sort of passageway or portal from a science fiction movie. There were occasional flickers of what looked to be electricity entering at the center of the portal, and then racing outwards towards the edges in a lightning-like manner.

When the circular opening had reached across the width of the entire warehouse there was a moment of absolute silence. Don looked back towards the woman lying on the table in front of him. She blankly stared upwards towards the dark mass hanging in directly above.

"LET IT BEGIN," she intoned.

Instantly, a dark black, cord-like tube sprang from the gaping darkness in the ceiling and tore into the side of Kim's body. Straight away a high-pitched scream exploded from her mouth, piercing the silence. It appeared as if some sort of object slid down from the ceiling, along the entire length of the tube, and entered Kim's belly. With a shriek, Kim strained as she grabbed the side of the table and violently pushed out the first child from her body.

Don quickly ran over, scooped up the baby in a clean hospital blanket, and wiped away some of the fluids which covered his face.

"It's a boy!" he triumphantly stated, turning the baby towards Kim so she could see him.

"Put him over in the circle...QUICKLY!!" she hissed. "The next one is coming!"

Don responded obediently and placed the baby into one of the six bassinets after cutting the umbilical cord. He stood quietly, staring at the table and observed that the child was oddly quiet. In fact, he hadn't made a single sound since he entered into this world.

Without any warning, Kim again shrieked, and another black, artery-like structure erupted from the ceiling and entered her side, immediately followed by another child entering the world. He once again took the noiseless child off the table, cut the umbilical cord, and placed it into one of the empty receptacles on the outer edge of the circular pattern on the table.

This process repeated a total of five times until a perfectly silent male child occupied all of the bassinets arranged in a circle. No crying...no fidgeting...they lay there quietly and almost motionless.

Again, the room was filled with a deep, loud rumbling. However, this time it was accompanied by a violent vibration. The windows and walls of the warehouse began to noisily shake. Even the table where the five children lay began to shake, as well as the bucket that sat on the floor underneath the table.

The next moment, a large, massive column of smoke descended downwards from the ceiling towards the table where Kim lay. Don stepped backward away from the center of the room, and the colossal shaft reached downwards until it completely surrounded and engulfed the table on which Kim was lying. He was not able to see what was going on inside of the dark column...and he wasn't sure that he wanted to know.

A loud scream, almost a howl, erupted from within the column, and he knew that whatever was taking place was causing excruciating pain to Kim. Looking downwards to where the edge of the column met the floor, Don could see what appeared to be a dark, oil-like liquid, spread slowly onto the floor. There was an ear-piercing shriek that came from somewhere within the dark column.

And then, without any warning, the room was again silent, and the dark column ascended and disappeared into the ceiling. Lying on the table was the sweat-drenched, exhausted body of Kim. Directly in front of Kim laid the naked body of a large, newborn female child. And without any warning, an almost haunting whimper came from the child who slowly began to cry.

Kim reached towards Don and motioned to him silently to come forward.

"Hurry," she softly hissed. "Take the child, and complete the ritual."

Don apprehensively reached forward and took the female child into his hands. As he lifted the baby from the table, he noticed that the child was no longer crying. Carrying the child towards the table where the other five babies awaited, he looked downwards and was met with a calm, steady gaze of the baby looking back into his own. Taking a deep breath, he laid the child into the sixth basket located in the center of the table and looked back towards Kim with an almost fearful expression on his face.

"FINISH IT!" she demanded.

Without a word, he reached down under the table and slid the bucket out on the floor. Reaching into it, he pulled out a large, almost mop-like brush that was saturated with a dark, thick liquid.

He glanced momentarily at Kim who was intently staring at him and then turned back towards the children. With the brush in hand, he slowly drew lines of blood connecting each of the five outer bassinets with one another. Once connected, he dipped the mop back into the bucket and circumscribed the points of the star that he had just drawn within a circle.

Sitting up from the table, Kim raised her arms slowly into the air. With beads of sweat trickling down the sides of her face she uttered the words...

"It is done Father...it is done."

CHAPTER 24
Extraordinary Announcement
(Eight and A Half Years Later)

It had been over eight and a half years since Mears Laboratories was founded, and the company had already made many significant advances. The groundbreaking procedure of therapeutic cloning that William innovated had nearly been perfected, so much so that he and his team were working feverishly toward their first set of human medical trials. Pending successful trials, they would quickly move toward FDA approval for widespread availability and application into multiple disciplines of medical science.

It was nearly noon on a Thursday, and the team of scientists and researchers were actively engaged in various experiments and tests in one of the three extensive laboratories located onsite at corporate headquarters. The company had grown almost tenfold over the past few years to a team of nearly one hundred employees. Fortunately, the local biotech incubator had available space and Mears Laboratories now fully occupied two floors, and part of a third.

William was working alongside a recent addition to the team to explain to her the intricacies of safely thawing a frozen embryo so as not to damage the cellular structure. Viable embryos for testing purposes had become almost impossible to come by, as the shortage that had begun eight years earlier had only gotten worse. The inventory of almost every frozen embryo bank in the United States had completely evaporated in a matter of months, forcing William to look overseas to offshore suppliers.

"Now carefully," William instructed, "very carefully, insert the pipette into the petri dish containing the vitrification solution."

The new scientist intently stared at the computer monitor at eye level above the laboratory table that showed an extremely magnified view of the fluid contained within the receptacle. Without hesitation, she confidently, but gently, squeezed the bulb affixed to the end of the pipette and transferred the few precious drops into the liquid. The image on the monitor blurred slightly then refocused, and the round shape of a perfectly formed, early-stage embryo came into view.

"It's beautiful," Amy expressed in an almost sacred tone of voice. "It really doesn't look like anything but a cluster of a few small cells contained within the larger cell. In reality, this is how all human life begins!"

William laid his hand lightly on the left shoulder of his employee in approval.

"Very nice work," he complimented. "Now we're ready to start the genetic imprinting process onto the host."

"But first we need to suppress the existing genetic disposition correct?"

A broad grin flashed across William's face.

"Exactly," he said in a satisfied manner. "You're a quick study."

Amy flashed him a quick grin in response and raised her eyebrows. She was in her late twenties and didn't resemble the 'typical' stereotype of a female biochemical graduate student. She had extremely blond hair, stood roughly five feet seven inches tall, and had an athletic build. Her eyes were a light blue color, complimented by her relatively tan complexion. William thought for a moment that he would normally expect to see such a woman lying on one of the sandy southern California beaches, rather than hunched over a microscope wearing a white lab coat and magnification glasses. But looks can be deceiving. She had been at the top of her class at the University and had a measured IQ of one hundred and eighty-two.

"I've had a great teacher," she gushed back.

William glanced around the room with an almost guilty expression on his face, barely managing to suppress a blush from rising on his cheeks. Satisfied no one else had witnessed the exchange, he quickly continued.

"Alright then," he practically blurted out, "let's start with the genomic imprinting."

Amy reached across the table and grabbed a syringe that contained a very small amount of greenish blue liquid. On the exterior glass was affixed a white label with the following details: 'Bacterial Artificial Chromosomes series 1.001.27.2 – January 27, 2012'.

"This one correct?" Amy confidently stipulated.

"That's the one," he replied.

Without hesitation, she took the syringe and turned back toward the table to insert it into the small robotic arm that would deliver the contents into the embryo.

The next moment, the stainless-steel doors leading into the laboratory from the exterior hallway sprung open in a loud clatter and in rushed Thomas, one of the male researchers, with a panicked expression on his face.

"WILLIAM!" he shouted, "COME QUICK! NOW! I MEAN...YOU'VE GOT TO SEE THIS, HURRY!"

Just as abruptly as he entered, Thomas darted back out of the lab without any additional explanation. William simply looked at Amy with a dumbfounded look on his face and was met with an equally perplexed expression.

"What was that all..." he attempted to say.

"HURRY UP!" a voice screamed from the hallway. "IT'S ON TV RIGHT NOW!"

Shrugging his shoulders, William started to exit the lab followed closely by Amy and the other three researchers who had all been equally startled by what had just occurred. Walking at a quickened pace, William saw two other employees running down toward the break room at the end of the hallway. Thinking that something horrible had happened, he too began to run down the hallway and entered the lunchroom.

Inside the break room, there were already two dozen or so employees, all gathered around a flat panel television mounted in the back corner of the room just below the ceiling. As William entered, several of the employees made a small path allowing him to stand directly beneath the monitor. The image on the screen showed the exterior of a nondescript business building with a series of three or four sets of stairs leading up from a walkway to a raised area directly in front of the exterior doors. A small, elevated podium was situated directly in front of the door with what looked to be a dozen microphones for various television stations and news providers. Television cameras were spread out in a large semi-circle around the podium, and a small army of men and women wearing business attire crowded into every available space. Standing close to the podium was the familiar face of Doctor Schmidt. A distinct sinking feeling hit William's stomach and his chest tightened. The newscaster on the television could be heard speaking, as the cameras remained affixed on the podium and image of Doctor Schmidt.

"We're just waiting now," the voice on the television announced, "for the news conference to begin. The man that you see standing next to the podium is Doctor Koenraad Schmidt, from the University of California. Doctor Schmidt has been catapulted to the top of scientific and medical discussions over the past several years, especially with his backing of the very successful biotech start-up Mears Laboratories."

The break room erupted into loud cheers and whistles in response to the recognition they just received.

"Quiet everyone," William implored. "I want to hear what's going on."

The room quickly settled down as they all intensely focused on the TV.

"Just eight years ago, Doctor Schmidt and the recently graduated doctor Mears founded Mears Laboratories based on the ground-breaking research that doctor William Mears had based his entire doctoral thesis on."

The room erupted into another cheer but quieted just as quickly as William raised his right hand in the air.

"We have all followed Mears Laboratories quite closely over the past several years as they have moved closer and closer toward trials and general availability of what most medical practitioners hail as the most astounding breakthrough in modern medicine. Well, we are here today at the request of Doctor Schmidt who has promised that he will to making an announcement that will change medical history, if not human history, forever."

Just then, a short, stocky man wearing a business suit ran into view on the screen and whispered something into Schmidt's ear. He simply nodded and motioned for the man to head back in the direction he initially came. Then, he purposely walked toward the microphone.

"It looks like the moment has arrived," the newscaster announced. "Let's all listen in as doctor Koenraad Schmidt addresses the world."

Standing directly behind the podium, Doctor Schmidt set both of his hands on the platform, interlaced his fingers, and stared directly into the camera.

"Ladies and gentlemen, I am honored to be here today to make what will undoubtedly be one of the most amazing, revelatory announcements of modern times. No, one of the most incredible declarations in human history," he pronounced in as matter of fact a tone of voice as possible. "I would like to introduce to you one of the leading medical minds in biochemical research, Doctor Don Clark.

William felt as if a truck had hit him. He hadn't heard Don's name, let alone even really thought of his past research partner, for at least six years. And now, he was listening to the man who he thought was his trusted business partner, give him an introduction as if he had known him for several years.

Schmidt turned to look over his left shoulder, reaching outward with his left hand, motioning the man to step up to the podium.

William had been focusing so intently on the screen that he didn't notice that Tara had joined him at his side and was tightly grasping his left hand between both of hers.

The familiar face of his previous friend Don Clark then came into view on the television screen.

Tara leaned up toward William and whispered in his left ear.

"He looks terrible! As if he hasn't slept for weeks!"

William simply grunted in reply, not wanting to take his

eyes or attention off the events unfolding on the screen in front of him. Tara was right though. Don's appearance had drastically changed from the last time he had seen him. His once neatly slicked back, jet-black hair was now streaked with tufts of grey hair and was loosely arranged on his head. He had deep, dark circles under his eyes that appeared sunken and somewhat hollow. His face was gaunt, and he looked as if he had lost at least twenty pounds.

Don lightly cleared his throat and apprehensively stared into one of the multiple television cameras aimed at him.

"Thank you, Doctor Schmidt. I'm thankful to be here today and especially grateful for all of the financial support and encouragement that you have given me over the past few years."

Without saying a word, William looked at Tara in complete disbelief, slightly raising his hands in an outward show of confusion.

"Past few years?" he silently thought. "Past few years?!"

"Ladies and gentlemen of the press. To all of the men, women, and children watching this broadcast both here in the United States and around the world, I'm thrilled to be here to make the first public announcement of a breakthrough so mind-blowing," he paused for effect, "so unbelievable, that it will cause you to question some of your strongest, most deeply held beliefs. Something so amazing that it will forever change how you view this world."

Don again paused for dramatic effect before continuing.

"It is with great excitement and enthusiasm that I announce here today, that my research team, along with the financial support and backing of Doctor Schmidt, have successfully created a human clone. Furthermore, we have not just accomplished this once, but we have created SIX clones which I would like to introduce to the world for the first time today!"

Don looked to his left and made a gesture beckoning for an unseen party off camera to join him at the podium. The picture on the television quickly panned over to the right side of the landing and paused on the all too familiar face of Tara's former roommate, Kim Dyson.

Tara let out another audible gasp which startled William.

Kim triumphantly stared into the television camera, and then took three steps to her right as she turned to look immediately behind where she was standing.

There, standing in a semi-circle, were five male children who looked to be ten years of age. Each of them had very pale complexions, were dressed in all white clothes, had blue eyes and long, extraordinarily white hair stopping just above their shoulders. Their facial features were highly angular in nature and their lips were almost a translucent red. They each stood about four and a half feet tall and held their hands behind their backs. None of them had much of an expression on their faces, but stood there silently looking at Kim.

At the center of the five male children stood one female child who looked to be fourteen years of age. She had a vibrant, almost angry looking expression on her fair, pale skin. In sharp contrast to the other five children, she had long hair, black as night that extended roughly six inches past her shoulders. Her eyes were also black, and she stood almost five and a half feet tall. Unlike the other children who were looking at Kim, this child stared intently into the lens of the television camera.

Kim started to motion to the children to come forward. The young girl took two steps forward before stopping momentarily to confirm the other children were following her. Satisfied with their action, she turned forward and starting walking slowly toward Kim while extending her hand in a manner that looked as if she held her in complete disdain.

Kim reached forward to take her hand, and then turned back toward Don and walked hand-in-hand with the young girl while approaching the podium. Once at the podium, Kim released the young girl's hand that slowly slid back down to her side.

Don looked forward again into the cameras and then continued.

"It gives me great pleasure to introduce the world to the first six human clones. The names of the boys from left to right are: Ash, Edgar, Jack, John, and Scott. And the name of the girl is Clarissa."

The television was completely silent, as was the break room at Mears Laboratories, as everyone stood there in absolute disbelief at what they had just heard. William could hear the blood pounding in his ears as his stomach tightened once again.

"For centuries, mankind has been trying to extend life; to cure diseases and treat illness. Yes, we have made great strides in curing many of the ailments that plague the human race. We've cured polio and smallpox. We have created artificial valves and hearts. We have even been able to map the human genome and unlock many of the mysteries of what makes us who we are. However, we have not been able to prevent the inevitable decline of the human body culminating in our demise. Well today, that is all about to change!"

Don paused momentarily again allowing for his words to sink in and then continued with his announcement.

"It gives me great pleasure to announce to the world the creation of 'Cenetics', a new genetic research company that will provide for the realization of that elusive Fountain of Youth that Juan Ponce de Leon sought after in the sixteenth century. When you look back over history, the average lifespan of most humans on this earth was between twenty-five and thirty years of age. Around the mid-eighteen-hundreds, average life expectancy increased to somewhere around forty-five as we began to understand the nature of disease and infection. Medical advances since that time have increased the overall average age of humans to almost eighty years. Think about that for a moment...that's really a quite miraculous accomplishment. In less than two hundred years, the average age increased almost three-fold."

William stared at the television screen with an expression of complete disbelief on his face. The few hushed whispers around the break room went by completely unnoticed as he waited for his former friend to continue.

"Well," Don triumphantly stated, "I'm here to tell you today, this day, at this very moment, that medical science is going to completely change the definition of old age. As you can see before you, we have successfully, not just once, or twice, but six times, replicated a human life form in all of its complexity. These six children represent the future for each and every one of us. It gives me great pleasure to announce, for the first time in human history, that we have the ability to extend life indefinitely."

Don gestured in a grandiose manner to his left, calling

attention to the six children that stood clustered around the podium.

"As our human bodies age, decay, and slowly die, our minds maintain more resiliency than the rest of our cells and organs. Sure, there are diseases such as Alzheimer's and dementia, which slowly deteriorate our cognitive abilities. But science is quickly advancing, and there will soon be a day where diseases of the brain will be no more. But that doesn't change the fact that our bodies grow old and tired. This is where Cenetics changes the game entirely."

"These six children share a commonality. They all possess an exact duplicate of my own genetic code. YES!" he shouted enthusiastically, "they are in fact, genetic duplicates of my own DNA. And as such, they offer up an option that we have never had previously in the history of the world. You're familiar with the adage 'the spirit is willing, but the flesh is weak'? Well, Cenetics has been able to combine biology and medicine to overcome the weakness of the flesh. We are now on the cusp of being able to transplant the mind of any human into an exact genetic duplicate, allowing for that individual to continue forward without being held back by a weak and aged body. We can essentially transfer their consciousness from a physical form that is at the end of life, into a new, vigorous incarnate, allowing for extended enjoyment of life. The *true* fountain of youth is not mystic belief or magic. Eternal life can effectually be ours. But not the kind described through religion and superstitions. Eternal life is now ours through the ingenuity of mankind!"

"Ouch," Tara exclaimed pulling her hand back from William's. "You're squeezing too tightly."

She looked up at William who was still staring blankly at the screen.

"Will?" she apprehensively inquired. "WILL," she stated more forcefully. "Are you ok"?

William stared blankly at the screen, muttering quietly to himself.

"What have you done, Don? What have you done?"

CHAPTER 25

Distressing Vision

(December 2016)

The once busy and bustling headquarters of Mears Laboratories was now only a distant memory. The vibrant and growing startup had been forced to lay off nearly ninety percent of their workforce over the past eighteen months given the mounting competitive pressure imposed by Cenetics and the dwindling public interest in William's company. While the science that William had pioneered still provided extraordinary value in the lives of humankind, it paled in comparison to the headline-grabbing press releases that came out of Cenetics on an almost daily basis.

The number of employees had shrunken to only fourteen comprised of the original eleven and three other scientists who had joined early on. The once expansive offices spread out across almost three full floors, comprised of state-of-the-art research laboratories, multiple offices, and storage facilities, was now relegated to occupy only a corner section of a single floor, including a smaller laboratory and moderate office space. Without William having been able to secure a small round of angel investment funding less than a week ago, the doors of Mears Laboratories might have already shut for good from the inability to meet payroll.

While it was only five fifteen in the evening, almost all the other employees had left for the day, leaving William alone in the lab. He was intently looking through the eyepiece of the microscope at a sample of damaged brain tissue. In the corner of the lab, a small flat screen television was tuned to a local news channel with the audio turned down very low, but still audible. Sitting up straight on his stool, William reached both arms above his head, stretching his back while he emitted a perceptible groan.

"Are you getting ready to call it a day?" Tara offered as she entered the lab through a doorway to the left of where William sat.

With arms still outstretched above his head, he turned towards Tara and a weak smile appeared on his obviously tired face. Tensing his body a final time, he lowered his arms and placed his hands lightly on the table.

"William, you look exhausted," Tara commented. "When was the last time you got a good night's sleep?"

William shrugged his shoulders and began to rub at his left eye with a closed fist. He had very dark circles under his eyes, his hair was disheveled, and his clothes were wrinkled from what looked to have been at least three days of continuous wear.

"I can't sleep," he meekly muttered in reply.

Tara slowly walked across the room, stood directly behind William and wrapped her arms gently around his neck, pulling him toward her as she leaned into his body. William tilted his head slightly to the left resting his face on the inside of her upper arm and sighed deeply.

"You know I love you?" she whispered quietly into his right ear.

"Yeah, I know it. And I love you too."

He paused for a moment, sitting upright on his stool, and Tara unwrapped her arms from around his neck and stood quietly on his left side.

"It's just been such a tough year!" he murmured. "Ever

since Don's announcement, everything has gone to hell in a handbasket. And it's not just for Mears Labs either."

"This isn't your fault!" she stipulated. "You couldn't have known what Don was going to do."

"I know. But it was my research that enabled Don to go down the path of creating clones in the first place. It was my research that enabled him to create...to create these clones that has everything turned completely upside down," he virtually spit out of his mouth with a disgusted look on his face.

Tara pursed her lips together and stared intently into William's eyes. Reaching up with both hands she cradled his face gently.

"Sweetheart, you need to cheer up. Over the past few weeks, you've become more and more depressed and it's starting to worry me."

She hesitated for a moment and then continued.

"So worried in fact that I asked my Dad for some suggestions on what I could do to help."

William let out another light sigh as he slightly shook his head from side to side. He set his right elbow on the table, resting his forehead on his hand.

"I know you don't believe in God," Tara cautiously remarked.

"It's not that I don't believe in God, I've just never seen anything empirical that proved he truly does exist."

Tara pursed her lips momentarily and then consciously relaxed them. She took a deep breath and responded.

"Will," she whispered tenderly. "There are signs of God all around us, all of the time."

She paused for a moment as she considered what to say next and finally continued.

"You're a scientist, right?"

"Yeah, so?"

"And not just any scientist. You're a molecular biologist, right?"

William crooked a speculative eyebrow that Tara quickly ignored.

"Well, as a molecular biologist, you're very familiar with cells, and atoms, and..." she struggled for a moment to choose the right words and finally, shrugged her shoulders before continuing, "...and all of that other scientificky stuff."

A big grin creased William's face.

"Scientificky stuff huh?" he chided her.

"Oh, you know what I mean!" she stated with a bit perturbed tone of voice. "Anyways, molecules and atoms, they all have a specific structure to them, right?"

William raised his eyebrows and simply nodded with a bit of a smirk on his face.

Tara ignored him and pressed forward.

"Well, atoms have a center to them. A...a...."

"A nucleus?"

"Yes, a nucleus. And that nucleus has little ball things that fly around it, right?"

"You mean electrons?"

"Yes, electrons! Stop interrupting me," she warned, "you're going to make me lose my train of thought."

William smiled again, slightly inclining his head as an indication that he wanted her to proceed.

"So, these electrons zip around the nucleus in a very ordered pattern, right? At a specific distance, and speeds. Kind of like planets that are zipping around the Sun in our galaxy."

"You mean our solar system," William corrected.

"Stop correcting me and just listen!"

"Sorry," he genuinely apologized this time.

"Thank you. Well, electrons are essentially like planets right."

William partly opened his mouth to say something and quickly clapped it shut when Tara threw a somewhat menacing glare into his face.

"Just work with me please," she begged. "Atoms and gala...I mean solar systems," she corrected herself, "are kind of similar. They have very specific paths and behaviors. In fact, they function in darn near a perfect manner. If they didn't, atoms would fall apart and planets would spin off uncontrollably into space."

"Ok, I'm following you. But what's the point you're trying to make?"

"Well, do you think that both of these things just figured out how to function so perfectly by themselves?"

William paused for a moment, carefully choosing his words before responding.

"I don't think they figured out how to function by themselves, but I believe that the laws of physics which govern everything in our universe provide an explanation for how planets orbit the sun, how they travel in elliptical paths...and even how they formed in the first place. It's not a surprise to me that atoms function in a similar manner."

A pained expression appeared on Tara's face. She was obviously getting frustrated with her inability to properly express her thoughts. Then, her countenance completely changed, as if a light bulb literally went off in her head.

"What about this?" she blurted out. "Imagine that you were an explorer, traveling on a spaceship."

William stifled a chuckle fearing that Tara was going to box his ears.

"Well, let's say that you were traveling in a completely different solar system, and you landed your spaceship on the surface of some far away planet. You stepped out of your spaceship and started to walk."

"What color is the sky on your planet?" William innocently inquired.

"PURPLE! GREEN!" she cried. "It doesn't matter! Just let me finish!"

William smiled and turned both of his hands upwards as an encouragement for her to continue with her story.

"So, you're walking on the surface of this never before seen planet, where the sky is purple. You walk for about thirty minutes and find that you are walking along an orange ocean with waves rolling onto blue sand beaches. As you're walking, a shiny object almost completely covered in sand catches your eye, so you stop and bend down to see what it is. After carefully brushing away sand from the surface of the object, you discover that it is a perfectly round, silver disk which you grasp in your hand to inspect closer. When you turn the object over, you notice that there is a clear glass covering on the other side, neatly framed by a thin border of the silver, and under the glass lay twelve odd-looking figures arranged along the outer edge of the circle at even intervals. At the center of the circle, you see two thin rectangular lines extending outwards towards the figures. One of the lines is noticeably longer than the other one."

Tara paused for a brief instant and realized that William was actually letting her talk uninterrupted.

"Next, you turn the object back over to inspect the side

that was solid silver and notice that there is a small latch of some sort protruding from what you deem to be the top of the object. Carefully you press it and the outer silver shell of the object opens with a quiet click. Very cautiously, you open up the backside of the disk and discover something amazing."

"What?" William asked with real interest. "What did you discover?"

"On the inside of the disk, you find multiple tiny pieces of metal. Wheels, gears, and springs, all moving in perfect unison, one with another. All faultlessly interacting with other objects to accomplish a task."

"Ah..." William expressed. "You're describing a hand watch or an old-fashioned timepiece, right?"

"Exactly! It's a pocket watch!" she exclaimed with great excitement.

"Ok, so it's a pocket watch. What's your point?"

"Will," she offered in a sincere voice. "You're one of the dumbest smart people I know."

William still had an expression on his face, clearly illustrating that he didn't have the foggiest idea of what the point of her story was.

"If you were a space traveler on a faraway planet, and came across something that I just described, which you correctly identified as a pocket watch, would you come to the conclusion that this object spontaneously occurred in nature because of physics or some other sort of natural laws?"

William thoughtfully paused for a moment considering what Tara had asked.

"Well, of course not," he finally responded. "This is something that would have needed to have been created by someone, or something, that had intelligence. That had a knowledge of manufacturing, mechanics, and how to bring together all these different components to work in unison with one another."

"You're right," Tara conceded. "It would have taken someone or something with intelligence to create this watch. It would have taken a plan or a design. There would need to be a purpose...right?"

This time it looked as if the light bulb went off in William's head. He finally understood the point that she was so patiently trying to make. Tara didn't wait for William to respond and continued with her story.

"If it's your opinion that this pocket watch had to be created by someone of intelligence, and it had a specific purpose, how can you look at our solar system, or at our entire universe, and come to any other conclusion? Are the planets not moving in specific, purposeful patterns around the Sun? Do they not react, interact, and interrelate to one another in just the right way so that they can continuously orbit the Sun? Is the Earth not at a specific distance away from the Sun to provide for 'ideal' conditions for life on earth to abound?"

She paused for a brief moment to give William a chance to respond, but William just sat there with an expression on his face that could only be described as dumbfounded and proud at the same time.

"How is our solar system any different than this pocket watch? It isn't!" she triumphantly declared. "And if something as simple as a pocket watch required someone or something with intelligence to have designed it, then how could our solar system, with all of its complexities, have just appeared by 'chance'...driven by a 'big bang'?

They didn't! The only logical conclusion is that there was a plan behind the creation of the solar system; it's planets, the Sun, and this very earth that we live on. And if there had to be some overall glorious plan that served as a blueprint for this universe to have been designed, created, and maintained, then what other possible option is there outside of a divine creator that created our world? And not just our world, but the entire universe itself? There isn't another option. To argue so would be an affront to logically minded scientists everywhere, wouldn't it?"

"Wow!" William chortled. "Who is this woman in front of me?! You should have been a lawyer or district attorney. That is about the most solid argument that I've ever heard regarding the existence of God."

"Well thank you," Tara expressed, almost out of breath.

"Ok...ok...you've made your point," William conceded. "What advice did your father give you about cheering me up?"

A broad grin covered Tara's face, extending virtually from ear to ear.

"Dad told me I should suggest you read the Bible."

"The Bible?" he asked in an incredulous tone. "That's it? Just read the Bible?"

"Dad always told me that when I was facing a hard decision, or was down in life, that all I needed to do was to turn to the scriptures. He feels that the answers to all of life's questions and challenges are in the word of God. All you need to do is to have an ounce of faith that you'll find help in the pages of the Bible, and sure enough, you'll end up finding something helpful."

William realized that Tara wasn't going to leave him alone unless he agreed to read some part of the Bible.

"Ok then," he surrendered. "What part of the Bible does your Dad recommend that I read?"

"He didn't give me a specific chapter or verse. He said that you pick up a Bible, open it to any page, and just start reading. And if you did that, with an expectation that you were going to find something that was relevant to your own life, that you would, in fact, find it! Something that was meant just for you, that would help you overcome whatever was confronting you in your life."

"Ok, I'll read the Bible when I get home tonight," William soberly agreed. "At this point, I'm pretty much willing to try anything and everything."

"Excellent!" she declared. "Now promise me...you are actually going to do this tonight when you get home, right? Before you go to bed. Promise!"

"Ok...I promise."

"Good! Now, why don't you and I get out of this depressing lab and go get something yummy to eat. Sound good?"

"Whatever you say, Tara...whatever you say!"

###############################

Later that night, William found himself resting in an upright position against two large pillows placed next to the headboard on his bed. Sitting directly in his lap was an unopened King James Version of the Holy Bible. He glanced over to his left to look at Tara lying comfortably on her pillow, sleeping peacefully. He noticed the digital clock on the nightstand and thought to himself that it was just after midnight. Turning his attention back to his lap, he hefted the somewhat heavy book in his right hand.

"Well," he quietly murmured to himself, "I might as well give this a shot."

With a light sigh, he opened up the book to the very beginning.

"I guess the best place to start would be the beginning."

Thumbing through the first few pages of the scriptures, he found himself staring at a page that read 'The First Book of Moses, called Genesis', and he silently began reading the words that lay on the page before him.

1:1 In the beginning God created the heavens and the earth.

1:2 And the earth was without form, and void; and darkness was upon the face of the deep. And the Spirit of God moved upon the face of the waters.

1:3 And God said, Let there be light: and there was light.

1:4 And God saw the light, that it was good: and God divided the light from the darkness.

1:5 And God called the light Day, and the darkness he called Night. And the evening and the morning were the first day.

1:6 And God said, Let there be a firmament in the midst of the waters, and let it divide the waters from the waters.

1:7 And God made the firmament, and divided the waters which were under the firmament from the waters which were above the firmament: and it was so.

1:8 And God called the firmament Heaven. And the evening and the morning were the second day.

He paused for a moment and reflected on the conversation he had with Tara earlier that day.

"Tara was describing this very same thing to me earlier," he thought to himself. "But could the entire universe, the heavens and the stars have been created in such a manner? What about how scientists have literally measured the ongoing expansion of the universe, emanating from an initial starting point? The 'Big Bang' is really the most logical explanation."

He paused and thought for a moment that he felt a warm sensation coming from his chest. Without thinking about it, he reached under the neck collar of his t-shirt and pulled out the Talisman that always hung around his neck, laying it carefully on the outside of his clothes.

"Let me be open-minded about this," he continued in his head. "Even if the 'Big Bang' really was the starting point of the universe, what caused the Bang to occur in the first place?"

The warming sensation in his chest intensified slightly as his mind began to ponder the possibility that the Big Bang, which truly has to be the moment at which the universe was created, was actually part of a larger plan or design.

"Is it possible that God *is* the cause of that event?" he postulated in his own mind. "Could this have been just the starting point of a grand design in which He created the galaxies, stars, and planets?"

William sat silently for a moment pondering this line of thinking.

"Well, let's put the old man's recommendation to the

test," he commented quietly to himself. "Let's see what fate wants me to uncover by turning to a random section of the Bible."

Bending the book across the forefingers of his right hand, he began to fan pages randomly with his right thumb for a couple of seconds and then abruptly stopped. Opening up the pages he noticed that he was now in the ninth chapter of Chronicles and he randomly pointed with his left index finger on the page to the thirty-eighth verse.

> 9:38 And Mikloth begat Shimeam. And they also dwelt with their brethren at Jerusalem, over against their brethren.

> 9:39 And Ner begat Kish; and Kish begat Saul; and Saul begat Jonathan, and Malchishua, and Abinadab, and Eshbaal.

> 9:40 And the son of Jonathan was Meribbaal: and Meribbaal begat Micah.

> 9:41 And the sons of Micah were, Pithon, and Melech, and Tahrea, and Ahaz.

William audibly laughed to himself.

"Well now, I'm not sure how this directly pertains to me and my depression, but maybe it's trying to tell me that I need to have children!"

Once again William fanned through the pages with his right thumb, and this time stopped in the tenth chapter of Job and began to read the eighteenth verse:

> 10:18 Wherefore then hast thou brought me forth out of the womb? Oh that I had given up the ghost, and no eye had seen me!

10:19 I should have been as though I had not been; I should have been carried from the womb to the grave.

10:20 Are not my days few? cease then, and let me alone, that I may take comfort a little,

10:21 Before I go whence I shall not return, even to the land of darkness and the shadow of death;

"Oh, that figures," he uttered sarcastically. "I open up to a section about Job wishing that he was dead!"

William closed the book in front of him and sat silently on the bed staring at the ceiling above him. After a moment, he closed his eyes and quietly, virtually silently, whispered the following words:

"God. If you really are there, I could use some help right about now. Everything in my life was going so well, but now nothing seems to be going right. I know that I'm not really a spiritual person, but I try to be a good man. Hopefully, that doesn't preclude me from getting some help from you."

"All of my research, all the work and time that I have spent on discovery, was for the betterment of mankind. I know that I'm not completely altruistic, but my intent was to help other people to ease their burdens and lessen their pain and suffering. And now, I feel like everything has been completely turned upside down and I'm being punished for some reason."

William stopped for a moment and opened his eyes. He looked around his bedroom and quietly sighed to himself. He felt sad and tired. Slowly he closed his eyes again.

"Please, God. I beg Thee that Thou would help me to understand what it is that I need to do. Help me to know!" he pleaded with every ounce of emotion.

The warmth that he had felt earlier returned, but this time it was much more intense. It was as if there was a burning sensation emanating from deep within his chest. He opened his eyes and glanced down at the amulet that was affixed to the necklace that laid loosely about his neck. He once again thumbed through the pages of the Bible, skipping over many chapters and books, trying to sense what it was that he could learn from this book to help him in his life.

Suddenly, he felt a strong inclination to stop flipping through pages. He slowly opened up the thick book lying in his lap and peered at the page before him.

"The Revelation of St. John the Divine," he silently read from the heading of chapter twelve.

He slowly ran his index finger down the page, across the various verses, searching – trying to sense what it was that he was supposed to read. As his finger slid downwards on the page the burning sensation in his chest intensified to a point that he had never felt before. At that moment, he felt as if there was someone or something else in the room influencing his action. He instantly froze his hand and glanced down at the words on the page lying before him.

> 12:4 And his tail drew the third part of the stars of heaven, and did cast them to the earth: and the dragon stood before the woman which was ready to be delivered, for to devour her child as soon as it was born.

> 12:5 And she brought forth a man child, who was to rule all nations with a rod of iron: and her child was caught up unto God, and to his throne.

12:6 And the woman fled into the wilderness, where she hath a place prepared of God, that they should feed her there a thousand two hundred and threescore days.

The sensation of warmth emanating from William's chest was almost overwhelming to the point of him feeling that he was going to pass out. He forced himself to continue.

12:7 And there was war in heaven: Michael and his angels fought against the dragon; and the dragon fought and his angels,

12:8 And prevailed not; neither was their place found any more in heaven.

12:9 And the great dragon was cast out, that old serpent, called the Devil, and Satan, which deceiveth the whole world: he was cast out into the earth, and his angels were cast out with him.

William paused and looked up from the book lying in his lap, and stared at the wall in front of him. The air in front of him suddenly seemed to shimmer slightly, and then more noticeably, so that he couldn't focus on the wall immediately on the other side of his line of vision. The blurring of the air seemed to swirl in a clockwise manner, and he thought that he could see something else in the room in front of him, but he couldn't clearly make it out. Slowly, those blurred images began to slide into focus as the one small shimmering section of air in front of him began to expand outwards in all directions. But not just upwards and down but it literally began to envelop the entire room until William himself was caught up in the expanding view, placing him in what appeared to be an entirely different location.

He looked to his left and right and realized that he was no longer sitting on his bed in his apartment. It appeared to him as if he had been transported to some faraway location that his eyes had never before seen. But even still, he felt as if what he was looking at was familiar in some way.

He saw a great, expansive field lying all about him. To his right, there were white, rolling clouds of smoke that were traversing across the landscape. Not only along the ground, but they seemed to be coming from the sky, from the very clouds themselves. They were moving slowly at first but started to pick up speed as they came closer to where he stood.

To his left, he saw dark, almost vile appearing smoke crawling across the land. It was moving as if in slow motion, in an almost liquid-like manner. There too he saw dark, ominous vapors of mist crawling through the air, coming from all directions. The black fog also appeared to be increasing in speed as it approached William's location.

Faintly, he began to hear what he could only describe as the sounds of horse hooves striking the ground, coming from the white vaporous mist to his right. Occasionally, he thought that he heard a voice shouting something unintelligible. Imperceptible noises also came from the dark clouds on his left. Gradually, he began to make out the obscure sounds of what he could only describe as a shriek or scream.

The billowing smoke on both sides of him was getting closer and closer. On his right, he thought he was able to see very faint images of what appeared to be winged horses. Straining his eyes to focus, he could discern that there were, in fact, two distinct images making up what he thought was initially just one. Unless his eyes were deceiving him, he thought that he saw horses mounted by winged men and women, who were wearing bright gleaming white armor, brandishing long spears and swords.

Glancing to his left he shuddered at the scene that was advancing directly toward him. There was what could only be described as some sort of demonic creatures flying through the air, mounted by equally gruesome beings of some sort. The winged personages flying in the air were donning dark, loathsome looking armor, similarly carrying spears and swords. However, these beings also had what looked to be some sort of object, almost as if it were a tail, trailing from behind each of them.

The noise from both sides grew louder and louder. The thundering of hooves and flapping of wings created an uproarious atmosphere. William was frozen in fear but could not take his eyes away from the tumultuous scene developing all around him.

Suddenly, the loud blare of a trumpet pierced through and above all the noise. William found himself crouching on the ground, grabbing his knees, and closing his eyes as the two opposing forces collided directly around and on top of his immediate position. He heard screams, and shrieks. Great clashes of steel, and whinnying of horses. The commotion intensified, grew louder, and William knew that he was about to be destroyed.

Slowly, he lifted his head and glanced toward some of the figures engaged in hand-to-hand combat close to his location. As he looked over he saw a man wearing bright, almost blindingly white armor, striking down a winged adversary with the edge of his sword. The man who delivered the fatal blow glanced in his direction and caused William's breath to halt in his chest.

The image before him suddenly began to swirl and spin. William quickly shut his eyes and grasped his knees again in a squatting position. The noise grew to a great crescendo and became almost unbearable. William felt as if he was going to go insane. In mad desperation, William stood up, raising his hand above his head and screamed in as loud a voice as possible.

"Save me!" he pleaded. "Save me!"

Abruptly he found himself back in his bedroom again, standing on top of his bed. His pajamas were completely soaked through with sweat, and his heart was beating wildly within his chest.

Tara immediately shot up on the bed, staring at William standing beside her with both fists clenched, held up high over his head.

"WILLIAM!" she cried. "ARE YOU OK?"

Realizing that he was back in his bedroom, William collapsed on the bed beside Tara. His muscles ached as if he had run a marathon carrying a fifty-pound bag of potatoes in each arm.

"William," she shouted. "What happened? William!"

William lay there silently for a moment trying to compose himself. After almost two full minutes he sat up on the side of the bed and turned to face Tara. Gathering himself he tried to speak but was unable to form words.

"William, you're scaring me," she pleaded. "Please, tell me what's wrong!"

William took another moment to slow his heart rate down and then stared directly into the face of the one person on this planet he felt he could tell anything. And he knew what he was about to say was going to sound completely, if not entirely, crazy. Tara simply sat there patiently, looking emphatically into his eyes.

"Tara," he finally uttered. "I think that I just had a vision."

"What do you mean?" she asked in a somewhat incredulous, but extraordinarily caring manner.

"I think that I just experienced a vision."

"A vision of what?"

He paused for a moment, took a deep breath and replied.

"I believe that I just saw a vision of a war of some type. A great battle between good and evil. And the strange thing is...that it wasn't as if I was seeing it for the first time. It felt..." he struggled to find the right words. "...it felt somewhat familiar. Like I had seen it before. And then..."

He stopped himself short knowing that what he was about to say would make him sound completely off his rocker.

"And then what?" Tara whispered with tears streaming down her face.

"And then...and then I saw one of the soldiers that was fighting in the battle – fighting on the side of good. And the face of the warrior was...my own!"

CHAPTER 26

Interpretation
(The Next Day)

William and Tara drove silently through the residential streets of Los Angeles. The morning sky was starting to illuminate with the sun rising in the East. William slouched behind the wheel of his car, exhausted from the events of the previous night and the fact that he wasn't able to get any sleep. Tara reflected almost a mirror image of weariness across her entire body. She had deep, dark circles under her eyes and her head slightly tilted forward as if her neck didn't have the strength to hold it completely upright. Occasionally, she would glance over at William with an expression of concern clearly evident on her face. She was very distressed about what she witnessed last night...and even more troubled about what William must be going through.

After coming to a stop at an intersection, William slowly pulled the car around a right-hand curve, and drove up the street a ways and then perceptibly slowed.

"I can never remember which house is his," he admitted in a quiet voice.

"It's just up on the left," Tara reminded him. "The third house with all of the bushes around the mailbox."

William willingly followed her instructions, slowly pulled into the driveway, and put the car in park. After shutting off the engine he inhaled a deep breath and held it in for a moment while he shut his eyes. The next moment, he loudly exhaled and turned to look at Tara.

"I'm totally drained!"

"I know," Tara replied sympathetically. "Come on," she

continued as she opened up her door, "let's go on in. Daddy is expecting us."

William took another deep breath as if he was going to say something, but then changed his mind and followed Tara's example, opening his own door and shutting it quietly behind him. Tara waited patiently by the front of the car for William to make his way to her, and after taking his hand led him to the front door.

As they approached the front door, Tara released William's hand and started to search in her purse for a key. Before she could find it, the door swiftly swung open revealing the familiar stocky figure of Tara's father. He was still wearing his pajama bottoms, along with a tight-fitting t-shirt, and a pair of tan leather slippers.

Without saying a word, Tara rushed into the doorway and threw her arms around her father, clinging tightly, and showing no sign of wanting to let go. Her father simply wrapped his thick arms around her and pulled her closely to the side of his scruffy face. After a brief moment, Tara released her grip from around her father's neck and reached up to her face to wipe away a couple tears.

Rich shifted his attention from his daughter and looked squarely into William's face.

"You ok?" he questioned.

"Yeah, I'm alright," he lied.

"Come on you two, let's get inside," he encouraged as he turned to walk into his house.

Both Tara and William followed him into the house and William shut the door firmly behind them.

Rich had already made his way into the family room and was sitting in his easy chair waiting for the pair to join him. He motioned toward the couch located directly across from where he was seated. Both of his visitors complied with the silent request and took a seat.

"Well," Rich stated after a brief moment, "Tara told me a little bit about what's going on, but I'd like to hear it from you son."

"I don't know where to start," he replied.

"Just start at the beginning, and we'll go from there."

William relayed the events of the past day with as much detail as he could remember starting with him and Tara's discussion at the laboratory in the early evening where she admonished him to follow Rich's advice to search the Bible for direction. He next recounted the uneventful evening as they went to dinner, stopped at a local ice cream shop for a quick treat, and then made their way back to William's apartment. He described how Tara indicated she was very tired and wanted to go to sleep, and how he felt she was just trying to give him some free time to start reading.

"Ok," Rich commented. "Nothing sounds too out of the ordinary."

William laughed out loud and soberly looked into his face.

"Well, strap on your seatbelt...it's about to get a little bumpy."

William then described how he began to read the Bible. How he followed Tara's suggestion of just starting to read wherever he opened it to.

"How did you feel?" Rich inquired.

"I didn't really feel anything."

He paused for a moment to reflect on the previous night's events and then continued.

"At least I didn't feel anything at first. I just opened the book and started to read in Genesis about the creation. As

I started to read the first chapter, it reminded me of the conversation that Tara and I had earlier that evening at the lab...about how the solar system, galaxies, and the universe were created by God. That He had a specific purpose for everything. And then..."

William paused for a moment, not really sure how to describe his thoughts.

"And then what?" he encouraged him.

"And then...I felt...I...I don't know how to describe it."

"Just try."

"I felt...warm. Almost, calm...at peace. I felt as if...as if heat was coming out of my chest."

Rich sat back in his chair and folded his arms across his large chest with a slight smile on his face.

"What?!" William demanded.

"William, what you're describing is a feeling that I have felt many, many times in my life. It is a feeling that I have when I'm in tune with the spirit of God. The best way to describe the feeling that you were experiencing was to say that you were sensing the Love of God through his Holy Spirit."

A look of consternation creased across William's face. He struggled for a moment trying to think how to word his response, but ultimately gave up and just stated it.

"But I don't believe in God! Well, at least I don't know for certain that he exists or not."

The smile on Rich's face grew even wider in response to his comments.

"Just because you don't believe in something, or don't know with a hundred percent certainty that it is true, or that it truly exists, doesn't mean that it doesn't. Man used to think that the world was flat, but we all know today that the earth is round. Just because they didn't believe it was round, or even considered it a possibility, doesn't mean that it wasn't so. And along that same line of thinking, just because you don't know that God exists, doesn't mean that He doesn't. It just means that you haven't discovered the knowledge for yourself yet."

William let out a light chuckle.

"Well, after last night, all I can say is that I've got a new perspective on the whole topic of religion!"

"At least one good thing has come out this," Rich proclaimed. "Ok, what happened next?"

"Well, I flipped through the pages and read a couple verses that made absolutely no sense, or at least, they were not relevant to me. So and so begat this guy, and so and so begat that guy."

"After reading those verses I shut the Bible and closed my eyes. After a couple minutes sitting there in silence..." he paused again struggling to find the right words to say.

"Go on," Rich encouraged him.

Tara reached over and placed her right hand on his leg as a show of support. She turned to William with a look of what could be best described as admiration.

"Tell him," she quietly prompted.

William shifted in his seat, obviously uncomfortable in describing the experience.

"I sat there in silence and tried to say a prayer in my head."

Rich simply smiled at William and inclined his head down as an indication for him to proceed.

"It really was the first time I think I've ever prayed in my entire life," he admitted with a confounded. "And I prayed with true intent...almost as if I had a tiny amount of faith."

"...for verily I say unto you, If ye have faith as a grain of mustard seed, ye shall say unto this mountain, Remove hence to yonder place; and it shall remove; and nothing shall be impossible unto you. Matthew, Chapter seventeen, verse twenty," Rich volunteered. "Even if you have but a particle of faith, anything can be made possible. The mysteries of God will be made known to you, and His will can be made manifest into your heart."

"How do I know if God is...trying to communicate to me, or tell me something?"

"That sensation that you described to me just now, that feeling of heat in your chest. That is the Holy Spirit working within you."

"Well if that's the case," William replied, "then he must have had a direct dial communication to me. I asked God if He would help me know what to do. And the very next moment, the sensation of heat coming from my chest," he stated while motioning with his hand toward his heart, "became almost overwhelming. It seemed to almost be emanating from this," he stipulated as he pulled the gold necklace that hung around his neck out from beneath his shirt, laying the amulet softly against his shirt.

Rich regarded the amulet and let out a barely audible grunt.

"This isn't the first time that you have experienced something odd with this Talisman, is it?"

"No," he admitted, "it isn't."

"Will," Tara blurted out with an incredulous expression on her face. "Why didn't you mention this before now?"

"I didn't think that it was important. Plus, I felt embarrassed to a certain degree," he admitted.

"Daddy," Tara spouted as she quickly turned to her

father. "I had almost an identical experience to what William is describing. The night of the Christmas party at the lab, when I passed out. I was looking out the window at those dark, ominous looking clouds that looked as if they were connected to the roof of a warehouse. When I was watching, I felt like the amulet around my neck was going to burn a hole in my chest."

Rich sat back in his chair, and brought his right hand up to face and grasped his chin tightly, deep in thought. After a minute, he crossed both of his thick arms in front of his barrel-like chest and let out an audible exhale through his nostrils.

"Remember how I told you that I had both of those Talisman consecrated by a Jewish priest? Well, the prayer that he spoke placed a blessing on those ornaments and infused them with *power* to ward off evil and evil spirits. If you both experienced the same sensation, then I would think," he paused again to choose his words, "then I would think that there is some sort of evil that is affecting the two of you."

"Well, that might explain the vision that I had then," William offered somewhat nonchalantly.

"Vision? What Vision?!" Rich virtually demanded.

"Well, as soon as I finished my prayer, I randomly opened the Bible up to the book of Revelations. Chapter twelve to be specific."

Both of Rich's eyebrows shot up so quickly that William thought they were going to pop directly off his head into the air above him. Leaning forward on the couch, he clasped both of his hands together as he rested his elbows on his knees.

"Go on," he asked with an intent expression on his face.

"Well, I started to read in verse four, and the sensation of heat intensified within my chest. And then...then...I know this is going to make me sound deranged, but air in front of me began to almost shimmer."

William paused again for a second to collect his thoughts. He didn't want to embellish the story, but he wanted to describe it in enough detail to get across the intensity of his experience. He leaned forward gripping his hands in front of him.

"At first, I couldn't figure out what I was seeing, but then it became apparent to me that it was as if I was looking into some sort of portal that was showing me images of some faraway place. Then, as the blurriness started to come more into the focus, the outer edges of the image began to expand in all directions until it completely encompassed the entire room and filled my field of vision."

"As I took in my surroundings I was certain that I was no longer in my bedroom, but I was in some far away landscape. A place that I had never seen before, but..."

He trailed off momentarily and bit his bottom lip lightly between his teeth. He looked over to Tara who was intently listening to every word that he uttered. William then turned back to Rich and continued.

"It was like I was seeing a location for the first time, but it also seemed eerily familiar...as if I had been there before. As I looked around I realized that I was standing in the middle of a very spacious field. There were sporadic trees scattered here and there, but for the most part, the ground was devoid of any vegetation."

"When I looked to my right, I saw a large grouping of pure white, billowing clouds, that was moving in my direction. To my left, I saw an almost equally large grouping of slow-moving clouds, but these clouds left an impression of a vile taint that I could literally feel, and almost taste."

"Then I started hearing faint noises which grew louder and louder. And images started to become visible within both sets of clouds. Within the white clouds, I beheld horses mounted by winged riders wearing brilliantly white armor, breastplates, helmets, and brandishing large silver gleaming swords. In sharp contrast, within the dark, ominous vapors on my left, I gazed upon creatures that exuded malignity. They were murky, almost shadowy entities that flew through the air on large, coarse wings and carried long black spears. It looked as if these creatures had some sort of tail trailing behind them."

The concern in Rich's expression was almost palpable. His eyes were squinting and his lips were tightly pursed. Further, he must have been gripping his hands in front of him with immense strength, as his knuckles were virtually white with no blood being allowed to flow into his flexed fingers.

William swallowed hard and proceeded to describe what he had experienced.

"Suddenly, I heard the pure piercing blast of a trumpet sounding off in the distance. Before the high-pitched tone of the trumpet had completed its formal announcement, I witnessed armed warriors colliding around me on all sides. I heard screams of anger and challenge. Clashing of steel upon steel. The nauseating sound of swords cutting through steel and burying itself into bone."

"I was frightened," William continued. "No, I was absolutely terrified. There was some sort of epic battle raging all around me and I had nowhere to go or hide. So, I crouched down, wrapped my arms around my knees, and tightly closed my eyes. I went on this way for no more than a minute, and then I reopened my eyes to view the horrific scene."

"At that very moment, I witnessed a soldier of some sort, wearing bright shining armor, flourishing an enormous broadsword over his head. He directed the force of his attack downward into some sort of creature that was cowering at his feet. As the sword sunk in and through the head, burying itself deep within the shoulders and upper torso of this...this animal, it let out a gurgling gasp of anguish as it fought to take in its last breath of life. Placing his right foot solidly onto the shoulders of the creature in front of him, the warrior violently pulled his sword directly from the body of his foe and kicked the lifeless form backward where it collapsed onto the ground in a clatter."

"This warrior seemed to have sensed that I was looking directly at him. He slowly turned his head toward my location, and that was when I realized that..."

Again, William paused, but this time for only a brief second.

"I realized that the face I was looking into was my own. That scared me even more than I had been already, and I squeezed my eyes shut again. The tumultuous noise grew louder and louder until I thought it was going to drive me completely insane. It was then that I stood up, raised my hands toward the sky and pleaded for someone, or something, to save me. To save me from what I thought was going to be my end."

Rich sat there in perfect silence and seemed to be holding his breath. Finally, he released his vice-like grip on the arms of his chair, allowing blood to rush back into his fingers. Leaning backward in his seat, he momentarily crossed his arms with a thoughtful expression on his face.

"Was that it?" he probed.

"Pretty much. What do you make of it?"

"William," Rich softly began, "I honestly believe that you experienced a vision. From what you just described, I can think of no other explanation than you witnessed the Great War in Heaven."

"A war in heaven?" he asked.

"No, not just a War, but The Great War in Heaven. You see, the Bible teaches us that there was a battle in heaven that ensued when Lucifer, who was once a choice angel, rebelled against God the Father. In fact, the very verses that you opened to and read in the book of Revelations describe that very event."

William had a dumbfounded look on his face and Rich immediately understood that he needed to provide more explanation.

"Let me try and explain this to you as succinctly as possible. God presented a plan to all of his children before we came to this earth. A plan that would allow us to learn through our experiences, and through the execution of our agency to choose between right and wrong. Good and evil. Lucifer didn't like God's plan because there would be many of His children that would be lost. So, Lucifer decided that he had a better idea, and that was that he would help man choose between right and wrong to ensure that we would not make bad choices. That we would not sin, and therefore, all of mankind would be able to return to God after this life."

"It doesn't seem that Lucifer's plan was necessarily an evil one," William postulated.

"On the surface, no. In fact, some believed that his plan was, in fact, a good one. And not just a few. There was a great number of the host of heaven that felt Lucifer's plan should be followed. This though was in contradiction to God's will. Lucifer sought to take the glory for himself and wanted to be the salvation for all mankind. When God rejected his approach, Lucifer became angry. So much so, that he enlisted that part of the host of heaven that supported his plan, and rallied them to his cause in so much that they raised up in rebellion against God himself. And that, William, is the cataclysmic event that you experienced in your vision. And from that event, we believe that one-third of the host of heaven was cast out of heaven. That Lucifer became the devil, and those who were cast out with him became his minions, as evil spirits and demons."

"And what about William seeing himself in that battle?" Tara cried. "What does that mean?"

"The only logical conclusion to come to," her father patiently replied, "is that William himself fought in that great battle against the forces of Lucifer."

William was clearly troubled by the explanation that Tara's father had just laid out in front of them. He took a deep breath, hesitated momentarily, and then blurted out his question.

"Why then when I asked...no, pleaded with God to help me to know what I needed to do in my life, did He show me this vision then? What does it all mean?"

"I don't know yet," Rich freely admitted. "However, I believe that God's purpose behind all of this will be made known to us shortly. And you, my dear boy, need to be ready to act when He asks you to take action."

CHAPTER 27

Second Chance
(April 2017)

Despite it being roughly ten thirty in the morning on a Wednesday, William found himself lying on his living room couch wearing a pair of sweats and a t-shirt, bundled up underneath a plaid patterned blanket. His hair was disheveled and he had what appeared to be at least five days of facial hair scruff growing on his cheeks and chin.

Tara confidently strode into the room, took the remote control from William's hand, and promptly turned the television off.

"Hey," William protested. "I was watching that!"

Tara temporarily ignored his comment, walked over where the flat panel rested and set the remote control on top of the counter. She turned back to face William with both of her hands placed firmly on her hips. The expression on her face was one that meant she was all about business.

"Yes, I know," she stipulated. "You were engrossed in this morning's broadcast of a riveting game show...right?"

William simply exhaled sharply while he rolled his eyes upwards.

"Seriously? Are you trying to tell me that one of the greatest scientific minds of this century, perhaps of all time, doesn't have a cleverer response than to just huff his breath?"

William's eyes shifted to meet the steady gaze that Tara threw in his direction, and averted them after a short moment.

Tara walked over to the couch and stood at the end where William's feet rested.

"Move'em or lose'em!"

Obediently, William raised his knees up toward his chest making enough room for her to take a seat. She sat down quietly and turned to face William, placing her hand on his leg.

"Sweetheart," she implored. "You've got to snap out of it. The last couple of months, all you have been doing is vegetating on this couch while your mind wastes away watching television. Will...are you listening to me?"

"Yes, I'm listening," he admitted while sitting up. "And I know you're right. But it's just so difficult. Only two years ago I was the CEO of an industry leading biotech startup with almost a hundred employees and millions of investment dollars flowing in. I was the talk of the scientific community. I was asked to write papers and make appearances. People respected and admired me. And then that all came crashing down when...Don," he virtually spat, "...announced to the world that he had created human clones. WITH MY STOLEN RESEARCH!" he shouted. "And then, my research wasn't of interest any longer. It seemed paltry in comparison to human clones. And as interest dropped, so too did the investment dollars and the company revenues. And then, three months ago all of our funding completely dried up and we had to close the doors for good on Mears Labs."

"All of my dreams came true and my greatest aspirations were realized. And now, everything is completely destroyed. And then that damned dream...that vision. That completely messed me up in the head, and I still find it hard to fall asleep at night, let alone stay asleep for fear of having nightmares. Your dad said that I had that vision for a reason. For some sort of purpose. Well, I'm failing to see what the purpose of that was except to make me a complete basket case, unable to motivate myself, figure out what to do next, or even just find a job."

Tara slid across the couch until she was sitting directly next to William, and wrapped her arm around his shoulders. Without any encouragement, William laid his head on her shoulder and let out a deep sigh.

"I know that you're depressed. Anyone would be! But there comes a time that it doesn't matter what I say, or anyone else for that matter, if you don't want to pick yourself up and try again."

She leaned back and framed his face between her two outstretched hands, gazing into his eyes.

"Will," she announced. "I love you. YOU! Not your research, not your fame or fortune, but you the person. I love your humor and your character. And I love that you love me back. I know that things seem overwhelming and you don't know where to start, but you're a brilliant man. All you need to do is put your mind to it and you can accomplish anything. I believe that with all of my heart!"

William responded with a half-hearted smile and took Tara's hands between his own.

"And what about the impact that the clones have had upon the world in general?"

He held up a newspaper that was lying on the table in front of him. In large letters, the headline on the front page read 'Violent Crimes Up 22%. Overall Crime Up 63%. Church Attendance Down 87%'. While holding the paper up he continued.

"This is not just happening here in the United States. This is occurring worldwide," he declared. "And my research paved the way for this. Every night when you turn on the news you keep hearing more and more about how the fabric of moral society is coming apart. I was at the mall last weekend and some lady recognized me and nearly accosted me. She started yelling at me about how my scientific breakthrough was killing God."

"You didn't kill God!"

"Really?" William disagreed. "It was because of my research that Don went down the path of creating a human clone. And his success in creating a clone brings into question whether or not God really exists. I mean, if man is able to create not just life, but human life, then what does that do to the idea that God is the creator of all things? And if man can create life, then what about the idea of a human soul? People will take that as proof that there is no such thing as a soul. Just a combination of electrical impulses and memories."

"It's not just a coincidence that the decline in church attendance and the increase in crime started to occur at the precise moment that the existence of a scientifically created human life form came to light. People were already rationalizing decisions between right and wrong. But now, I've indirectly put into question the very existence of God. The lack of a moral authority brings the age-old question of choosing between right and wrong to be one of complete personal choice."

"William," Tara quietly replied while gently stroking his hair, "you aren't the cause of what is going wrong in the world. If you had never thought of your research, someone else would have. It's inevitable that science was going to keep pushing the boundaries of cloning and ultimately someone was going create a human clone."

"So, does that mean there isn't a God then?"

"What does your heart tell you?"

"You know that I never believed in God before I had my...my vision. That experience changed my life forever."

"Well, I believe the same that you do. That there is a God. That He does exist."

"But what about science creating life? We aren't gods...we're just men and women."

"That's true, we're just men and women. But you have to remember that God gave us our minds to think, and the ability to learn, to be creative and to invent. Just because we're using the innate abilities that God gave us to our fullest potential, doesn't mean that God doesn't exist. In my mind, it actually means the opposite. I believe that every breakthrough in science, every invention, is something that He wanted us to achieve. Just because we figured out how to create a human life form doesn't mean that God doesn't exist. It just means that we have unlocked another mystery that until now, only God has known."

"But what about the human soul?"

Tara smiled at William, pulled him closer to her and placed a gentle kiss on his forehead. Leaning backward from him she looked sweetly into his eyes.

"Don't you think that God, who created the entire universe, the planets, stars, and all life forms, can place a soul into the body of a human form, even if he didn't create that human form? Our body is simply a vessel for our souls to dwell in."

A small smile appeared on William's face as he processed Tara's words. He took a deep breath and slowly exhaled with a slight sigh.

"Tara, you really are a wonderful woman. I don't think that I could get through all of this without you. And I really appreciate..."

The phone on the table next to the couch suddenly began to ring. William reached over and picked it up. An expression of utter disbelief appeared on his face as he looked at the caller ID. The phone rang a second, and then a third time.

"Will, who is it?" Tara prodded.

"Cenetics," he uttered in a hushed tone.

The phone rang a fourth time, and then the answering machine kicked in. After a couple seconds of silence, a voice on the other end of the phone started to leave a message.

"Ahhh...William. Hey, this is...Don. I know it's been a long time since..."

William quickly depressed the 'on' button and held the phone up to his ear.

"Don," he practically hissed into the receiver. "What do you want?" he demanded in a quiet voice.

William sat silently for nearly a full two minutes listening to Don's voice. Tara fidgeted back and forth nervously in her seat, straining to hear what was being said to no avail.

"I see," William finally stated. "How soon?"

Another brief moment of silence ensued, and William spoke again.

"Alright then. Tomorrow morning at nine. I'll see you then."

William slowly lowered the phone from his ear and pressed the 'off' button hanging up the line. His entire countenance had changed from just a few moments earlier where he seemed relatively lost, to one that now had renewed purpose.

"What was all that about?" Tara questioned.

"That was Don," he responded. "Something has happened at Cenetics with the clones...something bad. And he needs me to help him figure it out."

CHAPTER 28

Lion's Den

(The Next Morning)

The next morning, William found himself sitting on a black leather sofa located in the center of a large spacious lobby. In front of the couch, there was a low rectangular dark brown wooden table with numerous magazines and periodicals arranged in rows, lying neatly one upon another so the titles could be easily read. Flanking either end of the sofa were large silver pots roughly two feet in height, containing green, broad-leafed plants that rose approximately four feet above the level of dirt. To the right of where William sat was a smaller black leather love seat situated at the head of the rectangular table upon which Tara and her father were quietly seated. The lobby itself was nearly three stories tall, with enormous glass windows extending the entire length from floor to ceiling in massive panels, and had a revolving door situated directly in the center of the expansive wall.

To the left of the seating area, there was a large, dark cherry wood reception desk with two security guards sitting on raised swivel chairs. An attractive blond receptionist sat to the right of the guards and was busy surveying her face in a small mirror while she liberally applied a dark maroon lipstick.

William glanced down at his watch, noting to himself silently that it was nine ten in the morning. With somewhat of an exasperated expression on his face he turned toward Tara and her father.

"He's nearly ten minutes late," he stipulated in a level tone.

As if on cue, the door located behind the large reception desk swung outward, giving way to a man with dark, black hair splotched with grey here and there, khakis, brown shoes, and a neatly pressed white dress shirt.

William immediately recognized the familiar face of his old partner Don and his stomach tightened involuntarily. As William started to rise from his seat, the man called out to him.

"William!" Don nearly shouted. "It's so good to see you."

The sound of his voice made William visibly wince, but he quickly recovered as he straightened to a standing position and turned toward his greeter.

"Yes, it's good to see you again as well," he lied.

As the two men approached each other Don opened both of his arms in preparation to embrace his old friend. William had been intending to shake his hand and awkwardly hesitated in front of Don for a quick moment, but then responded in kind and the two men briefly embraced one another.

As William released his old friend, he turned back toward his two companions and motioned for them to come forward.

"You remember Tara of course," he asserted.

"Of course! How are you, Tara? It's wonderful to see you."

"And you as well," Tara politely replied.

"And this is Tara's father Rich Cline."

"Pleasure to meet you, sir."

"Likewise," Rich stated while extending his hand toward Don.

Don turned back to William with a somewhat puzzled expression on his face.

"I wasn't expecting that you were going to bring

company with you," he offered in as friendly a manner as possible. "It's not a problem of course, but I'd like for you and me to have a moment to discuss a few things in private before everyone can come back into the building. Is that alright?" he asked looking directly at Tara.

"Of course," Tara calmly replied. "We'll just sit out here while you two boys go catch up for a moment and take care of whatever it is that you need to."

"Are you sure?" William asked.

"Of course, we'll be totally fine out here."

"Thank you. We'll be as quick as possible," Don replied. "And then I'd be happy to give you both a personal tour of our facility."

Tara simply nodded in reply, and she and her father took a seat while both men disappeared back through the same doorway that Don had emerged from.

"What do you think that's all about?" Tara nervously questioned.

"Don't worry. I'm sure everything will be fine. The two of them have a quite a bit of history, and bad blood that they need to contend with. Give them a few moments and I'm sure they be back before we know it."

Tara picked up a random magazine from the table and diffidently starting thumbing through the pages as more of a distraction than actual interest in the content. Rich simply leaned back in his seat, folded his arms in front of him and closed his eyes.

About thirty minutes later William emerged from the same door he had previously entered. His countenance had completely changed from what one could have described as a combination of apprehension and hatred, to one of confidence and determination. He smiled broadly as he approached Tara.

"Ok," he stated. "Let's all head back into a conference room and I'll tell you what's going on."

Tara and Rich silently complied with William's request. They made their way back into the building, down a long hallway, and into a small conference room located at the end. Holding the door open William allowed his companions to enter the conference room and he quietly closed the door behind them.

"So?" Tara demanded. "What was all that about?"

"Please, take a seat first and I'll tell you all about it."

Both Tara and Rich took seats around a small circular table. William, however, remained standing, looking at both of them with a level of excitement in his eyes that Tara thought to herself she hadn't seen for a few months.

"Well? Are you going to tell us?" she impatiently demanded.

"Ok, ok...cool your jets. Everything is fine. Better than fine actually."

"What's going on?"

"Well," he began, "as you can probably imagine things were a bit uncomfortable at first. Neither of us really knew what to say or how to start saying it. I told Don that I was completely caught off guard, as was the rest of the world, with the news of his announcement about creating not just one, but six clone children. And how that announcement led to a decline in interest and the ultimate dissolution of Mears Laboratories. I told him that I was very angry with him and that he had dramatically impacted not just my life, but the lives of all of my employees."

"And how did he respond?" Tara inquired.

"He genuinely apologized for everything. He admitted that he leveraged, although he wouldn't go so far as saying he stole, the research that we worked on together, and that had been bothering him for quite some time. So much so that he decided to try and make things right between us."

"How so?" Tara pressed.

A big grin appeared on William's face in response to the question.

"He offered me a job!" he nearly shouted as he clapped his hands together. "And not just a job, but a leadership position here at Cenetics, with a large amount of equity in the company. And that's not even the half of it," he excitedly continued. "He said that I would be able to run my own research division and that I could hire back practically all of my prior employees at Mears. Isn't that wonderful?"

Rich who had been silently listening to the conversation unfolded his arms that were crossed in front of him and leaned forward placing his hands on a table.

"It almost sounds too good to be true," he cautioned. "Don't you think it somewhat suspicious that he didn't contact you about this before he needed you for some reason to help with the clones?"

"I know, it sounds almost too convenient. I told him as much when we were talking. But he already had paperwork drawn up detailing the specifics of my joining Cenetics."

"Will," Tara interjected, "that doesn't mean that he had them drawn up before the clone children started having whatever *problems*," she stated while making air quotations above her head to emphasize the word 'problems', "that they're experiencing. They could have been having issues for months and been unsuccessful in fixing things. And now they are bringing you in as a last resort."

"Well, whatever the reason, or the timing of the circumstance, all I know is that this feels right to me. Like

I'm supposed to be here. And I feel like I have a renewed purpose...and I'm finally excited again."

"Do you trust him?"

William pursed his lips thoughtfully for a moment as he looked down at the floor considering the question. Finally, with an audible exhale through his nostrils he looked back up at Tara.

"I can't say that I totally trust him...no. In fact, I would go so far as to say that I don't trust him at all. With that said, I don't know if I really have many options at this point to get myself back in the game. With Mears Laboratories a distant memory, and no active prospects on the horizon, this might be my best shot at being invited back to the rodeo."

Tara simply nodded toward William in response. The expression on her face was obviously one of doubt and suspicion, but she knew what William was saying was the truth.

William paused for a moment and then continued talking.

"Don actually called out that he knew I didn't have a good reason to trust him. Based on that, he had my contract drawn up in such a way as to provide me back-end protection."

"Back-end protection?" Tara asked. "What exactly is that?"

"Well, my agreement has specific language in it that clearly articulates that if Cenetics let me go, for any reason whatsoever, that I would be paid five years of salary, and ALL of my stock options would immediately vest."

"How much are they going to pay you?"

"Let's just say that I'll be pulling in north of three hundred thousand per year, with thirty-five percent yearly bonus, plus ever-greening of stock options to always keep me in the money."

Rich's eyebrows shot up on his forehead in response, clearly impressed by the size of the compensation package.

"That all sounds great," Tara responded. "So why exactly has he asked you to get involved in Cenetics? What's going on with the clones that has them so concerned?"

William pursed his lips momentarily before responding.

"He hasn't told me what exactly is going on with the children yet. Just that their behavior has changed somewhat dramatically over the past few weeks, and that there is something going on with them physically, at a cellular level, that they haven't been able to quite figure out."

A moment later there was a light tapping on the door which gently swung open revealing Don.

"How's everyone doing?" he inquired.

"Doing great," William replied. "I was just filling in Tara and Rich in on our conversation."

"I trust everything is good?" he anxiously asked looking directly at Tara.

"Everything sounds good so far," she coolly replied. Don visibly winced at the steady glare she threw in his direction. "I assume that William will have the opportunity to have a lawyer review the employment contract before having to sign anything, yes? You know, just to make sure that everything has been covered."

William threw Tara a somewhat annoyed sidelong glance, and then fixed his attention back on Don who was broadly smiling.

"Now I know why you brought Tara along with you.

She's here to represent your best interests and keep me honest." He laughed softly to himself before proceeding. "Of course, William can have the agreement reviewed. I actually encouraged him to do this to put to rest any concerns that he might have regarding my intentions."

Tara simply nodded in response to his comments.

"Of course," William interjected, "it will take a few days to get this reviewed. But I'd like to get started right away with trying to figure out what's going on with the children."

"Absolutely. Why don't the three of you come follow me?" Don offered as he started for the door. "Let's go to a different area of the building where one of our largest labs is located adjacent to the children's living quarters."

All three of the visitors complied with the request, closely following Don down the hallway. About twenty feet in front of the door leading back to the lobby, Don stopped short, turning to his left to face a large, white door with large black letters reading 'Security'. Pulling the badge that was hanging from his left pants pocket, he swiped it against a proximity reader, which was immediately followed by a high-pitched chirp and a loud clicking noise of the doors locking mechanism. Don grasped the handle, pushing the door inwards, and motioned for his three companions to follow.

Once on the inside of the room, Don closed the door behind them. The room itself wasn't that big, no larger than twelve by ten feet. On the right side of the room was a wall containing six enormous flat panel displays, each of which was segmented into twelve equally sized screens displaying various images from throughout the Cenetics complex.

"We'll need to get each of you set up with access badges before proceeding. Jim, can you set these fine people up?"

"Yes sir, Mr. Stafford," the security guard stated as he rose from a slightly raised swivel chair behind the table.

Jim was a young man, probably no older than twenty-five years of age. As he stood, William easily deduced why he had chosen the profession of security. The man was enormous, easily six feet, six inches tall. He looked to weigh at least two hundred and fifty pounds. His forearms were practically the size of William's thigh, and his all black, definitely XXL sized security shirt, looked one size too small. He reached into a drawer located on the desk in front of him and held out three access badges that appeared tiny as he cradled them in his gargantuan hands.

"Mr. Stafford," he continued. "Our guests will also need to be scanned if you are planning on taking them over to the children's quarters."

"Oh yes," he agreed, "thank you for reminding me. We have biometric scanners in addition to the proximity badges for the lab and living quarters. We take security extraordinarily serious here."

Don motioned to William to step up first.

"Just place your hand on this panel for a few seconds and we'll make a biometric fingerprint of each of you."

William, Tara, and Rich each scanned their hands, and within a couple minutes were back on their way heading down the hallway away from the lobby. After walking a short distance, Don took a right and an immediate left, stopping short of an elevator. He reached forward pressing the call button which resulted in an immediate 'ding' as the elevator doors slid open. Once inside, he pressed the '2' button on the elevator and after a brief ascent, they exited the lift and walked down a long hallway to their left.

Don led them all through a series of turns, doors, and hallways as they navigated their way deeper and deeper into the complex. As they walked Don commented anecdotally on the purpose of the various buildings and the different office areas and personnel located in each section. After what seemed ten minutes of hiking deep into the bowels of the Cenetics complex, the group turned a corner and came to a stop directly in front of two massive, stainless steel doors that reached the entire ten-foot length from floor to ceiling.

To the right of the door sat two grim-looking security guards behind a stainless-steel desk. The only thing adorning the desk were two flat panel displays, each accompanied by a keyboard and black mouse. One of the security guards immediately stood up and walked around from behind the desk, revealing a large handgun on his right hip strapped in a leather holster, and what appeared to be a Taser housed in a similar manner to his left hip.

"Hello, Mr. Stafford," he almost mechanically spoke. "I see you have visitors with you today. Everyone will need to be scanned of course."

He walked over to the left of the two doors where a large, black panel was located with the outline of a hand situated on top of an angled surface.

"Each of you will need to first swipe your access badge, and then firmly place your hand on the scanner. Once you hear a beep and see a green light, you will have successfully identified yourself."

"And if we don't get a green light?" Tara jokingly asked.

The security guard looked squarely at Tara and a thin grin creased his dry lips. Tara visibly shrank back from the enormous man, reaching for William's hand.

"Oh, don't worry," Don interjected, "everything is going to be fine. Let's get you all verified and we can proceed to the next area.

After about two minutes, all four members of their party had scanned their badges and successfully passed the biometric screening. Satisfied, the security guard nodded to the other guard still seated behind the desk, he responded by typing a few quick strokes on the keyboard in front of him, and then definitively hit the 'Enter' key with a solid thud.

Almost instantly, a loud 'CLICK' was heard from the two doors, and both slowly swung backward in an automated manner. Once the doors had opened sufficiently to allow access, Don quickly walked through them.

"Alright everyone, follow me."

This time, Tara was the first to respond. As she walked through the widening opening of the two massive doors, she cast a wary sidelong glance toward the massive security guard who was watching her with a smug expression on his face. Once everyone was completely inside the next room, the two doors methodically swung back to their starting position, accompanied by the same loud clicking noise signally that they were once again secured.

"This, my friends," Don stated in a somewhat grand manner, "is the entrance to the heart and soul of Cenetics."

The area inside of the two doors was actually quite small, roughly twenty-five feet wide and fifteen feet deep. Centered on the wall directly in front of them lay a set of stainless steel stairs approximately ten feet wide, leading up towards the third story level. Don immediately walked forward and started ascending the stairs, stopping momentarily on the third step to glance backward and confirm his companions were following.

After climbing the stairs, they found themselves at the end of a long, all white hallway that easily extended fifty feet in front of them.

"This way," Don uttered as he started walking.

As he followed Don, William glanced from side to side at the various photographs that were housed in massive, stainless steel frames every three or four feet. He immediately recognized the images in the photos as reflecting the various stages of the process that he and Don had perfected years earlier of the extraction of ESC cells and the imprinting process to create an embryonic clone. About halfway down the passageway the photos hanging on the walls showed tiny, newly formed embryos that he surmised were the six clone children. As they made their way further down the hallway the images continued to show the progression of the embryos through the various stages of the development lifecycle that every human child goes through as they are growing within their mother's womb.

"These photographs are of the clone children aren't they," Rich asked.

"Yes," Don agreed. "We wanted to make certain to fully document the entire process to remove any doubt that the children we created followed the exact same growth and development as any other child."

Rich responded by quirking his right eyebrow in a quizzical manner but held his tongue.

"When we get to the end of this walkway we have a series photographs of each of the six children showing what they looked like at birth, and then each year on their birthday."

As the group neared the end of the hallway they paused for a moment to survey the photographs hanging on the wall. Tara rested her index and middle finger of her right hand thoughtfully on the point of her chin as she regarded the photos. She turned slightly to her left to review another one, and then turned a hundred and eighty degrees to look at the frames on the opposite side. Finally, she turned toward William with a perplexed expression on her face.

"None of the children are smiling," she simply stated. "Even in the more recent pictures where the children have got to be ten or eleven years old, not one of them is smiling...not even a grin."

William furrowed his brow as he walked slowly toward the end of the hallway, and then stopped directly in front of a large, landscape, black and white photograph of all six of the children. In the center of the photo stood the one female child with the five male children clustered closely around her, reminding him of the first time he saw the children on television when Don announced them to the world.

The black and white photo seemed to accentuate the pale, white skin of each child. The hair of the children appeared so fair in the photo that it was difficult to delineate between where their skin ended and hair began. At least that was the case for the five male children.

The female child, on the other hand, had hair that appeared as dark as night, and equally dark pupils in her eyes. She stood almost a full foot taller than her five brothers, who stood with their bodies turned slightly in toward her. None of the five boys looked at the camera, but rather, they were cast in the direction of their sister in a furtive, almost deferential manner. She, however, was squarely facing forward with her head slightly declined, and her dark, black eyes boring into the lens of the camera through bangs that lazily hung across her face. William visibly grimaced as he felt as if the image of the girl was looking directly at him.

"Amazing, aren't they?" Don inquired breaking the silence. "I can't wait for you to meet them."

Without waiting for the group to respond, Don started making his way down an identical flight of stainless steel stairs to the ones they had climbed just moments before.

The group quietly followed him and ended up standing in front of another large set of stainless steel doors. This time, however, there were not any security guards or biometric scanners. As Don approached the doors, a soft click came from them as they unlocked, and silently swung outward allowing them to enter the next room.

As the doors swung open, it revealed a large, neatly arranged room with multiple rows of tables, upon which sat monitors, keyboards, and various pieces of scientific equipment. There were at least two-dozen men and women walking around the room wearing white laboratory coats, talking quietly amongst themselves. At the far end of the room, there was a large glass wall, stretching across the entire width of the room. Tables located directly in front of the wall were occupied with flat panel displays, and multiple cameras, all aimed at an angle down into the room on the other side of the glass.

"What is this place?" William inquired.

"This is what I like to refer to as Mission Control," Don announced in a grandiose manner. "And on the other side of that glass is our future."

CHAPTER 29

Observation Room

As the group made their way across the room, it became apparent to William that the space on the other side of the glass was actually two stories tall, with the observation area elevated above it so as to easily survey everything that was going on. As they neared the glass and looked down, they could see a room beneath them.

It was a large living space comprised of six smaller rooms, clustered around a large general-purpose area. The smaller rooms, approximately eight by ten feet, were separated by normally sized walls, however, none of them had a ceiling, allowing for anyone in the observation area to easily peer into them at all times. Each contained a twin-sized bed oriented on the wall opposite to the door leading from the common area. Each bed had a white comforter folded longwise along the base of the bed, a white bedspread, and two fluffy pillows with white pillowcases.

There was a small, light brown colored wooden desk situated at the foot of each of the beds. Each desk had a blue colored metal lamp extending up from a circular base of the same color, which curved out over the desk's surface. Arranged neatly across each of the desktops were various pencils, pens, and pieces of paper. A chair of the same light brown colored wood was positioned precisely in-between two sets of drawers. Against the same wall as the door sat a dresser containing four rows of drawers that extended across the width of the dresser. Each drawer had two large, blue, circular wooden knobs equally spaced from the middle. Situated directly above the dresser was a simple square mirror with a wood frame. A closet with two light colored wooden doors was positioned on one of the other walls.

Five of the rooms looked identical to one another with the exception of one whose closet doors sat wide open revealing neatly arranged white shirts and pants hanging from stainless steel hangers.

The sixth room stood in sharp opposition to the almost militant uniformity of the other five. The bed was unmade, with the white comforter and sheet hanging sloppily off the side of the bed closest to the door. One of the pillows was jammed into the corner between the headboard and wall, and the other one lay on the floor next to the dresser. Pens and pencils laid scattered across the surface of the desk and a few laid on the floor next to the chair which sat back about eight inches from the desk. Multiple pieces of paper were crumpled into balls lying across the desk. On the center of the desk sat a single sheet of paper with what appeared to be black, scribbled lines with various shapes drawn on it.

Rather than hanging neatly in the closet, white clothing laid in rumpled heaps on the floor, and one of the dresser drawers was hanging wide open revealing a drawer full of white socks that had been lazily thrown into it. And centered on top of the dresser was a black hairbrush.

The large area lying in-between the bedrooms looked to be forty by forty feet in size. In the exact center of the room sat a rectangular table with six chairs arranged neatly around it. In the back-left corner sat a large flat screen television sitting on top of a stainless-steel stand. Half a dozen beanbag chairs were arranged neatly in an arc on the floor about seven feet back from the television. Against the walls in-between the doors leading to the bedrooms were a total of six, stainless steel tables, each containing a twenty-seven-inch iMac computer, keyboard, and wireless mouse. Situated in almost a haphazard manner were three, dark brown couches with two burgundy pillows lying on top in opposite corners.

High up above the room were multiple rows of large, fluorescent light fixtures that illuminated the entire room. On the outside wall to the right of the living space were two large, stainless steel doors with the words 'Boys' and 'Girls' written on either one. On the wall located directly opposite the observation room were large, stainless steel double doors, each with a thin, rectangular window positioned vertically along the side of each door and directly above a stainless-steel doorknob.

"This," Don announced, "is where most of our research occurs. As you can see, the children have everything that they could possibly need."

"Except a little privacy," Tara commented in a sarcastic tone.

"Oh," Don lightly chuckled in response, "don't worry. The children are afforded all the proper accommodations to ensure privacy," he stated as he motioned over to the right side of the room. "There are absolutely no cameras and no personnel allowed into the bathrooms. Each has their own changing rooms, showers, and other accommodations that they require. "

"I guess," Tara replied obviously not convinced.

She looked around the room with a somewhat confused expression on her face and then turned back to face Don.

"Where are the children?"

One of the scientists sitting at the table on the right side of the observation room stood up and approached the group.

"The children are currently on a field trip," she

announced. "Each day we give them a few hours outside of this facility to go to the park, go to a museum, or any other different type of activity."

"Who is supervising them?" Tara pressed.

"That would be their mother of course," she casually replied.

William's stomach involuntarily clenched as he realized that she was referring to Kim. The thought didn't occur to him that he would in all likelihood need to interact with her on a somewhat regular basis.

"When do you expect them back?" Don asked in an excited tone.

"They should be back any minute now."

"Why are all the rooms neat and tidy except for that one?" Tara probed as she motioned to the left side of the room.

"Oh, that's Clarissa's room," the scientist responded in a flat tone. "We've given up on trying to get her to keep her things picked up. She's definitely marching to her own drum beat."

Just then, the large stainless-steel doors on the opposite wall started to swing slowly outward in an automated manner revealing a well illuminated, but empty, hallway on the other side. As the doors came to a gentle stop signifying that they were fully open, you could barely see a small, white pair of sneakers come into view at the far end.

While the first pair of sneakers started making their way up the hallway, two more sets flanking either side appeared behind the first, to be followed by another two pair a moment later. As the five sets of shoes made their way toward the living quarters, the identity of the wearers was gradually revealed.

Each of them wore neatly pressed, stark white slacks,

with crisp creases precisely down the center of each pant leg. A few moments later you could see equally whiter than white short-sleeved polo shirts, with sharply folded collars. The arms extending out of the sleeves looked as if they hadn't seen more than fifteen minutes in the sun, as they were extraordinarily fair and slightly pinkish in tone.

The faces of the children were finally viewable as they approached the opening into the living quarters, revealing that these were, in fact, the five male clone children. Their alabaster faces matched the fairness of their arms, and were framed by hair that would be considered long by a boy's standard, that was as white as freshly fallen snow. The expression on their faces was virtually lifeless. They all gazed down toward their feet, and as they shuffled into the room, each clasped their hands behind their backs and made their way silently to the table located at the center of the room.

A sixth pair of shoes suddenly appeared at the end of the hallway. But rather than being sneakers, they were a pair of white shiny leather, white Mary Jane style shoes. As opposed to the five male children, the legs of this sixth child were bare, as she wore a pleated white skirt that extended to her knees. As she approached the doorway she was wearing a similarly white blouse. When she came more fully into view you could see extremely dark, black as night, straight hair cascading about halfway down her torso.

As she neared the doorway her face came into clear view. In sharp contrast to the almost demure expressions on the boys, her visage was one of anger, almost outright aggression. Looking directly in front of her she confidentially strode into the room and stopped short after about ten steps. She brought her hands upward and rested them on her hips, while at the same time slowly inclining her head to survey the group of individuals gathered around the windows. Her gaze painstakingly shifted across the onlookers and abruptly halted when her eyes locked with those of Tara's father.

Rich involuntarily swallowed hard in response but managed to flash a friendly smile.

With an expression of disgust, the young girl's eyes narrowed slightly and she briefly shook her head. Her stare seemed to pierce directly into the back of the larger man's skull until he had to forcibly avert his eyes.

Seemingly satisfied by his reaction, the girl walked to the center of the room, however, about three feet from the table she veered to her right and walked straight into her bedroom and firmly shut the door behind her.

"Well then," Rich commented. "She's just a bucket of rainbows and sunshine, isn't she?"

Before anyone could respond, the faint clicking sound of a woman's high heels could be heard coming down the hallway. A pair of black leather, high-heeled shoes made their way toward the living quarters revealing olive colored skin that extended upward then stopped about one inch above the knee where a jet-black leather skirt began. She was wearing a deep, almost royal purple, long sleeve silk blouse.

William couldn't help but think to himself about how attractive her figure was. However, this feeling was abruptly halted the next moment when the individual entered the room, stopped and crossed her arms, as she surveyed the surroundings.

Trying his best to hide his emotions, William distastefully acknowledged the individual silently in his mind...."Kim Dyson."

CHAPTER 30

Meeting the Children

The group made their way down a short hallway, walking toward the set of two stainless steel doors that led into the children's living quarters. A motion sensor detected their presence roughly fifteen feet before reaching the doors and they began to slowly open outward. As they entered the room, William noticed that the five boys who had previously been sitting around the rectangular table in the center of the room had made their way over to the bean bags situated in a half circle around a large flat panel television screen watching some sort of nature show. Each of them had a clipboard on their lap with a few sheets of paper, and each held a pencil in their left hand.

An attractive female scientist, with brown, shoulder length hair wearing thin, black-rimmed glasses, sat on a small wooden chair to the right of the television quietly giving them directions for what they needed to be watching for in the program. Her white lab coat was hung across the back of her chair, and she wore blue jeans and a reddish colored blouse with small blue dots. Leaning forward, she rested her forearms on her knees with her fingers interlaced together.

Kim Dyson was not in the common area, and William surmised that she must have gone back into the girl's room. As the group approached the children, the scientist paused to acknowledge their visitors.

"Children," she intoned with perfect enunciation, "it looks like we have some visitors today."

The heads of all five boys swiveled to their right in

virtually perfect unison to look at their visitors. None of them spoke, smiled, or showed any emotion of any kind whatsoever.

"Good morning children," Don stated. "How are we doing today?"

There was a moment of awkward silence while everyone waited for some sort of response. However, after a period of about ten seconds, each of the children turned their heads back toward the television in unison to continue watching the program on the screen.

Don showed a momentary grimace but quickly recovered himself before continuing with introductions.

"Nancy, let me introduce you to William Mears."

A startled expression flashed on the research scientists face, followed immediately by a bright, broad smile.

"Doctor Mears," she gushed. "It is an absolute pleasure to meet you. I have followed your work very closely over the years. You have completely changed the field of therapeutic cloning. I'm so honored to meet you," she stated as she rose from her seat and extended her hand toward William.

"Well thank you, Nancy," William responded as he grasped her hand.

William noted to himself that she had relatively large hands for a woman and an almost bone-crushing grip as she gripped his hand.

"That's quite a grip you have there," William joked.

"Oh, I'm so sorry," she replied with a slight flushing to her face. "I'm just so excited to meet you! Your research has had such a significant impact on the medical community."

William's face slightly reddened at the woman's over the

top reaction. To cover his own embarrassment, he turned to his left to introduce the rest of his party.

"Let me also introduce you to my wife, Tara Cline, and her father Rich."

"Pleasure to meet both of you," she responded, taking a moment to shake each of their hands.

"Nancy is one of our lead biochemists. She also has a degree in advanced children's psychology which gives her the unique opportunity to not just work behind the scenes looking into a microscope, but also to engage directly with the children."

"That's quite an impressive resume," William replied.

"I think I've got some extraordinarily good news for you Nancy," Don continued. "William has just agreed to join our team, and is going to help head up the research division."

Nancy's face lit up as she loudly clapped her hands together in excitement.

"That's wonderful!" she gushed. "It's going to be wonderful working closely with you!"

Tara shot William a sidelong glance with a crooked eyebrow, causing him to involuntarily swallow in response. He turned his attention back to Don giving him an excuse to break eye contact.

"Why don't we all take a seat over in the middle of the room to discuss the children," Don stated. "Nancy, are you alright leaving the children for a few minutes to bring William up to speed on them?"

"Absolutely!"

"Dad and I can sit over here with the children while you go talk shop a bit," Tara offered.

"You sure?" William replied.

"Not a problem," she assured him. "Is it ok for us to talk with the children?" Tara directed toward Nancy.

"That would be fine. With that said, don't expect a whole lot of interaction with them. With multiple childbirths, especially in the case of quadruplets or higher, the siblings tend to have a single, dominant child...an alpha if you will. With our group, that would definitely be Clarissa. And with her back in her bedroom, the boys are likely to just keep to themselves."

Don, William, and Nancy made their way to the center of the living quarters, leaving Tara and her father with the children. Tara took the seat that Nancy had been occupying moments earlier and turned her attention to the children, while Rich stood slightly outside the grouping of beanbags.

"Hello children," she chimed in a friendly, high pitch voice. "My name is Tara. It's very good to meet all of you."

Not one of the children showed any response to her voice.

"Would you like to tell me your names?"

Silence.

"This is a pretty neat setup that you boys have here with your beanbags and television, don't you think?"

None of the children showed any acknowledgment of either Tara or Rich, but rather, sat there staring intently at the screen that flashed images of some wild animals on a plane likely on the African continent.

Tara pursed her lips momentarily while she thought silently to herself. The next second, her eyebrows shot up as if she had a brilliant idea.

"I know...why don't we play a game? What game would you like to play?"

Not one of the children showed any reaction to anything that Tara said. One of them scribbled a note on the sheet of paper pinned on his clipboard and glanced at the other boys. As if by some sort of silent communication or telepathy, the other four boys lifted their pencils and also scrawled something on the paper in front of them, then returned their gaze to the television set.

Tara looked up at her father with an expression of helplessness, to which he responded with a slight shoulder shrug and a thin smile.

Turning back to the children Tara slowly rose from her seat, clasping her hands in front of her.

"I tell you what boys," she continued in as equally bright a tone of voice as she had initially, "I'm going to go stand over here for a moment to talk with my Dad. If you need something, just let me know."

Each of the children continued to stare at the screen showing absolutely no emotion on their faces.

"Alright then, I'll just be right over here," she stipulated as she walked to the left of the bean bags and motioned for her father to join her about ten paces away from the children.

As Rich approached Tara, he flashed a quick grin at his daughter.

"Well," he whispered in a hushed tone of voice, "she did say not to expect much in the form of interaction, didn't she?"

"I know. But that was ridiculous," she replied in as equally a quiet voice. "I don't think I even saw them blink," she jokingly commented.

Rich furrowed his brow momentarily before continuing.

"I can't quite put my finger on it, but there's something

slightly off with those boys. It makes we wonder," he paused.

"Wonder what?" Tara pressed.

Rich stood there silently for a moment as he considered the situation before responding.

"It makes we wonder if it has something to do with the fact that these 'children' were cloned. Makes we wonder if...if there's something different about them. You know...different than a normal child."

"They seem like normal children to me. Maybe a bit socially awkward, but who wouldn't be," she stated motioning to the room around them, "growing up in an environment like this."

Rich stood there quietly for a moment considering his daughter's words.

"Maybe you're right," he finally agreed. "It is quite a sterile environment."

Tara simply nodded in response.

"Why don't you check in on William to see how much more time they need?" Rich offered. "I think I'm about ready to leave Cenetics."

"Ok. You stay here and I'll go check."

Rich watched as Tara walked back over to where the other three were sitting, actively engaged in a conversation. She walked up and stopped short behind them, waiting for an opportunity to interrupt.

With Rich's focus on his daughter, he didn't notice that one of the five boys had risen up and made his way noiselessly over to where he stood, stopping roughly one foot directly behind him. He stood there silently for almost a full sixty seconds before Rich felt his stare on the back of his head.

As he slowly turned around, he looked down and into the eyes of a boy that looked to be ten years old. He was blankly staring up directly into the eyes of the large man. His expression remained as placid as it had previously been when the children were first introduced to their visitors. However, this time there was an almost imperceptible difference...one that could only be described as a faint awareness.

Rich stood there motionless, in an almost trancelike state, finding himself unable to move much less breath. As he stared into the black, abyss of his eyes, he thought he could see a slight swirling of motion reflected in the pupils. The spinning seemed to intensify, and then abruptly stopped.

Caught up in the gaze of the small child, Rich was completely unaware that the boy's right hand was reaching forward and slightly upward until it gently rested on his own left hand which loosely hung by his side.

Instantly Rich felt a strong sense of nausea sweep over his body starting from the top of his head, down through his stomach and legs, and out of his toes. He consciously blinked, and when he opened his eyes, the child appeared as if he were wrapped in a dark, thick, undulating mist, that seemed to envelop the outline of his figure. The vapors slowly oozed in a counterclockwise direction around the boy, slightly extending outward, and then contracting upon itself. Slightly darker swirls appeared in the dark mist momentarily and then disappeared again.

It took all of Rich's will to squeeze his eyes shut, and when he reopened them he felt as if he would shriek in absolute terror at what stood before him. The dark, seething mist remained, but rather than encircling the boy's body, it now encased what could only be described as a translucent shell...an almost cocoon-like structure. Within the semi-transparent outer casing resided a massive, hulking entity that Rich could only describe as demonic in nature, seemly bound by a shell that was three times too small.

The creature had broad, muscled shoulders that extended down to large biceps, sinewy forearms, and enormous hands. On the end of almost skeletal like fingers extended five-inch jagged nails that were as black as the dead of night. Wing-like appendages wrapped around the torso and extended halfway down the legs of this unnatural beast, each tipped with what appeared to be long, sharpened hooks. Due to the constrained space, the demon was squatting down on massive, rippled legs, that sat atop almost eagle-like feet, each sporting three finger-like toes and opposable thumbs ended with blunt black blades.

The head appeared to have almost been compressed downward upon itself. It was unnaturally short in length and abnormally wide. There were long gashes located on either side of the head where ears would have been expected to reside. The long, slack mouth, adorned with dark, vile lips was tightly closed and drawn downward in more of a grimace than a frown. The head itself was slightly inclined down toward the floor, and Rich frantically searched the face for some sign of life.

As if in response to his thoughts, the eyelids of the creature cracked open slightly and nostrils sitting upon a broad, grotesque nose seemed to flare as if it was taking in a breath of the vile, seething vapor. The head then began to slowly angle upward as if a predator were zeroing in on its prey. The narrow, eyeless slits, appeared as if they were staring into Rich's wide gaze.

Suddenly a deep rumble seemed to collide with the air immediately around Rich, causing him to feel as if he were going to be thrown back across the room and into a wall. Instead, he remained standing, frozen in place, unable to breathe or avert his eyes from the events playing out. Both eyes of the evil creature then widened, exposing large black eyes with deep, almost blood colored, diamond shaped pupils. Rich opened his mouth to scream, but no sounds came out. The demonic animal then opened its gaping maw exposing rotten, decaying razor teeth and emitted the most horrific shriek that Rich could have ever imagined possible, carrying with it a sense of hatred, despair, and death.

Rich clenched his eyes shut and opened his mouth, but this time he surprised himself by the sound of his own shriek piercing his ears. He immediately opened his eyes and found himself standing in the middle of the room, completely by himself. He stared in amazement at the boy who had been standing in front of him, but who now sat back amongst the other four children around the television set.

Tara looked at her father with an expression of fear and concern, while the others sitting around the table all jumped up and starting to make their way toward the trembling man. But before they could get to his side, the large man's eyes rolled back into his skull, and he tumbled backward unconscious onto the floor, lying there motionless as if he were dead.

CHAPTER 31
Aftermath

A small group was clustered around a dark brown couch located off to the side of the living quarters situated directly beneath the observation window perched high above the room. Tara sat sideways on the couch clasping the right hand of a large, unconscious man with tears streaming down her reddened cheeks. A few moments earlier William and Don had physically dragged Tara's father roughly fifteen feet from the spot where he had collapsed on the floor. Don was speaking harshly into his cell phone requesting paramedics be brought as quickly as possible, while William nervously paced the floor.

"He seems to be breathing," Tara cried, "but he won't wake up. Oh, Daddy, please wake up," she pleaded while tightly gripping his large hand.

"Did anyone see what happened?" William demanded.

"Nothing," Don admitted. "One moment he was just standing over there," he stipulated while pointing with his right hand toward where the five boys still sat in their bean bags, "and the next thing we heard was the sound of him screaming just before he fell to the ground."

Tara reached up with her left hand to gently stroke the side of her father's head. Cautiously, she touched a slightly reddened, raised area close to his right temple.

"Looks like he's going to have quite the goose egg," she offered in as light-hearted a manner as she could muster, like a mother reassuring a child.

The two stainless steel doors leading into the living quarters suddenly started to open, revealing two emergency medical technicians pushing a wheeled gurney that had two large black bags sitting on top. The children momentarily turned to watch the gurney zip by and then turned back again to focus on the television.

"Ok everyone, please make way and let us do our jobs," one of the technicians announced.

Tara obediently complied with the request and stood up, although she only moved about two steps from where her father lay.

One of the technicians unzipped a black bag, removed a blood pressure cuff and quickly slid it upward on Rich's right arm being careful to place it in the correct position. He then began to vigorously squeeze the black bulbous pump connected to the cuff to increase the pressure on the arm. The room was totally silent except for the monotonous narration that could be faintly heard coming from the television.

"Eighty-five over forty," the man called out.

"That's really low, isn't it?" Tara exclaimed.

"It's lower, but not too low as to overly concerned us," the other technician stated.

An instant later, Rich's eyelids fluttered slightly, and then both slowly opened. The pupils of his grey colored eyes constricted in response to the bright room, and he shifted his head from side to side to see where he was. As he tried sitting up, the technician who had just taken his blood pressure placed his right hand lightly on his chest.

"Easy does it," he instructed. "You've had a bit of a spill, and we want to make sure that everything checks out before we let you up and about."

Rich complied with the request and eased himself back gently to the couch.

"What happened?" he demanded. "And why is my head

throbbing?" he barked while lightly touching his right temple.

"We're not really sure," William admitted with a perplexed expression on his face. "We were going to ask you the same thing. All of us were discussing the current situation of the children, and the next thing we heard was you screaming right before you fell to the floor. What do you remember?"

Rich sat for a second quietly racking his brain to try and remember. After a brief moment, he shook his head slowly from side to side with an exasperated expression on his face.

"I don't remember anything," he finally stated. "Not a single dang thing."

The door leading into Clarissa's room suddenly opened and Kim noisily stomped out and approached the group.

"What's all the commotion about?!" she demanded. "I was trying to talk with Clarissa about something that was bothering her."

Tara spun on her heels to face Kim with an appalling glare in her eyes.

"Oh, I'm sorry we bothered you," she spat at her former friend. "We didn't mean to inconvenience you with my Dad's medical emergency."

Kim glared directly back into Tara's eyes, and then shifted her gaze to take in the scene playing out in front of her. Finally, both her expression and tone of voice changed to one that could best be described as moderate compassion, sprinkled with sour grapes.

"I'm sorry. Is your father alright?"

Stepping directly in-between the two women, William tried to diffuse the situation before it escalated any further.

"Alright, now...I'm sure she didn't mean anything. She just didn't know the situation."

Tara let out a light huff and Kim icily stared at her with a thin, almost snakelike smile. After a brief moment, Kim turned around and walked slowly back to the girl's bedroom.

The medical technician continued to survey Rich from head to toe, trying to identify if he had any other injuries besides the bump on the side of his head.

"Go ahead and sit up," he politely ordered.

As Rich began to sit up his head started to swim a little bit. Ignoring the disorientation, he sat completely up and faced his examiner.

"Let me take a look at you to see if you have any other injuries."

He quickly scanned his right arm and hand, and then shifted his attention to Rich's left arm. He stopped for a moment to examine his left hand.

"What's this?" he politely questioned. "Was this there before?"

On the top of his left hand, there were four small, reddish colored ovals arranged in a slight arc, with a fifth red dot sitting slightly off to the side. Rich looked down at his hand and returned a puzzled expression to the medical technician.

"I don't know," he admitted.

The examiner lightly touched the discolored skin.

"Does that hurt or feel uncomfortable at all?"

"Nope."

"It might just be a rash of some sort," he finally commented in an unconcerned tone of voice. "Do you feel ok enough to try and stand?"

Without replying, Rich placed both hands on either side of his legs and pushed himself up into a standing position. Once fully erect he felt another brief spell of disorientation that quickly passed.

"How's that?" Rich offered.

"Very good. Can you walk?"

With his head feeling clearer, Rich tentatively took one step...then another...until he was cautiously walking from side to side in front of the group.

"I feel fine," Rich stated.

"Are you sure Daddy," Tara inquired.

As he walked back toward the couch, another dizzy spell swept over Rich causing him to stagger slightly.

"Pretty sure," he stated. "But just to be safe, why don't I just sit down here for a moment to rest, and then we can go home."

Rich took a seat back on the couch, folding both of his arms in front of him, and Tara sat next to him.

William walked over to Don, taking his left arm in his right hand to pull him close.

"Your guys were recording everything from the observation room, right?" he whispered into his ear. "Let's take a look at the tape to see if anything out of the ordinary happened."

"Great idea," he agreed. "Come with me."

Both men made their way back to the observation booth leaving everyone else in the children's living quarter. Once in the room, Don walked over to the right side of the observation window where a man wearing a white cloak sat in front of a bank of three flat panel screens.

"Can you bring up the last thirty minutes of recording on the monitors?"

"Sure thing," he replied. "Just one second."

The images on the screen flickered as he rewound the recording to thirty minutes earlier. On the screen, you could see the five male children sitting around the table at the center of the room, and Clarissa was just entering the living quarters. As she placed her hands on her hips the images on the screen flickered momentarily, but then were normal again as she started to make her way toward to the table and ultimately her own room.

"What was that," William asked the scientist sitting at the table.

"Looks like some sort of electrical feedback or something," he guessed.

"Ok. Go ahead and fast forwarded to the point where Rich collapses," Don ordered.

"Sure thing."

The images on the screen danced forward at five times normal speed as they zipped forward on the recording.

"There!" Don stated. "Play it at normal speed now."

The images on the screen showed Tara standing close to her father. The next moment, she turned and walked over to where William, Don, and Nancy were seated. Rich simply watched as she made her way over to the table. Suddenly, the images on all the television screens flickered and showed nothing but grey static.

"What happened to the picture?"

"I have no idea," the scientist commented in a slightly flustered tone.

The static images on the screens lasted for approximately forty seconds and then went away showing the room as it was before, but this time Rich lay unconscious on the ground. The scene continued to play itself out with William and Don lifting Rich and dragging him over to the couch.

"Rewind the tape to where we lost the image," Don ordered.

Without comment, the man sitting at the table complied with the request and the images on the screen flickered momentarily and then showed Rich once again facing the table. Just as it played out the first time, monitors showed multiple angles of him standing, watching his daughter walk back towards the group, and then, exactly as it occurred the first time, all the screens showed static at the exact same moment lasting roughly forty seconds, until they once again showed a clear image of Rich lying unconscious on the floor.

"Whatever it was, it affected all of the cameras at the exact same time."

Turning back to others sitting in the observation room Don continued.

"Was anyone watching the floor?" he called out.

All of the research scientists remained silent, a few of them negatively shaking their heads from side to side. Clearly frustrated, Don spun back around to address the man sitting in front of the monitors.

"See if you can do anything to get those images, and let me know the instant that you do."

The man simply nodded and turned back to face the monitors.

Looking down into the room, William saw that the medical personnel had already departed. Nancy had returned to sit with the children who continued to stare at the television screen, and Tara sat in a chair across from her father who sat leaning forward with his large forearms resting on his knees.

"It's the strangest thing," Rich commented. "I don't remember a single thing. One minute I was watching you, and the next I was waking up lying here on this couch."

"Don't worry about it," she sympathetically responded. "I'm just glad that you're ok."

Rich shook his head back and forth as Tara stood up and walked over to where the children were located.

He paused for a moment and glanced down at the top of his left hand where the five red dots remained. The skin on his left hand started to feel slightly warm and then became a little itchy as the intensity of the heat increased. Instinctively, he rubbed the top of his left hand in response and looked over at his daughter who was now standing to the side of the children.

He shifted his gaze to the children who all sat facing away from Rich. As he scanned from right to left, he paused as his line of sight fell upon the fourth child. Almost as if the child knew that he was being observed, the boy turned his head back over his right shoulder and locked his eyes with those of Rich.

Rich blinked and when his eyes reopened it looked as if a dark aura appeared around the outline of the boy who was still staring back at him. A feeling of nausea swept over him once again, and the burning sensation on his left hand intensified. He clenched his eyes shut and when he opened them the black haze had disappeared from around the child.

Rich's mouth stood slightly open in disbelief at what he had just experienced. Seemingly aware of his thoughts, a brief grin creased the corners of the boy's mouth who then turned back to face the television screen. Rich continued to stare at the boy, not noticing that the burning sensation had ceased emanating from the red marks on his hand.

CHAPTER 32

Dark Influence
(Six Months Later)

William found himself working in a laboratory at Cenetics around nine o'clock on a Thursday evening. The lab was completely empty except for William and his assistant Nancy. Both of them were hunched over the same table looking through the eyepieces of two different microscopes.

"Oh...that's it," Nancy announced, sitting up in her chair and raising both arms above her head as she stretched out the aching muscles in her back. "I need to take a break or my eyes are going to pop out of my head and explode right here on the counter."

William simply chuckled in response.

"Do you want something from the kitchen?"

"No thanks," William replied. "I'm probably going to spend about another thirty minutes and then call it quits for the day."

"Ok. I'll be right back."

Nancy stood from her chair and exited the lab from a door located at the back of the room.

William continued to peer into the microscope at the specimen in the glass. Sitting back in his seat he took a deep, revitalizing breath then removed the slide sitting on top of the microscope stand and placed it on the tabletop to his right.

Reaching into a box of microscope slides, he removed a new, clear slide without any specimen. After gently placing it on the table in front of him, he reached forward and grasped a test tube with a rubber stopper affixed to the top, and raised it in front of his eyes to read the label.

'Blood Specimen #00101821 – Clarissa – April 7, 2015', he silently read to himself.

While holding the test tube in his left hand, he picked up a syringe from the table with his right hand and carefully inserted the long needle into the test tube. After removing about three cubic centimeters from the vial, he carefully placed the test tube back into its rack.

Holding the glass slide on the table between the thumb and index finger on his left hand, he placed two small drops of blood onto the center of the glass and immediately capped it with a clear plastic slide cover. The drop of blood on the center of the glass slide immediately spread outwards toward the edges of the slide cover making a very thin layer of blood for him to examine.

Carefully, he lifted the newly created slide specimen and set it on top of the microscope table, pinning it beneath two metal brackets to ensure it stayed in place. Satisfied that the slide was secure, he turned the magnification filter on the rotator to select the least powerful magnification lens.

Looking through the eyepiece he regarded an indistinguishable blurry image. With his right hand, he gently turned a large knob causing the image to gradually shift until he saw a red colored liquid. Carefully turning a smaller knob, he adjusted the view until the image was crystal clear.

William made a barely audible 'humph' to himself and then rotated the lens to the next level of magnification. After going through the same steps as before, the image through the eyepiece finally revealed a much closer view of the liquid. This time, however, he could see some of the outer structures of the blood cells contained within the sample.

Finally, he rotated the magnification filter to the highest setting and repeated the same steps. As the image came into sharp focus William could clearly see individual blood cells floating within the plasma, as well as the interior structures of each red blood cell, including the hemoglobin.

As he gazed through the eyepiece at blood cells freely floating through the plasma, he noticed something that didn't look exactly right.

'The blood cells appear to be darker than normal', he thought to himself.

Sitting back from the microscope he scribbled a few thoughts into his notebook, paused to gaze back through the eyepiece, and then continued to write a few more. After committing his comments to paper, he sat back in his chair pinching his chin pensively between his index finger and thumb.

An idea suddenly popped into his head. Leaning over, he picked up a stand containing seven similar test tubes from another table and placed it directly in front of him. Searching through the vials he found the one he was looking for and held it to easily read the label.

'Blood Specimen #07204831 – Don Stafford – March 2, 2015', he read silently in his head.

Taking a new syringe, he carefully withdrew three cubic centimeters and placed it onto a clean microscope slide. After covering it with a clear cover he placed it on a separate microscope located on the same table. After going through the same process, he found himself looking at an ultra-magnified view of red blood cells floating across the field of view.

"The color of these blood cells is much brighter...even

though the sample is older," he quietly whispered to himself. "The newer sample should be brighter given a higher oxygen content level."

Leaning forward in his seat, he once again wrote down a few comments in his notebook regarding his observations.

"I wonder," he softly spoke.

He took a third microscope slide and introduced a single drop of Clarissa's blood, and a single drop of Don's blood directly next to it, and very carefully covered them both with a slide cover. The two samples of blood slowly oozed together.

Removing a slide from off of one of the microscope decks, he quickly replaced it with the combined sample. Just as before, he repeated the steps until he was able to clearly see red blood cells floating across his field of view.

Carefully looking through the eyepiece, all of the blood cells appeared to be of the same, brighter red color. For a moment, he thought he caught a brief glimpse of a somewhat darker object, but it quickly disappeared.

William was focusing so intensely on the microscope he didn't notice that Nancy had quietly entered the lab. She paused at the table in the back of the room staring suspiciously at William. After a few seconds, she gently placed a plastic bottle of water along with a chocolate bar on the back table and noiselessly crept toward William until she stood directly behind him.

Completely unaware of Nancy, William continued to gaze through the lens. His patience finally paid off as he spotted a darker red blood cell moving into the field of view. It meticulously floated across and toward the brighter colored red blood cells. He strained his eye and carefully adjusted the fine focus knob of the microscope to see as clearly as possible the collision that was about to occur, completely unaware that he was holding his breath.

Then it happened. As the two blood cells collided, he couldn't help but think of two planets slamming into one another and releasing an enormous amount of energy. Having seen this occur multiple times before, he expected that they would merely bounce off of one another heading in different directions. However, instead of peacefully rebounding in different directions, the two cells appeared to adhere to one another and began to float along together.

What happened next was almost unbelievable. At the connection point between the two cells, a dark, almost vaporous mist appeared to transfer out of the darker cells and through the membrane wall of the brighter one. Once inside the outer membrane, it expanded in every direction until the cell had been completely consumed.

At that moment, the two cells separated from one another. William continued to focus on the once brighter red blood cell that started to gently float backward. Suddenly, the outer membrane of the blood cell appeared as if it was thinning, until it completely disappeared and the cell erupted ejecting its contents into the surrounding plasma.

"Unbelievable!" he exclaimed.

He continued to look through the eyepiece, still completely unaware that Nancy, who had taken position directly behind him, was now standing only inches from the back of his chair.

She slowly, methodically, lifted both of her hands above William's head and lowered them in as equally painstaking a pace to hover directly above his shoulders. Purposely, she placed both hands softly on his shoulders as she leaned forward placing her mouth directly adjacent to the left side of his head.

"See something odd?" she virtually hissed into his ear.

Startled, William lurched backward with his head and torso, to which Nancy responded by tightening her grip on his shoulders to hold him in place.

William immediately felt a burning sensation emanating from his chest. A bright flash suddenly filled his view of vision and he looked downwards towards his right shoulder. But instead of the hand of his female co-worker, he saw a massive, almost animal-like paw clutching his shoulders. It had four massive, large-knuckled fingers that were dark black, tipped with long, curved fingernails that looked a putrid dark brown.

He tried to move but was unable to wrest himself away. Exerting every ounce of energy he could muster, he looked over to his left shoulder only to find an equally menacing claw. The grip of whatever was holding him seemed to tighten and he felt as if the bones in his arms and shoulders were going to shatter under the pressure.

Not knowing what to do, he struggled with his right hand to locate the chain hanging around his neck onto which the talisman was affixed. After what seemed an eternity, he was able to grab the chain and quickly pulled it out from beneath his shirt, exposing the amulet. Instantly the room was filled with a bright, blinding light, which seemed to erupt from the adornment itself. Instantly the two massive hands released William and he was able to stand up, launching his chair backward as he straightened his legs.

Turning around he expected to see some sort of vile

creature facing him. However, he found his coworker lying on the floor, holding up her hand to catch blood that was pouring out of her nose.

"Nancy!" he exclaimed. "Are you alright? What in the world were you doing?"

"Nothing," she responded from behind her blood-drenched hand. "I had come up behind you, and must have startled you when I placed my hands on your shoulders because you slammed your head backward into my face and..." she held up her hand to emphasize the damage, "...and this is the result!"

"Oh Nancy, I'm so sorry," he quickly apologized. "You scared me for sure..." and then he hesitated. He took a deep breath and then continued. "I thought you were...well...something..." he paused again.

"You thought I was what?" she pressed in an annoyed tone.

"I thought...I thought..." then hesitated momentarily. "Oh, never mind. It doesn't matter what I thought...what matters is that we take care of you."

After running over to a counter on the side of the room, he returned with a handful of paper towels.

"Here, hold this to your nose. It will help stop the bleeding."

Nancy grabbed the paper towels and held them up to her face.

"I'm so sorry Nancy," he continued. "It's just that you scared me."

Nancy held the towels away from her face, and then blotted it a couple times to make sure, then placed them into the garbage.

"I think it stopped," she remarked. "Does it look bad?"

William had to consciously not cringe at the rumpled mess he had made of her face. He took a deep breath before he responded.

"I think I need to take you to the hospital," he finally admitted. "Come on, let's go."

Seemingly having calmed down, Nancy nodded her head in agreement, and the two of them started making their way out the back of the lab and down the hallway.

"Crap," Nancy commented. "I forgot my purse."

"Let me grab it for you," he replied.

But before he could respond, Nancy had already started making her way back towards the lab.

"It's ok," she called back. "You go grab your car and I'll meet you out front."

"You sure?" he yelled at her as she was about to enter the lab.

"Yes, just go," she shouted over her shoulder as she was about to enter the room.

"Ok...I'll be right back."

And with that, William started sprinting down the hallway to make his way to the parking structure.

Nancy paused at the doorway to ensure that William was not following her into the room and then continued into the lab.

Once in the lab, she purposely walked over to the table where William had been examining the different samples of blood. Stopping in front of the microscope where he had combined the two different samples, she removed the microscope slide and held it up directly in front of her.

The slide which had previously held the red color blood samples was now darkened as if soot from a fire had been rubbed onto it, and there appeared to be a black, almost oil-like substance oozing from beneath the sides of the slide cover.

With a hideous sneer, she clenched her fist around the slide, shattering the glass into dozens of pieces. When she opened her hand, jagged glass shards protruded from her palm that bled profusely. She held her hand open momentarily and a black, oil-like substance, began to coalesce and appeared to be absorbed into her own blood which slowly flowed back into her wounds.

Casually, she plucked the glass shards from her hand and the wounds began to seal inwards. After a brief moment, there was absolutely no sign of any trauma.

With a slight huff, she turned on her heels and started making her way slowly towards the back of the laboratory and out the back door.

CHAPTER 33

Emotional Upheaval

(The Next Night)

Tara and her father were talking with each other in the kitchen as Rich was busily preparing dinner. William sat on a comfortable couch in the family room aimless switching channels in an attempt to find something interesting on the television.

"Crap...crap...uhhh...total crap."

"What was that dear?" Tara called from the other room.

"Oh, nothing. I was just trying to find something interesting to watch, but there is absolutely nothing on."

"Why don't you switch over to ESPN? I think the Dodgers are playing tonight," Rich offered.

William silently complied and set the remote down on the low coffee table situated in front of him. Leaning backward crossing his arms just beneath his chest he stared at the television.

"It's the top of the third, and the Dodgers are down three to nothing already!"

"Figures!" Rich called back. "Do you mind finishing up here?" he asked his daughter.

"Actually, I'm having dinner with a friend that is in town this weekend," she gently reminded her father. "All you really have left to do is to slide this into the oven for thirty minutes and you should be all set."

Tara walked over to the sink to rinse her hands, blotted them dry with a kitchen towel hanging over a knob on one of the cupboard doors, and set it down on the countertop. With a satisfied nod of her head, she walked into the family room and leaned over William to plant a kiss solidly on his forehead.

"You out of here?"

"I sure am."

"Alright then...have a fun time. Your Dad and I are going to hang out for a while, eat some food, and possibly watch the ball game."

"Sounds fun."

Tara stood up and made her way towards the front door, pausing just short to look back at William.

"It seems like FOREVER since you've been home at a reasonable hour in the evening, let alone ate dinner with someone other than a research scientist."

"Oh, come on," he weakly protested. "It hasn't been that long."

Tara simply crooked an eyebrow in his direction with a half-smile on her face.

"Uh huh...whatever you say," she called back as she made her way out of the apartment and closed the door behind her.

Turning back to the television William kicked his shoes off and placed his feet on the table in front of the couch. A moment later Rich walked into the room, took one look at William, and let out a chuckle.

"Tara's going to have your hide if she catches you with your feet on her table!" he comically scolded.

Unfolding his arms, William reached upwards, lacing his fingers together and resting them on the back of his head.

"Well, what she doesn't know won't hurt me!"

"Very true," Rich agreed as he sat in the armchair situated at the head of the low table and just to the left the couch.

Both men sat silently watching the television as the ballgame played out to completion of the third inning. As the commercial came on, William hit the mute button and turned towards Rich.

"I want to talk with you about something that happened at the lab last night."

"Is everything ok?" he responded leaning towards William. "Tara mentioned that you didn't get home until eleven thirty. That's late even by your standards."

"No everything is ok. Well...I think it's ok. I didn't say anything to Tara because I didn't want her to worry, but something...unexplainable, happened last night. And I thought that you might be able to help me make sense of it considering what you experienced at the laboratory."

Rich's eyes widened slightly as he sat backward in his seat crossing his arms firmly in front of himself.

"What happened?" he encouraged.

William began to describe the events that occurred the evening before. How he was working in the lab, examining specimens under the microscope, and what happened when he combined different samples together.

"You've never seen anything like that before?" Rich interrupted.

"No. Never. And that's not even the half of it!"

William then began to recount how Nancy had seemingly sneaked back into the lab to stand directly behind him.

"The next thing I knew, I felt a pair of hands grip both of my shoulders. I tried to struggle, but couldn't move a muscle. I was finally able to look down towards my right shoulder, and..." he hesitated.

"And what?!" Rich demanded.

"And...I saw what I could only describe as...as...the hand of some kind of a creature or an animal. It was dark black, and had...."

William paused for a moment, staring at Rich with a look of concern on his face.

Rich sat motionless in his chair as the blood drained from his face.

"Are you ok? You look like you're going to be sick," William pressed.

Rich was completely unresponsive and sat staring forward for a period of almost thirty seconds. Suddenly his eyes fluttered, he stood up and ran towards the bathroom, nearly tripping on the corner of the coffee table.

From the other room, William could hear horrific retching sounds that clearly indicated that the other man was emptying the entire contents of his stomach into the toilet. William rose and was about to follow after Rich when he heard the sound of flushing coming from the other room. He paused for a moment until he saw Tara's father start to make his way back down the hallway.

Rich walked back into the family room and noisily flopped himself into the armchair. A bit of color had returned to his cheeks, but to say he looked healthy would have been a tremendous exaggeration. Beads of sweat poured off of his balding head and ran down across his brow and cheeks.

"Are you ok?" he anxiously repeated with real concern in his voice.

Rich leaned back looking directly into William's eyes as he gently shook his head from side to side.

"Rich, you've got me really scared. Do you need to see a doctor?"

"No," Rich responded. "No doctor is going to be able to help with this. As you were describing what happened to you last night, I had a terrible sensation of déjà vu. And then...it was like I was transported back six months ago to our first visit to Cenetics."

"The day you passed out?"

"Exactly. Except for this time, I had extremely vivid memories of what happened, or at least what I think happened. It all seemed so real that it had to have occurred."

"What?"

"I was watching Tara walk over to where you and the others were seated. Then I felt, like someone...no," he corrected himself, "like something was staring at me. When I turned around I found one of the five children standing in front of me, except..." he trailed off.

"Except what?"

"...except, I don't think that it's really a child."

"What?" he incredulously demanded.

"This THING standing in front of me reached forward and touched my hand," he stated while holding the backside of his left hand in front of him. "And the instant that it touched my hand I experienced what I can only describe as some sort of vision. The child that was standing in front of me was no longer there, and in its place, was some sort of creature...almost an animal, that was pure evil. It appeared somehow as if it were trapped inside of the child, and...."

Rich paused for a moment as he realized that the expression on William's face had distinctly shifted from that of concern to one that could be best described as speculative suspicion.

"You don't believe me, do you?"

"It's not that...it's just that..."

"I'm not making this up!"

"I know, I was just about to tell you..."

But Rich had already stood up and was making his way to the door.

"Rich! Seriously, come back and sit down," William shouted as he stood up. "I don't think you're making this up, in fact..."

William was cut off by the sound of the front door slamming shut, and he could hear heavy footsteps bound down the stairs leading to the ground level. He sat down heavily on the couch letting out a large sigh.

"I was just about to comment on the similarities between your experience and mine."

CHAPTER 34

Abominable
(Later That Night)

Frustrated by the events that just occurred, William walked into the kitchen and simply turned the oven to the 'off' position. He then made his way over to the kitchen table, grabbed a light jacket from the back of one of the chairs, and clipped his Cenetics ID badge onto his shirt pocket.

"I guess I might as well make it a late evening at the lab!" he sarcastically stated to himself.

After roughly a fifteen-minute drive, William found himself walking through the almost entirely empty hallways of the Cenetics facility. He had taken this path so many times previously that he didn't even consciously notice all the twists and turns.

Suddenly, realizing that he was in an area that he didn't recognize, he paused to look around. A short hallway to his right led up to a stainless-steel door, with the words 'Top Secret – Authorized Personnel Only' in large red letters across the front. He walked up to the door and noticed the familiar proximity reader located on the wall, adjacent to the handle.

"I wonder," he thought silently to himself.

He lifted his ID badge up to the reader and immediately heard the all too familiar clicking sound of the door unlocking. William quickly glanced behind him to make certain that no one was there. Satisfied that he was in fact alone, he turned the handle, quickly made his way into the next room and shut the door behind him.

The room in which he was now standing was initially

dark, and then a motion sensor detected his presence and automatically turned on all the fluorescent lights overhead. There were long tables arranged end to end in three neat rows across most of the width of the room. A single chair sat in front of each table facing the opposite wall that housed two massive windows and a large, sliding glass door.

As he approached the glass door on the opposite wall, he noticed yet another card reader located next to it. Instinctively he placed his ID card against the reader. This time, however, it resulted in a distinctive buzzing sound and a red light illuminated on the reader.

Despite the denial of access to the room, a few lights in it turned on revealing a massively sized, square laboratory, at least seventy-five by seventy-five feet. It had multiple rows of tables all situated around the center of the room, each covered with different types of scientific equipment and computers. Around the outer perimeter of the room, there appeared to be a raised walkway of some sort, with additional cabinets and storage shelves. And in the very center of the room, he couldn't quite make it out, but he thought that he saw a massive silver cylinder surrounded by what looked to be massive empty test tubes.

"What is this place?" he suspiciously whispered to himself. "And why won't *my* access badge grant me access?"

Realizing that he wasn't supposed to really be here, he quickly made his way back out of the room and retraced his steps back to a familiar looking hallway. This time he went the right direction, and after a few moments was sitting in front of a table inside the observatory room overlooking the darkened living quarters of the children.

After hitting the spacebar on the keyboard in front of him several times, the computer screen illuminated, prompting him for his user ID and password. Within a few moments, he was busy typing out his experience from the night before in an email to document the events.

Suddenly, he thought that he saw something out of the corner of his eye, and he looked up from his keyboard and into the room below. Satisfied nothing seemed out of the ordinary, he turned back to his computer and continued inputting his recollection of the previous night. Again, out of his line of sight, something grabbed his attention and he looked back into the children's living quarters.

This time he painstaking searched the room to see if anything looked suspicious. The central living area looked virtually identical to how it had appeared previously on multiple occasions. The rectangular table in the middle with six chairs neatly surrounding it, couches, chairs, beans bags...it all looked normal. Then he shifted his gaze to the sleeping quarters of the children. The bed in each room was arranged in such a way that he could see the children lying down, peacefully sleeping.

"Three boys...four boys...five," he silently counted in his head. "All boys accounted for and present."

Then he shifted his gaze towards Clarissa's room. Being in the back corner, her room was darker than the others, but there was enough light for him to make out the interior. Her closet door was left open, and he could faintly make out the outline of clothes hanging within. Then he focused on what he expected to be the shape of a sleeping girl on her bed and his breath caught.

Rather than lying peacefully on her bed, it looked as if Clarissa was sitting up on her bed, wearing a white nightgown. As she sat there it looked as if she was rhythmically swaying from side to side, as she tilted her head backward towards the ceiling.

William sat there stunned, not knowing what he should do next. He stood up and leaned closer to the glass in an attempt to get a better view, and as he did, he felt a slight tingling sensation on his chest. He glanced downwards at his shirt where the amulet was most assuredly located, and then cast his line of sight back towards Clarissa's room, and blinked.

When his eyes refocused, it appeared as if the shape of the little girl shimmered, and then appeared to have dissolved away, leaving in its place, or more accurately described, contained inside of the girl, the outline of some sort of dark, horrific creature. He could see the rough outline of the girl's arms lift up and outwards, however within the figure of the arms he could have sworn that he saw large, massively muscled arms. It appeared as if wings rose directly out of the back of the child opening outwards revealing rough, leathery looking flaps, tipped by sharpened hooks or blades.

He breathlessly stared at the image before him, caught precariously between a desire to understand what was going on, and an instinct to run as quickly as possible in the opposite direction.

Unconsciously, William reached to the chain hanging around his neck and withdrew the amulet hanging onto it, gently lifting it in front of his chin and towards the window.

As if the entity in the child's room felt the presence of the Talisman, it lifted its grotesque, broad head towards the observation room. Blood red eyes glared menacingly towards William, and its mouth drew open revealing dark brown, razor-sharp rotting teeth.

What happened next would haunt William for the rest of his life, which at that moment he thought might be ending at any second.

A deep, rumbling sound seemed to emanate from every side, and the already dark room appeared to darken further as if a diseased plague had just been released into the air around it. With his eyes locked on those of the vile creature, his stomach began to churn.

"IT'S TOO LATE!"

The thunderous words pounded into his chest and ears as if he was experiencing the launch of a massive rocket first hand.

"THE END IS COMING...AND YOUR FATE IS SEALED!"

His skull nearly split open and he felt as if blood poured from his ears.

"THERE IS NOTHING THAT WILL HINDER HIS COMING...NOTHING!"

A dizziness fell over him and his stomach lurched. He felt like he was going to drown to death in his own vomit.

William clenched his eyes and held his hands over his ears, waiting for what he surely knew was the end of his life. After a few moments, it was dead silent. He cautiously squinted through his eyelids, and then slowly opened them revealing a dark, calm room, with no sign of what he had just witnessed.

He looked back towards Clarissa's room and found her lying silently, supposedly asleep, on her bed.

He blinked...then blinked again.

With great resolve, he turned and ran from the observation room and made his way into the living quarters of the children. Standing in the main room, his eyes wildly darted, searching for any indicated of what he had just seen. All he found was the dark, deathly quiet of an empty room.

He turned towards Clarissa's room, determined that he was going to wake the girl up and demand an explanation. This, unfortunately, was not to be.

As he took his first step towards the child's room he heard a loud crack of thunder that shook him to his very core. His heart raced, pounding within his chest, and his eyes opened so wide he thought they would pop right out of his skull.

He took a second step, and this time felt the ground shake beneath him, nearly causing him to lose his balance and stumble to the floor. This time he froze expecting the shaking to continue and the room to literally crumble around him. However, as he stood there the shaking ceased and the room became as quiet as the inside of an ancient mausoleum.

Taking a deep breath, he forced himself to try and take another step.

As he began to lift his right foot, the air in front of him shimmered as if he was trying to look through the air directly above a raging fire. Then suddenly a dark, thin line appeared directly in the center of the hazy image and spread out towards the edges revealing an absolute black, dark abyss on the other side. A shadow suddenly erupted from the darkness in front of him and he felt a sharp pinch on the left side of his chest, causing him to fall backward and onto the floor.

Instinctively, he reached with his right hand and touched his left side, which immediately sent mind-numbing pains throughout his entire body. Staggering, he got to his feet and stumbled out of the living quarters and into the hallway on the other side of the two large stainless steel doors.

Under the light coming from fluorescent fixtures in the ceiling, he lifted up his dress shirt revealing four, evenly spaced scratches on his left chest, approximately three inches in length, that cut deep enough to have drawn blood to the surface of his skin and stain the underside of his shirt.

"What in the world just happened?!"

###############################

Rich was jolted awake from a deep sleep by a loud banging and continuous ringing of his doorbell. He sat there for a moment when the thumping and clanging stopped.

"Was I imagining..."

THUMP THUMP THUMP!!

Angrily, he threw the top covers off of himself and onto the floor while flinging both legs off the side of the bed in a single motion. Pushing himself up on his mattress he started to stagger from his bedroom and towards the front of the house.

DING DONG! DING DONG! DING DONG!

"ALRIGHT ALREADY!!! ALRIGHT!!! I'M COMING...STOP WITH ALL OF THE NOISE!!!"

THUMP THUMP THUMP!!!

Fully awake and angered beyond belief, he stomped across the entryway towards the front door, grabbing a baseball bat that was leaning against the wall next to a small table. Upon reaching the door, he didn't even bother to look through the peephole to see who was causing this racket at one thirty in the morning. He grabbed the deadbolt, gave it a quick counter-clockwise twist with his left hand, turned and jerked the handle, and just barely jumped out of the way of the door as it flung open.

The next thing he knew, a man fell inwards across the threshold of his home and onto the tile floor with a loud crash. Rich hefted the baseball bat high above his head with both hands ready to deliver a bone-crushing blow if the situation required.

"WHAT IN TARNATION DO YOU THINK YOU'RE DOING!!!" he screamed at the intruder.

The man on the floor turned onto his back and stared up at the massive man threatening to crush him with eyes so wide that he thought they would literally pop out of his head.

"RICH!!!" the man yelled. "RICH!!! IT'S ME...WILLIAM!!!"

Rich paused as he recognized the man strewn out on the floor in front of him as his son-in-law, and then dropped the bat behind his head and onto the tile in a clatter.

"WILLIAM!" he thundered. "What in the world are you doing here at this hour of the morning...making all of that noise?!"

William hastily got to his knees and stood up beside Rich. His pulse was racing and he thought he would pass out from the amount of adrenaline coursing through his veins.

"Rich! You scared me to death!"

"I scared you?!" he incredulously scoffed. "You woke me from a deep sleep making all of this noise, and you darn near got your skull caved in the process."

"I'm sorry," he honestly offered. "I didn't mean to scare you...but I had to talk to you as soon as possible."

"Well, come on in I guess," he relented. "I'm not going to be falling back to sleep again any time soon...let alone at all this evening."

Rich shut the front door and followed William into the kitchen.

"Have a seat," he anxiously implored. "You're going to want to be sitting down for what I'm going to tell you."

Rich raised his eyebrow and was about to protest, but then acquiesced to his request and took a seat across from him.

"Alright...tell me what this is all about."

William started to describe to Rich in extraordinary detail the events of the evening after he had stormed out of his apartment. He explained how he wasn't doubting his story, but was in fact surprised at the similarities between Rich's experience and his own.

He then recounted how he had stumbled upon some strange, obscure looking laboratory that he had never seen before, and how his access badge, which was supposed to grant him access to the entire Cenetics facility, was restricted from entering a particular room.

Next, he described the horrific image that appeared where Clarissa had been sitting on her bed. How this creature that could only be characterized as pure evil, looked at him and spoke in a heinous, depraved voice, issuing threats of being too late, and how something or someone was coming.

Rich raised his hand with a questioning expression on his face.

"What did you do that got this 'beast's' attention?"

"Oh," he admitted, "I nearly forgot. As I was observing this monster, I must have unconsciously reached down and removed the Talisman you had given me from beneath my shirt. As I held the Talisman in front of me, the eyes opened and look directly at me."

Rich furrowed his brow and pursed his lips in deep consternation. Then with an audible harrumph, he placed both of his hands in front of him flat on the table and stared directly into William's eyes.

"Do you remember what I told you when I gave you that ornament?"

"Yes. You said that it would serve as a protection. That it had been blessed by a priest to protect the wearer against..." he wavered momentarily before finishing his sentence, "...to protect the wearer against evil."

William's chin nearly hit the floor as the depravity of the situation sunk into his mind. Rich simply nodded at him in acknowledgment of his unspoken conclusion.

"Is there more?" Rich finally prodded.

William then conveyed to him how he had tried to confront the little girl, and how when he tried to enter her bedroom that something unseen tried to stop him. He detailed the deafening crack of thunder that came from nowhere and how the ground roiled beneath his feet. Finally, he disclosed that something had literally struck him.

"ARE YOU CERTAIN?! DID IT ACTUALLY MAKE CONTACT?!"

Rather than responding, William stood up from his chair and lifted his shirt to expose the four small gashes that had already scabbed over on his left chest.

Rich's eyes widened in terror and he let out an audible gasp.

"What is it?!"

Rich closed his eyes for a moment shaking his head slowly from side to side. Finally, he opened his eyes and clasped his hands in front of him. Intently staring at William, he finally responded.

"A POLTERGEIST!"

"A WHAT?!" he demanded. "You mean like the movie?"

"No, not like the movie at all. This one is literally happening, and I think I finally understand what has been bugging me this entire time about the children."

Rich sat there silently for almost a full minute.

"What is it?"

Swallowing hard, Rich looked across the table at William with an extremely severe look, nearly making William's skin crawl.

"The biggest controversy that the religious community has raised about these clones is that they don't have a soul. That man is trying to destroy God by proving that we can create life ourselves based on our own ingenuity. That science can explain the existence of man, and that there isn't a greater Being. But through Man's Creation…Abomination!"

"What are you trying to say?!"

"What I'm saying is that these clones do in fact have souls. I would go so far as to speculate…no, to definitively conclude, that these clones have been possessed by the angels of the adversary."

"But why?"

Rich halted again thinking to himself, and then finally responded.

"Revelations, Chapter twelve, verses four through nine. Do you remember it?"

"That was one of the sections of the bible that I was reading when I had my...my vision," William was barely able to utter.

"Exactly. Those verses described the War in Heaven, and how Satan was cast out of the presence of God, along with a third of the host of heaven. How those that were cast out with him became his angels."

"I'm not understanding what you're trying to say."

"Will, the Book of Revelations describes the events leading up to the end of the world. The fact that your dream was about the War in Heaven is not just a coincidence. I believe, in my heart of hearts, that what is occurring right now is a clear indication that the end of times is close at hand. That the evil one and his angels are preparing for the final battle. Good against evil. And that these clones are the key to the entire thing."

As Rich finished his supposition, William realized that he felt warmth emanating from deep within his chest. He instinctively placed his right hand directly over the amulet and he could physically feel heat radiating directly from the Talisman.

"I don't know how, and I don't know why, but I believe you," he stated as a matter of fact.

William closed his eyes, and after a brief moment reopened them, staring directly into those of Rich with an expression of absolute certainty on his face.

"What do I need to do?"

CHAPTER 35

Unimaginable
(4 Months Later)

It was nearly seven thirty on a Friday evening, and William found himself traversing down and empty stairwell leading to the basement of a Medical Research Facility at the University of Southern California. This was the same path he had taken virtually every Friday evening for the past six months and he knew that tonight would likely be his final undertaking.

After his harrowing encounter at the Cenetics facility, and what he could only explain as a revelatory insight during his discussion with Rich, he had come to the conclusion that it was his moral responsibility to put an end to the heinous activities that were being conducted by Don and his company. While he knew that he needed to do something, he wasn't certain how he could eliminate any trace of the research and development that Cenetics was conducting. Furthermore, he knew that in order for his actions to have any real meaning, he needed to ensure that he eradicated not just the ability of Cenetics to create clones, but that he needs to wipe out any trace of their research – he needed to destroy the clones themselves.

He had struggled at first to come up with a realistic plan to achieve his goals, but the ultimate path became readily apparent to him as he learned more and more about Cenetics and the overly suspicious nature of his former colleague Don.

Don was an absolute paranoid about corporate espionage. So much so, that he had taken extreme measures to ensure that no research relating to any part of the cloning process, or related to the clones themselves would ever be at risk of threat. Built into the very design the research facility were unique precautions to prevent any data from being stolen or leaked. All of the data relating to this research was maintained on an isolated network protected by no less than five military grade firewalls. There were multiple authentication and biometric safeguards to ensure that only authorized individuals were let anywhere near a computer that could access this closed network. Taking advantage of new encryption techniques, all of the data was stored and transmitted leveraging leading-edge Quantum cryptography, based on a quantum key distribution that changed every sixty seconds. In addition, the network itself that connected these systems leveraged optical fibers and packet technology that only had the capability to transmit signals over a maximum distance of five thousand feet.

The net result of all these safeguards was that information was essentially bound to the facility itself. This meant that any data warehouse backups and redundancy needed to be housed on site. And as far as William knew, the data didn't exist anywhere else on the planet outside of the Cenetics walls. Once William understood this, he knew that destroying the entire facility in one cataclysmic event would eliminate any record of the work that had occurred there.

This left him with solving the problem of creating and transporting an explosive that was powerful enough to destroy the facility into the very heart of Cenetics without being detected. The only possible solution that he could come up with was to create a portable, nominal yield nuclear device.

Coming up with a design for the device really wasn't that difficult given the vast amount of information that is available online. Constructing one was a completely different matter entirely.

William had spent two months acquiring the various components and materials that would be required to create a compact nuclear apparatus. He needed to come up with two different types of explosive materials that detonated at differing speeds. This was necessary to create an explosion that would compress the energy inwards upon a solid core, resulting in criticality of the fissile material.

After perfecting the design and acquiring the assorted ingredients from somewhat less than scrupulous sources, he was still faced with the challenge of acquiring the fissile material capable of sustaining a nuclear chain reaction. After only a week of research, he discovered how he could acquire this material in one of the most unlikely sources possible.

As it turns out, Plutonium is used as a fuel for cardiac pacemakers due primarily to its long-lasting life. Once you go through the efforts of installing a pacemaker, you don't want to have to reopen the patient every four weeks to install fresh batteries. Based on his research, he needed at least 300 grams of Plutonium 238 to achieve critical mass under the right conditions. Each pacemaker contained .5 grams of Plutonium – the maximum amount of material that the U.S. Government permitted to be transported by air travel. If William were to steal twenty pacemakers each week – small enough to go unnoticed at a large medical research facility – he would be able to amass 250 grams in six months. This would mean that he would need to pilfer more than half the remaining stock on this final night, or one hundred pacemakers, in order to have sufficient material.

As William rounded the corner at the bottom of the stairs he nearly ran into a security guard that was making his way down the hallway of the basement.

"Doctor Mears," the guard apologized. "Sorry about that."

Realizing that the security guard was someone that he knew, William was able to quickly steady his nerves.

"Alan...it's Alan right," he responded in as calm a voice as possible. "I nearly knocked you over. Aren't you normally over in the science laboratories?"

"Normally," he responded. "However, about two weeks ago we discovered that someone has been stealing pacemakers of all things from the storage area in this building." He paused for a moment and raised a quizzical eyebrow towards William. "By the way, what are you doing here so late?"

William's heart nearly jumped out of his chest as his mind raced to come up with a believable excuse to explain his presence. Finally, he thought of something that should get him out of this bind.

"I'm doing some research right now, affiliated with the University of course, and I realized that I had done something similar when I was at USC for my doctoral research. I couldn't find it anywhere in my own notes, so I thought I'd come take a look in the storage archives in the basement."

William's stomach tightened and he felt queasy as Alan stood there silently considering his response. If he caught onto him right at the very end, all his efforts would have been for nothing, and he wouldn't be able to stop Don.

After what seemed a veritable eternity, but in reality was only a few seconds, Alan responded.

"No worries," he casually stated shrugging his shoulders. "Do you need any help?"

"Oh no, it's not a problem," he assured him in as uninterested a voice as possible. "It will only take a few minutes and I don't want to take you away from your rounds."

"Alight then. Good luck finding what you're looking for."

And with that, Alan slowly walked past William and up the stairs to the first level of the building.

When he was totally out of earshot, William let out an audible exhale as he leaned against the wall of the hallway.

"That was too close," he admitted to himself in a whisper.

Roughly five minutes later, William was walking down a narrow aisle of one of the side storage rooms in the basement of the building. With a small LED pen flashlight, he briefly searched the shelves until he found a large box in a familiar location.

Opening up the top, he peered inside and his heart nearly sunk at what he saw.

"Where are they?" he cried.

The box was completely empty.

He spent the next fifteen minutes frantically searching through each of the aisles trying to locate the supply of pacemakers to no avail. He finally sat down against the back wall of the room on the cold concrete floor and buried his face in his hands.

After a few moments, he jerked his head upwards and looked to his right. In the corner of the basement, there was a door that led into a small storage closet. The only way to gain access to this closet was to swipe your ID badge, and he didn't know if his University ID would grant him access. And even if it did, it would place William on the very top of the list of suspects to talk to when they discovered that additional pacemakers had been stolen.

"Well, I'm too far into this to stop now."

He stood up and approached the door. As he was about to swipe his ID badge on the reader he paused for a second.

"I wonder."

Reaching forward he grasped the doorknob and gave it a hopeful twist with his right hand. Much to his happy surprise, the doorknob freely turned. He gently pulled the door and it swung outwards providing him access to the closet.

He quickly jumped inside of the doorway and found three shelves of boxes on the right-hand side of the small room. Utilizing his light, he searched the labels on the outside of the containers until he came to a large box with the words 'Medratus, Inc.' printed on the outside.

"Thank God!" he exclaimed.

He quickly pulled the box towards him far enough so he could open up one of the flaps to peer inside. Much to his great relief, it appeared as if the University had just received a new shipment of devices. Inside the box there appeared to be no fewer than two hundred small packages, each containing a state of the art Medratus pacemaker. And most importantly, there would be more than enough of the vital substance to make his explosive device work.

William slung his backpack from off his shoulders, opened it and began to fill it with about half the contents of the box. Satisfied that he had sufficient quantity, he pushed the box back into place on the shelf and struggled to zip the top of his pack shut. With a little bit of effort, he closed the bag, and quickly made his way back out of the storage room, up the stairs and into his car.

It took William about five minutes to make his way over to the engineering building at the University. He had decided that it would be much safer to construct his device at a location other than his apartment, mostly due to the fact there would be no way he could keep it a secret from Tara.

William had decided that it would be in the best interest of everyone if he kept his plans completely secretive, even from Rich, with whom he had initially discussed how this evil work needed to be brought to an end.

It was almost nine o'clock in the evening when William made his way into a remote corner of the engineering design and fabrication facility. He carefully placed his bag on a table and pulled out a cart from behind several boxes. On top of the cart was a large throw cloth that William thoughtfully removed, being certain not to upset any of the contents laying directly beneath it.

Precisely laid out on the top of the wheeled cart was a large steel tube approximately ten inches in length and four inches in diameter. One end of the tube was capped by a large steel end piece that had already been tightly fastened. Precisely arranged in two separate rows were a total of forty hexagons that were fashioned out of a clay-like material. The sides of the shapes in the first row were exactly 1.63 centimeters in length, .5 centimeters in thickness, and were lying on top of a thin sheet of wax paper. The second row of hexagons were exactly 2.13 centimeters in length and had the same thickness.

Set off to the side was two halves of a hollow sphere made of tungsten. It was crucial to house the explosion within as dense a material as possible to reflect as many of the neutrons inwards towards the fissile material. The diameter of the sphere on the outside was just shy of 10 centimeters and had a thickness of .25 centimeters. This was necessary to ensure that it could be snugly slid into the center of the steel pipe that would house it. There was also two halves of a spherical mold with which William intended to shape the exactly 3.5 centimeters in diameter plutonium core.

Finally, there were two six-volt lantern batteries, some wire, a digital clock, a small circuit board, and two small explosive triggers.

William opened the backpack, removed the packages, and quickly went to work opening up the pacemakers to get at the power supply cases. Within roughly twenty minutes, he now had over one hundred tiny cases, each containing .5 grams of plutonium.

Next, William went to a small storage closet nearby, carefully retrieved a steel container, and placed it on top of the cart. He pulled out another cart from behind the boxes in the corner of the room that housed a state of the art nuclear safe glove box. It had two portals on one side of the box, on the inside of which were fastened large, black rubber gloves, coated with a material that would protect William from being exposed to the radiation from the substance he needed to shape into a solid core.

Opening up the glove box, he placed the small steel container and the newly removed power sources inside. Being certain to seal the box, William then prepared to fashion the fissile material into a perfect sphere.

Placing his hands into the protective gloves, William spent the next hour removing the plutonium from the protective casing and began shaping it. Luckily, plutonium is mostly malleable at room temperature. Very carefully, he compressed the plutonium into the two halves of the sphere, and then applied a moderate amount of heat to bind the separate pieces of plutonium to each other. As the material began to fuse, William could feel the heat energy emitting directly from the material itself. He then combined the two halves of the sphere together, and after about three minutes was able to remove the outer casing, revealing a silvery, brightly colored marble, precisely 3.5 centimeters in diameter.

Next William introduced the components on the other cart into the glove box by placing all of them into a chamber connected to the container. Once everything was in the container, he slid open a door allowing him access to reach the contents wearing the protective gloves.

Over the next two hours, William diligently worked at completing the assembly of his device. He carefully placed the smaller hexagon shapes onto the outside of the plutonium core he had just manufactured until they completely covered the entire surface, and then repeated the same task with the larger ones in an equally diligent manner. Satisfied with the end result, he then painstakingly placed the object into the interior shell of one-half of the tungsten casings and completely enclosed it with the other half that had an industrial grade chemical sealant delicately applied to the rim. After about sixty seconds the two halves were permanently sealed to one another.

Beads of sweat were profusely rolling off his forehead

and the armpits of his shirt were completely drenched with sweat.

"No stopping now," he muttered to himself as he wiped his brow with the sleeve of his shirt.

Very carefully William completed the construction of his device by screwing the triggers into the two locations on the outside of the tungsten sphere, connecting the wires to the capacitor, and connecting the circuit board to the digital clock. With a satisfied nod, he slid the sphere into the steel tube and screwed the end piece onto the open end.

"That should about do it!"

Stepping to the left of the box, William carefully opened the door with his left hand and held the measurement end of a radiation detector inside the box next to the device. The digital display on the meter read '0.0013 ppb'.

"Well, at least I won't kill myself from the radiation," he jokingly commented with a small grin.

William carefully withdrew the device he had just created and held it in front of him to inspect it. The ten-inch long metal pipe had two tightly fastened end caps on either side, with two wires leading out of one of the ends. The digital clock was fastened to the outside of the steel pipe, and the small circuit board was located directly on top of the clock.

"All I need to do now is to connect the power supply, set the clock, and then get as far away as possible."

William meticulously placed all the various components into his bag and gently slung it onto his back. After glancing around at the room one final time, he turned and started making his way out to his car with the most determined look on his face that he had ever worn.

CHAPTER 36

Detonation
(Early Morning Hours)

With his heart pounding in anticipation, William opened his car door and stepped into the chill temperature of a February night. It was almost two a.m. and he hadn't slept for the past 48 hours. He knew what he had to do, what absolutely had to be done, but that didn't make things any easier for him. Silently he shut the car door and donned his black hat to help conceal him in the darkness. Running from his car and keeping to the shadows he made his way to the side of the complex where a few trees stood on the outside of a ten-foot-tall fence topped off with barbed wire. Looking around him to make certain that no one had seen his approach, he climbed up a tree about fifteen feet off the ground and made his way out on a branch that extended just over the perimeter of the fence line. At this point, he remembered the duffle bag that he was carrying with him, unzipped it, and took out a nylon rope. Quickly he tied one end of the rope around the two handles of the bag, securing it with a knot, and zipped the bag shut again. Slowly he lowered the duffle bag down to the grass on the other side of the fence, being certain to set the bag and its contents down gently.

"Dropping the bag would make this a very short trip" William chuckled to himself quietly.

With the bag on the ground, he tied the other end of the rope to the four-inch branch that was supporting his weight, and then slowly climbed down to the grass below. Reaching the ground next to the bag, William crouched and untied the rope from the handles of the bag, and inspected the contents. Nothing seemed to be out of place. The display was dark and the wires were still tightly wound with black electrician's tape to ensure that they didn't accidentally make a connection with the battery prematurely.

Quickly he zipped the bag shut again. Grasping the handles tightly between his clenched right fist, he trotted across the grass and paused at the edge of a parking lot, hiding next to a small group of bushes. The parking lot was empty except for a white security pickup truck parked close to the entrance of the building with the words "CENETICS Security" on the side door.

From this distance, William could clearly see the two security guards sitting inside the building at the front desk. He could not make out their faces, but he was certain he knew exactly who the two guards were. Sitting lazily in front of a bank of video monitors with his feet resting on the desk in front of him was Jim Tramble. His bald head reflected the light from the fluorescent lighting directly overhead, and his 300-pound frame seemed to ooze into the chair itself. The other man was Karl Trent. All 6 feet 5 inches of him stood back behind Jim leaning up against the wall, although you wouldn't have been able to guess he was that tall at first sight. Karl always hunched considerably as if trying to hide his height. Despite his height, Karl was a frightfully skinny individual, probably weighing no more than 180 pounds. William figured that Jim and Karl would be on duty tonight as they were pretty much every night. He had become acquainted with both of these men in his previous visits to the Cenetics facility.

Taking three deep breaths, William readied himself to make the sprint across the parking lot to the back corner of the main building. But before he could take action a pair of headlights swung into view and shined directly at the spot where he was hiding. A white windowless van pulled up to the front gate. William froze and held his breath for what seemed an eternity. Finally, he heard a loud clank of the fence as the motor turned on and began to slowly pull the gate to the right of the vehicle making it possible to pass. As soon as the gate fully opened the van pulled forward and drove along the main road up to the front entrance. The lights were no longer illuminating William's place of hiding, but he was still gripped with fear as he watched the van pull to a complete stop. The right front door opened almost immediately.

A man dressed in blue jeans wearing a dark leather jacket stepped out of the van and immediately lit a cigarette. After taking what were probably just two puffs, he tossed it onto the ground and stepped roughly on it to extinguish it. He muttered something inaudible to the driver of the van and about three seconds later the motor of the van was turned off. The man in the leather jacket walked slowly to the side of the van, opened the door, and reached inside. As he drew his arm back out of the van he held a metal step and set it upon the ground immediately in front of the open door.

"Alright, we're here," the man grunted at the open door. "Come on now, let's get going."

As William intently watched, a child's hand reached out of the inside of the van and grasped the armrest of the opened door. Slowly, a small figure clothed completely in white emerged from the van and stepped out onto the metal stair that sat on the ground. The figure stopped momentarily and tentatively looked around the parking lot, pausing when its line of sight looked across to the area where William had concealed himself. William's heart pounded so hard in his chest that he thought that the others would be able to hear the noise beating in his ears. He knew who the figure was. It was Clarissa.

Pausing briefly on the metal stair, Clarissa cast her gaze over to the fence where William was frozen motionless. It was as if she knew William was there, but she was completely unconcerned by his presence. She briefly pursed her lips and she stepped off the metal step.

In almost the exact same manner as the first, five additional small figures emerged from the van dressed identically to the first and stood outside the van in a small cluster. Although not completely identical in appearance, it was obvious that each of these five males shared virtually the same facial features and characteristics as one another. It was clear that they were all from the same "mother" from a single pregnancy.

William's stomach tightened and he nearly threw up as he realized that the six individuals in front of him were the targets of his attack.

The man who opened the door grabbed the metal stair and noisily tossed it back into the van and slammed the door. "Alright you kids, let's get a move on," he barked. "I'm not going to stay out here all night while you stand around staring at each other."

William's heart raced again as the man's voice confirmed for him that these were, in fact, the six children that he meant to destroy before the night was over.

Without a word, Clarissa began to walk towards the front of the building and the other five followed closely behind her still in a tight cluster. The gruff man motioned impatiently at the children as if to push them forcefully towards the building to get them to go faster. Seemingly aware of the man's impatience, Clarissa slowly turned her gaze back to the man until her eyes met his. Immediately he averted his eyes and his entire demeanor changed.

Having seen the children approaching the building, Karl, who was previously leaning up against the wall slowly loped to the front door and swiped his ID badge to unlock it. Holding the door open, each of the six children entered the building and stood in a semi-circle around the front desk. The bald man behind the desk picked up the phone, and while William could not hear his voice, he knew that he was announcing the arrival of the six visitors. Moments later, a large door beyond the front desk swung open and a woman walked out with her hands outstretched towards the children.

William grimaced at the sight of her. "Kim," he spat. He knew without a doubt that the figure that walked towards the children was Kim Dyson...their unholy mother. While most men found her attractive, William cringed at the sight of her.

The small grouping of children walked up to their mother and oddly stared up at her face. Kim looked back at them and then motioned at the man who had escorted her children in to go back to the van. The front door of the building opened again and the man walked quickly back to the van, opened the front door, and slammed it shut as he hopped into the front seat. The window of his door immediately rolled down and William saw a flash of light as the man lit a new cigarette. The engine of the van turned over and the driver backed the van up and slowly drove back towards the gate they had originally come in through. Pausing long enough for the gate to reopen the van drove roughly over a speed bump at the exit and sped back down the street and out of site.

Looking back at the building, William saw the group of children walk back into the building through the door that Kim had come out, with their mother following closely behind them. As the door began to slowly swing shut, William noticed Clarissa glancing back through the open doorway in the direction where he still sat motionless. William could have sworn that he saw a smirk on her face just before she vanished as the door closed shut.

William let out a whoosh of breath and rolled onto his back on the slightly damp grass.

"I don't think I can do this," he thought to himself. "But I have to. If I don't, I won't be able to live with myself. And why are the children out so late?" he pondered. "No matter...at least I know that they're here."

Rolling forward to a sitting position, William got back on his feet and readied himself again to run towards the backside of the building. Checking to make sure that both Jim and Karl were working hard at not paying attention, William grasped the duffle bag and sprinted across the parking lot to the side of the building. He threw his back into the brick exterior trying to dissolve into the wall itself. He wildly looked around to make certain that no one had seen him. Satisfied that he was undetected, William slinked down the wall to the rear of the building and slid back behind a six-foot wall concealing a diesel-powered backup generator.

Despite having access to the building, he knew that he needed to break in so as not to announce his presence. Jim and Karl would have been immediately notified if he swiped his badge to gain entrance. Behind the generator was another concrete wall only 4 feet tall with two large metal-hinged doors facing the rear parking lot. As quietly as possible, William lifted the metal rod that held the door in place and raised the end up out of the ground where it normally rested. Slowly twisting the metal rod backward to lock it in the up position, the steel gave a gentle groan. After pausing momentarily to look around, William turned the rod the remainder of the way to ensure that it would stay in the raised position and silently pulled the metal door outwards just far enough so he could squeeze by. Once inside the low enclosure, the sickening smell of rotting garbage filled his nostrils from the dumpster.

With the lid of the dumpster already closed, William climbed up onto it so he could climb a ladder secured to the side of the building allowing him to get to the rooftop. He easily scaled the ladder with the duffle bag in his right hand, sliding from the top of the ladder onto the rooftop where he crouched down. Making his way across the roof he reached an exterior vent that allowed for fresh air to enter the building. Unzipping the duffle bag, William reached in and grasped an electric drill with a hex nut adapter already secured to the end. Placing the tip of the screwdriver bit softly against the vent he silently removed each of the four fasteners holding the metal cover in place. When the fourth screw was removed he cradled the vent casing and laid it quietly on the rooftop. Silently, William hoisted himself up into the ventilation shaft.

Once inside the four by four-foot shaft, he sat down and secured a headlamp from his duffel bag to his forehead, turned it on and pulled a schematic of the ventilation system for the building that was folded into fourths from his front pocket. It only took a couple of moments to get himself oriented and he began to prepare to slide down the first eight-foot drop to the main air duct running along the full length of the top floor of the building.

Securing the duffle bag to a loop on his pants with a carabiner clip, he rolled over onto his knees and carefully inched his way back toward the opening of the air duct. Very slowly he lowered his feet and legs down the length of the air duct until the lower half of his body was extended down the shaft and he was lying flat on his stomach. With his hands pressed solidly against the metal air duct close to his waist, he raised his upper body until he was holding himself up. Slowly he lowered his entire body down the shaft by bending his elbows until he was almost in a pull-up position with his hands directly beneath his chin. Tightly gripping the corner of the shaft, he began to lower his body further down by extending his arms until his entire body was fully outstretched and he could barely touch the bottom of the horizontal shaft beneath him. At this point he slowly let his grip loosen above him, gently dropping down onto the floor beneath him.

"Piece of cake," he thought to himself. "Too bad that wasn't the toughest obstacle for me to overcome this evening."

William knew that was probably one of his easier tasks.

After approximately five minutes of crawling on this level of the ventilation system, he had negotiated his way to the center of the building where the path he had been following abruptly ended in front of him as it intersected an equally sized shaft running perpendicular to the one he had been navigating.

"This is where things start to get interesting," he ruefully thought to himself.

Pulling a second nylon rope from his bag he carefully unraveled it and began lowering it down the shaft. Almost immediately he realized that he had made a dreadful mistake.

"Dang it!" he muttered.

William became conscious of the fact that he had used the wrong nylon rope to lower the bag from the tree when he first entered the Cenetics complex. The tree limb was approximately 15 feet above the ground and would have required no more than the 20-foot length of rope that he now held in his hand. Most likely a result of all the adrenaline, he inadvertently used the forty-foot length of rope by accident. He now needed to decide if he was going to call off this night's endeavor.

"It's now or never," he firmly told himself. "If I call it off now, I might not get another chance."

With his resolve renewed, William now began to reason through the mechanics of using twenty feet of rope to make his way down a thirty-five foot drop off. Unfortunately, the dimensions of the ventilation shaft extending downwards into the pitch black beneath him were the same dimensions as the rest of the building...too wide for him to brace his body against either side and inch his way down slowly.

There was no way around it – he was going to need to drop himself fifteen feet to the bottom of the air duct, and pray to God that the noise didn't announce his presence to the security guards. Or, that the bottom of the air duct didn't give way to his weight, dropping him another 30 feet to the concrete floor of the main laboratory.

Using the electric drill and a carbide drill bit, he made a small hole at the juncture of two air ducts where he would get the most support. He twisted in a hook screw with a half-inch opening into the hole and secured a knot to the hook with one end of the rope. Another thought occurred to him at that moment that he didn't think of before. Would the impact of a fifteen-foot drop detonate the bomb that he was carrying in his bag?

"It doesn't matter. If the bomb goes off I will still accomplish my goal of destroying this building, everything inside, and put an end to this evil work."

Slowly, William began to climb down the nylon rope straight down the ventilation shaft. He quickly realized that his hands were beginning to slip on the rope because of sweat now beading off his body. About five feet from the end of the rope, which would have still been about twenty feet above the bottom of the shaft, the unthinkable happened. William's hands lost their grip and he plummeted helplessly down the ventilation shaft. He frantically reached out to grab something to slow down his fall to no avail. With a tremendous crash, his body slammed into the bottom of the shaft and he immediately felt a sharp twinge in his right thigh.

With a low groan, William pushed himself up to his side and listened intently to see if he could hear anything. The sound of sirens or alarmed voices would have been an indication to him that his presence had in fact been detected, and that it was only a matter of time before the security guards located him. Fortunately, there were no alarms or sirens, only the sound of the metal air duct creaking.

"Keep moving," he groaned to himself. "You've got to keep moving."

Slowly he got back on his knees and looked down the shaft extending in front of him approximately twenty feet. He could see a faint light break through small horizontal slits at the end of the shaft. With his right thigh throbbing in pain, he starting to crawl down the shaft towards the light.

After about thirty seconds, William found himself kneeling in front of an end cap of the airshaft. The light coming from the room on the other side was breaking through what looked like a giant heat vent William had in his apartment. There were approximately ten large steel slats that were partially open to allow for air to freely enter the room.

Rolling backward into a seated position, William scooted himself forward the remaining couple of feet until he was located directly in front the air vent. Reaching forward he wrapped his right hand firmly around the top slat and his left hand around the bottom slat. Bringing his knees back towards his chest he took a deep breath and extended both feet simultaneously into the vent dislodging it from the end of the shaft that he sat in.

With his hands tightly gripping the shaft, he was able to prevent it from falling thirty feet to the laboratory floor beneath him. He positioned his body sideways to the opening, still holding onto the air vent. Slowly he began to twist the vent so as to bring it back into the ventilation shaft diagonally. He moved his legs carefully behind him and started to move his body over to the right side as he began to draw the metal vent into the shaft. After about thirty seconds of effort, the vent cover lay diagonally inside the opening, angled directly over William's body. With his hands free, William inched towards the opening and peeked out over the edge.

The room beneath him was the same room that he had seen previously. It was approximately seventy-five by seventy-five feet in dimensions. Large by any scientist's definition for a laboratory, it was packed with state-of-the-art scientific equipment. In the center of the room, there was what looked like twelve, over-sized glass test tubes, all situated in a raised circle about five feet off the floor. The bottom of these cylinders was rounded glass, and the top was covered by a stainless steel covering, into which multiple tubes and wires protruded from the exterior into the tube. Each of tubes had a small nozzle at the end with a fitting that would allow it to be snapped into place. The wires were connected to various electrodes that hung lazily inside the tube. All the tubes and wires on the outside flowed back into the center of the circle and into the top of a large, stainless-steel canister. Scanning each of the cylinders William audibly gasped when he saw that one actually had contents inside of it.

"Unbelievable," he remarked with disgust. "They're actually trying to create more. But what's worse, it looks like they're trying to create an adult-sized clone."

Inside one of the cylinders on the far side of the circle was what looked like a gelatinous, pink mass extending lengthwise down into the container. Probably no more than three and a half feet in length, and about nine inches around, this fleshy looking matter really didn't resemble anything familiar. At least not at this point. William knew that eventually this would grow into something quite different than what he was currently staring at, and would provide a vessel to be possessed by dark angels.

Clustered around the glass cylinders and stainless-steel canister in the center of the room was a series of tables covered with computer screens and endless piles of papers. In addition, countless scientific instruments occupied the tabletops. Test tubes, microscopes, centrifuges, and syringes comprised the majority of the equipment.

It was the soft glow from the computer screens that was providing most of the illumination in the room. All the other lights were off given it was the middle of the night, with the exception of two fluorescent lights that remained on at all times to provide emergency lighting. The tables were arranged in three rows extending backward from the middle of the room. Desk chairs were sitting here and there without really any rhyme or reason, indicating that the cleaning staff had not made their rounds to clean up after a day's worth of work. The chairs and tables circling the cylinders in the middle of the room appeared as if they were sitting down in a sunken pit of sorts. This was emphasized by the fact that the floor beyond the chairs and table were raised about four feet higher, forming a large-sized square approximately forty feet by forty feet.

The edge of the raised floor had a stainless-steel railing around it to prevent someone from accidentally falling to the recessed floor beneath it. At the center of each side of the square were five steps providing easy access to and from the different levels. On the other side of the railing around the edge of the interior square was another series of tables, again covered with multiple computer screen and stacks of paper. Larger pieces of scientific equipment were located on tabletops including flasks, beakers, Bunsen burners and test tube racks. In addition, small sized Cryo Fridges were located on the sides of the tables, as well as incubators and blood shakers. There were two rows of tables on this second level with about ten feet of space in-between each row, allowing for medical carts and other mechanized transport equipment to freely navigate to the various workstations bringing raw materials and other supplies needed. The second level extended back approximately fifteen feet from the railing.

Another raised level, this time only about twelve inches higher, surrounded the second level. Again, a stainless-steel railing surrounded the end of the platform, but rather than stairs a gradually sloping ramp connected the two levels. The third level had about ten feet of open space on the other side of the railing, leaving the remaining ten feet of the floor space in the room to be filled by storage units, refrigeration units and large, walk-in Cryo Fridges, all of which had glass fronts allowing for viewing of the various contents contained inside.

These units lined the entire length of the walls except for a section in the middle. Two of the walls, opposite of each other, possessed a large, ten by ten hydraulic lift platform in the center that allowed for items to be transported from an almost mirror-like image of the storage, refrigeration units, and Cryo Fridges that sat directly on top of the first level of storage units around the perimeter of the large lab. Like the first level, there was ten feet of open space in front of the units with a stainless-steel railing at the edge. In addition, access ladders were located on either end of each wall for people to navigate from one level to the next without having to use the slow-moving hydraulic lift. One of the other walls had secure access doors that led to a small room with another set of security doors to ensure that only authorized personnel could come into this room. It is from this small room that William had first seen this lab.

The other wall, the one that William was very aware of, contained in it the means for his escape. Located in the center of the wall was a large metal door, approximately four feet tall by six feet long, hinged on the bottom edge, with a steel handle located at the top. This was the debris chute that was used to discard boxes and other packing materials easily from the laboratory thirty feet straight down into the basement of the building. This was William's route once he had completed his task. Fortunately for William, there were no security cameras allowed in the laboratory because Don was paranoid that someone was going to try and steal his work.

Glancing up towards the ceiling, William could see the rows of fluorescent lights that ran parallel to the ventilation shaft, spaced approximately ten feet apart from one another. The ventilation shaft essentially ran in-between two of these rows, leaving about a three-foot distance from either side of the opening. Reaching back into his duffle bag, William pulled out a final piece of rope that was five feet in length and had a heavy-duty steel hook fastened to one of the ends. William wrapped the end of the rope without the hook around his right hand three times to ensure he didn't accidentally drop it.

"That's all I need to do," he muttered to himself. "Drop the hook and rope as I try to climb over to the lights. Falling down the ventilation shaft was enough pain for the evening, thank you," he ruefully thought. "The concrete floor of the lab wouldn't be quite as forgiving as the ventilation shaft was."

Carefully, William leaned his upper body out of the shaft. His right arm was hanging over the edge gripping the rope and hook, while he used his left hand to press up against the top of the shaft to ensure that he didn't lose his balance. Gradually, he loosened his grip on the hook letting it hang approximately nine inches beneath his right hand, dangling at the end of the rope.

"Here we go," he huffed as he brought his hand slightly backward causing the hook to swing away from him.

He lowered his shoulders and swooped his hand forward swinging the hook towards the light fixture on his left. When he knew that the hook was moving directly at the top of the light fixture he released it. The hook immediately shot forwards towards the top of the fixture with the extra slack of rope trailing behind it.

It made a loud 'CLANK' as it stuck home on the top of the light fixture. William pulled his right hand back slightly causing the hook to slide along the top of the fixture, neatly resting itself around one of the steel conduit pipes extending from the ceiling that housed the electrical wires. With another firm tug, William verified that he had a solid connection.

Letting out a sigh of relief, William looked around the room again to make sure that the noise hadn't alerted anyone to his presence. Satisfied that he was still undetected, William positioned his body so his legs were dangling over the edge of the vent, being diligent to keep the rope slightly taut so the hook would not slip.

With the rope still wrapped tightly around his right hand, he firmly grabbed the rope with his left hand, pulling it strongly to ensure that the light fixture would be able to withstand his weight hanging from it. With his feet dangling from the shaft, he cautiously slid his body out. The instant that he was no longer in the shaft he dropped about three feet downwards until the rope stopped him short with a violent jerk. William now found himself hanging precariously from the light fixture, gently swinging back and forth. Quickly glancing upwards, he saw that the entire light fixture was gradually swaying as well.

Without hesitation, he quickly climbed up the rope towards the light fixture. Reaching the top, and while still gripping the rope with his left hand, William slowly unwound the rope from around his right hand. Once free, he reached for the outer edge of the light fixture and gripped the top with his right hand. Firmly holding onto the fixture, he reached for the left edge with his other hand and grabbed hold.

"I don't want to hang around here all day."

There was about fifteen feet from where he was currently hanging to the outer edge of the upper level. Slowly, but deliberately, William began sliding his hands one after another towards the edge of the room. After sixty seconds, William found himself almost to the outer edge of the upper level and his feet were nearly able to touch the top of the security railing at the edge of the floor. Moving forward a few more inches, William found that he could rest his feet on the top of the railing, allowing him to take some weight off his hands, which by this point were aching from the strain of his body weight.

With his feet now solidly on the railing, he easily slid his hands forward about six more inches and prepared to jump onto the floor of the second level. Releasing his hands, he hopped forward and gently landed on the floor.

"Keep moving," he told himself again.

Confirming that the duffle bag was still securely fastened to his belt, William darted towards the first ladder that would allow him to climb down to the main floor of the lab. Reaching the ladder, he turned himself around, grasped the top of the ladder and stepped down to the main floor.

Turning around slowly, William looked around the room as his gaze again met with the glass cylinders in the center of the room. William now purposefully made his way towards the center of the room. He quickly descended the stairs into "the pit" surrounding the glass cylinders. Moving forward, he found himself standing directly in front of the tube with the fleshy mass hanging within. This close he was to able see the contents in much more detail.

The fleshy mass was comprised of a thick, cloudy outer covering that was slightly transparent. Beneath the surface, he could see different shapes slowly writhing with no specific pattern or purpose. Leaning forward, he now stood with his nose only about four inches away from the glass. Almost as if sensing his presence, the indistinct objects seemed to coalesce directly in front of his line of vision, as if trying to reach towards William through the glass.

Suddenly William felt a strong wave of dizziness fall over him and the room seemed to darken. A sense of queasiness almost overwhelmed him as he bent forward and reached upwards with his hands to hold either side of his head in an effort to stop the room from spinning. The next instant, a sharp, screeching noise, almost like the sound of glass being shaved off a window with the edge of a knife pierced his ears, and he felt as if something roughly grabbed his wrists. Jerking himself upright, he stared again at the glass tube in front of him and noticed distinct etches in the glass that almost resembled the marks that a wild animal would have made if it tried to grab its prey.

In bewilderment, he looked at the tops of his hands and everything seemed normal. However, as he slowly turned his hands over he noticed small scratches on both of his wrists that seemed to match the spacing of those that were etched into the glass, with blood slowly oozing from the wounds.

Incredulously, William stumbled backward. "What the heck was that!" he exclaimed.

His wrists felt hot, almost as if they had been burned. Rubbing his wrists with his hands, William continued to stare at the glass container in front of him. The undulating mass looked as it had before, but the scratches in the glass remained.

"Time to get this done," he resolutely stated.

William reached for the duffle bag hanging at his side and unzipped it. After reaching into the bag, he withdrew the explosive device that he had painstakingly completed.

Resembling what could be described as a pipe bomb, but significantly more powerful, the device was approximately ten inches in length and four inches in diameter. Hanging out of one end were two wires – one red and one green. Each end was covered with electrician's tape to prevent them from accidentally connecting. Carefully, William set the device on one of the tables he was standing next to along with the duffle bag. Reaching back into the bag, he removed the two six-volt lantern batteries that would provide the power.

"Red to red, green to green," William silently thought to himself.

William laid the two wires parallel to each other and tightly twisted the ends to ensure a very good connection. Satisfied with the red wires, he carefully rewound electrical tape around them to prevent the green wires from accidentally touching them. Focusing on the green wires, he repeated the same steps as before.

As William completed assembling the device, a brief feeling of doubt and regret rushed over him. For an instant, he doubted his courage to see this through. However, looking again at the wounds that had somehow been inflicted upon his wrists by something that wasn't there, he knew he had to push forward.

William picked the device back up and cradled it in his left hand. With his other hand, he grasped a key attached to the digital clock and firmly turned it 90 degrees in a clockwise motion. Instantly, the display of the unit turned on with all the LED lights illuminating for two seconds. The display read "0:00:00." Depressing the black button on the top and holding it down, the numbers began to increase in order, slowly at first and then gradually increasing in speed.

Thinking he had accounted for enough time, he released the button and the display read "0:12:04." This number had meaning to William and reminded him of one of the scriptures that he had previously read. Pressing and holding the top button for a moment and releasing again, the display now read "0:15:07."

Having decided previously that he needed to set the timer to fifteen minutes to assure that he had sufficient time to get to a safe distance of roughly one and a half miles, William left the timer at "0:15:07" and readied himself.

Taking a deep breath, he reached again for the key with a visibly trembling hand. Without hesitation, as soon as he gripped the key he turned it another ninety degrees clockwise, which was immediately followed by a high-pitched chirp. The device was armed! William closed his eyes for a few seconds, opened them, then depressed the green button on the base of the device, and the clock began to count down from "0:15:07."

"Time to move," he barked.

Reaching in-between two of the glass tubes in the center of the room, one of which contained the pulsating material, William placed the device as close to the center canister as possible and out of view.

"Can't have someone walk in here and find a surprise," he mused.

Turning quickly, he now darted back across the lower level, up the stairs, and made his way to the far side of the room where the door to the debris chute beckoned. Hastily he reached down and snapped the door upwards, making a loud metal clank. Holding the underside of the door with his right hand, he slid down into a seated position and moved towards the gaping hole extending down into complete darkness beneath him. At this point, he realized that he had left his duffle bag on a table in the center of the room.

"No time to worry about that now," he said in an exasperated tone. "When the bomb goes off there will be nothing left."

Holding the door with his right hand, William readied himself to jump into the debris chute.

Pausing briefly, William thought to himself. "I sure hope they're still using this to dispose of *only* cardboard boxes and packaging material. Otherwise, this could be a very painful trip."

William was counting on the fact that garbage from the facility was picked up in the morning on the next day. This meant there should be several boxes and other material to cushion his thirty-foot drop straight down.

Without another thought, he pushed his body forward with his left hand and fell downwards into the darkness without any way to slow his descent. Almost immediately after he lunged forward he heard the loud BANG of the debris chute door slamming behind him. Holding his breath, William braced for what he hoped would be a relatively soft landing in the dumpster located at the end of the garbage chute exactly 1.36 seconds later.

William landed in a mostly full dumpster amongst cardboard boxes, paper, and Styrofoam. Despite the dumpster being relatively full, he hit the garbage pile with a distinct thud. Not being able to control his descent, the fall caused William to wince in pain as his right thigh once again began to throb in pain.

"No time to lose!" his mind raced. "Go Go Go!!"

Scrambling to get to the edge of the dumpster, William realized that the headlamp that was secured to his head now hung lazily around his neck. Holding the side of the dumpster, he replaced it back onto his forehead and switched it on to illuminate the basement. Quickly scanning the room, he noted various boxes stacked on the side, some pallets, blue plastic drums containing chemicals, and other miscellaneous items. Holding onto the side of the dumpster with both hands, he pushed himself upwards to his waist and slung his right leg over the edge. Again, a sharp twinge of pain emanated from his right hip.

"Oof!" he grunted. He knew that he likely had at least pulled a muscle, or had possibly even torn something. "This is going to slow me down."

Shifting his weight, he pulled his left leg over the side of the dumpster and jumped down to the concrete floor. Again, pain ripped through his right side but he barely noticed it this time. He sprinted across the basement towards a small corner where he could see light coming in from outside through a window placed high on the wall. He pulled a box over to the wall just beneath the window, crawled on top of it and peered out the window. Immediately he turned his head away with a sharp jerk.

"STUPID IDIOT!" he screamed silently to himself.

He had forgotten the lamp on his head was still on. Quickly he reached up and turned it off, and cautiously looked out the window again.

"Too close," he muttered as he exhaled in relief. "Way too close!"

Fortunately, there was not anyone within view of the window. He just had to hope that no one had noticed the light reflecting off of anything outside.

Reaching for the bottom of the window he unhooked the latch and silently pulled the window towards him. A cool breeze ran over his face as the night air softly passed through the open window. Reaching outside of the window he grabbed the side of the building and gruffly pulled his body up and out through the opening. He quickly got onto his feet in a crouched position and looked around. He was in approximately the same area where he was thirty minutes earlier. About twenty feet to his left lay the four-foot-tall brick wall concealing the dumpster that he had initially climbed on to reach the ladder.

Glancing around he checked to make sure that no one was within sight. Satisfied that he was still alone, he ran over to the dumpster wall and made his way around to the side of the wall concealing the generator. Peeking around the corner he could see the front of the building and into the main lobby of Cenetics. Both Karl and Jim were in essentially the same positions that William had left them. Karl stood lazily to the side of the front desk, leaning against the wall and inspecting his fingernails, while Jim sat in the chair, again staring blankly at the monitors in front of him. The only difference was that Jim now held a large Styrofoam cup in his right hand, undoubtedly filled with a caffeinated beverage.

At that moment William again felt a sudden rush of queasiness fall over him and his vision seemed to darken again. He looked around wildly as if expecting to find someone or something close by, but found nothing at all. Still feeling sick to his stomach William started to sprint back across the parking lot towards the spot by the fence where he had lowered himself from a tree limb. After going no further than ten steps William was suddenly struck on the left side of his body and fell roughly to the parking lot's hard blacktop. Excruciating pain shot out of his left shoulder that he tightly gripped with his right hand. As he slid his hand beneath his sweatshirt to rub his shoulder he felt the slickness of warm blood. Terror gripped him as he picked himself up off the ground, looking around to discover what had struck him.

"Show yourself," he demanded. "By God, show yourself to me now!"

William looked down roughly ten feet in front of him. The ground was illuminated by the lights affixed to the top of the poles in the parking lot. The ground slowly began to darken as if a cloud had materialized below them. As the cloud began to thicken and move, the shadow cast on the ground in front of him became starkly dark and looked as if it was growing in size, sliding in an almost purposeful motion towards William. The shape of the shadow continued to shift in size and became so dark that William thought it looked as if the ground had opened up revealing a pitch-black bottomless pit. With the shifting shape getting closer, William's head began to ache and his wrists that had been scratched earlier began to burn from an unseen heat. A distinct feeling of torment swept over William and he felt as if he was trapped and unable to move.

It took every ounce of strength for him to reach back inside his sweatshirt and again pull out the Talisman from around his neck. Holding the symbol directly in front of him he felt as if he were pushing against an insurmountable weight that was trying to crush him. Forcing his arm to hold the amulet, he took a step towards the murky dark shape on the ground in front of him. The shifting shadow that lay just in front of him on the ground seemed to recoil from the advance, and shrunk away from William. With great exertion, he took another step forward and thrust his hand forcefully toward the ground. As if it were a sheet of glass struck by a rock, the shadow immediately shattered upon itself with light once again returning. The final specs of shadowy shapes slid out to the periphery of his view and completely disappeared. The dizziness left him and his head stopped aching, but the sickness in his stomach remained.

"I don't believe that this is really happening," he exclaimed in utter disbelief.

Looking at his hand holding the amulet he could make out the distinct color of red covering his palm and fingers.

Reaching back toward his left shoulder he stretched the neck of his sweatshirt down revealing his shoulder. He was not prepared for what he saw next.

There were six gouge marks of approximately the same size on the front of his shoulder, close to his chest, and blood was slowly oozing from each of the wounds. Shrugging his shoulder forward he saw six, virtually identical marks on the back of his shoulder.

"They almost resemble teeth marks," he puzzled to himself. "But how is that possible?!"

He sprinted the remaining distance to the spot where he had traversed the fence and found the end of the rope still hanging lazily where he had left it. Still feeling sick to his stomach, he turned back to look at the building which stood about seventy-five feet from him. Slowly his eyes shifted upward toward the sky directly above the building. He was absolutely not prepared for what he saw next.

In the darkened sky above the facility, William could make out a swirling motion of clouds, no, more like vapor, moving in a counterclockwise direction. There was no wind to speak of, but the vapor appeared to move rapidly, constantly shifting and changing shape. Continuing to examine what appeared to be almost a vortex of sorts, he could make out distinct shapes veiled by the vapor, moving in the same direction. Starting out very quietly he could hear what sounded like the faint flapping of wings of some sort. He intently listened while he stared at the spectacle in front of him. Gradually the flapping sound grew stronger and he began to hear what he could only describe as shrieks of pain. The cries became louder and louder, and the dark spinning mass appeared to increase in speed. The louder the sounds became, the faster the motion of the vapor and shapes. Suddenly, a bright light, almost like a bolt of lightning, flashed directly in front of his eyes, causing William to clench them shut in response. When he opened his eyes he could clearly, vividly see what was lying shrouded by the vapor just moments earlier.

Numberless dark, shadowy creatures were clearly visible to William flying in a massive cluster directly above the Cenetics building. Each of them had thin, almost frail looking wings on their back, extending several feet outward directly from their shoulder blades. Each wing came to three points on the front edge, tipped with what looked to be a sharp claw. These wings flapped slowly in a rhythmic motion, powered by massive muscles flexing and relaxing across their backs and upper shoulders. Long thin tails extended backward from what could be described as a small torso, ending in a hook-like tip. Short, stocky legs trailed behind the creatures, each having four toes tipped by four-inch claws. Strong, stocky arms extended in front of the creatures, with three fingers and a short stubby thumb, each topped with razor-sharp four-inch long nails. Each of the hands was opened as if ready to grasp or attack.

A long, thick neck extended out from the torso for what seemed to be half a foot. Thick veins were standing up on both sides of the neck just beneath the surface of the skin. Resting on top of the neck lay a stout, almost triangular shaped head. There were no ears visible, but rather small, snake-like slits located where the ears would have likely been placed.

Large, bulbous eyes lay toward the outer edge of both sides of the head, with a broad, flat nose situated squarely between them. Extending down from the nose, the head narrowed toward the point of the triangle and formed an elongated mouth. Almost as if there were no lips, the teeth of these beings were bared and easily visible. William could clearly see six, sharply pointed teeth of about two inches in length on both the upper and lower jaws, exactly matching the six gouge marks that William had seen and felt on his left shoulder.

The faster the swirling mass spun in front of William, the stronger the sense of sickness he felt in his stomach, almost to the point of becoming uncontrollably ill. As the mass continued to spin, the noise became louder. William felt a warm trickle down the right side of his neck, and as he reached up to the side of his head, he felt a slight wetness of blood the was weeping from his ear. As the sound became almost unbearable another bright flash of light filled William's sight and the very next instant the vision was gone.

A strong sense of urgency hit William as he glanced down at his watch. Almost six minutes had passed since he had set the timer on his device.

"YOU HAVE TO MOVE NOW!" he exclaimed.

He grasped the rope hanging from the branch and started to climb it back to the branch overhead. The pain in his left shoulder was severe, but he ignored it altogether given the fact the clock was ticking. Reaching the branch, he swung one leg over it, then the other, and slid his body along the length back towards the trunk of the tree. Looking beneath him, he saw that he had cleared the barbed wire fence. Instantly he unwrapped his legs and hung down towards the grass beneath him by his hands. Letting go he landed softly on the grass standing upright. Without wasting a second, he immediately turned and sprinted away from the building down the driveway leading back to the main road.

The Cenetics facility was located in an industrial section of downtown Los Angeles. There were light and heavy manufacturing facilities, warehousing, and food processing plants. Being nearly three-thirty a.m. the streets were abandoned and everything was quiet. William ran directly away from the Cenetics building. After running for about ten minutes as fast as his legs would carry him his right hip began to cramp, undoubtedly from the falls he experienced not long before. As the seconds ticked away his sprint turned into a run, which ultimately turned into a jolting jog.

"You've got to keep going!" he angrily shouted at himself. He knew he needed to get as far away from the building as possible or he wouldn't survive the night.

A few moments later he thought to himself that it must be getting close—his time was almost up. Despite his injury, William was now approximately a mile and a half away from the laboratory. The pain was now almost unbearable as he tried to press forward. Suddenly, his hip gave out on him and he fell hard to the ground. With great effort, he pushed himself back up to his knees, readying himself to start moving again.

He then turned back to glance in the direction of Cenetics, and at that moment a tremendous flash of light burst into his field of vision. Blinded by the white beam, he turned his head away and braced for the shockwave that would inevitably follow the explosion.

Traveling at two thousand meters per second, a shockwave erupted outward from the center of the blast along with incinerating heat. Everything within a one-quarter mile radius of the blast was vaporized. At 10,000 degrees Kelvin, not much was going to survive even a small nuclear blast. Buildings, steel, concrete and trees...all gone. The blast dug a massive, bowl-shaped gouge into the earth about four hundred feet in diameter and almost twenty feet deep.

Extending out to a half-mile radius was a scene of absolute destruction. The heat blast instantly ignited almost everything in sight. The heat was so intense that buildings were literally engulfed in flames. Walls of large, concrete structures were toppled to the ground, and large chunks of concrete were strewn everywhere. Streets and roads were twisted and torn exposing deep gouges and cracks. What few trees remained standing were set ablaze or sat smoldering from the intense heat that had literally ripped the life out of them. It virtually looked like hell on earth.

Stretching out to a one-mile radius from the blast there were obvious signs of the intense level of energy and heat released by the explosion. The paint on cars and buildings was blistered, peeling and bubbling on all surfaces. Trees and other landscaping were burning or smoldering. Buildings were on fire and secondary explosions occurred as gas mains or containers of chemicals detonated, sometimes in rapid succession. Glass was everywhere from windows of buildings and automobiles. Several cars were sitting on their rims, their tires combusted in flames or melted altogether. Beyond one mile there were fires that were lit by burning debris of wood and steel that rained down from the sky. Not one window facing the explosion within a three-mile radius remained intact.

Exactly one point two seconds after the detonation of the nuclear device, a shock wave traveling at two thousand meters per second hit William, throwing him sideways into a dumpster behind a two-story brick building. He momentarily heard the explosion but then all sound vanished as the piercing noise hit his eardrums. With a struggle, he slowly got to his knees and looked back in the direction that the explosion had come from. As he took in the devastation, blood oozed from both of his ears, and darkness slowly entered in from the outside of his vision, until everything completely blacked out as he lost consciousness.

CHAPTER 37

Rude Awakening

It was approximately eleven o'clock in the morning and while the December sun was shining down on the city of Los Angeles, it didn't seem to carry much warmth with it to the ground below. There was a slight haze that covered most of the city and some of the surrounding areas. The streets were mostly devoid of traffic, excepting an occasional car or city vehicle here and there, and very few pedestrians could be seen. An eerie, almost deathly hush fell over the large metropolitan city that would normally be bustling late on a Saturday morning.

Tara and her father sat anxiously in the emergency waiting room of the hospital. Rich sat in one of the small chairs with his arms tightly folded against his chest and had a stoic expression on his face. Tara sat in the chair immediately next to him, nervously wringing her hands while she unconsciously bounced her right leg. After about three minutes, Rich glanced over at his distraught daughter and placed his left hand solidly down on her right leg, not so much to stop her from moving it, but to show her support.

Tara glanced over at her Dad as giant tears began to well up in both of her eyes. She had been trying to keep her emotions under control, but she just couldn't contain them any longer. With a deep gasp, she flung her arms outward and wrapped her arms around her father, burying her face between his neck and left shoulder for a few moments.

"Oh, Daddy! I just don't understand what is going on," she spouted out as fast as she could speak. "First, there was a major terrorist attack on the city of Los Angeles in the middle of the night, and then the hospital calls me at three thirty to let me know that William has been seriously injured. I come down here to see how he is doing and they don't let me in to see him at first because he is in surgery. They tell me a few hours later that the surgery went fine and that I would be able to see him in thirty minutes. Then, a whole bunch of police and FBI agents head back into the recovery rooms, and the next thing I know they tell me that I can't see William right now because he is being questioned."

Tara was literally sobbing uncontrollably at that moment, and she buried her face again in Rich's tear soaked shirt. He sympathetically hugged his daughter and started gently stroking the back of her hair.

Suddenly, Tara jerked back from her father with an expression of horror on her face.

"They think that William had something to do with this, don't they?! There's no way that he had anything to do with this!"

Again, she hugged her father and continued to sob.

"It's ok Tara," Rich gently consoled. "Let's not jump to any conclusions until we find out exactly what's going on here. I'm sure it's just some sort of big misunderstanding."

Rich sounded sure enough in the words that he spoke, but deep inside he knew that William most likely had something to do with what had occurred the night before. The images on the television in the waiting room showed footage shot from a helicopter circling over the warehouse district. On the center of the television screen was a massive crater approximately a quarter of a mile wide and at least a couple hundred feet deep. The proximity of the crater to the river and what he could make out of the buildings that were left standing relatively close by led him to the conclusion that this was the location of where the Cenetics research facility once stood. The headline on the bottom of the television screen confirmed his conjecture.

"Terrorist attack on Cenetics completely obliterates research facility."

A moment later, an armed policeman accompanied by an FBI agent solemnly approached the area that Rich and his daughter were seated.

"Mrs. Mears," the FBI agent politely inquired. "You are Mrs. Mears correct?"

Tara simply stared at the large federal agent but seemed incapable of responding. Rich leaned backward slightly, allowing him to look at the two men while keeping his left arm protectively wrapped around his daughter.

"My name if Rich Cline, and this is my daughter Tara. What exactly is going on?"

"If you would, please come with us. We have a number of questions that we need to ask you...both of you actually."

Tara helplessly looked at her father who managed to produce a somewhat reassuring smile in response.

"Its ok sweetheart...let's go on back with these two gentlemen. I'm sure that we'll find out exactly what's going on as quickly as possible."

Both Tara and Rich rose from their seats and followed the two law enforcement personnel out of the waiting room, down a hallway, and into a small conference room. Once they had entered the room, the policeman shut the door behind him.

"Please," the FBI agent stipulated, "take a seat."

Rich and Tara both took a seat around a small circular table, looking expectantly at the two men standing on either side of the closed door.

"I'm special agent Stevens," the FBI agent announced. "I am assigned to a tactical anti-terrorism unit in the Los Angeles area. As I'm sure you've heard on the news there was a massive attack last night on the Cenetics facility. Horrible actually. The entire area is completely devastated, and we are quarantining a one-mile radius around the blast."

"Quarantined?" Rich asked. "Why is it quarantined?"

"They are shutting down the area due to the risk of radiation contamination. You see...that explosion last night wasn't from an ordinary bomb. We have reason to believe that it was nuclear in nature. Not a full blown atomic explosion, but more of a controlled, tactical strike."

Tears began to well up again in Tara's eyes and she tightly gripped her father's hand. She took a brief moment to get herself under control and then began in as calm a tone of voice as possible.

"You don't think that William had something to do with this, do you?" she finally blurted out. "There's no way that he could have been!"

A tight-lipped frown creased Agent Stevens face and he looked down at the floor immediately in front of Tara. He then cast his eyes upward with a stern expression on his face.

Tara wheeled to face her father with tears freely streaming down her reddened cheeks. Her mouth hung open as if she was trying to speak, but no sound came from her mouth except for a non-comprehensible crackle.

"Mrs. Mears," the Agent continued, "I can give you five minutes to speak with your husband, but then we need to isolate him from any visitors. You understand why of course?" he questioned without expecting any real response.

Tara simply looked at the man and nodded silently. She then turned to her father, whose hand she was still tightly clutching, and then looked back at the FBI Agent.

"Can my father come with me?" she implored.

The Agent took a deep breath with a somewhat conflicted expression on his face. As he opened his mouth to respond he seemed to change his mind before speaking, and then addressed the question.

"Yes," he relented. "I suppose that would be alright. Please follow me."

Agent Stevens opened the door and led Tara and her father back down the hallway to one of the recovery rooms. As they approached the room a nurse carrying a clipboard exited from the room, paused for a moment to glance at their party, then continued on her way.

"I can give you five minutes, no more."

"Thank you," Rich responded.

With his arm around his daughter's shoulders, he accompanied Tara into the hospital room.

As they walked into the room, the sound of a heart monitor could be heard. The room itself was quite large but looked to be completely empty. On the right-hand side, there was a large white hospital curtain hanging from a small track on the ceiling. Tara walked over and grasped the end of the curtain and slowly slid it to her left revealing a hospital bed with William lying on it with his eyes closed.

Several wires attached to electrodes were affixed to William in multiple locations to measure his vital signs. His right arm was encased in a large, plaster cast that extended from his shoulder down to the second set of knuckles on his hand. A large bandage was holding a gauze pad in place on the left side of his head. There was a bump on his left cheek, and his skin on his arms, face, and torso was black and blue from injuries that he had sustained. He wasn't wearing a shirt and a large bandage was tightly wrapped around his torso. In addition, a second bandage was tightly wrapped around his left shoulder holding gauze in place on both the front and back.

Sensing that someone was in the room, William's eyes fluttered momentarily and then opened. He stared into the eyes of the love of his life and a tear slowly trickled down his right cheek. Swallowing hard, he took a deep breath readying to speak.

"Tara..." he whispered as he cast his eyes down to the floor.

Tara quickly stepped over to the side of his bed, taking his right hand her between both of hers as she sympathetically looked into his eyes.

"William, they said that there was a terrorist attack!" she spoke in almost an inaudible tone. "They made it seem like you had something...something..."

Tara broke off as her breath caught, unable to continue speaking.

"Tara, you have to understand that I didn't have a choice. This was the only way that I could make certain that..."

"WHAT!?" Tara cried, releasing his hand as she took a step back away from the bed.

"Tara, please!" he implored. "Let me explain!"

The look on Tara's face vacillated between apprehension and panic, and after a brief moment solidly expressed what could be best described as disgust.

"Tara..."

"Don't talk to me!"

"But Tara, you have to let me..."

"I don't have to let you do anything. I don't know who you are! You destroyed that facility. You...you..." she nearly choked on her own saliva between sobs. "You killed people. You killed those children. You..."

Tara took a large step back staring at William. She had so many feelings coursing through her brain that she thought she was going to pass out from emotional overload. She stood there, staring at the man lying on the hospital bed like she had never seen him before.

Then, without another word, she turned and ran from the room leaving William and her father behind. The sound of her sobs trailed away as she made her way down the hallway and away from William.

CHAPTER 38

Due Process
(May 10, 2018)

The weeks leading up to the trial were the loneliest that William had ever experienced in his life. The courts had denied his bail primarily on the basis that he would likely be at risk of physical injury or worse if allowed to be in public. The majority of his days were spent in solitary confinement. Tara refused to make contact of any kind, and it seemed as if Rich had abandoned him. The only personal interaction that he had was with the police officer who brought him his daily meals and the hours that he spent in a conference room with his court-appointed public defender.

William had opted not to hire his own defense lawyer and asked that the court simply assign him an advocate to try his case. He had decided that he wasn't going to try and mount a defense. He freely admitted to the FBI and police that he was responsible for the destruction of the Cenetics facility and that he had orchestrated it entirely by himself.

He spent hours upon hours in his six by eight-foot cell lying on a simple mattress that didn't provide much in terms of comfort, staring up at the concrete ceiling. Occasionally he would thumb through a magazine or book. But for all intents and purposes, he had consciously shut himself off from the outside world.

The trial itself was not expected to last long at all. Based on the fact that he openly admitted to the heinous act, it didn't take much for the prosecution to lie out a damning set of evidence. They had spent the better part of the first day of the trial detailing the massive destruction that William had caused both in terms of life and property. The blast from the device had completely obliterated nearly four square city blocks, including the state of the art Cenetics research center, and left in partial ruin another ten blocks immediately adjacent to the blast. The total cost of direct monetary loss for the destruction of property was in the area of two hundred million dollars. However, because the explosion was nuclear in nature it had created a quarantine zone of nearly six miles from the epicenter, and experts estimated the loss of real estate value and business activity to be in the billions.

There had been a total of seventeen lives lost that evening in February. Those among the dead included the six clones, the children's mother Kim, seven security guards, two cleaning staff, and an unfortunate driver of a city bus who was heading home after a long shift. The bodies of those killed in the Cenetics facility were never found, having been utterly vaporized by the amount of energy released in the explosion.

The state attorney spent the majority of the second and third days explaining in detail the nature of the relationship between William and Don. They described their former friendship and how they had split ways over differing opinions when it came to their research. They painted a picture of William being humiliated by Don's success, and how that disdain had festered over a period of years. How when Don tried to make amends over the supposed injustice that William had suffered, that he seized on that as an opportunity to exact his revenge.

They described in gory detail the premeditation, the planning and all the concerted efforts that were required to conduct such a deplorable act. They detailed how his conduct showed absolutely no concern for the lives of others.

The final piece of evidence that they presented was a taped video confession from William himself admitting to having committed the crime. He matter-of-factly described all his planning and preparation, and how he not only intended to destroy the Cenetics complex, but that his aim also included the destruction of the six clone children.

On the fourth day of the trial, William was escorted into the same courthouse that he had been on the three previous days. Upon entering the courtroom, he glanced around taking note of the audience that had assembled to witness his public castigation. No fewer than twelve news-related organizations were feverishly snapping photos and capturing video as he made his way up to the front of the room. The jury box was empty as he expected, knowing that they would not be asked to take their seats in the courtroom until the judge was about to enter. But then he saw something that he hadn't expected.

To the left of the room, situated directly behind his court-appointed attorney was the familiar face of Rich, sitting with his arms folded as they customarily were in front of his chest. The countenance on his face clearly communicated the emotions he was experiencing— sadness, anger, grief, and a touch of empathy. As the large man leaned back in his seat, William nearly choked as he realized who had accompanied him to the court that day.

Tara quietly sat in the chair next to her father. She wore a simple, black silk dress, and large rimmed sunglasses that didn't do much to hide the fact that her eyes were swollen from having cried so much. Silently, she stood up from her seat, removed her glasses and faced William.

"Tara," William whispered in disbelief. "Tara, you came!"

He approached Tara with the intention of holding her in his arms, but stopped short and froze where he stood, not knowing if she would reject him. He took a deep breath preparing to speak, but couldn't find the words to even begin.

Tara didn't waste a second and she flung her arms outward and embraced William in a tremendous hug. Burying her face into his chest he could barely make out what she was saying.

"Oh William, I've missed you so much!"

"Tara, my dear Tara! I'm so sorry for all of this."

The two of them fiercely embraced one another for the next two minutes. William could barely believe that Tara had come to the trial. He thought that she had completely written him off because of the deplorable act he committed.

Finally loosening his vice-like hug slightly, he leaned back and looked into her eyes.

"I don't understand," he admitted. "Why did you come?"

"Daddy told me everything," she whimpered with tears welling up in her eyes. "He told me why you did what you did!"

William glanced momentarily over at Rich and silently mouthed the words 'thank you' in his direction, and then redirected his gaze back toward Tara.

"I understand you wanting to take some sort of action," she continued, "but I don't agree with what you did. There had to be another way."

William closed his eyes and exhaled slowly. When he looked back into Tara's eyes, tears were welling up and he could barely keep his composure.

"I...I didn't know what else to do. No one would believe me if I tried to explain what was going on. They would think that I was totally off my rocker, or that I was just retaliating for my company going under."

Rich stood alongside the two who were still embracing one another. Placing his hand on William's shoulder, he leaned close to whisper something to him.

"What is your defense going to be?"

"I wasn't planning on saying anything. I did what I did, and that's that. There's no reasonable or logical defense than I could possibly mount."

Rich stood staring at William for a moment, and then the expression on his face dramatically shifted from one of resignation to one that reflected hope.

"Will...you need to tell them exactly why you did what you did. You need to tell them everything. Tell them about the visions and the physical marks. Explain to them about the demons that you saw possessing the children. Confess that you felt it was not just your will, but the will of God that the children, facility, and everything else needed to be destroyed."

"But if I do that..."

"They will think you're crazy!" Tara blurted out, catching her father's logic.

"Exactly," Rich agreed. "And the thing is, you wouldn't be lying. You would be telling the absolute truth. And Will...there never would have been a better example of the truth setting you free!"

"Do you think it will work?"

"If I hadn't witnessed the same type of vision, I would think that you were totally mad. So yes...I think it will actually work."

The bailiff then entered the courtroom, followed immediately by the twelve members of the jury who took their respective seats in the jury box. The bailiff was a rather small, unintimidating man, whose shirt looked two sizes too large.

William reluctantly released Tara from his arms, taking his seat next to his defense attorney.

"All rise. The Los Angeles Superior Court is now in session, the Honorable Judge Eli Jacob presiding."

A mostly unassuming man wearing the traditional black robe customarily worn entered the courtroom. He had a mostly balding head and wore thin, silver-rimmed glasses.

"Your Honor, today's case is The City of Los Angeles versus William Mears."

"Thank you, you may all be seated." Turning to face the accusing attorneys he continued. "Does the state wish to call any additional witnesses."

A slender, attractive woman in her mid-forties stood up to face the judge. She was wearing a dark navy-blue dress suit and a white silk blouse.

"Your honor, the State does not wish to call any more witnesses to the stand, and the State rests."

"Thank you."

Turning to his right he faced the small desk behind which William and his attorney were seated.

"Defense, I understand that you have decided not to call a witness at this time. Does the defense rest?"

William's attorney slowly stood and was readying himself to reply to the judge.

"Will," Tara insisted in a sharp whisper. "WILL!!"

William glanced back at Tara who was virtually jumping out of her seat. The expression of panic on her face, obviously driven by love, inspired William to speak.

"You honor," he interjected in a loud voice. "I would like to take the stand in my own defense please."

The courtroom noisily buzzed about the change of events, and the judge raised a quizzical eyebrow toward William's attorney who merely shrugged his shoulders in response. After a brief moment, the judge continued.

"Does the defense wish to call a witness?" he formally inquired.

Still standing, William's attorney responded in an equally formal manner.

"Yes, your Honor. The defense calls Doctor William Mears to the stand."

William stood up from his seat, straightened the suit that he was wearing, purposefully approached and took his seat on the stand. The bailiff approached William and placed a Bible on the table directly in front of him. Standing up from his chair, he placed his left hand on the Bible and raised his right arm to the square.

"Do you swear to tell the truth, the whole truth, and nothing but the truth, so help you God?"

William took a deep breath and the confidently responded.

"I do!"

"You may be seated," the Judge responded. "Doctor Mears, I understand that you would like to make a statement in your own defense is that correct?"

"It is."

"Alright. Please proceed."

William clasped both of his hands in front of him on the table, as Tara anxiously watched holding her breath. After taking a moment to gather his thoughts, he proceeded to address the jury.

"Ladies and Gentlemen of the jury. I freely admit that I am responsible for conceiving, planning, and carrying out the detonation of a nuclear device within the Cenetics facility. I do not wish to argue that point at all. However, the reasoning that the prosecution has laid out is completely false. I want to explain to all of you, and to everyone in the world, why I did what I did."

William then proceeded to chronicle in vivid detail all of the events that he experienced. He described the multiple visions that he witnessed including his observance of the Great War in Heaven, and how he saw himself as one of those fighting against Satan. He described the multiple instances where he saw demonic personages trapped within the bodies of the clones, possessing their bodies. He recounted the real interactions that he had had with unseen entities and the physical marks that they left on his body. He described the absolute truth of the events, scenes, and situations that he witnessed, and how this unseen evil had been fighting against him.

William paused for a moment scanning the faces of the jury. All of them had an incredulous expression on their faces intimating that they didn't believe a word he was saying. In sharp contrast, the countenances on Rich and Tara's faces glowed with agreement and approval.

Shifting his gaze to the audience in the courtroom, he was startled when he locked eyes with his once close friend Don Stafford.

With narrow eyes, a furrowed brow and pursed lips, a look of absolute hatred exuded from his face. William hadn't expected to see him at the trial but understood why he would want to be present. He had killed the woman with whom he had fathered those six, unholy vessels.

After averting his eyes and taking a reassuring breath, William continued with his narrative.

"I knew that I had to do something," he stipulated. "It was my moral obligation. No...it was more than just that. I had a personal revelation from God himself that I needed to take action. That these vile creatures needed to be eradicated from off the face of the earth. My life's work had been perverted...twisted...made evil. Out of Creation...Abomination. This is why, ladies and gentlemen of the jury, I did what I did. I swear that this is the truth. I swear by the very name of the Great God Almighty that this is what happened, and I cannot deny, nor will I ever deny that this did, in fact, occur."

The courtroom was dead silent as William paused to let his words sink in. The perplexed expressions on not just the jurors, but pretty much everyone else in attendance, clearly relayed bafflement and disbelief. That is, everyone in the room except Don.

Don continued to glare at him with a tightly locked jaw. William could see the anger building to a crescendo from within—an escalation of pressure in preparation to eject all of the searing enmity that he held for the man who ruined his company, destroyed his work and murdered his girlfriend.

The judge paused for a moment to consider the testimony that William had just delivered and then turned toward the defendant with a perturbed look.

"Doctor Mears, with your testimony is it your intent to change your plea in this case?"

William pondered the question for a minute, considering how best to reply.

"Your honor, it is not my intent to try and sway the court one way or another. I simply wanted to state, for the benefit of all, the truth of what had happened, and why I acted in the manner that I did."

"I would like to ask that the defendant please return back to his seat and that both counsels please approach the bench."

William obliged his request, slowly making his way back to his seat. He didn't have to look in the direction of Don to know that he was bitterly staring at him. As he approached his seat he glanced at Tara who was attentively sitting on the edge of her seat, while she tightly gripped her father's left hand.

Both of the attorneys gathered closely around the judge, ardently listening to his quiet whisper. After roughly three minutes, they turned and returned to their respective seats. The countenance of the state attorney plainly expressed her irritation at the judge's words. When both the counsels were once again seated the judge took a preparatory breath before addressing the court.

"Doctor William Mears, in light of your most recent testimony, I have no choice but to recommend a continuance of this trial. Further, I propose the you be remanded into the custody of the Greater Los Angeles Mental Health Center for an indeterminate period of time in order to assess your mental state over the time period leading up to, and during the committal of the attack against Cenetics Research, and to determine if you are competent to stand trial."

The courtroom immediately erupted in a loud cacophony as jurors, news crews, and others sitting in audience noisily responded to the judge's announcement.

"Order in the court...I *will* have order in the court!" the judge warned slamming his gavel against his desk.

"MURDERER!" Don screamed as he stood in the rear of the courtroom. "THIS IS RIDICULOUS! HE CONFESSED TO THE CRIME! FIND HIM GUILTY AND PUT HIM TO DEATH!"

"Doctor Stafford!" the judge ominously warned as he stood from his seat. "If you do not immediately sit down and remain quiet, I will find you in contempt of court!"

"FIND ME IN CONTEMPT?! I HOLD YOU AND THIS ENTIRE PROCEEDING IN CONTEMPT! THIS TRIAL IS A FARCE!"

"Bailiff, please take Doctor Stafford into custody and escort him from the courtroom."

The bailiff was already making his way down the aisle towards where Don was seated. Despite Don's obvious agitation, he didn't make any effort to resist the bailiff who efficiently cuffed the man's hands behind his back, and led him out of the rear of the room.

The room filled with noise again, but immediately subsided in response to the sound of the gavel loudly rapping against the judge's desk. The next moment later, the bailiff entered the court and took his spot next to the judge.

"Bailiff, please take the defendant Doctor William Mears into custody, to be held at the county jail until such arrangements can be made to transfer him to a mental health facility for observation. This court will convene again once Doctor Mears has been sufficiently evaluated, and based on the recommendation of certified psychiatric professionals, we will continue with these proceedings."

The judge slammed his gavel down again, resulting in a reverberating clap throughout the courtroom.

"This court is now adjourned!"

The bailiff immediately approached William and

motioned for him to stand so he could take him into custody. Within a few seconds, William's hands were secured behind his back and he was about to escort him to the county jail.

"William!" Tara blurted out. "William...wait!"

William twisted to face Tara who had a panicked expression on her face and then turned back to the bailiff.

"May I say my goodbyes," he politely requested.

"Make it quick," he simply grunted.

William leaned up against the railing that separated the gallery from the front of the courtroom, and Tara fiercely wrapped her arms around him. With his arms handcuffed behind his back, he could only lean his head sideways against hers.

"I don't want you to go! When will I see you again," she whimpered.

"It's ok," he assured her. "I'm sure once I'm admitted that I will be able to have visitors."

Rich laid his hand on his daughter's shoulder reassuringly.

"Ok, now sweetheart...you need to let him go. We'll see him again."

Tara reluctantly released William from her embrace and securely held onto her father's arm. William nodded to Rich in acknowledgment of his appreciation.

"Take care of her for me!"

Rich simply nodded in reply.

William then turned back toward the bailiff, who firmly grasped his arm and escorted him out a door located to the left side of the judge's bench. Tara silently watched William as he exited through the doorway, and then burst into tears as the door solidly closed behind him.

CHAPTER 39

Prophesy
(September 2018)

It was nearly three o'clock in the morning, and William lay uncomfortably on a narrow cot in a room that was not much larger than the jail cell he had occupied while being held at the county jail prior to his trial. There was a small wooden desk on the opposite wall from his bed, with a painted wooden chair sitting directly in front of it. The room was completely dark except for a faint light that trickled in from a narrow window, approximately two feet wide by less than one foot tall, sitting high on the wall in-between the bed and desk, nearly eight feet from the floor.

Turning onto his right side, he closed his eyes in an attempt to find the sleep that had been eluding him for the past six hours. He lay there silently on his bed, listening to the sound of his own heartbeat slowly thumping in his ears.

He lay there quietly for approximately three minutes, and then noisily flipped himself over on his left side, exasperated by his inability to doze off. A few seconds later he flipped his covers off the bed in frustration, slid his feet off the side of the bed, and pushed himself up into a seated position.

"This sucks!" he muttered quietly to himself.

He stood up, took a couple steps across the room, noisily pulled the chair back from the desk and sat down. Reaching across the desk he depressed a small switch on a lamp, and with a quiet click, a light illuminated a circle approximately two feet in diameter on the workspace.

Reaching across the desk he grabbed a small, leather-bound notebook, opened it and found the page where he had made his last entry. With his right hand, he grasped a small ink pen and began to write on a blank page of paper.

"September 7, 2018: It's been almost four months since I was admitted to this nuthouse. I've been poked, prodded, analyzed, and medicated. It's obvious that the doctors all think I'm completely delusional. I have explained to them over and over again the things that I experienced, what I saw, and I never waiver on my description of the events. They just sit there and say 'I see. And why do you think these creatures are after you? Why is it that no one else can see them?' And then, of course, my favorite, 'How do you feel about having hurt so many people'. Of course, I feel bad, but it had to be done. The research and children had to be destroyed or else an evil would have been unleashed on the earth, and then no one would be safe.

It's frustrating beyond belief. They haven't let me see any visitors yet, saying that they want me to make more progress before interacting with anyone else. MORE PROGRESS! WHAT PROGRESS?"

William set the pen down on the surface of the desk and reached above his head with both arms as he stretched his back. Flexing his muscles momentarily, he let out a whoosh of breath and his shoulders slumped forward as he set both hands in his lap.

Unconsciously he reached up and scratched the scruff on the right side of his face, bowed his head down toward his chest and closed his eyes. He sat silently for a period of about two minutes listening to the deafening silence permeating the mental hospital.

His eyes opened suddenly in response to a very faint noise that sounded like the muffled screams of a woman. Holding his breath, he strained with his ears trying to pick up the noise again but to no avail. He turned his head back and forth searching the dark room, but nothing seemed out of the ordinary. With a sigh, he reached forward and turned the lamp off.

The room was essentially pitch black while his eyes adjusted to the darkness. He could begin making out the familiar shapes of the desk and bed, and he glanced up toward the window resting high on the wall. The same faint light seeped into the room from the outside world.

William let out another sigh and closed his eyes.

His eyes suddenly shot open again, this time in response to the sounds of a deep, bellowing growl that seemed to come from nowhere and everywhere at the same time. He excitedly turned his head from side to side, but he couldn't locate the source of the sound that had halted almost as quickly as it began.

"Maybe I really am going crazy," he jokingly considered.

Standing up, he made his way back to his cot and as he started to sit down, something caught his attention out of the corner of his left eye. Freezing in a half-seated position, he slowly turned his head to the left and desperately searched the dark recesses of the room. As he shifted his gaze to the right corner of the room his breath caught.

A foreboding sensation swept across his entire body as he faintly made out a murky, ominous shadow, seemingly growing out of the dark angular corner of the room.

Very consciously, he reached up towards his neckline and removed the Talisman that loosely hung around his neck. This was the one personal item that he was allowed to retain upon being admitted to the hospital, and he momentarily thought to himself that he was fortunate to have it with him.

Holding the necklace tightly in his grasp, he extended the Amulet towards the dark, nebulous shadow, which seemed to recoil backward, oozing back into the corners of the wall, until it completely disappeared.

While holding the necklace, William looked around his room trying to determine if something else was present, but he found nothing. Taking a deep breath, he sat back down on the cot and gently laid the Talisman against his chest on the outside of his shirt. As he reached up to wipe his brow, he surprisingly found that he had been sweating profusely, and he could feel his heart racing in his chest.

After sitting there for a few minutes to calm his nerves, he became acutely aware of how extraordinarily tired he was. He slowly lowered himself back into a laying position on his back, and gently closed his eyes. Within a few moments, he was quickly drifting into a deep, deep sleep.

As he lay there with his eyes shut, he could almost visualize dark swirling clouds of darkness flickering across his vision. As he breathed in, he felt the sensation of his body gently rising above his bed, and as he exhaled, it seemed as if he was falling downward, literally seeping through the bed itself. This sense of rising and falling seemed to intensify as he continued to deeply inhale and exhale, breathing in and breathing out.

As he took a deep, deep breath, his lungs expanded outward and he had the impression that he was literally rising above his body. He felt as if his very soul had escaped from his body, and he was actually suspended several feet above his mortal vessel.

As he exhaled, the feeling of falling swept over him in a much different manner than before. As he seemingly fell backward, he could feel the wind rushing around him, brushing past him as he plunged down into darkness. But this time, no matter what he did, he couldn't stop falling. And as he plummeted downward, he felt as if he was speeding up, falling quicker and quicker, deeper into and through the earth itself. Down through rock and stone...fire and darkness.

He tried to scream, but no noise escaped from his mouth. He shrieked in his mind, but no one could hear. Perilously and continuously he plunged through the blackness. He thought it would never end. He wished he could die.

Then, the feeling of air rushing past him halted, and he found himself standing alone, on a large rocky surface, in a deep, dark cave. He feverishly looked around him and could not make out any details, or discern anything that would give him an understanding of where he was.

Seemingly out of nowhere, there appeared to be a dark, red glow coming from somewhere beneath him, and all around him at the same time. Turning his head from side to side in a frenzied manner, he strained his vision to see where the light was coming from. And then he saw it.

Coming up from the ground around him there appeared to be liquid fire, boiling up from the very surface of rocks. Gurgling and roiling upward, the broth thickened, spewing forth bubbles and noxious gases. As the level increased, it began to encroach closer and closer to where William stood. He took a step back in an effort to escape what he was certain to be his death and then realized that the fiery elixir was completely encircling him. He felt the searing heat penetrating his skin and piercing into his very soul.

A large, deep rumbling noise erupted through the air nearly knocking William off his feet. His eyes darted to the right and to the left and then focused directly in front of him.

Ostensibly rising directly from the roiling sea of fire, William perceived a massive shadow extending from the surface. As it arched up to a nonexistent sky, massive black wings spread outward from a nondescript hulking center, extending at least one hundred feet in either direction. The wings were capped with enormous razor-sharp hooks spaced in uneven intervals.

Centered between the wings the features of a massive torso came into focus. Large, clearly defined muscles rippled beneath the exterior of what looked to be a thick, leathery skin. A broad, extensive chest flexed in unison, as colossal, powerful shoulders appeared. Gargantuan, sinewy arms reached upward, each with extraordinarily large hands, and fingers ended with five-foot-long, jagged nails.

Finally, almost as if sprouting out from the chest, a broad neck appeared and a grotesque, massively broad face appeared. The cheeks were sunken and possessed multiple scars extending in every direction. Hideously shaped horns protruded forth from the sides of the heads, twisting out and upwards, coming to sharply pointed ends.

The eyelids of this great, demonic creature were closed momentarily, but then abruptly opened, revealing what appeared to be an opening into the very bowels of hell. A flame flickered from within the sockets, and you could virtually feel pain and suffering emanating outward.

The beast's massive right shoulder shifted as the creature extended its right hand toward William, and lazily pointed at him with a monstrous claw. Then the demonic entity gaped its great mouth and spoke.

"THERE IS NO ESCAPE...NO MATTER WHAT YOU DO!" it bellowed in a maniacal voice so overwhelming William thought it would literally tear his body into pieces. "YOU THINK YOU HAVE THWARTED ME? YOU THINK YOU HAVE WON?" it taunted. "I AM EVERLASTING, AND I AM ALL POWERFUL. THERE IS NOTHING THAT YOU OR ANYONE CAN DO TO STOP WHAT IS COMING. AND IF YOU TRY, I WILL CONSUME YOUR SOUL, AND THE SOULS OF ALL THOSE YOU CARE ABOUT."

William feared for his very being. He didn't know what he could do. He felt like he was doomed and this was the very end.

"ALL WILL BOW TO ME AND I WILL HAVE MY DOMINION OVER THE EARTH. NOTHING CAN STOP THIS NOW!"

As William struggled to escape somehow, he snapped the Talisman from around his neck and cast it into the seething flames all around him. With his last ounce of energy, his raised his hands above his head and howled, clenching his eyes shut.

As he opened his eyes, the beast that he could only conclude was the devil himself, was gone, and he was surrounded by darkness.

He blinked again, but this time when he opened his eyes, it was as if he was in the air above the ground in some far away land. He glanced around but could not make out where he was.

He blinked again, and this time his eyes focused, he saw a large, dark grey building, sitting on the other side of a ravine. The building was four stories tall and was covered in many windows. Straining his vision, he was able to make out the word 'Cenetics' written in large letters on the side of the building.

He blinked again, and this time he was inside the facility, staring at tables covered with computers and various pieces of scientific equipment.

He blinked again and found himself inside of what he thought was the most massive laboratory that he had ever seen in his entire life. Row upon row of what could only be called massive test tubes was spread out across the entire floor. And within these containers, he could distinctly make out the gelatinous forms of human bodies that were being grown by the hundreds. These were the bodies of clones being produced on a massive scale. They were designed from the beginning to be formed into adults.

Looking to his right, his gaze seemingly cut through walls and the outside of the building. William felt as if he would vomit from what lay before his eyes. He saw long, endless rows of dark, demonic creatures, moving toward the facility with the intent of possessing the bodies that were being created to house them.

Like lightning striking its target, William was suddenly aware of the adversary's plan. And that was to build an army large enough to battle humans on the face of the earth. To conduct a war for the very souls of all humankind. To lead a conflict that would bring an end to the reign of God, and to issue in a new era, where the devil himself would rule supreme from the hills to the valleys, from the mountains to the depths of the sea. There would be nothing on the entire earth that would escape his power, and he would destroy all mankind, bringing to them the same pain and misery that he was brought to endure.

Not able to take the visions and boundless emotions any longer, William cried out in a loud, mighty voice.

"GREAT GOD ALMIGHTY! FREE ME FROM THIS DARKNESS! BRING ME BACK INTO THE LIGHT! MAKE ME WHOLE AGAIN AND I WILL SERVE THEE UNTIL THE VERY END OF TIME!"

Instantly, as if he had been teleported from the opposite side of the planet, William found himself again lying on top of his small cot inside the mental facility in Los Angeles. His clothes and bedding were completely sweat-sodden like he had run twelve marathons at a full sprint. But rather than being exhausted, he felt invigorated. He felt revitalized.

Shooting his feet off the side of the bed, he abruptly stood up and stared at the wall on the other side of the room.

He knew that he had been shown a vision. He knew that there was another facility. He knew that the devil himself was the master puppeteer behind everything that occurred. William knew that he was the one that needed to take action to put an end to this madness.

But he couldn't do this locked away in a mental facility. William knew…that he needed to escape!

##############################

Here ends the story of the first installment of the Creation Abomination series. The next book describes William's escape from the facility and his trek to destroy the plans of the adversary. We discover the extent to which Don has been consumed by evil spirits and the exact details of the deal that he has made to become rich and powerful. As William works to end that which he had initially begun, evil forces take a more deliberate part in influencing the world's events, leading up to a cataclysmic confrontation between good and evil. However, William will find that the forces of good are beginning to intervene, in what ultimately leads up to the Second Coming and Armageddon.

##############################

Note from the Author

Thank you so much for taking time to read Creation Abomination. I truly hope that you loved the characters, storyline, and overall experience! If you have enjoyed this book, please consider writing a review on Amazon.

Best!
Alan W. Thompson

Made in the USA
San Bernardino, CA
30 June 2018